Sharon Kendrick once won a national writing competition by describing her ideal date: being flown to an exotic island by a gorgeous and powerful man. Little did she realise that she'd just wandered into her dream job! Today she writes for Mills & Boon, and her books feature often stubborn but always to-die-for heroes and the women who bring them to their knees. She believes that the best books are those you never want to end. Just like life…

Irish author **Abby Green** ended a very glamorous career in film and TV—which really consisted of a lot of standing in the rain outside actors' trailers— to pursue her love of romance. After she'd bombarded Mills & Boon with manuscripts they kindly accepted one, and an author was born. She lives in Dublin, Ireland, and loves any excuse for distraction. Visit abby-green.com or email abbygreenauthor@gmail.com.

D0522697

STOLEN NIGHTS WITH THE KING

SHARON KENDRICK

THE KISS SHE CLAIMED FROM THE GREEK

ABBY GREEN

MILLS & BOON

First Published in Great Britain 2022
by Mills & Boon, an imprint of HarperCollins*Publishers* Ltd,
1 London Bridge Street, London, SE1 9GF

www.harpercollins.co.uk

HarperCollins*Publishers*
1st Floor, Watermarque Building,
Ringsend Road, Dublin 4, Ireland

Stolen Nights with the King © 2022 Sharon Kendrick

The Kiss She Claimed from the Greek © 2022 Abby Green

ISBN: 978-0-263-30085-7

06/22

FSC™
www.fsc.org

MIX
Paper from
responsible sources
FSC® C007454

This book is produced from independently certified FSC™ paper
to ensure responsible forest management.
For more information visit www.harpercollins.co.uk/green.

Printed and Bound in Spain using 100% Renewable Electricity
at CPI Black Print, Barcelona

STOLEN NIGHTS WITH THE KING

SHARON KENDRICK

MILLS & BOON

This book is dedicated to the amazing anthropologist
Winifred Creamer, who I was lucky enough to meet
on a long-distance train journey in Australia
(Darwin to Adelaide, if you're interested!).

Her skill is in explaining the past
and making it come alive with breathtaking clarity.
It's what helps make this story extra-special.

CHAPTER ONE

AGAINST THE GLARE of the beach, the man seemed to blaze more brightly than the sun. His tall body was bronzed. The sunlight caught his thick hair and gilded it with licks of fire, making him appear almost incandescent. But unlike everyone else on the beach, Rosie wasn't particularly mesmerised by his presence. She wasn't trying to get him to notice her, or stare at her. Mostly she was trying to melt into the background and pretend she wasn't there, wishing she were back home in England.

She glanced across the sand, where everyone looked like models you might see within the pages of a glossy magazine. She'd always been taught to concentrate on the similarities rather than the differences between people, but here there *were* no similarities and never had she felt it more keenly than today. She was different from everyone else who frolicked on the fine-grained silver sand.

She wasn't royal.

She wasn't even well connected.

And she certainly wasn't rich.

Fiddling with the strap of her black swimsuit, she continued to observe the action playing out on Monterosso's most desirable stretch of beach, where the assembled gathering was paying homage to the man in their midst.

The man with a mane of hair which some called russet, or titian, but was often described in gushing newspaper profiles as resembling dark fire. He exuded an aura of poise and power. Of arrogance and assurance. Every woman was in love with him and every man strove to be like him.

Corso.

Or, more accurately, Corso Andrea da Vignola, Prince and heir to the fabulous kingdom of Monterosso, with its casinos and nightclubs and the famous red mountain which had given the country its name.

Women wearing bikinis, which looked as if they had been constructed from dental floss, opened their glossy mouths and roared with laughter whenever the Prince spoke. They thrust out their perfect breasts and sucked in already concave stomachs as they unsubtly vied to capture his interest. They looked like thronging cattle in a market stall, Rosie thought in disgust, quickly quashing the thought that she might perhaps be *jealous* of them. Of course she wasn't. For a period in her life she'd felt almost close to him, before time and circumstances had intervened. These days she felt as if she didn't know him, apart from the fearsome reputation he seemed to have acquired in the press—*the playboy with the heart of stone*, they called him, although Rosie thought that was a bit cruel. Just because a man of twenty-five hadn't chalked up much in the way of long-term relationships, didn't necessarily mean he had a heart of stone, did it?

Her bottom pressing into the sand—for all the loungers had been taken and she was too shy to ask for another—she folded her arms around her knees, hoping the pose struck a confidence she was far from feeling. She wondered how much longer she was going to have to stay here with her head getting hotter and hotter be-neath her cheap sunhat. Probably until Corso decided he wanted to leave—because it was forbidden for a guest to leave a function before the royal Prince.

Why *had* she come here?

She should have let the past go. Let it slip away like a silent stream, into the hidden backwaters of her mind.

She stared down at the grains of sand, which looked like crushed diamonds as they glittered in the sunshine. Had she been hoping to find a sense of peace, of belong-ing—here in this Mediterranean paradise where she had spent so many happy summers, before life had hurled a series of grenades into her life? Perhaps she had. But, like all daydreams, her hopes had dissolved the minute they'd made contact with reality. She had no place here, not really. Her imaginings had been nothing but illusions. Although her father had been considered Monterosso's most respected archaeologist and the Prince's favoured mentor, when it boiled down to it, he had been nothing more than a servant.

And she, a servant's daughter.

'Now, the question I am asking myself is what you're doing over here, hiding away in the shadows like a lynx in the forest. Why aren't you joining in with the party?'

Rosie was startled by the sound of a richly accented drawl, which had always been the most distinctive voice she'd ever heard. She glanced up to see Corso standing in front of her and quickly turned to look behind her to see who he was talking to, but there was nobody there.

'Yes, I'm speaking to you, Rosie.'

His deep voice was tinged with amusement but it sounded as if it might be underpinned with a faint sense of impatience and Rosie realised that she must have looked the odd one out among all the supermodels, world-class sportswomen and other over-achieving females who were on the beach-party list. She should have listened to her sister, who had told her she would be insane to pitch up at one of the most glittering social events of the year, taking her hopelessly inadequate wardrobe with her. But Rosie had felt drawn back to Monterosso, as if she were being tugged there by an insistent and invisible string. Was that because some of her happiest times had been here, in this beautiful mountain kingdom—or because the current reality of her life was grey enough to make her want to lose herself in the past?

And, of course, Bianca had been right, because everything *did* seem strange and different—which was probably more to do with the way Rosie was feeling, rather than the way she looked. Had she imagined that she might have some sort of special bond with the Prince, just because he used to enjoy her mother's chicken pie and had taught her how to tie knots? Because if she had, then surely *that* was the real insanity.

Once she might have chattered to him with the lack of inhibition of a child, but now she didn't dare. She couldn't think of a single thing to say. She shifted awkwardly, self-conscious of her under-developed body and how gauche she must seem compared to all the stunners who were draped across the sand. Which was why she stayed exactly where she was, unwilling to stand up and subject herself to the scrutiny of the royal Prince, who suddenly seemed like a stranger to her. How could it be that the man she had once regarded as a quasi-big brother—if their positions in life hadn't been so dramatically different—now appeared so distant and remote? She could feel her cheeks growing hotter and she swallowed. If this was what growing up was about then she didn't want it.

'Happy birthday, Corso,' she said awkwardly.

'Thank you,' he responded, with a regal inclination of his head.

But his dark brows remained raised in question and Rosie realised to her horror that he might be expecting her to bow down before him. Was he? As a child, she had only ever curtseyed to his father, the King, and the Corso she had known would have loathed such formality. Cheeks still burning, she scrambled to her feet, painfully aware of the plain swimsuit which emphasised her bony ribs and skinny legs. As she sank towards the soft sand, she wished it would swallow her up.

'Forgive me for my lack of protocol,' she said as she rose to her feet once more. 'I'm not quite sure what to do. Not any more.' He was looking at her in bemusement—as if he was unused to someone saying exactly what was on their mind—and something about the molten quality of his golden gaze made her blurt out the truth. 'It's so weird being back here.'

'Yes, I can imagine it must be.' There was a pause. 'How long has it been?'

'Six years.'

'Six years? Is it really?'

Was that a sigh she heard? Surely not. Sighing was something she associated with sentiment or nostalgia—and the steely Corso was not the type of man to indulge in either.

'Time passes with the speed of a tornado,' he continued, with a frown. 'How old are you now? Sixteen?'

Rosie shook her head. She knew she was young-looking for her age, but for some stupid reason his comment hurt. Surely she hadn't expected him to remember how old she was! 'Eighteen,' she amended. Which made him twenty-five. But Corso looked like a fully grown man, in the first great flush of his vibrant prime, whereas she felt gawky and naïve in comparison.

His handsome face grew grave. 'I miss your father,' he said suddenly.

Rosie nodded, her heart giving a sudden wrench. 'We all miss him,' she said, and the thought of the man she had idolised made her remember her manners. 'It was very…very kind of you to invite me here, to your birthday celebrations.'

'I thought it might please you all to revisit a place he loved so much.' His eyes narrowed into a metallic gleam, which was suddenly tinged with hardness. 'Although I was surprised your mother and sister were unable to accompany you.'

Rosie bit her lip. It was a statement which managed to be a question and a rebuke all at the same time because clearly the Crown Prince of Monterosso wasn't used to people turning down one of his coveted invitations. 'Er, no,' she said. 'I'm afraid they couldn't make it.'

There was little point in enlightening him that her mother had gone to pieces ever since her husband had died, or that Bianca had sworn never to set foot on Monterosso again. She remembered what her sister had said when Corso's gilt-edged invitation had unexpectedly thudded onto the mat.

'Who wants to be reminded of a place where we had to be grateful for every damned thing we got?' Bianca had demanded. 'Which robbed us of everything that mattered to us?'

Deep down, Rosie disagreed with Bianca's anti-Monterossian views, but she didn't attempt to talk her out of them, because her older sister was far too strong-minded. And besides, Bianca was at university now. She had talent and ambition. She was destined for bigger and better things.

Unlike you, mocked a voice inside Rosie's head.

'A pity,' mused Corso. 'I thought they might have enjoyed seeing the island again.' He fixed her with a curious look. 'Are you looking forward to the ball tonight, Rosie?'

Not really, since I'm certain my dress will stand out like a sore thumb and I'll look like an absolute fright next to some of the other women who are here.

'Of course. Can't wait,' she said, forcing a smile.

Corso repressed a click of irritation, because it was obvious she wasn't speaking the truth and he found that disappointing, because hadn't he always thought that Rosie Forrester was completely straightforward? It had been one of the things he'd most liked about her.

The last time he'd seen her she had been gangly and ungainly—and unfortunately, she still was. There had been no transformation or blossoming in the intervening years, as so often happened to women in the time between adolescence and womanhood. Her legs were still long and skinny—her knees as knobbly as a teenage boy's. She was the only woman on the beach without the adornment of jewellery and if you factored in her plain swimsuit and unflattering straw hat, she was someone you noticed for all the wrong reasons. Yet for a moment, Corso found himself admiring her refusal or inability to conform to an invitation to today's picnic which had read: *Beach party chic.*

He wondered if it had been a mistake to invite her.

When her father had finally died last year, he had wanted to reach out to offer the family more comfort than a formal letter of condolence. But he hadn't known how and, naturally, there was the thorny issue of royal protocol to consider. The relationship between him and the Forrester family had always been too imprecise to fall into any recognisable category, but his own father had been unequivocal when Corso had brought the matter to his attention.

'Lionel Forrester is dead,' the King had announced, with the dismissive attitude he applied to everyone, including his own son. Corso gave the ghost of a smile. *Especially* his own son. 'And yes, he was the greatest archaeologist Monterosso has ever known and a good teacher to you, but our association with his family is now at an end. The palace has paid the school fees for his two daughters and provided a generous stipend for his widow. We can do nothing more for them, Corso, nor should we.'

But Corso had disagreed. To the King's anger, he had invited Rosie, Bianca and their mother to his birthday ball, thinking it would be an enormous treat for them to revisit the country after so long—something to tell their friends about back in England. After all, how many commoners were invited to stay in one of Europe's most lavish royal palaces and be entertained by a crown prince?

He had imagined gratitude and a satisfactory sense of closure. He certainly hadn't expected two refusals in rapid succession—and for the only attendee to be a sulky-looking teenager who looked as if she were being subjected to a particular type of torture.

'Try to look as if you mean it, Rosie,' he advised acidly. 'Most people would kill to go to one of my balls.'

'Let's hope not. I'd hate to witness any form of homicide on your birthday,' she answered, with a sudden return of her customary spirit. 'And I think someone over there is trying to get your attention.'

A touch impatiently—for he did not care for flippancy *or* her sudden change of subject—Corso turned his head to follow the direction of her gaze and saw one of the most beautiful women he'd ever laid eyes on heading their way. Tiffany Sackler, with her flawless skin and all that long, dark hair which tumbled to her tiny waist. A small smile edged his lips as she sashayed across the sand towards them, a pair of sunglasses perched provocatively on the end of her nose.

As well as her very obvious physical attributes, the brunette had played hard to get from the moment he'd met her. This was rare enough to excite his interest—despite him never doubting that it was anything other than a game on her part—for Corso was familiar with the plotting of women. And although Tiffany's occupation as one of the world's best-paid supermodels meant she was popular tabloid fodder, her arrival on Monterosso had been as discreet as he could have wished for, which was another point in her favour. Her credentials as a prospective lover were therefore impeccable, which left only one question in Corso's mind.

Did he want her?

He felt the beat of something like indecision before ruthlessly eradicating it. Yes, of course he wanted her. He had been spending far too much time on affairs of state lately, as he prepared himself for his eventual accession to the throne. He wondered if his appetite for women had simply become jaded the more avidly he was pursued—as had happened for most of his life. Yet surely it was a sad day when a man allowed work or caution to subdue his legendary libido. And since he was determined to follow his father's example of enjoying a long and faithful marriage, then surely it only made sense to sow his wild oats before that day came around.

A slow rush of breath escaped from his lungs. Tonight, he decided. After the ball was over. That would be the perfect time to take Tiffany Sackler to his bed.

'Tiffany,' he murmured. 'Good to see you.'

'I'd... I'd better go.' Rosie's voice broke into his thoughts and he realised he'd forgotten she was still there. He turned to see that her cheeks were the colour of a morning sunrise.

'Goodbye, Your Royal Highness,' she added, bobbing another awkward curtsey to him, before grabbing an ugly-looking beach bag and rushing away across the sand before he could stop her or give her permission to leave. Not that he had any intention of stopping her, but still—she should have known better than to go before he had dismissed her.

He frowned.

A man was only a true man if he was able to acknowledge his mistakes and Corso saw now that he definitely should *not* have invited her. The boundaries between them had become blurred. The sunny child he remembered had been replaced by an awkward and self-conscious young woman, who was no longer comfortable mixing in royal circles. Rosie Forrester had no place here—that much was glaringly obvious. His jaw tightened in a moment of exasperation, but at least there

were only a few more hours for her to get through before she boarded her flight back to England.

Because the sooner she was away from Monterosso,
the better.

Rosie didn't stop rushing until she was back in the
grounds of the palace and the crushed diamond glitter
of the beach was far behind her. Skirting the less used
paths she knew so well, she was able to move unseen
through the fragrant foliage, towards the turreted creamy
patina of the soaring royal residence. And it wasn't until
she was safely back in her room and had closed the door
behind her that she drew in a shuddering breath of relief.

And anger.

She found herself staring into an enormous mirror
without really seeing herself, because the only things
which dominated her thoughts were those piercing amber
eyes which gleamed like purest gold.

Had Corso *always* been so hateful? First of all he'd
looked her up and down with faint incredulity and then
started behaving as if she were invisible—while his
jaw had practically dropped to the ground when Tiffany Sackler had appeared with that foxy look on her
face. As soon as the supermodel had arrived, the whole
atmosphere had changed, making Rosie grow increas-
ingly uncomfortable. Or was she just being naïve and
unrealistic? What had she expected? That the Prince
would prefer to talk to her, when one of the most lusted-
after women on the planet was in the vicinity, batting
her super-long lashes at him?

But of all the women he could have had—why choose
Tiffany? Or was it her own lack of self-esteem which
made Rosie suspicious of the American model, whose

eyes she thought resembled shards of blue ice? Her suite was right door next to hers and, since the thick palace walls meant the phone signal was hopeless, Tiffany would sometimes wander out onto her terrace, wearing an eye-poppingly tiny bikini, chattering into her phone and surveying the magnificent scenery around her with a hungry expression. Surely Corso could have found himself a less *in your face* girlfriend than that?

But his relationship with Tiffany was nothing to do with her and Rosie forced herself to focus on the pale face which was staring back at her from the ornately scrolled mirror. She needed to get things in perspective. Tonight was the Prince's birthday ball and after that the clock would start ticking down towards her departure. Just a few more hours to get through and then she could fly back to England and decide what she was going to do with her future.

But the future was scary. She knew that better than anyone. Thank heavens no one was ever given a crystal ball, because if you knew some of the things which were waiting for you—you'd never get out of bed in the morning. She hoped that her mother would start becoming the warm, loving woman she'd grown up with, rather than the pale and haunted widow who seemed unable to cope with her husband's death.

In an effort to distract herself from reality, Rosie began flicking through the bookshelf until she found a book she recognised. A record of early Monterossian art, written by the man who had introduced her to the subject almost before she could walk. The man who had been her hero and the lynchpin on whom the three Forrester women had depended—perhaps a little too much—until his spirit and body had been crushed by an underwater arch which had collapsed on him. The density of the water had meant he hadn't been killed instantly, as would have happened if it had occurred on dry land. Instead, he had lain in a coma for four long years before his eventual death, which had given the family time to reflect on the fact that Lionel's enthusiasm had stupidly led him to undertake a dangerous mission, single-handedly. It had been a slow kind of suffering for them all—and now his work and his two daughters were all that remained of him.

It had been a long time since Rosie had been able to bring herself to look at this particular book, but it was comforting as well as poignant to read the familiar words, for it conjured up her father's voice and his presence. Lost in tales of ancient battles and of jewelled crowns forged for royal princesses, Rosie was oblivious to the hours drifting by until she heard a noise coming from the direction of Tiffany's terrace. With a shock, she glanced down at her watch and realised there was barely an hour left before the ball began. She hadn't even thought about getting ready—and no way should she be late.

A quick shower washed all the remaining sand from her body but there wasn't enough time to wash and dry her hair. Never mind. She could twist it into an intricate knot, high on her head, and hopefully that would conceal the fact that some of the strands were still covered in suncream. At last she plucked her dress from the ornately carved wardrobe, her heart hammering nervously as she pulled it over her head.

'Keep it simple,' her sister had advised, and, since Bianca always looked totally amazing, Rosie had taken her at her word. She suspected that the only reason she'd been able to afford the dress was because the unforgiving white fabric would have revealed every lump and bump on most people, of which Rosie had none. The gown was silky and fell to the ground, pretty much covering her feet—which was a good thing as she was wearing a pair of red ballet pumps which still fitted her and which she had never really used, since she'd always been hopeless at dancing. She still was. The most daring thing about the outfit was that it draped over one shoulder, leaving the other completely bare. Her only adornment was a delicate choker of gold, a replica of an ancient Monterossian necklace which her mother had lent her. But the catch was fiddly and Rosie's fingers much too nervous to secure it...

Couldn't she go and ask Tiffany to fasten it for her? Forget her prejudices about the American supermodel and perhaps have a friendly chat with her before the big event. Wasn't that the companionable kind of thing women sometimes did before parties? Maybe they could even go to the ball together—because that would be infinitely better than having to enter the luxurious palace ballroom on her own.

Her ballet pumps were silent as she crossed the marble floor and she was going to approach from the shadows of her own terrace, when she saw Tiffany standing with her back to her. Her phone was held to her ear and Rosie was just about to retreat and return once the call was finished when her ears pricked up as she heard a name she recognised.

'Oh, don't worry. I have Corso *exactly* where I want him,' Tiffany was purring.

Rosie had been taught never to listen to other people's conversations because nothing good ever came of it, but a faintly troubling quality in the supermodel's voice was making her body grow tense.

Leave, she told herself, but she remained rooted to the spot all the same.

'Because I've made him wait and he's hot for me, and my timing couldn't be more perfect.' Tiffany was whispering, before letting out a soft and triumphant laugh. 'Yes, you do. You know exactly what I mean. And if the stars align themselves properly, you're going to be organising a baby shower before the year is out. Yeah, yeah...'

The rest of her words were lost as Rosie slipped back into her room, her thoughts spinning.

Disbelief washed over her as she thought about what she'd just heard. Could Tiffany have meant what it *sounded* as if she meant? As if she was planning to trap the Prince by getting herself pregnant? Surely she wouldn't do something as crass and as underhand as that.

But she wouldn't have been the first woman in the history of the world to have stooped to such an action. Rosie might have been completely innocent of men, but she knew that much. Her face grew hot and she wanted to squirm. Because if that *were* the case, then surely she couldn't just remain silent about it, because in essence— that would be condoning it. Did Corso *realise* what was on Tiffany's mind? Did he have any idea what might be waiting in store for him?

Because she knew very well that the Crown Prince had always been a traditionalist and his royal legacy was hugely important to him. And yes, his sexual exploits might give people the idea that he was a playboy, but he was also the type of man who would marry only when the time was right—to a woman of a similar exalted royal background. He certainly wasn't the kind of man who would have a baby out of wedlock, with a commoner.

Trying to keep her fingers steady, Rosie fiddled with her necklace until at last it was fastened and she wished she could just crawl underneath the embroidered covers of the magnificent bed and sleep the night away until her flight home tomorrow. But she couldn't do that. She couldn't.

What *should* she do?

She swallowed.

She and Corso went back a long way—even if he *had* been unable to conceal his faint disdain for her today or the fact that, inevitably, they had grown apart. And anyway, this was about more than her own hurt pride. Surely she owed it to the Prince, to his land and his people to confide in him the truth. She *had* to tell him. Before it was too late.

She heard the first of eight sonorous clangs as the palace clock began to ring in the hour.

Despite all her best intentions, she was late.

The final chime was just dying away as Rosie burst into the ballroom to confront the Crown Prince of Monterosso.

CHAPTER TWO

SITTING BENEATH THE glittering chandeliers which hung from the vaulted ceiling of the ballroom, Corso did his best to stifle another yawn. The lavish birthday feast was almost over and as soon as the cake had been cut, the dancing could begin. And not a moment too soon, in his opinion. Why the hell had he agreed to celebrate his quarter-century with a glittering party? Had he forgotten that these affairs could feel interminably long, as well as tediously predictable? Forcing his expression into one of benign approval, he nodded as an enormous cake was wheeled into the ballroom and the entire room burst into song.

He could feel the heat from the candle flames as the extravagant concoction reached him and, with one mighty expulsion of air, he leaned forward to extinguish them, to the accompaniment of rapturous applause. With an air of apparent enjoyment, he took a mouthful of wild strawberry and cream gateau and washed it down with a sip of vintage champagne, but afterwards pushed the plate and the glass away. It occurred to Corso that for each year that passed, he enjoyed his birthday less and less.

During the banquet itself, he had sat between two

high-born women from neighbouring countries—a countess and a duchess—but this had solely been a nod to propriety. A reassurance to his father—who was not present—and to the courtiers who feared he wasn't giving proper consideration to his future and, more importantly, an heir. And you could not have an heir without first finding a royal wife to bear him.

But the women had bored him, as they so often did. Corso had not been dazzled by their perfect manners, nor their jewels. He certainly hadn't been tempted by their coy references to the bloated coffers of each of their kingdoms. Presumably intimating at the large dowry which could be his, should he request either of their hands in marriage, for in this part of the world tradition still prevailed. He knew that when the time came, he would take a wife of a noble lineage which resembled his own and he was okay with that. It was just the way things were and he had long ago accepted his destiny.

But this evening he had been far more interested in observing Tiffany Sackler busily chatting with the handsome man on her right and not looking in Corso's direction once. Several times she had thrown back her head and laughed, as if her companion were the single most amusing person in the world. Yet her actions had irritated him and her evident game-playing had quelled a little of the hunger in his blood.

A sudden movement caught his attention and he looked down the far end of the banqueting table to see Rosie Forrester staring at him, chewing her bottom lip as if she were worried about something. Her eyes looked huge and she was pursing her lips together, as if trying to silently convey something to him. As their gaze met, she half lifted her arm to wiggle her forefinger at him in a wave and Corso expelled a sigh of irritation.

What was the *matter* with the girl?

First, she had arrived after everyone else—bursting into the ballroom all out of breath. To have been late at the birthday party of the Prince of Monterosso was bad enough, but her social gaffe was compounded by the fact that she was wearing what appeared to be a repurposed bedsheet. He had stared in brief amazement at the silky white material which had skimmed her slender frame, unable to miss the crimson ballet shoes exposed by the flying fabric. With its one-shouldered nod to a Grecian goddess, she had looked as if she were going to a down-market fancy-dress party. And now she was trying to get his attention! Wasn't she aware that her behaviour was totally out of line? Very deliberately, Corso turned away from her and began to speak to his aide, Rodrigo, who had appeared by his side and was enquiring about the commencement of the dancing.

'Let the music begin,' Corso said, with a swift inclination of his head. The violins began to play as he rose to his feet, the orchestra not quite managing to drown out the collective holding of breath as the assembled gathering waited to see which woman he would choose to open the dancing. He was aware that his choice of partner was significant, knowing if he selected either the countess or the duchess then the media would go wild and wedding-dress manufacturers would be giving non-stop interviews to the broadcast media tomorrow morning.

He observed that by now Tiffany's eyes *were* on him but, still irritated by her game-playing, he decided to let her wait and fret for a moment or two, before walking over to where she sat and extending his hand.

'Would you do me the honour?' he questioned carelessly.

Her curtsey was deep and practised and she held the submissive pose just long enough for him to get ample exposure to the creamy swell of her cleavage, which no doubt had been her intention. 'I would be delighted, Your Royal Highness,' she replied huskily.

The guests made a circle around them as they began to move in time to the music and Tiffany began to talk, as if determined to make the most of this rare public one-to-one with the Crown Prince. Corso listened while she prattled away in her sultry drawl, extolling the virtues of his country, the magnificence of the view from her suite of rooms and the lavishness of the meal she had just eaten. Her body was light yet strong and she was an accomplished dancer. He could feel the occasional brush of her erect nipples against his chest, as he was certain he was meant to, and it had the desired effect of arousing him. Yet he felt curiously…*detached*, and he frowned.

Maybe a bout of energetic sex would cure him of his ennui.

'I will see you later,' he promised, his voice growing husky.

She looked up at him with teasing provocation in her blue eyes. 'Oh, really?'

'*Si… certo,*' he murmured, lapsing into Italian, rather than his native tongue. 'But for now I must play fair and give other women the chance to dance with me, or I will have a riot on my hands.'

'I understand perfectly, Your Royal Highness. Until *later*, then.' She bowed her gleaming head and dropped another graceful curtsey, before retreating in a swish of lavishly embroidered silk.

Corso began what he thought of as his duty, working his way through as many of the female guests as possible. He saw their expressions of joy, of hope, and the pure delight which greeted his invitation to dance and knew that the majority of them longed to be his bride. Who could blame them? He was young and virile and had been told more times than he could count just how devastating sexy women found him. That he was heir to one of the most wealthy kingdoms on the planet only increased his worth in the eyes of the opposite sex.

Towards the tail end of the evening, he supposed he really ought to partner young Rosie in a duty dance but when he looked to find her, she was nowhere to be seen. More champagne was poured and an ensemble of acrobats from Monterosso's leading circus performed a series of awe-inspiring routines, in dramatic costumes which resembled flames. Finally, everyone moved out onto the wide veranda to engage in a little stargazing before the firework display, which was timed to start at exactly midnight, the official end of the Crown Prince's birthday.

But just as Corso was preparing to take his place at the front of the balustrade, he felt something tugging at his sleeve. Or rather, someone. With a scowl, he looked down to discover who'd had the temerity to touch him in such a fashion—knowing that if Tiffany was attempting to draw attention to their proposed liaison, then she would be history before they'd even begun—when he saw Rosie looking up at him.

In her bedsheet dress she looked even paler than usual and strands of hair from her updo—although admittedly a magnificent shade of moonlight—remained wild. It looked as if she'd been running anxious fingers through it all evening, which, judging from her expression, was entirely possible. Her only jewellery was a replica of an ancient Monterossian necklace—the beaten metal gleaming softly against her milky skin. And something about that simple choker made Corso's equilibrium falter for a moment. She was no match for the society guests here tonight, he thought, yet her careless appearance caused a peculiar awareness to shimmer through his body, which made him feel decidedly *disconcerted*. It whispered featherlight fingers over his flesh. It hinted at something delicious and unknown. But it was gone almost as soon as he had acknowledged it, banished by a swift shake of his head.

'Corso,' she whispered.

Now she was addressing him without waiting for his permission to speak—and in a highly insubordinate manner! 'What is it?' he snapped.

'I need to talk to you.'

'Well, you can't.'

'But—'

'Not only is your request highly inappropriate,' he bit out, from between gritted teeth, 'but it is also untimely. In case you hadn't noticed, this happens to be my birthday party and there are many guests craving my attention. Princes and sheikhs who have travelled many miles to be here, as well as many old friends.'

'But I need to speak to you,' she said, with an oddly stubborn note in her voice. 'I'll never forgive myself if I don't.'

Scarcely able to believe her audacity, Corso considered his options. If he sent her away there would be a scene and, besides, the mulish expression pinned to her face made him doubt she would obey him—he had never seen her look that way before. What was the *matter* with her? Having her removed by Security remained an option, of course, but the forced removal of a troublesome guest was hardly an auspicious end to his party—and would doubtless cause gossip and speculation. And since this was doubtless the last time he would ever see her, why not tolerate her request and hear her out?

Knitting his brows together, he glanced up at the illuminated dial of the mighty clock as the hour ticked irrevocably towards midnight. Would five minutes be long enough to allow her to get whatever it was off her chest before he dismissed her?

He dipped his head so his words couldn't be overheard, their silky tone failing to disguise his irritation. 'Very well. I will grant you a few minutes. What is it?'

Rosie hesitated, glancing this way and that, terrified someone would be able to hear what she was about to say. 'Not here,' she whispered. 'Can't we just go over there, where it's quiet?'

'No.'

'Yes, we can, Corso,' she persisted stubbornly. 'You're the most senior royal here tonight. You can do anything you please.'

'Good to know that you're able to remember protocol when it suits you,' he answered testily.

But to her relief, he waved away the aides who were hovering anxiously nearby and strode over to the velvet-curtained recess she'd indicated, where indigo shadows replaced the bright glitter of the ballroom, and Rosie followed him—steeling herself against the fierce look on his face.

'Well? What is it?' he demanded. 'I'm waiting.'

But now that the moment of revelation was here, Rosie couldn't work out how she was going to say it, because this was something way outside her experience. Way outside most people's, she guessed uncomfortably. How did you tell any man—let alone a hugely important royal—that you thought someone was attempting to trick them in the most underhand way possible?

'It's Tiffany,' she said, at last.

He stilled. 'Tiffany?'

Rosie nodded. 'That's right.'

'What about her?'

'I don't think… I don't think she has your best interests at heart.'

'No?' He gave a short, disbelieving laugh. 'But you do, I suppose?'

Again, she hesitated as the hard light from his eyes lanced through her. 'Yes, I do. Of course I do.'

'So what is it about her which makes you think I should be on my guard?' he questioned sarcastically. 'Surely you're not jealous that I had the first dance with her and didn't find time to dance with you? Is that why your eyes were following me round the ballroom so reproachfully all evening?'

Rosie froze. Did he really think this was about *jealousy*—or imagine he was so gorgeous that all a woman could think about was craving his company? She was so outraged by his assumption that she nearly turned on her heel and fled, because it would serve him right if he created a love child with Tiffany Sackler on the very night of his twenty-fifth birthday. And then a feeling of nausea rose up inside her as she acknowledged her own dated terminology. *Love child?* Nobody said that sort of thing any more. What if she *had* got it all wrong?

She had zero experience of sex, or relationships. What if she'd misread the situation and was sticking her nose in where it wasn't needed? For all she knew, he and Tiffany might already have had long and avid discussions about planned parenthood. She had read the textbooks at school, along with everyone else. Who was to say they hadn't spent the last three days taking her temperature and deciding which would be the best sexual position to adopt?

Her fingers strayed to her lips because that particular thought made her feel queasy and she wasn't quite sure why. But the Prince's eyes were narrowed with exasperation and she thought he was about to stride away and she'd never get another chance. Maybe it was that which made it all come tumbling out, her words almost tripping over themselves. 'I don't want to be the one to have to tell you this, Corso, but Tiffany and I have suites next door to each other. Our terraces are connected and I overheard her talking on the phone earlier.'

'You mean you were eavesdropping?'

'Yes. No.' She shook her head, knowing that she probably deserved the withering disdain she could hear in his voice and knowing she needed to justify it. 'I never intended to stay and listen but then I heard… I heard her talking to someone—'

'That is usually what happens when you're on the phone to someone,' he interrupted sarcastically.

'And she was saying…' She shrugged her shoulders with helpless embarrassment. 'She was saying that she'd made you wait and you were hot for her. And…'

A sudden chill seemed to have entered the atmosphere. 'And?'

Rosie could see that his face had changed. The irritation had vanished and been replaced by a look of cold, quiet danger.

For a moment she questioned the wisdom of what she was about to do, but somehow she knew there wasn't any other choice. Because not only was Rosie spurred on by the certainty that the da Vignola lineage was too long and revered a line to be continued in such a potentially destabilising way, there was another factor, too. No way should Corso Andrea da Vignola become a parent. Certainly not at this stage in his life—perhaps not ever. Because how could a man ever raise a child when he was so proud and unfeeling and downright arrogant?

'She said it was perfect timing.'

'Perfect timing?' he repeated slowly.

It occurred to Rosie that his innate superiority might prevent him from understanding the harsh truth of what she was telling him. He probably imagined that any woman would think it perfect timing to have the royal Prince in their bed and that she, for all her innocence, had misunderstood what Tiffany had been alluding to. So enlighten him—even if it's the most embarrassing thing you've ever had to do.

'She said something about there being a possible baby shower before the year was out,' she whispered. 'I got the feeling that was what she meant. That she wanted to…that she wanted to have your baby.'

A ragged breath erupted from his lungs. It sounded like a caged beast breaking free and Rosie had to concentrate very hard not to take an instinctive step back. She had seen Corso many times during her life—admittedly only through the eyes of someone who was young and untutored—but she had never seen him look anything like this before. Naked fury darkened his brilliant eyes, followed by a spiky glint of anger. She wondered if he was going to thank her for telling him before it was too late, but maybe that was naïve because there was nothing resembling gratitude on his hard features. He looked utterly magnificent but also utterly terrifying.

Don't shoot the messenger, she wanted to say, but of course—she didn't dare.

He was nodding his head, like someone doing sums inside their head, before coming to some kind of calculation. His words were slow and measured. 'This is the beginning and the end of this conversation. Do not ever speak of it again. Not to anyone,' he instructed. 'Believe me, I will know if you have broken this confidence and I will make you pay. Do you understand what I'm saying to you, Rosie?'

She nodded. He was asking her to keep this a secret. To collude with him.

She thought how differently he could have put it. He could have made it sound like a strengthening bond between them, but it was nothing like that. His words were a warning—maybe even a threat. As if the already wide chasm which existed between them had opened up even wider. As if he were standing on the deck of a giant ocean liner which was moving slowly but irrevocably away from her.

And she should not forget that he had also insulted her. He'd accused her of jealousy. Of mooning around and being somehow offended because he hadn't asked her to dance. As if! She'd rather scrub the palace floor with a toothbrush than dance with *him*. Somehow she couldn't imagine ever seeing him again after tonight, let alone speaking to him. And wouldn't that be for the best? To finally put Monterosso and all its bittersweet memories behind her. To forget that once she had eaten chicken pie with a crown prince, and try to get on with the rest of her life, wherever that took her?

'Yes, Your Royal Highness,' she emphasised sarcastically, but her formal acknowledgement of his title must have reassured him that she meant what she said, because he nodded with patriarchal acceptance.

'Good. I think that is all. And now, if you will excuse me, people are expecting fireworks and I must signal for them to begin.'

And that was that. No thanks. No further acknowledgement. Nothing but a cool gaze before the Prince swept out from within the curtained recess. After a couple of moments Rosie did the same and watched as he walked towards the front of the palace balustrade, and people parted to clear a path for him, as they always did. She could see Tiffany glancing towards him as he lifted his hand in command for the fireworks to begin.

But he did not look in Tiffany's direction. Not once. Rosie saw a trace of discomposure cross the supermodel's exquisite features, just as Corso brought his hand down with the rapid and irreversible movement of a guillotine blade.

As the palace clock struck midnight, fireworks exploded and Monterosso was lit up with silver and pink, with green and blue and crimson. The colours splintered the dark blue sky like bright, kaleidoscopic comets but as the chimes began to die away, Rosie could hear the sound of boots coming towards them...and they were running.

Running.

She knew something was wrong the instant she saw the marble-white faces of the King's inner guard as they sped towards Corso, who was regarding them impenetrably—though in the moonlight she thought she could see the dawning of comprehension hardening those rugged features. And suddenly Rosie guessed what was happening as, to a man, the guard sank to their knees before him, their solemn pronouncement echoing through the shocked silence of the partygoers.

'The King is dead!'

And then.

'Long live the King!'

Corso's strained features reflected the enormity of what was taking place and Rosie wondered if she had imagined the bitter acceptance which briefly darkened his extraordinary eyes.

CHAPTER THREE

Seven years later

THE WOOD WAS dark and dense and it was easy for Corso to remain concealed as he waited for her, beneath the shaded canopy of leaves. There was nobody else around, he had insisted on that—despite the words of warning and handwringing on behalf of his security people. There were guards stationed discreetly throughout the woodland—that much he had conceded—but he had been afforded the privacy he wanted, because he was the King, and in the end everyone always did what the King wanted.

Would it be contrary of him to wish that sometimes they wouldn't?

The woodland was quiet. Everything was quiet, save for the rustle of a nearby squirrel, or the whisper of the breeze in the leaves overhead. There was a sense of green and sylvan calm, for this was England and it felt a long way from the warm beaches of Monterosso. Yet it was curiously life-enhancing to be completely on his own in a foreign country—for solitude had become an almost forgotten luxury since he had inherited the throne, along with so much else. A deep breath escaped his lungs. Was he imagining the brief sense of peace which had washed over him as he had walked through the forest towards Rosie's cottage, or was that simply wishful thinking? A brief moment of anonymity seducing him into thinking that a better life existed than the one he had.

His mouth hardened. Because didn't everyone think that, to some degree? Surely the fantasy of the unknown had always been more seductive than the demands of the here and now.

The sudden cry of startled birds scattering from the treetops warned him of someone's approach and Corso tensed as, several minutes later, he saw a figure on a bicycle weaving its way along the uneven path towards the cottage.

It could only be Rosie but he would never have recognised her—not in a million years—and not just because her skinny shape had filled out. A safety helmet was crammed down over her head and she wore dark and unprepossessing clothes.

He wondered what her reaction would be when she saw him, and whether she would approve of this covert method of contacting her. He supposed he could have picked up the phone, but instinct had urged him to choose an element of surprise—because in many ways he knew her well enough to break with convention, and wasn't there something *exhilarating* about such an unorthodox approach? Usually his timetable was calculated right down to the precise second and the rigid regimentation of his life inevitably made him feel constrained. But not so today. Today he was master of his own destiny.

Plus, he suspected she wouldn't exactly be overjoyed at seeing him again after their last meeting—particularly as his dramatic accession to the throne meant he hadn't spoken to her since. And that state of affairs would probably have continued, if he hadn't realised that Rosie Forrester was the one person who could provide him with what he needed. Some men might have felt a shimmering of doubt about what he was to ask of her, but not Corso—for he was certain that she would bend to his formidable will. Her father had been a loyal man of service—and his daughter was undeniably cast from the same mould.

She dismounted the bike and disappeared inside the humble house and he crunched his way up the path and knocked on the door. A couple of minutes later the door was opened to reveal Rosie Forrester standing staring at him, with disbelief on her face.

He was prepared for her surprise, but not her dislike. That much was evident from the sudden flash of fire in eyes whose colour he had never really noticed before, which was grey. Grey as the wings of the doves which sometimes darkened the skies over Esmelagu, Monterosso's capital city. He felt momentarily startled—as if he had just stumbled on something unexpectedly beautiful—but her shuttered lashes quickly veiled their stormy hue.

'Hello, Rosie,' he said softly.

She was shaking her head. 'I can't...'

'Can't, what?'

'I can't believe it's you.'

At this, he smiled but he noticed she didn't smile back. 'You are surprised I have awarded you such an honour?' he questioned benignly.

'That's not exactly how I would have described it,' she said, before adding, as if she had only just remembered, 'Your *Majesty*.'

Corso felt her unfriendliness crash over him in almost tangible waves and he narrowed his eyes, because such a reaction was rare. Even if they hated him—as he was sure many did—his position always daunted people. Thus, they presented what they thought he wanted from them. Grovelling and deference were high on this list—usually delivered in obscene amounts, which sometimes amused him—because those who fawned over him clearly had no idea just how much such an attitude bored him. But Rosie clearly had no such ambition to impress him. Her lips remained set in a mulish line and Corso's brow knitted together for women never reacted to him this way. He was used to provocation. To guile and glamour. Perhaps it was down to the awkwardness of their last conversation when diplomacy and convention had been eroded by her startling disclosure about Tiffany, and he shuddered now to think how careless he had been up until that night.

But that experience had been a wake-up call and perhaps he should be grateful to her for enlightening him. Alongside his sudden accession to the throne, Rosie's revelation had changed him. Hardened him. Made him acknowledge there were few people in this world you could trust. His mouth twisted. But it had also made him better able to withstand the even more bitter truths which had been hovering in the background like malignant forces. Unpalatable facts just waiting for him, once he had begun to delve into the late King's affairs.

And ultimately, that was what had brought him here today.

Once again, he smiled. 'I would like to talk to you,' he said.

But she seemed oblivious to any kind of charm offensive, or indeed to the unthinkable reality that he remained standing on the doorstep, like a cold-call salesman! And now she was peering suspiciously over his shoulder.

'Where is everyone? Your security detail? The armoured car and the heavy mob? The men with suspicious bulges in their jackets?'

'They are present, but concealed throughout the woods. There's no need to worry about my safety, Rosie.'

'It's not your safety I'm worried about, Corso—it's my privacy.'

'Your privacy?'

'Yes.' She bit down on her lip, hard. 'I don't want tomorrow morning's papers carrying some kind of cloak and dagger story about a Mediterranean king paying a surprise visit to a quiet English hamlet.'

'King being the operative word and one which you might do well to remember,' he prompted lazily.

Their gazes clashed, and perhaps she responded better to authority than persuasion for she seemed to pull herself up—stepping back within the confines of the small cottage.

'You'd better come in, I suppose.'

'I am bowled over by your enthusiastic invitation,' he drawled sarcastically.

'Nobody's forcing you to come in, Corso,' she said, but so quietly that he almost missed it and, since he wanted something from her, he was prepared to overlook her rudeness.

Dipping his head, Corso entered the cottage, narrowly missing an overhanging beam, straightening up to find himself standing in the smallest room he had ever seen, and he looked around, curious to see how she lived.

Modestly, it would seem. His sources had told him as much but the evidence of his own eyes spoke volumes.

The woodland setting of the cottage was perfect, but its interior suggested that money was scarce. A small, battered sofa with shiny arms. On an equally small table—next to her discarded cycling helmet—stood a vase filled with a yellow sunburst of daffodils—a quintessentially English touch. But it was the vase which captured his attention more than the spring flowers, for it was decorated in different shades of blue—the distinctive pottery for which Monterosso was renowned. One of his country's more wholesome trades, he thought bitterly—before turning his attention to Rosie herself. And now it was his turn to be surprised and not just because she was regarding him with that same unwelcoming stare. She had unzipped her bulky waterproof jacket so that it was flapping open and he found himself taken aback by the glimpse of abundant curves which lay beneath. And Corso swallowed.

What had happened to her?

Gone were the angular lines and skinny ribs of her boyish frame and in their place was the swell of generous bosom, demurely covered in a navy-blue sweater on which was embroidered a tiny red logo of a train. Her legs—once bony—were now slender and shapely, despite the workmanlike fabric of her trousers. But it wasn't just her physical appearance which had changed. This was a Rosie he didn't recognise, for the look on her face was almost…*insolent*.

She would never have looked at him like that before yet somehow her defiance was heating his blood. He could feel the sudden quickening of his pulse and his mind began to stir with forgotten memories of how delicious sex could be, before he curtailed his errant thoughts. Hadn't he embraced celibacy for the last seven years, ruthlessly sublimating his healthy libido with hard work and exercise? It had been a long time since he had allowed the warm curl of lust to fire his blood and that was the way he had wanted it.

So why the hell was he thinking this way about someone as unsuitable as Rosie Forrester?

His throat dried.

Because denial created hunger. And in the end, wouldn't a starving man sooner devour the hunk of dry bread lying on the table before him, than hold out for a banquet which might never materialise?

So dial it down. Be pleasant. Formal. Remind her—and yourself—of the natural order of things. 'How are you, Rosie?' he questioned, with the same polite distance he might use if he were greeting someone standing in the official line during the opening of a sardine factory.

'Honestly? I'm confused. Bewildered, even.' She shrugged. 'If you must know, I'm wondering why you're here. Why the King of Monterosso has turned up on my doorstep without any kind of warning.'

Corso frowned. Shouldn't she be displaying a little more excitement than this? He had been expecting to have been offered a very English cup of tea—which he would almost certainly have refused—and to have been invited to sit on one of the uncomfortable-looking pieces of furniture. He hadn't been anticipating this cool reception on her part, despite the awkwardness of their last meeting.

She had changed, he thought, before wondering why he'd ever thought otherwise. Of course she had.

They had all changed.

His mouth hardened.

Seven years was a long time.

'I need a favour,' he said.

Rosie was careful to keep her expression neutral, though inside she wasn't feeling a bit like that—and for once it wasn't worry about her mother, or fear of the future which was making her pulse race. An unfamiliar sense of disorientation was unsettling her and it had nothing to do with the shock of protocol being blown away by the King's surprise appearance. It had nothing to do with his lofty position in the world and everything to do with the man himself.

Because Corso Andrea da Vignola had somehow acquired the ability of making the humble dimensions of her cottage shrink even further. It felt as if the walls had started closing in on her. She was finding it difficult to breathe, or think, or concentrate. It was impossible to look anywhere other than at him, yet she had no desire to look anywhere else.

Her gaze drank in the angled planes of his sculpted features and aristocratic cheekbones, as if she needed to commit them to memory. The arrogant curve of his sensual lips and metallic blaze of his eyes. She'd always been aware that his body was strong and powerful—his physical prowess was legendary—but suddenly it wasn't easy to be quite so objective about it. With a sudden flash of insight, Rosie understood why women used to swoon whenever he was around. Why their faces would contort with desire when they thought he wasn't looking.

Her heart skipped an uncomfortable beat. Had she too fallen victim to his allure after years of being immune to it? Was she fated to join the bloated ranks of women who desired him, who humiliated themselves in their desire to get him to bed them, or wed them?

She gave herself a mental shake. No, she was not.

Only a fool would wander down that path. She needed an urgent encounter with reality and to remember their last encounter, when all traces of the old Corso seemed to have vanished. He had been cold and cruel, accusing her of jealousy when she'd told him what she'd overheard. He had looked her up and down as if she were something unpleasant he'd found clinging to the sole of his boots. And then he'd dismissed her—making her feel small and inconsequential—before the night had descended into total chaos. His father had died unexpectedly and Corso had been pronounced King, right before her eyes. The ball had ended abruptly and the whole country had been plunged into mourning.

On her flight back to England the next day, Rosie had wondered if Corso had gone ahead and spent the night with Tiffany anyway, because hadn't she read somewhere that people found comfort in sex, during times of intense grief? But if he had, there had been no apparent consequences. No baby and certainly no wedding. Tiffany Sackler had gone on to marry some hedge-fund manager and was living between Manhattan and the Hamptons. And if occasionally Rosie had seen articles about Corso in newspapers, which took great pains to report that he remained resolutely single, she genuinely hadn't cared.

She needed to remember that she was a different person now. She was seven years older and had cut her ties with him and his homeland completely. She had grown up—in all ways. Physically, she had been a late developer, but at twenty, her body had suddenly filled out. Almost overnight she'd stopped being skinny and gawky and had acquired curves and she'd had to get used to having breasts, and hips. She had found a job she enjoyed, even if it didn't pay quite as much as she would like. But she supplemented her income with extra work *and* she was almost at the end of a perfectly respectable online arts degree, even though she hadn't been able to utilise it yet. She had made something of herself and didn't have to hang onto his every word, or agree with him, or bow down to him. She didn't even have to talk to him if she didn't want to. She wasn't his subject and she owed him nothing.

Nothing. Not even the cowering deference which he probably thought was his due.

'I did you a favour once before and you threw it back in my face,' she reminded him.

'That was wrong of me.' He hesitated, like a person who was about to use unfamiliar phraseology. 'I was— am—very grateful to you.'

Her gaze was suspicious. 'Really?'

'Really.' His words were dry. 'Unfortunately, you didn't choose the most opportune moment to tell me.'

'It was the only one I had. I couldn't get near you all evening, or work my way through the adoring crush.' The unreasonable accusations of jealousy he had thrown at her had rankled for a long time, and Rosie subjected him to a steady stare. 'Anyway, that's all in the past. I'm puzzled why you think I could do you a favour, Corso. What possible use can I be when you're one of the best-connected men in the world while I am just an ordinary woman?'

'Perhaps that is the key to your usefulness,' he mused. 'The sheer ordinariness of your life.' His rich gaze seared over her. 'Forgive me if my words offend you.'

'Why should they?' she questioned, though of course—they did. 'Like me, you are only stating facts.'

'Indeed. You have a job on the railways, I understand?'

Did he really? Rosie wondered acidly. Could a man in his position ever *understand* what it was like to work for a living, or worry about where his next meal was coming from?

She nodded. 'I'm in charge of the catering trolley on the long-distance line which operates between Paddington and Cornwall.' She stabbed her finger against the little red train logo above her breast. 'This is my uniform, in case you were wondering.'

'Indeed.' He inclined his head. 'I confess I was surprised when they told me. It isn't the profession I would have mapped out for you.'

Instinctively, Rosie's eyes narrowed. He must want something very badly if he was prepared to indulge in meaningless small talk like this. 'Is that so?' she questioned innocently. 'What did you imagine me doing, Corso? I'm sure you must have given the matter a good deal of thought over the years.'

His brows narrowed, as if correctly sensing sarcasm. 'Something to do with antiquities, perhaps,' he suggested. 'Or with art, or literature—fine-tuning the gifts you might have inherited from your father. Didn't you used to help him? I often used to see the two of you dusting and polishing precious artefacts around the palace?'

She felt vulnerable then and wished she hadn't challenged him. Of *course* she would have loved to have followed Lionel Forrester into his rarefied field of archaeology, but jobs like that were few and far between. And life had had other plans for her, waiting to emerge from the shadows, like spectres. Those same spectres swept into her mind now and she thought about the constant nag of debt. Of bankruptcy. Of human frailty and the depths to which someone would sink in their pursuit of love. A terrible sadness pierced her heart and it took a moment or two before she trusted herself to speak. 'Yes, I used to help him in school holidays. He taught me all about Monterosso and its rich history and I was very grateful for that. Actually, I've been doing an on-line arts degree.'

'So I understand.'

'Your people found that out for you as well, did they?'

He shrugged. 'That's what I pay them for.'

'I've submitted my dissertation,' she explained, not quite knowing why she was telling him all this, other than the fact that—amazingly—he actually looked as if he were interested. 'I just haven't had the final degree yet.'

'Which is why I am here today,' he said. 'If you are prepared to hear me out?'

It was so out of character for Corso to seek permission to speak that for a moment Rosie was startled into silence. She wanted to tell him no. To go away and leave her alone—taking his newly distracting presence with him. But she felt as if she had a duty to listen to what he had to say, because her dad had loved him. He had loved him like the son he'd never had and hadn't she sometimes been jealous of that? And she was curious, too. Of course she was. Who wouldn't be, in her position? 'Very well,' she agreed. 'Why don't you sit down and make yourself comfortable?'

But he didn't sit—as if the concept of comfort was irreconcilable with a place like this. He just continued to stand there, dominating the space around him with his hard and brilliant allure, and suddenly Rosie wanted to be as far away from him as was possible. She took off her bulky jacket and hung it on the back of one of the dining chairs, before perching on it, and from here it was impossible not to study him as she waited for him to speak.

He looked older, she thought—and his air of cynicism seemed even more pronounced. The lines around his lips were deeper and his flame-dark hair was flecked with the occasional strand of silver. His body had always been lean, but never had it looked harder than it did right now. As if he'd spent the last seven years banishing every ounce of softness from his frame. As if he were determined that each muscle should be honed and defined. And although he had clearly made an attempt to dress down in jeans and a dark leather jacket—presumably in an attempt to blend in and look 'normal'—he had failed spectacularly, because his aristocratic lineage radiated from him like a precious aura. He exuded charisma and power and something else. She swallowed. Pure, raw sex appeal—there was no other way to describe it.

Rosie's breasts tightened and she felt the wash of something warm and seductive, slowly unfurling inside her. Her breasts began to grow heavy and prickle at the tips. It was a deliciously distracting feeling and because she liked it too much, she wanted it gone. Unseen on her lap, she clenched her fingers, because she didn't want to think of him this way. She didn't want to think of him in *any* way. She wanted her old immunity back and to be protected from this sudden aching awareness of her neglected body.

'Okay, then. Enlighten me.' She laid her palms flat on the table, directly in front of the vase of daffodils. 'I'm all ears.'

Corso nodded, momentarily distracted by the gleam of her hair, which was a slightly paler shade than the flowers, before cursing the random nature of his thoughts. What a ridiculous thing to preoccupy him at a time like this!

He forced himself to concentrate.

How much to tell her?

How much did she need to know?

He felt the sudden clench of his heart.

As little as possible.

Because information was power—and right now he needed all the power he could retain. Wasn't that one of his greatest fears—that the knowledge he had acquired spelled danger, not just to him, but to his country? That the past was going to rear its ugly head and impact dramatically on his future and the future of his people?

'Your father was responsible for the discovery of Monterosso's most significant and ancient artefacts,' he said. 'In particular, the jewellery collection of the country's tragic young Queen, who died in childbirth, over four thousand years ago.'

'Do you really think I need to be reminded of that?' she answered quietly. 'When the pursuit of that treasure was responsible for his own untimely death. If… if he hadn't been so keen to get back to that underwater burial chamber a second time and had waited for back-up, he might still be alive today.'

Corso saw the way her face had paled. Heard the pain and sadness in her voice. But he detected accusation, too—trembling at the edge of her words as subtly as a night-time breeze—and his eyes narrowed. Did she hold Monterosso responsible for his death?

'Lionel was a passionate archaeologist, Rosie, and sometimes men like that take risks,' he said, more gently than was usual for him. 'That was the life he chose. A life he loved and thrived on. Which drove him. He was impatient to see what that cave contained, which was why he went in on his own. It may not have been what you or I would have done but it was what he wanted.'

Tears pricked the backs of her eyes as Rosie stared down at her fingers, determined that Corso wouldn't see them, because his words were chipping away at her defences and making her feel...*vulnerable*. And instinct told her it was dangerous to feel that way—especially in front of him. Oh, why had he started talking about all this after so long? Didn't she have enough to deal with, without him reminding her of a time when life had been peachy?

'Yes, I know that,' she said, composing herself before lifting her face to meet his gaze. 'But sometimes it seems as though he died for nothing. The treasures he uncovered have never been seen, or even written about. His discovery seemed to have faded into insignificance, as if it had never happened. As if it didn't matter.'

'My thoughts exactly,' he breathed. 'And the reason I am here today.'

The smile which accompanied his words was disturbing and Rosie couldn't work out why. Because it felt strangely *manipulative*?

Or because it was making her blood slug around her veins, as sweet and heavy as honey?

She blinked. It was almost as if Corso were playing with her, in the way an expert angler played a fish, before bringing it dry and gasping to the shore.

'I want the world to see these jewels and marvel at their splendour,' he continued softly. 'I have a vision for Monterosso's future, Rosie, and the collection will help me achieve that vision. I plan to take it on a whistle-stop tour of Paris, New York and London. Some of the most beautiful cities in the world, which will showcase our finest treasures.' There was a pause before his gaze became shuttered by his thick lashes. 'And I want you to come with me.'

CHAPTER FOUR

THE KING'S SILKEN words shimmered through the confines of her tiny sitting room and Rosie stared at him in disbelief.

'You want to take the Monterossian burial jewels around the world and for *me* to accompany you? I'm sorry, but you've lost me, Corso. Why? I mean, why me?'

He frowned with the exasperation of a man not often required to repeat himself.

'It's simple,' he said, not very patiently.

Rather alarmingly, he pulled out a chair and sat down opposite her at the table, so close that Rosie imagined she could feel the warmth of his breath. Close enough to see the dark amber flecks in his golden eyes. And the faux intimacy made Rosie remember when he'd occasionally appear at the door of her parents' grace-and-favour house in Monterosso, and they would invite him to join them for a family meal, soon after his mother had died. Her own mother had urged Rosie and her sister to treat the Prince 'normally' and they had been young and unselfconscious enough to comply. Rosie remembered sometimes thinking how *alone* he had seemed, and her heart had gone out to him.

But that was an erroneous impression, she reminded

herself fiercely. Corso was the least lonely person on the planet. He was idolised and adored and always had been. It was well known that from the moment he had lain in his cradle, he had been waited on hand and foot, for he was the only child of the royal marriage and a precious son and heir. From the moment he was born, he'd had only to lift a chubby little fist and one of his adoring nurses would rush to his side. It was true that his father had been away a lot and in the latter years his mother had been very sick, but day and night he was surrounded by people, eager to fall in with his every wish. Which made it even more inexplicable why he had turned up *here*, at her little cottage deep in the forest. But perhaps it was her memory of those earlier times which made her lean back in her chair and humour him.

'Carry on,' she said.

Corso nodded, aware of needing to choose his words carefully because Rosie wasn't the walkover he'd been expecting. He had anticipated her eagerness to agree with whatever it was he suggested, not for her to survey him with that faint air of scepticism. He was here because, essentially, he trusted her, which meant he could tell her some things. He felt his throat dry. Just not everything.

'When I inherited the Kingdom seven years ago, I had to look at my country with different eyes,' he said. 'As a ruler, rather than an heir—and these positions are very different. I was to discover things which had never been apparent to me before...'

'What kind of things?' she interjected curiously as his words tailed off.

Corso shot her a reprimanding look. He wanted to tell her that *he* would be the giver of information, rather than her attempting to take it from him. But something warned him that if he wanted her to fall in with his wishes, then he needed to be diplomatic. And so he nodded benignly, as if he weren't in the least bit irritated by her interruption.

'My father's way of ruling was not my way, Rosie. And the legacy he left me was not...ideal. Now that I have properly settled into my reign, I intend to do things very differently.'

'A new broom,' she suggested quietly.

'If you like.' He got up from the chair and walked over to the window and stared out at the seemingly impenetrable green of the forest outside, before turning back to see her grey eyes fixed on him. 'I did not realise, until the mantle of the throne came upon me, how much I really loved my country. Or, rather, the country I want it to be. I want to forge a new Monterosso. One which is no longer solely dependent on gambling, or providing a tax haven for questionable sources of income. I want an inward investment for my land, which will benefit my people. High-end eco-tourism, among other things. The tour is to showcase some of the historic culture of the nation, but will also serve as a backdrop for my meetings with business leaders and investors. It will act as a reminder of Monterosso's great history, as well as all the possibilities of a great future.'

There was a pause while she absorbed this, touching her fingers to the ends of her thick plait. But her no-nonsense hairstyle was having precisely the wrong effect on him. He imagined himself loosening it, seeing it falling like pale silk between his fingers, and, as he experienced another jerk of unwanted desire, he scowled.

'There's no need to glare at me like that, Corso,' she

said. 'Because, while all this sounds very commendable, I still fail to see how I can help you. I may *almost* have a degree in art, but I have no real experience of mounting an exhibition. In fact, I don't have any experience at all.'

'You don't need any.' Corso felt his jaw tighten as the image of a face swam into his mind. A face similar to his own. *An unknown half-brother who lived on the other side of the world. A man he had never met nor wanted to meet. But he knew that state of affairs could not continue. He couldn't continue burying his head in the sand and pretending his sibling didn't exist.*

His pulse accelerated. And wasn't that the real reason why he wanted to take the jewels on tour—to conceal a potentially threatening assignation behind a cloak of cultural respectability? He shuttered his eyes as he returned her gaze because Rosie didn't need to know that. His mouth hardened. Perhaps nobody needed to know. 'My historians have collated the entire collection.'

'So take *them* with you.'

'I don't want them. I want you. You're the one who can bring the jewels to life because you are Lionel's daughter—and that will add a personal touch like no other. Your presence will ensure the kind of publicity which is impossible to buy, as well as being a fitting testimonial to your family name. Obviously, there will be challenges. But you are young and have potential.' His gaze swept over her assessingly. 'Naturally, you will need to do something about your appearance.'

'What's the matter with my appearance?' she demanded.

'Nothing. I am sure it's completely appropriate for the life you lead but not...' He paused, speculatively. 'Not for a member of the royal party.'

'Are you *trying* to insult me, Corso?'

'Not at all.' He met the stormy flash of her eyes. 'Would you prefer weaselly words of flattery instead of hearing the truth? Especially when beauty can be such a curse,' he added, his words rough.

'Yet one possessed by every woman you've ever been associated with! Funny that.' She pulled a face. 'Well, I must say that the last thing I imagined on my way back from work this afternoon was to find you here, waiting to make me such an extraordinary offer.'

He gave a reflective smile. 'Which, now that you've heard, you are happy to accept?'

As she met his metallic gaze, Rosie gave herself just long enough to imagine what it might be like if she agreed to his bizarre request. She remembered some of the perks which accompanied involvement with the Monterossian royal family. You never had to wait—not for anything. According to her dad, you always got the best rooms and the best service. People tried to get near you and they were prepared to grovel if they thought you had the ear of the King. But that wasn't her world. It never had been, not really—and it would be dangerous to allow herself to be lured back into it.

Yet it was more than that which made her realise she was going to send Corso away without the answer he desired. Mostly, it was because of the way he was making her feel, which was freaking her out. He was doing it right now, with that lazy smile which was drawing attention to the curve of his lips. She'd never found him in the least bit attractive in the past, but something had happened to make her completely reverse that assessment. Because he wasn't just hot, he was dangerous. Way too dangerous for an innocent like her.

She smiled, trying to refuse as tactfully as possible because he wouldn't like it. He wouldn't like it at all. Well, that was tough. It might do him good if someone actually had the nerve to refuse him. 'Flattered as I am to have been asked,' she said, 'I'm afraid my answer has to be no.'

'Are you serious?'

'I'm very serious.'

'Because?'

'Because I already have a job, Corso. It's decent work,' she added defensively, when she saw the incredulous look in his eyes. 'And it pays me an honest wage. I can't just announce that I'm about to fly off with the King of Monterosso on a whim.'

There was a pause which went on a little too long to be entirely comfortable. 'And there's nothing I can do to change your mind?' he said at last.

'Nothing,' she said firmly.

'Are you quite sure about that, Rosie?' he said, in a voice she'd never heard him use before. 'Because I'm thinking your salary must be very modest and probably not enough for your current needs. Am I right?'

Instinctively, Rosie sat up straight because although the words weren't exactly a *threat*, they were definitely underpinned with something disquieting. 'What does my salary have to do with *you*?'

Corso gave a reluctant sigh as her defiance washed over him and for a moment he felt something close to regret. Because he hadn't wanted to do it like this. He'd hoped she would demonstrate the compliancy which was as familiar to him as the sound of his own heartbeat—of people doing what he wanted them to do, without question.

'Why don't you just think of it in terms of an opportunity?' he questioned silkily. 'The tour would take less than a month. You could request unpaid leave and go back to your job once it's over. If you like, I can easily have my people sort that out for you.'

'How very convenient,' she said faintly.

'Or you might think about leaving the railway altogether and trying something new. I have connections you could utilise. You could use the degree you have worked so hard for,' he continued smoothly. 'And I am prepared to be generous, Rosie. Very generous.' The sum he mentioned provoked an instinctive widening of her grey eyes, but just as quickly the look vanished—to be replaced by a quiet fury which he found strangely *attractive*.

'You think I'm someone you can just move around the place however it suits you, like a pawn on a chess board?' she demanded. 'You can't just rearrange my life for me and you certainly can't *buy* me. I'm not one of your adoring subjects, Corso—in fact, I'm the very opposite!'

Again Corso felt the frisson of unexpected heat, because he was finding her truculence intensely provocative. Her rosy lips were parted. Her cheeks were flushed pink. And despite the thick sweater and workmanlike trousers which flapped around her ankles, he was moved by an urgent desire to take her in his arms and kiss her.

'I would advise you to consider two things,' he said unevenly, as the blood pounded hot and sweet around his veins.

'Which are?'

Briefly, he savoured her challenge before preparing to quash it, because surely to reprimand her would remind her of the natural order of things. 'Firstly, I do not expect to be spoken to in such a manner.'

'Well, there's a simple solution to that. You can always leave.' She tilted her chin. 'Nobody's stopping you.'

'And secondly,' he continued, trying to ignore the thick plait swaying like a blonde snake against the luscious curve of her breasts. 'I think you'll find that interest rates on credit cards are very high. And if you're not careful, you could spend the rest of your life servicing your debt.'

He got a reaction then and it was more profound than he had expected. All the fight went out of her. Like a hot needle lancing into a balloon, she seemed instantly to deflate. As she slumped back onto the chair, her face grew even paler. Her grey eyes were filled with alarm and a look of fleeting reproach, which somehow made him feel guilty. But not for long.

'What are you talking about?' she husked.

'If you like, we could play games all evening, Rosie.' He shrugged. 'You could feign ignorance and outrage. Or you could accept that I know all about your current difficulties.'

'What...?' she whispered. 'What do you know?'

'I know about your large credit card debt. That the reason you're able to live in this cottage is because you help clean the big house of the estate on which it stands. I gather you have a wealthy absentee Sicilian owner to thank for that. And living rent-free enables most of your salary to reduce the money your mother owes to the courts, which is a frightening amount, by most people's standards. I know that you and your sister are guarantors and committed to paying it off.' He paused, and suddenly he was curious. 'What did she do, Rosie?'

He saw the faint flicker of fear which crossed her pale features. 'I'm surprised you haven't found that out, too.'

He shrugged. 'My investigation threw up only the bare facts, which were sufficient for my needs.' He narrowed his eyes as he looked at her. 'But I'm advising you that if radical action isn't taken quickly it could ruin your and Bianca's future, because long-term debt can grind you down.'

'And someone in your position would know all about long-term debt, of course,' she said sarcastically.

But Rosie's heart had started racing like one of the high-speed trains she rode every day of her working life. *How* had he found out their secret, when she and Bianca had done everything possible to keep the whole affair quiet?

And then she wondered how she could have been so naïve.

His advisors would have rooted around to discover stuff about her—just as they must have known exactly when she would arrive home today. They would have studied her shifts to ensure that the King didn't turn up to an empty cottage. He was simply using the knowledge which was always available to him.

'Are you…are you trying to *blackmail* me, Corso? Is that what this is all about?'

He laughed then, but she thought it sounded as empty as the cruel wind which sometimes howled in the trees outside her cottage, during the long months of winter.

'Don't be so melodramatic,' he remonstrated silkily. 'What would be the point of that? I am not in the business of destroying lives. I'm just pointing out that if you do me a favour, I could return the compliment and do one for you. It could be mutually beneficial, don't you think?'

Her head was spinning but, despite the magic wand temptation of having the Mediterranean king cancel the debt, Rosie knew she had to refuse—because warning signs were leaping up in front of her like road blocks. She didn't *need* his help. She and Bianca were managing on their own...just. She didn't *want* to make herself beholden to his immense privilege and power. She had weaned herself off Monterosso and its spurious glamour. She'd turned her back on her former life and put it in the past.

Plus, she didn't like him. Not any more. She found him proud and cold and arrogant. It didn't help that she had started wanting him in a way she'd never wanted anyone before. But the things you wanted and the things you got were two very different things.

'My answer is still no,' she said, ignoring the disbelief which made his autocratic features grow so cold. 'And now, I'm going to have to cut this visit short, I'm afraid. I need to do some cleaning over at the big house because Signor Corsini is flying a bunch of guests over from Palermo next weekend and he likes everything looking its best.'

But to her surprise Corso didn't react to the kind of dismissal he was unlikely to have experienced before. He just put his hand in the breast pocket of his leather jacket and pulled out a card, his expression still unyielding. It was the same stony countenance which was stamped on the front of every Monterossian coin and, for a moment, Rosie felt slightly intimidated.

But then he wrong-footed her and afterwards she wondered if it had been deliberate. He walked across the room towards her, covering the tiny space in seconds until he was standing directly in front of her—tall and golden, dominant and beautiful. A glowing god of man, pulsing with life and virility. Rosie gazed up at him as he took her hand, slipping the card into her palm before gently closing her fingers around it, and the resulting spark which fizzed over her skin was just...

Electric.

It was the briefest of touches yet her body rippled in instant response—as if she had spent her whole life waiting for him to touch her like that. Did he feel it too? Was that why he suddenly tensed, as if someone were about to land a blow on his solar plexus? Why he fixed her with that questioning golden gaze which seemed to burn right through her? She held her breath—almost as if she were waiting for him to do something else. Like what? Pull her into his arms and kiss her? Wasn't that what her fevered imagination was conjuring up?

But he didn't.

Of course he didn't.

His lips simply curved with a hint of mockery as he let go of her hand.

'Why don't you think about what I've said, Rosie? In my experience, it's always better to sleep on a proposition, before coming to a decision.'

His words hung in the air like silken baubles as, noiselessly, he let himself out of the cottage.

CHAPTER FIVE

'HE SAID *WHAT*?'

Rosie very nearly pulled a face but she didn't want to irritate her sister any more than she was already. She didn't want to repeat herself either, because she suspected that Bianca had registered every word she'd said and just wanted to mull them over.

That was the trouble with these video phone calls, she thought gloomily. You couldn't pretend. Your reaction was there for all to see—no matter how fuzzy the pixilation on the computer screen, or the fact that you were talking to someone in faraway Venice.

'I told you,' she said dully. 'Corso knows about Mum.'

'*What* does he know?'

'That she owes masses of money.'

'Does he know why?'

'It appears not, although that could just be an act. With Corso, you never know.'

'Tell me again what he said.'

Rosie swallowed. 'He wants to make full use of the Forrester name—to cash in on Dad's reputation and the fact that he discovered the jewels. He wants to exploit the fact that I'm Lionel's daughter and that I've got a degree in art history—well, I will have soon, hopefully. Which is presumably why he's offered me a ridiculous amount of money to go on a tour of the collection with him.'

'How much money?' asked her sister quickly.

As Rosie repeated the incredible sum, she was greeted with complete silence—which was rare. On screen she could see Bianca chewing her bottom lip, the way she used to do when she was at boarding school—studying harder than anyone else in her year. The dazzling star student Rosie had spent her life being unfavourably compared to.

'And you said, what?' Bianca demanded.

'What do you think I said? I refused, of course.' Rosie tried to iron out the defensiveness in her voice and to silence the thought which was telling her she was being unreasonable. 'I don't want to go anywhere with *him*,' she added fiercely. 'Especially not on a whistle-stop tour of three big cities I've never been to before.'

'Why not?'

Because suddenly I've started to fancy him. Because he makes me want to do things I've never done before and feel stuff I've never felt before. Because, because, because...

'He's insufferable!' she breathed. 'I'd forgotten just how arrogant he can be.'

Bianca gave her a look. 'Good heavens. How things change! I always thought the sky went dark whenever he sat down. It was always "Corso this" and "Corso that".' She huffed out a great big sigh. 'But that's all irrelevant.'

Rosie screwed up her face as she looked at the screen, because there was something in Bianca's tone which she recognised of old, and it was making foreboding creep over her skin. 'I'm not sure what you're talking about.'

'Then let me enlighten you, dear Rosie,' said Bianca—her studiedly patient tone morphing into the natural bossiness of a big sister. 'Corso's wealth can wipe out this debt for us—and that can't come a moment too soon. I'm fed up with scrimping and saving, just because of the stupid mistake our mother made. I don't want to be saddled with money worries for the rest of my life and neither should you. So here's what you do. You ring him and tell him you'll agree to do what he wants.' There was a dramatic pause. 'Only you ask for twice as much money.'

If Rosie had been on a conventional phone call, this would have been the moment when she probably would have dropped the handset and smashed it. 'Are you out of your mind?' she breathed. 'I can't do that! What he's offering is more than generous!'

'Rubbish! It'll be like small change to him. Think about it. Wouldn't it be nice to use the extra to get Mum a decent place of her own, near her sister, where she can lick her wounds and find some kind of peace?' On screen, Bianca swept a glossy handful of black hair away from her face. 'I don't see why Corso Andrea da Vignola can't dig deeper into his pockets—he is one of the richest men in the world, after all.'

'I know he is.' Rosie swallowed, but her throat still felt like sandpaper. 'But I don't feel comfortable asking for more.'

'Why not?'

What could she possibly say? That she didn't want Corso to think she was greedy and grasping? It didn't *matter* what he thought of her, did it? Or maybe the truth was more insidious. What would Bianca say if she admitted that her major reservation was far more frightening? How would her worldly sister react if Rosie blurted out this stupid desire which seemed to have come out of nowhere? Which was that she wanted to melt into the King's powerful arms and offer her virginity to him, despite his arrogance and deep sense of entitlement?

Wouldn't that be enough of a let-out clause?

But she couldn't do that. For a start she would never admit that to anyone, not even her sister. And if she forced herself to discount Corso's physical impact, his offer made nothing but sense. Because Bianca was right. Sometimes Rosie felt as if the regular repayments were chipping away at her soul as well as her bank account. Why should *her* weakness around the Monterossian king prevent her from taking a step which would liberate them both?

She sighed. 'I suppose I'll have to do it.'

'Excellent.' Bianca flashed a cat-like smile. 'Keep me posted, little sister.' Suddenly there was a pinging noise and the screen went blank.

Rosie rose from the little desk which was shoved next to the wardrobe in the cottage's only bedroom. It was all very well to be bullish when she was talking to Bianca, but now she was filled with an overwhelming sense of dread at the thought of what lay ahead. She stared down at the discreetly expensive card he'd given her. It said simply: Corso of Monterosso, and next to his name was a phone number. All she had to do was to ring him.

But it took ages for her to pluck up the courage and, in the meantime, she procrastinated. She went over to the big house to check that everything was in place for Lucio Corsini's visit, before the temporary housekeeper, chef and butler arrived to cater for the tycoon's weekend party.

And that was another thing. Her cottage accommodation was provided free in return for keeping an eye on the property of the wealthy Sicilian. How would Lucio react when she told him she intended to be absent for a whole month while she waltzed off with the King of Monterosso?

Before she had time to change her mind, Rosie grabbed her phone and tapped out the number he'd given her, holding her breath as she prepared herself for the velvety onslaught of his voice. But instead of getting Corso, it went straight to one of his assistants, who introduced herself as Ivana.

'The King would like you to come in and see him in person.'

'But, I—'

'The embassy is in Belgrave Square,' continued Ivana, with the calm delivery of a woman who never deviated from her boss's wishes. 'I understand that you work in London, so it shouldn't be a problem. Just tell me what time suits and I'm sure we can work something into His Majesty's schedule. And please don't worry about transport. We can easily send a car to pick you up.'

'No, thank you,' said Rosie grimly. Imagining a royal car turning up at the Paddington train depot! What on earth would all her co-workers say if they saw the Monterossian flag fluttering on the bonnet? 'I'll make my own way.'

Which was how she found herself cycling through the drizzle to the quiet tree-lined streets of Belgravia the following afternoon. Past the imposing houses she rode before chaining her bike to a railing outside the beautiful, white-stuccoed building which housed the Monterossian embassy, where the two burly-looking men who guarded the entrance stared at her askance. But Rosie didn't care. So what if she was dripping rainwater onto their pristine marble floor, or was already getting hot and sweaty beneath her waterproof jacket? Corso had demanded to *see* her—so see her he would, warts and all.

Nevertheless, she felt sticky and crumpled as she was shown to the King's grand suite of offices on the first floor, past sleek women and equally sleek men who didn't lift their gazes from their computer screens. Over an endless expanse of pale wood she walked until at last she was shown into the inner sanctum of the monarch's office and, to her surprise, Corso was alone.

He sat behind a monster of a desk—ancient, carved blackwood by the look of it—and her attention was captured by a crystal paperweight which threw vivid rainbow light across the polished surface. Behind him were a couple of exquisite paintings of Monterosso—one depicting the silvery shimmer of the iconic lake which edged the country's capital and the other a landscape view of the wild mountain range which lay to the north of the country. She didn't want to feel a jab of nostalgia but there it was, all the same.

And when Rosie could distract her gaze no longer, she allowed it to fall on the flame-haired man who was leaning back in his chair, studying her with amusement quirking the edges of his lips, as if he was perfectly aware that she'd been trying to look anywhere other than at him. She couldn't deny that he looked delectable—or that the roof of her mouth had dried with instant desire, but hopefully she disguised her reaction well enough with a small, forced smile.

At first glance, his dark suit, pale shirt and a tie of amber silk made him seem the embodiment of the contemporary man, but a portrait of one of his ancestors on a nearby wall and the identical glint in Corso's eyes reminded her of his background. He was privileged. Ruthless and powerful. He didn't care about her, or her feelings. He just wanted what suited him.

That was how royal dynasties managed to survive.
And to dominate.

'Rosie,' he purred, and she could hear the satisfaction in his voice. 'Why don't you remove that dripping garment and come and sit down?'

She didn't want to sit down. She didn't want to be here, but her skin was tingling as if she were standing in front of a naked flame and so she peeled off her sopping cagoule and hung it on the back of the chair. Sinking into the surprisingly comfortable seat on the other side of the desk, she looked at him questioningly. 'I gather you wanted to see me in person?'

'I did. And I will take your presence here as acceptance.' His eyes narrowed. 'You will do as I ask?'

'Yes. I've spoken to my sister and she thinks...' She shrugged. 'We both think I should accept your offer.'

'Excellent.'

Rosie opened her lips to speak, but she was finding it harder to replicate Bianca's demand than she'd imagined. 'But on one condition.'

'On one condition,' he repeated, only now his voice had taken on an edge of something she didn't recognise. 'And what might that be, I wonder?'

'I want more,' she blurted out into the awkward silence which followed his question.

He raised his eyebrows. 'More?' he echoed unhelpfully.

'Money.' She tried not to flinch as she saw contempt hardening his features. 'I... I want more money.'

Corso felt a slow rush of anger invading his blood—but the feeling was underpinned with something else. Something he hadn't expected, nor wanted to feel—and that was a deep sense of disappointment. Because yes, he had pushed hard to get Rosie Forrester to agree to his offer—but he had justified his behaviour with the knowledge that, ultimately, his generosity would benefit her family. She was her father's daughter after all, and part of him had hoped Lionel's liberal attitude might have percolated down to his younger daughter. Had he imagined that she might regard him as a person, rather than just a symbol of power and wealth? That, having had time to think about the many benefits his offer would bring, she might also wish to accompany him for old times' sake, and even be grateful for his intervention? Yes. Stupidly enough, he had.

Silently, he cursed his foolish idealism, focussing on her true nature as a way of sidelining the sudden stab to his heart. Why, she was as avaricious as any other woman he'd ever met! And perhaps not quite as clever as she imagined. Wasn't she aware that her attitude would destroy any lingering traces of affection he'd held for her? Yet in many ways it was easier to be angry with her than to desire her. And definitely easier to concentrate on her blatant greed, rather than the brother who awaited him in New York.

The brother whose very existence is a testament to the sham of your parents' supposedly perfect marriage.

'How much do you want?' he demanded harshly, but at this she blushed and the brief flicker of hurt which clouded her grey eyes was confusing. He shook his head in frustration. She ought to make up her mind about the part she was trying to play. About whether she wanted to come over as acquisitive or sensitive. About who she really was.

'Er, I haven't quite worked it out yet,' she prevaricated.

'Which is just about the most hopeless piece of negotiation I've witnessed in a long time,' he snapped. 'What exactly do you want the money for, Rosie?'

She moved a little awkwardly, which had the unfortunate effect of making his gaze want to stray to the luscious swell of her breasts, which managed to transform a perfectly ordinary sweater into one of the most provocative pieces of clothing he'd ever seen. But, with a huge effort of will, he kept his eyes fixed firmly on her face.

'I'd rather not say.'

'Tough, because I'd rather you would. I might even make it a condition.' He flicked her a disdainful look. 'Or maybe you think you have the monopoly on conditions, Rosie?'

For a moment she seemed about to object, but maybe she realised she was on shaky ground because she chewed her bottom lip, before nodding in silent assent.

'It's to pay off the debts and buy Mum a house,' she said at last. 'Once the court judgement against her has been settled. She's renting a cheap bedsit in the middle of London at the moment and we'd like her to have a little cottage in the country, near to where her sister lives.'

Corso leaned back in his chair, her selfless declaration taking him by surprise, reluctantly forcing him to reassess his jaundiced view of her. Because he didn't want to think of her as thoughtful, or caring. In fact, he didn't want to think about her at all. 'Don't you think it's time you told me how she got herself into so much debt?' he probed. 'Since you're expecting me to bankroll her future.'

Rosie wanted to tell him it was none of his business, but she could see that maybe it was. In a way, she had *made* it his business, by asking him to increase his offer. And if she didn't tell him, he would find out soon enough—if he were so inclined. So why not give him her version—even if there wasn't really a way of conveying the facts which didn't make her mother look a little sad?

She hoped her shrug hid the pain—because that was the trouble with remembering. It hurt. 'My mother was never the same after Dad died.'

'They were that rare thing,' he observed. 'A married couple who seemed genuinely to care for one another.'

She wondered if she had imagined the bitterness in his voice—but it wasn't exactly the sort of thing she could ask him about, was it? 'Yes, they did. They cared for each other very deeply. That's probably why she missed him so badly after he died. She felt lost without him. She went to pieces and never seemed to put herself back together again. Way too soon after his death she went onto an online dating site to try to find herself a new partner—desperately looking to replace what she had with Dad.' She hesitated. 'So that, unfortunately, the predictable happened.'

He narrowed his eyes. 'The predictable being, what?'

She wanted to tell him to use his imagination, but what was the point? She didn't think Corso would have a clue what she was talking about. He didn't operate in the same kind of world she lived in and she doubted whether he even *had* an imagination. 'She lost her heart to a man she'd never even met. How insane is that?'

'*Losing* your heart to anyone is something I've never understood,' he said, his voice edged with acid. 'But yes, that kind of behaviour is particularly insane.' He leaned back in the sumptuous leather chair, the spring sunshine streaming in from the tall windows and setting the thick mane of his hair on fire. 'So what happened?'

'She gave him money every time he came up with yet another excuse about why he wasn't able to meet her in person.' Rosie gave a hollow laugh as the long-repressed words rushed from her mouth and she realised she'd never talked about it with anyone else, other than her sister. She had hidden it away, like a dirty little secret. 'It was the usual story. He was expecting a bank transfer which had been held up. He was due a huge inheritance any day. An ex-partner owed him hundreds of thousands of pounds. To an outsider it would have sounded exactly what it was—a blatant lie and a scam. But whatever he told her, she believed him. She was putty in his hands— blinded by longing and influenced by the three most manipulative words in the English language.'

'Those words being?'

'Oh, come on.' She met the question in his eyes. 'Do you really not know *that*, Corso?'

He lifted his shoulders expressively. 'I love you?'

And the craziest thing of all was that Rosie started wondering what it would be like if the flame-haired King were actually making that statement to her and that he *meant* it—rather than as a scornful query. She shuddered. What was the *matter* with her? Was she in danger of behaving as foolishly as her mother?

'You've got it in one,' she answered flippantly. 'By the time Bianca and I found out, it was too late. She'd lost everything—and more.' It had made her think a lot about grief. About loneliness. And for a while it had made her think that maybe she was lucky to have escaped all that. That maybe relationships weren't everything they were cracked up to be, if you could hurt so badly once they ended.

She looked at Corso and perhaps she was hoping for a smidgeon of understanding or empathy in his eyes, but she could read nothing in that hard, metallic gaze.

'Then perhaps we should acknowledge that my intervention is timely,' was all he said. 'And think about where we're headed, going forward.'

Rosie sat up very straight. 'Does that mean you agree to my price?'

'You might want to think carefully about how you express yourself,' he advised caustically. 'Unless your intention is to make yourself sound like a commodity in the marketplace, being offered to the highest bidder.'

Corso heard her shocked intake of breath and, though something was urging him to go gently on her, he did not heed it. She was not the Rosie he remembered. She had become someone he didn't know. She looked different. She sounded different. 'Yes, I agree to your price,' he continued coldly. 'And because of that you will agree to my terms.'

A soft knock on the door interrupted him in midflow and, with a flicker of irritation, Corso looked up to see his assistant standing in the doorway. 'Yes, Ivana— what is it?'

'I have the Maraban ambassador on the line.'

He waved an impatient hand through the air. 'Give me five minutes.' As the door closed behind his assistant, he returned his gaze to Rosie. 'You will meet me in Paris in exactly one week's time.'

'No way. I can't just walk out of my job that quickly,' she protested.

'This is the deal. Take it or leave it. It's not up for negotiation. We are showing the collection in three major cities—Paris, New York and London—and I want you there from the start. One of my assistants can liaise directly with your employers about temporarily replacing you, if that makes it simpler.'

'You think I am so easily replaceable?'

'Everyone is replaceable,' he said wryly. 'Even kings.'

'Even you, Corso? Surely not!'

Corso was tempted to tell her not to talk to him like that. He didn't want fire and feistiness, or teasing. He wanted her to be greedy and calculating. He wanted her to help reinforce his prejudices about women, which were deeply engrained—especially now. He didn't need her words to remind him of a different time, when life had seemed so simple. When he had been able to regard her as something close to a friend.

But it wasn't friendship he was feeling now. It was lust, pure and simple.

His gaze travelled over her. Her sweater was plain, her jeans faded—but the cheap clothes failed to conceal the fact that her body was strong and healthy. Or that her firm curves had obviously been acquired through hard work and natural exercise—not from narcissistic hours spent gazing at her own reflection in the mirror of a gym. Her thick hair was as pale as the dawn and the soft dimple in her cheek oddly compelling. But that kind of thinking was deeply unhelpful. *He needed to concentrate on her inadequacies, not on the way she was inexplicably turning him on.*

'We also need to find you some new clothes,' he said abruptly.

'You're assuming I have nothing appropriate of my own?'

'I really have no idea,' he drawled. 'Do you?'

Rosie glowered. Of course she didn't have anything suitable for an international royal trip. Her railway uniform and the casual clothes she favoured when she wasn't working would hardly go down a storm. Why, she only owned one dress and she couldn't remember the last time she'd worn it.

'Sorry, I'm fresh out of diamonds and lace!'

'You won't need those for TV. Simple works best for television.'

'*Television?*' she echoed, sitting bolt upright. 'Are you out of your mind?'

'Careful, Rosie—my aides might not take kindly to you casting doubts on my sanity.'

'Corso.' She cleared her throat. 'Listen.'

'I'm listening.'

'I can't possibly go on TV. I don't have any experience.'

'You've got the only experience anyone ever needs. You know your subject, don't you? You know all about your father…' There was a faint crack in his voice, before he recovered his velvety delivery. 'And all the treasures he unearthed,' he concluded.

'It isn't as simple as that. How can I possibly go on television? Me, of all people! I'm not a media personality—I'm a railway worker. I serve cups of tea and sandwiches on the train.'

'Don't worry. These days everybody gets their ten minutes of fame. We'll make sure you get a crash course in media training before we throw you to the lions.'

'Corso—'

'Rosie, I really don't have time for this.' He gave an impatient click of his fingers. 'If I feed your fear, it will only grow. I'll see you in Paris. My office will be in touch about the arrangements.'

He was staring at her pointedly and Rosie realised that the door had silently opened and Ivana was standing on the threshold, waiting to escort her from the premises, like a gatecrasher at a party. Her face hot, she rose to her feet, picking up her helmet and dripping cagoule. Her hand was shaking, she realised—and not just because Corso had ended the conversation so abruptly. Nor even because he'd high-handedly announced that he was going to provide her with a brand-new wardrobe. No, it was nothing to do with that. It was all to do with *him*. With his gleaming eyes and flame-kissed hair and a hard body which no amount of fancy clothes could disguise. How dared he make her want him like this?

Outside, she unchained her bicycle and stared up at the enormous first-floor windows of his offices, in time to see a silhouetted figure appear. It was too shadowy to be able to make out his features with any degree of clarity, but the hard-bodied frame was unmistakably that of the King as he stared down at her. She waited for him to lift his hand in a wave of acknowledgement—but no such sign came and she felt an undeniable twist of disappointment as he turned away from the window, as if dismissing her.

Rosie's heart raced as she wheeled her bike away. Didn't he realise how difficult it would be for someone like her to go on television, wearing stuff somebody else had chosen? Maybe that was the kind of magnanimous gesture which would thrill a certain kind of woman— but that woman wasn't her. She wasn't going to act like some grateful Cinderella, if that was what he was expecting. She would accept what she was given in a very grown-up way and afterwards she would hand every-thing back—borrowed clothes for a borrowed life. She would conduct herself appropriately because she knew how—she'd watched how royal circles operated often enough. And she would work her socks off, because she'd never been afraid of hard work.

Somehow—she wasn't sure how—she would over-come her fears and be an asset to Monterosso and its people. She would bring pride to the Forrester name. All she needed to do was to focus on the big prize which awaited her, which would liberate her and Bianca from the constant worry of debt and give their mother the type of home they thought she'd lost for ever.

Most important of all, she would keep her desire for Corso hidden.

Actually, she was going to do more than that. She would trample it ruthlessly underfoot, until it was noth-ing but a dusty memory of her own stupidity.

Somehow that seemed like the biggest ask of all.

CHAPTER SIX

THE TELEVISION STUDIO was buzzing with activity and people were running around in every direction. Impossibly glamorous people in ripped jeans, jabbering in French and gesturing excitedly with their hands. Rosie felt another stab of apprehension as she glanced around.

'Is it always like this?' she asked nervously, twisting her fingers together and wishing the palms of her hands weren't quite so sweaty.

The producer—who looked about twelve but was probably about the same age as her—shook his head. 'It is because we have a king here,' he said, giving a conspiratorial grin as he thumped his fist against his chest in a crude attempt to mimic a rapidly beating heart. 'All the women—they want him to notice them. I think that they want to be his queen—despite the fact that we are a proud republic!'

Rosie looked up at the monitor, where Corso's sculpted features dominated the screen, beneath which a small crowd of women were standing, watching him avidly. His skin glowed like old gold, his metallic eyes lashed with ebony and his dark hair lit with fire. She could see exactly why they were watching him because he really *did* look like an old-fashioned matinee idol

as he conducted the interview—but all she could think
about was the ordeal which lay ahead. She was up next
for her interview in front of the camera and already she
was frozen with fear. Despite the make-up artist dab-
bing her brow every other second, it remained hot and
clammy and her heart was pounding like mad beneath
the horrible black dress they'd given her to wear.

Half sick with dread, she turned away from the monitor and walked carefully to the far end of the studio,
desperate to be alone. For a moment she stood there in
blissful solitude, drawing in ragged gulps of air as she
tried to calm herself, though it did little to quell her spiralling fears. How could all those articles on deep breathing be so wrong, and how on earth had she ended up
here—in a Parisian television studio, waiting for one of
France's most respected art historians to quiz her about
the ancient jewels of Monterosso?

She couldn't do it.

She *wouldn't* do it.

Already events had taken on the surreal air of a
twisted fairy tale—but instead of a travelling in a
souped-up pumpkin, she had been plucked from her cottage in the forest before being whisked by limousine to
London, then flown to Paris on the King's private jet.
From the airstrip she had been taken to the Monterossian
embassy on the fancy Rue du Faubourg Saint-Honoré to
a suite of almost unimaginable splendour. She'd scarcely
had time to brush her teeth before a scarily sophisticated
stylist had turned up with a bunch of clothes for her to
try on, which were the last thing Rosie would ever have
chosen to wear herself. Silk, chiffon and leather were
very definitely *not* her thing and she'd nearly passed out
when she'd spotted a couple of the price tags.

Even worse was the accompanying lingerie because surely underwear was supposed to cover you up—rather than revealing more of her body than she was comfortable with. She had tried to refuse them, but, once again, had been overruled. It seemed that the palace was controlling everything—or rather, Corso was. He seemed to have been orchestrating things from a distance—and it was all too much. She felt like a puppet having its strings tweaked by an unseen master, which should have made her deeply indignant. So why did a scary shiver of excitement skate its way down her spine, every time she thought about it?

'Rosie? Ah. It *is* you. Once again, I find you hiding in the shadows. This is getting to be a habit. Is it a deliberate ploy, I wonder? An attempt to force people to seek you out?'

Rosie tensed as Corso's sardonic question rippled through the air like a brush of velvet and she turned to face him, resenting the sudden rush of awareness which sizzled through her as he walked across the studio floor to join her. She had convinced herself she was going to feel nothing but detachment when she saw him again, but her conviction was fast disappearing—melted away by the powerful heat of his presence. No man had a right to be this gorgeous, she thought despairingly. On the small screen he had been captivating—but up close he was positively *distracting*.

His dark designer suit hugged the contours of his muscular frame and he'd left the top two buttons of his silk shirt open, making him appear far more relaxed than usual. It was the first time she had spoken to him since arriving in France, because he'd been meeting with politicians and CEOs or so closely surrounded by his security people that nobody could get near him. She'd tried telling herself it was a bonus not to have to endure his company, or to have to gaze into the mocking distraction of his metallic gaze. The only trouble with that statement was that it wasn't true.

'I came over here because I wanted a little time on my own before my interview,' she said pointedly.

But he refused to take the hint. 'Are you ready?' he questioned, jabbing a finger against the face of his watch. 'They'll be calling you in a minute.'

'No,' she mumbled, his effect on her forgotten as her throat grew dry with renewed panic at the thought of what she had to do. 'If you want the truth, I'm nowhere near ready. If I could, I'd walk out of here right now. Get the earliest flight back to London and go back to my old life.'

She expected him to snub or berate her, or tell her to pull herself together, but maybe she had misjudged him. Because beneath the subdued light of the studio, the King's eyes narrowed thoughtfully.

'What's the matter, Rosie?' he questioned softly.

She wished he wouldn't use that tone with her because it reminded her of the past, when he'd been kind to her. It made her feel vulnerable—and that was the last way she could afford to feel right now. 'Is that a serious question?' she demanded. 'You mean, apart from the fact that I'm trussed up in this dull dress which makes me look so frumpy? Or that these shoes are so high that I can barely walk in them without risking a fracture?'

Corso frowned, because her self-assessment was so off the mark, it was almost laughable. When he'd walked into the studio today, he hadn't recognised her. The inevitable ripple of excitement followed by total silence must have alerted her to the fact that the royal party had arrived, but Rosie's back had remained turned to him, for she had been engrossed in reading something. Yet for once he had been prepared to overlook the huge breach of protocol. He remembered his gaze homing in on her, as if something outside his control were compelling him to do so—and that was unusual. Her black dress was deceptively simple, yet somehow it managed to emphasise her incredibly curvy shape, which reminded him of an old-fashioned movie star. Just as the high-heeled black shoes showcased a pair of beautifully toned legs, which gleamed beneath the studio lights. Her hair was caught back in an elegant chignon and, as he'd registered the few strands of palest blonde which had tumbled onto the slim column of her neck, he was hit by a powerful thunderbolt of something he didn't recognise.

Because this really was Rosie.

A remarkably different Rosie from one he'd ever seen before.

And one who was completely out of her depth, he realised, with an unusual degree of insight.

'You look sensational,' he said slowly.

'No, I don't.'

Corso wondered what made him seek to reassure her further. The knowledge that a flurry of nerves had the potential to ruin her interview and garner adverse publicity for his tour? Possibly. Or maybe it was more fundamental than that. Because the truth was that he hadn't been able to stop thinking about her and he couldn't work out why. She'd been invading his thoughts at the most inappropriate moments. Those cushion-soft lips and cloud-grey eyes. Her defiance. Her compliance. Different sides of a woman who was fascinating him more than she should.

And yet her physical transformation from duckling to swan had only managed to highlight her inherent freshness and lack of guile—and since these were qualities he rarely came across in his daily life, shouldn't he help preserve them?

'Believe me when I tell you that you do. You look amazing,' he contradicted. 'And that perpetrating a negative attitude about yourself is a waste of time.'

'It's easy for you to talk.'

'And just as easy for you to listen,' he admonished sternly.

'You were the one who told me I needed to change my image,' she mumbled. 'How is that going to do anything for my confidence?'

'Surely you're able to take a little constructive advice,' he came back coolly. 'You've got to start believing in yourself, Rosie. As of now. The camera has the power to pick up every single one of your insecurities and magnify them—and that won't do you any favours.'

'If that's supposed to be encouraging, I'd hate to hear you being negative,' she said moodily.

Corso had almost forgotten what it was like for someone to speak to him as an equal—even though she would never be his *real* equal. Nonetheless, her words provoked an unexpected flicker of a smile as he fixed his gaze on the high-heeled black shoes which made her legs look so deliciously long. 'If you really can't walk in those,' he added, 'then I can offer my arm to support you.'

'I'm twenty-five, not a hundred and five! I don't think I've quite reached the stage of needing to use you as a crutch, Corso—though obviously I'm extremely grateful for the offer.'

But she smiled and it was the first time he had seen a genuine smile from her in a long time. It split through the intervening years like a knife ripping through a closed curtain, taking him by surprise. As did the sudden punch of his heart and the rush of something shockingly potent which was making his blood grow heated. Something he recognised with confusion and annoyance—because he'd never wanted her that way in the past.

I don't want to desire her, he told himself angrily.

I don't want to desire anyone, until the time is right.

His focus must be on finding his brother. *Not on how much he would like to spread open Rosie Forrester's soft thighs and put his head between them and lick her until she was crying out his name.*

With an effort, he adopted the mask of indifference which usually came so easily to him and flicked another glance at his watch. 'They're calling you. Just go in there and give it everything you've got. I'll wait for you in the car out front.'

She blinked at him. 'You'll wait for me?' she verified slowly. 'But the King waits for nobody.'

'Don't labour the point, Rosie,' he drawled. 'We can share a car back to the embassy. It makes perfect sense. If we save on fuel, it's so much better for the planet.'

His lazy words were so unexpected that Rosie giggled and she saw people turning to look at them, as if startled by the sound. Come to think of it, she was pretty startled herself—given her current state of nerves. She watched hungry female eyes following Corso as he swept from the studio and, as his entourage moved quickly to surround him, she warned herself never to join their adoring ranks. She mustn't start thinking he was funny, or sexy, or clever.

But maybe his words had been more comforting than she'd realised because her panic seemed to have evaporated as she sat down to face the interviewer. It helped that the niche arts programme had relatively modest audience figures and that the questioner knew loads about her dad. Which meant she was able to speak with genuine passion about the exquisite pearls and beaten gold jewellery which he'd discovered all those years ago. She spoke for longer than she'd anticipated and felt almost high with relief when finally she exited the studio. She felt more confident now in the skyscraper heels, and the heady atmosphere of springtime Paris helped lift her mood even further.

The TV studios were situated eight kilometres outside the city centre and she could hear birds singing amid the dark pink blooms of the horse-chestnut trees which lined the street. Bathed in bright sunshine, she looked around without much expectation, doubtful Corso would have hung around for this long and deciding that maybe she should walk for a while before taking the Metro back to the embassy. But no, there was the dark-windowed royal limousine parked by the edge of the pavement, the turquoise and purple of the Monterossian flag fluttering proudly on the gleaming black bonnet.

A member of the King's security detail stepped forward to open the door for her and Rosie slid inside, the fitted dress making her movements unusually cautious and slow. The door clicked shut to enclose her and her heart began to hammer as her eyes became accustomed to the dim light and she became aware of Corso's shadowed presence on the seat beside her, writing something by hand in a notebook.

He'd told her he would be here—so it was no big surprise—yet his impact on her was shockingly visceral. Suddenly she was glad she was sitting down. His muscular body was so powerful. His shoulders were so broad. Even the fingers which held his pen were gorgeous. What would it be like if those long fingers were stroking their way over her skin—lightly grazing her burning flesh? Her throat dried as his gaze washed over her and, to her horror, she realised she had started to tremble. Was it that which made her blurt out the first stupid thing which came into her head?

'You waited.'

He raised his eyebrows. 'I said I would.'

'I know, but…'

'But what, Rosie?' She heard the faint edge of exasperation in his voice. 'You don't consider me to be a man of my word?'

Rosie realised she had no idea what kind of man he was because most of the things she knew about Corso were things she'd read or heard from other people, and everyone knew that hearsay was unreliable. Yet she remembered the younger version very well. The Crown Prince whose mother had died. Who had hidden all his pain and grief behind an impenetrable mask, because that blanketing of emotion had been demanded of him— by his father, and by his royal destiny. Had that been the moment when the first layers of cynicism had started building around him, separating him from other people, or was that just inevitable when you inherited a throne and people always wanted something from you?

'Actually, I *do* believe you're a man of your word,' she said, the words more fervent than she had intended.

Corso was silent as he studied the gleam of her lips, for he was unused to receiving such heartfelt praise. Yet he had sought her good opinion of him, hadn't he? Now he found himself wondering why—and why he had dismissed his bemused aides to sit waiting in his limousine while Rosie Forrester finished her interview, he who had never waited for a woman in his life.

He knew why. It was obvious from the tension which was thrumming in the air between them, so powerful that he felt he could have reached out and touched it.

Desire.

Inexplicable, intense and unpredictable.

He might have successfully kept his sexual hunger at bay for the last seven years—but that didn't mean he didn't recognise it when it came along to hit him with the force of a sledgehammer. He stared unseeingly out of the window as the limousine began to move through the traffic, his thoughts coming thick and fast. Inheriting the throne had been a double-edged sword. First had come his realisation of the damage done to his country by his father's greed—and later still, the discovery of his duplicity and its grim legacy. Sickened by the revelations and determined to repair the destruction the late King had wrought, Corso had decided to wholeheartedly embrace celibacy, like the knights of old. Because women were a distraction and extra demands on his time were something he didn't need.

He had banished desire from his life through sheer effort of will and a determination not to be sucked in by its sweet promise. Employing a masochistic element of self-control, he had allowed himself a brief sense of satisfaction at successfully banishing the carnal needs of his body. It was as though he had acquired a special immunity against sexual hunger. But that hunger was washing over him now and it was taking him prisoner. Unremitting and unrelenting—it flooded through his veins like a rich rush of honey. It felt unbearably sweet to be alone in the back seat of a car with Rosie Forrester and he wondered if it was curiosity which had made him take this potentially risky step, or just his body's yearning to feel properly alive again.

He observed her stiff posture as she sat beside him. The way she kept crossing and uncrossing her legs, before resting her hands on her knees. She was probably trying to blot up the stickiness of her palms, but all she was doing was drawing his attention to her luscious thighs. And even though they were demurely covered in black linen, he couldn't stop thinking about the soft flesh beneath and how much he would like to press his fingers against it.

His mind played a speeded-up version of what could happen next, if he pulled her into his arms and began to kiss her. It would be so easy. He gave a grim smile. It always was. The atmosphere between them was so electric that he imagined little would be required in the way of foreplay. Sometimes hot and urgent was best for the first time, he mused.

But *he wasn't going to have sex with her* and not just because of his determination to remain celibate. Because this was Rosie he was thinking about. *Rosie.* The tomboy he'd once rescued from a tree. Who he'd taught how to tie knots. Who had been kind to him at a time when nobody else had known how to behave around him. What right did he have to contemplate intimacy with her and then inevitably break her heart?

So focus on something else, he told himself fiercely. Focus on the only reason she's here today—as the star turn for Monterossian PR and nothing more. Leaning back, he spoke from lips which were suddenly bone-dry. 'You did very well in there just now.'

'How do you know that, if you were waiting in the car?'

'My aides usually relay initial feedback from the interview, but in this instance…' He leaned forward to tap the blank screen of a TV fixed to the screen separating them from the driver. 'I watched you live.'

'You watched me live,' she repeated, before turning those grey eyes on him, and Corso felt as if he could have fallen straight into them, like diving into a silvery lake. 'Honestly?'

'Honestly,' he echoed gravely.

'And?'

'You were excellent. Much better than I had anticipated. As seasoned as a pro, in fact. Lionel would have been very proud.'

She bit her lip. 'That means a lot. I can't tell you how much.'

He wanted to tell her not to look at him like that—so wide-eyed and grateful that it was threatening to burrow beneath his defences. Nor to draw his attention to the succulence of her lips, which made him badly want to kiss them. He felt his fingers uncurl so that the pen he was holding slid to the floor of the car and only the clattering noise it made broke the fraught silence, alerting him to the fact that he had dropped it. Pleased by the distraction, Corso bent to pick it up himself but so, too, did Rosie. As they bent down to retrieve it, they reached towards the gleaming object at exactly the same time, their fingertips touching and briefly lingering. It was the faintest and most innocent of contacts and yet it was like…

Corso felt the pounding of his heart.

It was like a bolt of lightning forking through his body. It was making him grow hard. Making him want to pull her into his arms and pull the clips from her silky hair and then lay her down on that wide seat, and kiss her.

Her face was so close but he made no attempt to move his head away, even as his fingers closed around the pen before she could reach it. He could feel her warm breath on his skin and smell her scent—something subtle yet earthy, like sandalwood. The crackle of attraction between them was so strong he could almost hear it. And something stabbed at his heart as well as his gut as she looked at him with those wide grey eyes. As if he were the only man she had ever looked at like that.

Her lips were crying out for the press of his. The hard peaking of her nipples demanding he touch them. Temptation rippled over his skin and the urge to kiss her was overwhelming. But he would not give into temptation. He would not become a victim of desire. If this was a test of his own inner strength, he would pass it.

And wasn't denial good for the soul—if such a thing existed?

Abruptly, he sat up, distancing himself physically as well as emotionally—and emotional withdrawal was something he excelled at. Putting the pen away, he opened his notebook to study it—as if he were able to make sense of the indecipherable blur of his own handwriting—before glancing up to offer her a bland smile.

His official smile. The one which reminded people never to get too close. 'Haven't you got a cell phone or something to play with, Rosie?' he murmured. 'Now that I've massaged your ego by complimenting you on your performance, I have some things which really need my attention.'

Even the most dense of people would have recognised his words as a dismissal, and Rosie Forrester was not dense. He saw the flicker of consternation which crossed her features and the way she chewed on her lip, as if distressed. Why was she looking so damned kittenish all of a sudden? he wondered angrily. Was she hoping for all the things he'd just been fantasising about?

But her thoughts were irrelevant.

All she needed to be aware of was that nothing was going to happen between them.

Nothing.

CHAPTER SEVEN

'I'M WAITING FOR my guided tour, Rosie.'

A pair of dark brows were raised in arrogant query and Rosie's smile was nervous as Corso stood in front of her, looking mouth-wateringly delectable in his dark designer suit. With a minimum of fanfare, he'd arrived at the Musée des Antiquités moments before and been escorted straight into the exhibition room where she'd been working with Phillipe le Clerc, the museum's curator, for most of the day.

She tried to steady her suddenly ragged breathing, but it wasn't easy. None of this was easy. It was the first time she'd seen him since he'd driven her back from the TV studios yesterday afternoon, when for a moment the sexual tension between them had been so heightened that she'd thought he was about to kiss her.

Corso?

Kiss her?

Her?

How sad was that? As if Corso—having the pick of any woman he wanted—would choose to get intimate with her. Deciding she needed to put as much space as possible between them for the sake of her own sanity, she had slunk upstairs when they'd arrived back at the embassy. Then she had busied herself preparing for the upcoming exhibition, before picking at the meal she'd asked to be delivered to her room—a request which seemed to perplex the French maid who had delivered it. As if nobody in their right mind would choose to eat their dinner off a tray.

But she couldn't hide away from Corso for ever—especially not when he was towering above her beneath the bright lights of the museum, a faintly impatient look glinting from between his narrowed eyes as he demanded her attention. Bobbing a small curtsey in an attempt to highlight their difference in status, she produced her most efficient smile. 'I'm sure Monsieur le Clerc is far more qualified to show you around than I am,' she said. 'He is, after all, one of the greatest experts on ancient Mediterranean jewellery in all of Europe.'

'But it is you I want,' emphasised Corso—his silky command enough to make Phillipe melt away into the background, with a very Gallic shrug.

The King's words were distracting—his presence even more so. Suddenly Rosie felt as if she were alone with him again. As if they were the only two people in the world—even though the usual phalanx of guards were standing a respectful distance away. But that was the undeniable power of the man. He had the ability to make everyone else seem like shadows around him. And that was nothing new. She had always recognised that quality in him. What had changed was *her*—and the effect he was having on her. Despite her having elected to wear the most sensible components of her wardrobe, her body was reacting in ways she couldn't seem to control. Beneath the sawn-off linen trousers and silk shirt, her skin felt sensitised and prickly. Her breasts seemed to have acquired a new and alarming life of their own—their tips pressing uncomfortably against her new bra—and there was that distracting curl of heat again, low in her belly.

She needed to get a grip of herself before she did something stupid. She was supposed to be doing a job of work for him, that was all.

That was all.

'Very well,' she said crisply. 'Let me show you around. We've made some changes to the order of the display cases.'

Indicating he should follow her, Rosie started at the first glass-covered case, beneath which were a set of small bracelets, intricately inlaid with amethyst, turquoise and lapis lazuli. 'We've decided to show the pieces chronologically,' she explained. 'And since the collection isn't very big we were able to contain it all within this one space, which makes it very accessible for the public. Look. These are the bracelets which were made for Queen Aurelia when she was just a baby—though it's doubtful if she ever wore them. See how tiny they are.'

But her professionalism dissolved the moment Corso stepped closer to study the contents of the display case and Rosie felt a terrifying desire to reach out and touch him. To run her fingertips over the shaded jut of his jaw to see how rough it felt.

She cleared her throat as they made their way towards the next exhibit. 'As we move through the room,' she said quickly, 'we can see the magnitude and size of her jewellery collection increasing—culminating in the precious suite she was given on her marriage and then on the birth of her first child.' She paused. 'But we saved the best for last, which isn't jewellery at all. Because here we have the only known statue of the young Queen—probably carved during the first year of her marriage. It's…it's beautiful, isn't it? So incredibly clear, and detailed. It's almost as if she's here with us.'

Corso inclined his head, admiring her fluency and knowledge and noticing the way her face came to life when she spoke about the ancient artefacts—her features filled with fire and passion.

With an effort, he dragged his attention back to the statue. He had seen it before—many times, for it had been languishing in airtight storage in Monterosso for years—but here it seemed to assume a special poignancy when assembled with the burial jewels. It seemed to emphasise the terrible awareness of hindsight, knowing the shadow of death was already hovering over the young Queen. He wondered, if he were to die now, what his lasting legacy would be and whether the brother he was seeking would choose to inherit the heavy mantle of the throne. Had he made Monterosso as good as he possibly could? Wiping out some of the damage done to it in the past? Had he done the best he could?

Suddenly he thought about his mother, unprepared for the shaft of pain which clenched at his heart. His recent discovery of an illegitimate brother made an already complicated relationship with his past even more so—and usually, he controlled access to his memories with steely rigidity. But not so now. Was it Rosie's familiarity, or the strangely informal relationship he'd once shared with her, which made him want to confide in her the secrets he carried with him, despite knowing how misguided such a confidence would be?

Attempting to quash the muddle of his thoughts,

he asked a question to which he already knew the answer. 'How old would the Queen have been when this was modelled?'

'Twenty-five.'

'The same age as you,' he observed.

'Well, yes.'

He heard her miss a beat—as if she was surprised he'd remembered, or that he had deigned to mention it. 'And by then she had already given birth to one child and was pregnant with the second,' he continued.

'That's right.'

There was a pause and afterwards he found himself wondering what made him ask a question which had no relevance at all. 'Haven't you ever wanted to marry and have a family of your own, Rosie?'

He saw her face working awkwardly, as if he had put her on the spot.

'I'm not a big fan of the institution,' she said, at last. 'I've seen very few examples which make me want to rush to join in.'

'Not even your own parents?'

She shrugged. 'You can never be objective about your parents' marriage, can you? Anyway, you make marriage sound like a choice. Like something you can just decide to do—like picking a can of beans off the supermarket shelf.'

'I guess, for me, it is a bit like that.'

'Because you're a man?'

'Because I'm a king.'

'How easy you make it sound, Corso. Like clockwork! Any idea when this auspicious event might take place, so that I can buy myself a hat?'

'You might not be invited to the wedding.'

'Well, tell me anyway—so at least I can start saving up for a toaster!'

He failed to hold back the glimmer of a smile. 'There is no definite time-frame, but it is going to happen,' he said resolutely. 'When I am satisfied that my country is finally on the right track for a prosperous future, then it will be time to take a bride.'

'And where are you planning to take her?' she asked.

He ignored the flippant interruption, finding himself in full flow as he answered a question nobody had ever dared ask before. His courtiers wouldn't dream of being so presumptuous and he had spurned close relationships for so long that keeping his own counsel had become second nature. 'She must be of royal blood, of course,' he continued thoughtfully. 'That is a given to a man in my position. I have always found it ironic that, although an eligible king can have his pick of almost any woman he desires, his choice of whom he can marry is, by necessity, limited.'

'I can't believe you're saying all this,' she breathed.

'I'm saying it because it's the truth,' he retorted. 'Even if it isn't a particularly fashionable one.'

'And does the lucky, high-born woman have any say in your decision to marry her, or is her fate sealed like a sacrificial lamb?'

'You don't think most woman would be delighted to marry me, Rosie?'

Rosie could hear the mockery in his voice but also the unmistakable arrogance. And the most annoying thing was that he probably *was* speaking the truth because she could imagine there were plenty of women who would want to marry him. He was, after all, a golden-eyed sex god who ruled one of the most powerful kingdoms in the Mediterranean. What was not to like? She met his gaze. 'If they have a penchant for patriarchal men with archaic views, then yes, I'd say they'll already be forming a long line to your door.'

His eyes narrowed and for a moment Rosie wondered if she'd gone too far. If he were about to reprimand her for her outspokenness, but he didn't. Instead, he gave her a lazy smile, which was far more lethal than his anger. She didn't want him to smile at her like that—and, of course, she did. She wanted it far too much.

'Are you planning to join us for dinner later?' he questioned. 'Or intending to do another disappearing act?'

'Actually, I'd prefer to have a tray in my room, if that's okay.'

'Actually, it isn't okay,' he said tightly. 'And not just because it's an insult to request *"le sandwich"*, night after night when the embassy chef provides some of the finest cuisine in the city. You are here as part of my delegation so you can damned well put in an appearance, if I command it. Which I do. Do you understand what I'm saying to you, Rosie?' he finished coolly.

'I think you've made yourself pretty clear.'

'In that case, I will take my leave.' He paused and inclined his head. 'But be in no doubt that I like very much the changes you've made to the exhibition.'

'Is that a compliment, Corso?'

'Indeed it is. Accept it with grace.' He gave a cool smile. 'I'll see you at dinner.'

He turned and swept away and Rosie was left gazing after his retreating form, her heart still racing with unwanted longing. As the King's party departed to the flash of affiliated press cameras waiting outside, Phillipe le Clerc made his way back across the room towards her, his dark hair flopping attractively over one eye.

'Mon dieu, le Roi est magnifique!' observed the handsome curator, his voice dropping to an appreciative purr.

'Magnificent indeed,' agreed Rosie woodenly, because how could she possibly deny his words? Yet despite all the jewelled beauty which lay beneath the gleaming glass of the display cabinets, the room seemed empty and lustreless now that Corso had gone. She forced herself to smile at Phillipe. To flick her blonde plait back over her shoulder as if she didn't care about anything other than the upcoming exhibition. 'Shall we just have a last-minute look at the brochures—and then we could grab ourselves a coffee?'

CHAPTER EIGHT

ROSIE WISHED SHE were somewhere else. Anywhere else but here, in this grand embassy dining room in Paris, feeling more awkward than she could ever remember feeling. Yet she had grown up on the periphery of the Monterossian palace, so she was used to fancy surroundings and knew how to feel relatively comfortable in them. But here she couldn't get rid of the sense of being an outsider. An interloper.

Because she was.

Which presumably was why she'd been stuck down at the furthest end of a very long table and about as far from Corso as it was possible to be. She played with the linen napkin on her lap. Of course, she was always going to be seated at the unimportant end of the table! Unless she'd really been expecting to be at the King's right hand—when that honour had been given to the French President's wife, who was nodding her head in blissful agreement with everything Corso was saying.

Rosie tried to smile and listen to the conversation taking place around her. Talking was pretty impossible because her schoolgirl French didn't extend much beyond asking where the bathrooms were. But the general hubbub of the evening was too loud for her to be able to concentrate on anything other than how utterly amazing Corso looked in his Monterossian military regalia, which made the most of his spectacular physique. The dark jacket hugged the broad width of his chest, its row of medals glinting in the guttering light of the candles.

Like every other woman in the room, she had curtseyed when he'd made his grand entrance and then wondered whether she'd imagined his eyes lingering on her as she'd sunk to the marble floor in her silken gown.

The wine was excellent, the food superb. Chandeliers like diamonds suspended in mid-air glittered down on silver cutlery, sparkling crystal, and low bowls of fragrant flowers, which scented the air with heady perfume. But all the pomp and splendour was wasted on her because all Rosie could think about was Corso—like a one-track song playing invasively inside her head.

She pushed away her dish of *Îles flottant*—untouched mounds of soft meringue, floating in a sea of custard. Such a waste. What was the *matter* with her? It was as though someone had flicked a switch, or cast a spell on her. As if she were in the middle of an enchantment—unable to prevent her gaze from straying to the man who was sitting at the top end of the table. And the mortifying thing was that Corso had actually caught her doing it. Several times, their gazes had locked and the last time it had happened she had flushed, causing the third or fourth secretary—or whatever his position in the embassy was—beside her to remark that they really should improve the air-conditioning in the building.

It didn't help that she was wearing an outfit which made her feel exposed, even though it was probably one of the most modest in the room. A low-cut silvery fitted gown which skimmed her ankles, to allow the peep of gleaming silver stilettos. The stylist had assured Rosie that the dress really suited her and, on one level, she knew it did—she just wasn't used to the brush of silk next to her skin, nor for a lavish borrowed sapphire and diamond necklace and earrings to sparkle like a firework display above her breasts and at her ears. Maybe that was the reason she had let her hair down for once. Usually, she preferred the thick tresses tamed and neat but tonight they tumbled in a newly washed sheen about her bare shoulders, allowing for some welcome concealment.

At least now the toasts and speeches had been made and the guests were following the King's lead and rising from the table. Rosie waited until she was certain she wouldn't be noticed, then slipped away from the banqueting hall, though the relief she had expected to find once back in her suite eluded her.

She sighed. She felt restless. Empty. As if some vital component of her life was missing. An image of flame-kissed hair and amber-flecked eyes taunted the edge of her consciousness—and she wondered how she was going to get any sleep tonight.

Kicking off the silver shoes, she removed the necklace and earrings and put them in the safe, before padding barefoot over to the window to stare out at the Eiffel Tower. Dominating the Parisian skyline, the enormous structure was lit with coloured lights, which were reflected on the wide stretch of the river Seine, and which flashed like fireworks into the bedroom.

She went into the bathroom to brush her teeth and was just thinking about getting undressed when she heard a light tap at the door. She frowned as she spat some peppermint foam into the sink. Who would come looking for her at this time of night? Would the embassy have thought to send up a cup of late-night hot chocolate? Unlikely.

She opened the door and her heart thudded because Corso was standing there, still in his military uniform. Vibrant and handsome and oozing sex appeal, the King of Monterosso was standing on *her* doorstep. She should have felt nervous, or outraged, or indignant, or angry or… But she felt none of those things. The only thing which was fizzing through her veins was the overwhelming certainty that there was nobody else in the world she would rather see. But Corso must not know that. Definitely not. She must remain calm. In control. Maybe he was here to discuss an aspect of the exhibition he'd forgotten to mention earlier.

'Goodness,' she said coolly, clutching the door handle tightly for support and hoping he didn't notice. 'This is unexpected.'

For a moment Corso couldn't bring himself to answer.

He hadn't been able to keep his eyes off her during the formal dinner. Unassuming Rosie Forrester—who seemed to have become a thorn in his flesh. He'd registered her curvy body clothed in a gown the colour of starlight. He'd been mesmerised by the lustrous fall of hair cascading down around her shoulders and the alluring flush of pink in her cheeks. There had been a captivating air about her, which had set her apart from everyone else in the room—a watchfulness and solitude he had found completely mesmerising. Had that been deliberate? Was she aware that those wordless looks she'd been directing at him had made it impossible for him to concentrate on a word the French President's wife had been saying? And now she was standing in front of him like some incandescent angel in her silver gown. 'Can I come in?' he questioned throatily.

'Really?' she verified, with a slightly bemused rise of her eyebrows.

Outraged that she should have the temerity to challenge a question which would have made any other woman melt, he glared. 'Yes, really. Unless you wish to have this conversation with me on your doorstep, which would not only be extremely indiscreet in the circumstances—but also highly discourteous.'

'Oh. We're having a conversation, are we?' she questioned, but she opened the door wider all the same, allowing him to step inside, and then closed it quietly behind him. She headed towards a tall lamp and switched it on in a very busy manner, before turning to look at him, her eyebrows still raised. 'Okay. What do you want to talk about? The exhibition? The dinner? It all seemed to go very well tonight and I thought your speech was great, if that's what you're… Corso?' The prattle of her nervous words halted and she looked at him in confusion, as if she had only just noticed the tension in his face and body. 'Is something the matter?'

'I just think we need to establish a few boundaries,' he said unevenly. And since he was aware that visiting her room at close to midnight was almost certainly in direct breach of the boundaries he was about to propose, he moved as far away from her as possible.

'Right,' she said slowly, still with that faint look of perplexity. 'Go on, then. Let's hear them.'

For a moment Corso's resolve faltered because, in the apricot light spilling from the lamp, her lips were parted and her eyes were glittering like dark stars. That unbelievable hair was brushing against her cheeks and he found himself wanting to use one of those pale, silken strands as an anchor. To wind it round his finger and use it to draw her face close to his, so that he could kiss her. He wanted to kiss her so much. Angrily, he pushed the thought away but traces of it lingered in his mind.

Was it seven years of self denial which made him answer her with such a marked lack of finesse? 'It's infuriating, but I can't stop thinking about you.'

He saw her brief look of uncertainty before she shrugged. 'Well, we go back a long way, don't we?'

'That's not what I'm talking about.'

'No. I guess not.' Suddenly all the uncertainty was gone. Her gaze was clear and he was reminded of the focus she had demonstrated when she'd been showing him around the exhibition earlier. 'Perhaps you'd like to tell me exactly what it is you *are* talking about.'

'With pleasure.' He could have kicked himself for his inappropriate choice of word as she stood there, bathed in the light from the Eiffel Tower. 'It isn't going to happen, Rosie.'

'What isn't?'

'Please.' He didn't bother to keep the impatience from his voice. 'We're not teenagers. Let's at least be honest with ourselves. We need to work and travel together and at the moment I'm not finding it particularly easy to do either.'

'Why not?'

'You know damned well why,' he gritted out. 'Unless you are denying the chemistry between us?'

She blushed. She actually *blushed*. 'Wouldn't acknowledging it be a teeny bit presumptuous, Corso?'

'So you feel it, too?' His words were a silken challenge.

'Yes, of course I do,' she admitted and pulled a face

which made him think of a younger Rosie. 'I find you extremely attractive. Along with every other woman with a pulse, no doubt. It's a pity really. All those years of not understanding what anyone saw in you seem to have come to nothing—which is annoying to say the least. Happy now?'

Happy was the last adjective he would have used to describe his current state of being. Frustrated? Yes. Aching? Certainly. Resentful? Possibly. 'I agree, it's…annoying.' He paused. 'But you do realise that nothing is going to happen.'

Her brow clouded. 'So you just said, although you haven't made yourself very clear.'

Afterwards he would justify his next remark by convincing himself she'd goaded him into it. 'We're not going to have sex.'

'Have sex?' she echoed, the cadence of her voice rising in disbelief. 'Have you taken leave of your mind, Corso? I don't want to have sex with you!'

'Oh, really?' he challenged, but deep down he knew his challenge was layered with provocation. 'You're either distorting the truth or deluding yourself if you think that, Rosie.'

She flew at him then—and wasn't that exactly what he wanted? Her blonde hair was streaming like a banner behind her as she hurled herself against him, her balled fists drumming uselessly at his chest, and he felt a jolt of something he didn't recognise as he stared down at the pale gleam of her head. He suspected she wanted a physical outlet for her rage, and couldn't decide whether to let her just get it out of her system, or capture one of her wrists before telling her to calm down. But her fists were no longer drumming, they were kneading at his flesh in a way which was distracted yet inciting, and he was no longer trying to decide how to react. Because suddenly he couldn't help himself. He could battle with himself no longer. Or maybe he had just surrendered because he was no longer thinking, just *feeling*.

Heeding nothing but the siren call of her body, he pulled her into his arms, her breathless gasp of assent reinforced by the way she was reaching up to cling to his shoulders, as though he wasn't the only one in need of an anchor. Impatiently, he brushed her hair aside and began to kiss her. His tongue teased her lips apart and she was the most delicious thing he had ever tasted—coffee and toothpaste and something else, something which was uniquely her. Something which made him grow even harder. Her breasts were pushing against his chest—their tips like diamond bullets pushing against the delicate fabric of her gown. He made one last attempt to resist—at least, that was what he tried to tell himself—but her soft moan of incitement made resistance impossible. He felt like a man who'd been lost in the desert, stumbling upon a deep well of cool water and being told he wasn't allowed to drink. As he deepened the kiss, he found his hand straying towards her breast and she gripped his shoulders even tighter. Was that his name she was whimpering?

He cupped her breast, his thumb circling the thrusting nipple, and never had he wanted to lick and suck an area of skin so badly.

'Corso,' she gasped.

'You want this?'

'So much. I can't… I can't tell you how much.'

And neither could he. It was because it had been so long since he'd had sex that his heart felt as if it were on fire. It must be. His hands skated hungrily over the contours of her body—firm curves covered by the soft silk which defined them. She writhed as he stroked her, the subtle, almost indefinable scent of her desire filling the air and reminding his starved body of everything he'd been missing. He knew if he touched her she would be wet. Just as if she touched him, she would find him rock-hard. He swallowed. He had to have her. It seemed as inevitable as the sun which rose every morning over the red mountains of Monterosso. Yet surely to do so would be the height of recklessness?

He didn't care. The only thing he cared about right then was the pressure of her lips as they kissed frantically. He could never remember a kiss like this—so deep, so drugging, so unbelievably *erotic*. His fingers were tangled in her hair. He pressed his body against hers and she whispered his name. He pushed her up against the wall and felt her thighs part. And he knew then that he could take her. That she wanted him to take her.

'Rosie,' he husked.

'Yes,' she breathed. 'Yes.'

It was an answer and an incitement melded into one delicious word and Corso bent to clasp the hem of her dress. The fabric trickled like liquid silk over his hand as he began to ruck the gown up, eager to tease his finger against her molten heat until she pulsed helplessly beneath him. But he tried to pace himself. To spin it out for as long as possible in order to luxuriate in these long-forgotten feelings of lust.

And then, just as abruptly, he stopped, his hand coming to a halt on the jut of her knee which caused her to make a slurred objection. His heart was crashing against his ribcage as the unwanted voice of reason began to clamour inside his head, asking if this was how seven years of denial were going to end.

He let the hem of her dress fall back down. 'We're not going to do this,' he ground out.

Her eyes looked huge and troubled and disappointed. 'We're…we're not?'

'No.' He saw she was trembling and appeared unsteady on her feet and Corso convinced himself it was simply courtesy which made him lift her up and carry her towards the large bed he had avoided looking at when he'd first entered the room.

She was lighter than he had expected and he missed her warm weight as he laid her down against the snowy white counterpane. But this was the right thing to do. They weren't teenagers and there was no reason for them to behave that way—fumbling at each other's clothes, then having sex because they couldn't stop themselves. He had called a halt to it just in time and he should commend himself for his steely self-control.

But her pale hair was spread like moonlight over the pillow and he wanted to stroke it. And her lips were parted and he wanted to touch them with his own.

'I should go,' he said.

With the tip of one finger, she reached up to trace the outline of his mouth and never had such a simple gesture felt so powerfully hypnotic. Damn you, Rosie Forrester, he thought resentfully. *Damn* you.

'Go, then. If that's what you want.'

He could barely breathe, let alone speak. 'You know damned well it's not.'

There was a pause. 'Well, then.'

Deliberately, Rosie made her comment sound like an invitation, or an acceptance—it all depended on how you looked at it. But inside she was praying and hoping as she saw an agony of indecision distorting Corso's carved features and she wondered which way he would go. Deep down she knew he didn't really want this, and on one level neither did she. Because nothing but trouble was going to come from it. Instinctively, she recognised that. Every sensible atom of her body was urging her to send him away, and she had spent most of her life being sensible.

Yet tonight Corso Andrea da Vignola had ignited something in her. Something which was making her body ache with an unbearable kind of longing. It wasn't so much about wanting him—it was more about *needing* him and feeling that the rest of her life would seem incomplete if she didn't have him. She wanted him to douse the flames of desire which were threatening to consume her. To free her from the burden of never having tasted physical pleasure before—a burden which grew heavier with every year that passed.

But it was his call.

It had to be.

'I don't have any condoms with me,' he said.

His words were the antithesis of romance and his brutal declaration should have been enough to kill Rosie's passion stone-dead, but, ironically, they made her feel more comfortable. Because he wasn't pretending. He wasn't saying stuff he didn't mean in order to get her into bed. He wasn't talking about moonlight and roses, he was talking about contraception. It felt like a grown-up thing they were engaged in—a very adult way of approaching sex.

'I do,' she said.

She saw his look of surprise and, yes, disappointment—he didn't manage to disguise that in time and she didn't know whether to be pleased or insulted at his silent judgement. But it didn't matter whether he thought she was being bold, or whether it wasn't the 'done thing' for a woman to be quite so assertive. She wasn't seeking his good opinion of her. She just wanted him so badly that she felt she might die if she couldn't have him.

'Where?' he demanded.

She ought to fetch them herself, but the thought of getting up from this bed—exquisitely aroused as she was—to parade in front of him in her unfamiliar evening gown was more than she could bear. Better she was lying here if he changed his mind.

'In the back of the wardrobe,' she said breathlessly, 'is my suitcase. They're in a little red purse in the inside section.'

He found the suitcase and flipped it open, frowning for a moment as he saw the neat piles of clothes. 'Why haven't you unpacked?'

'Because they're my normal clothes. You know. The ones which were deemed redundant after your stylist provided me with a new wardrobe for the royal tour.'

For a moment Rosie wondered if she'd said too much. If her sarcastic words would reinforce the difference between them and remind him of how eminently unsuitable she was to be the King's lover. But wasn't she jumping the gun? She wasn't his lover yet and she still might not be. Not when he was regarding the pack of condoms with an expression of bemusement.

'Are these still in date?'

'Of course.' No way was she going to start explaining why she was carrying them around, because he had started to undress and every sane thought flew straight out of her mind. He took off his military jacket and hung it on the back of the chair. Next came the long, polished boots—so that all he was left wearing were his dark trousers with the scarlet stripe down the sides and a close-fitting shirt of white silk. He came back to the bed and sat on the edge of it, his free hand stroking her cheek with a hypnotic movement, before tracing the outline of her lips so that they trembled beneath his touch.

'Now,' he said.

Too unsure of herself to know how to react, she suspected she was probably much too passive as he peeled the dress from her body, his gaze roving appreciatively over the delicate lace of her new push-up bra and matching French knickers, which he removed so slowly that she wanted to urge him to hurry up. But when he bent his head to lick at each exposed nipple he gave a groan which sounded almost helpless and Rosie began to feel a sense of her own power growing alongside her mounting excitement. Her inhibitions melted like butter in the midday sun and soon she was unbuttoning his silk shirt and spreading her fingers with glorious abandon over the warm, beating satin of his chest.

He made a little sound in the back of his throat as he began to unbutton his trousers, before briefly kicking them away. And it occurred to her—though only briefly—that the King's military clothes really ought not to be lying in a crumpled heap on a bedroom floor, but by then Corso was back on the bed and pulling her in his arms and kissing her, and the concern flew straight out of her head.

Dimly, she was aware of him reaching for the protection he had retrieved from her suitcase but by then nothing else mattered other than thinking she would ex-

plode if he carried on stroking her like that. She thought
that, compared to her own sense of wild abandon, his
own movements seemed to be cloaked in an element of
fierce control. His face was a shadowed mask she could
not read and his lips were hard and tense.

He took her to the brink so many times before at
last he entered her with one long, deep thrust and Rosie
couldn't hold back her small cry, which was more about
rapture than pain. He stilled only fractionally, his narrowed eyes glinting, before continuing with those long
and incredible thrusts.

It came upon her when she wasn't expecting it. When
she was so lost in the experience that she relaxed enough
to let go. She'd read about it, of course. Descriptions of
starbursts and fireworks she'd always considered slightly
fanciful. But not any more. If anything, they were under-
statements. As she began to spasm around him, Rosie
felt as if she were being sucked up in a warm jet stream
to the top of the mountain, before tumbling blissfully
back down to earth again. And that was when the King's
own movements became more rapid. She felt his powerful body jerk as his head fell back and the cry which
erupted from his lips was like nothing she'd ever heard.
But he drove his mouth down on hers in a hard kiss, as if
he wanted to disguise the sound—and for the first time,
Rosie wondered where his bodyguards were.

For a while everything felt perfect. She wrapped
her arms tightly around his back, with her head resting against the broad width of his shoulder. Almost absently she dropped a kiss onto the satiny skin there and,
almost immediately, she felt his body tense as he with-
drew from her.

She tried to convince herself it was normal for a man

to roll to the opposite side of the bed after having sex with a woman for the first time, but instinct was contradicting her because there was something about Corso's body language which warned her that whatever was coming next was probably going to be unwelcome.

Because his expression had darkened, and he was actually *scowling*, and Rosie wondered what had caused him to look that way. Maybe she had been a disappointment. Maybe he was already regretting it. Until she told herself to stop being so *wet*. If she had been confident enough to point him into the direction of a packet of condoms, then surely it was pointless to shrink back into the shadows now.

She wriggled back against the pillows. 'Is something wrong?'

'Wrong? Doesn't that qualify for understatement of the year?' He gave a bitter laugh. 'You mean, other than that it was your first time and you didn't bother to tell me?'

CHAPTER NINE

CORSO TENSED AS he waited for Rosie's answer, trying to ignore her pink and blonde beauty as she lay back against the pillows. Ravishing Rosie. Rumpled Rosie. Innocent Rosie. His groin tightened and he willed the exquisite aching to subside because this kind of thinking wasn't helpful.

'Why should I have told you it was my first time?' she demanded. 'I'm not sure how these things work because I'm a novice—obviously. Is it a prerequisite of having sex that you're supposed to run through a list of your previous partners first? Bit of a passion-killer, I would have thought. Anyway, it's not a big deal.'

Corso grabbed the bedsheet and hauled it over his throbbing groin, unwilling to let her see the evidence of his rapidly growing desire. He felt a multiplicity of emotions. Sated, yes. But he felt baffled too—and more than a little angry with her. And with himself. Because, without putting too fine a point on it—why her?

Having successfully resisted the lure of women far more appropriate than Rosie Forrester during the past seven years, he was wondering what had made him fall so eagerly into her bed just now. Maybe it was just a question of timing. Or the need for distraction as the meeting with his brother approached. Was that why all his control and determination seemed to have deserted him? He had hungered for her, and she for him—but she had neglected to tell him something vitally important. Why had she done that? To trap him?

Pernicious guilt washed over him, for no way could he underplay his own role in what had just happened. On the contrary. He should have *known* she was innocent. Should have guessed. Should have run a mile from the indefinable allure she exuded and which had so effectively snared him. Were the clues there all the time and lust had simply blinded him to them? Or had he allowed their undeniable camaraderie to gnaw away at his defences, leaving him so vulnerable to her voluptuous blonde beauty that seven years of celibacy had been annihilated in the space of a few minutes?

'Don't try to be funny, because you're not succeeding,' he snapped. 'Of course it's a big deal. You were a virgin, for God's sake.'

'But everyone's a virgin at some point in their life,' she pointed out. 'Even you. When did you first have sex, Corso? Why don't we talk about *that*?'

Impatiently, he shook his head. It was so long ago that he could barely remember the details. Only that the woman had been older and had known every damned trick in the book. And it had felt nothing like this. Nothing ever had. *And wasn't that the most galling thing of all?* That this innocent young woman he'd known since she barely reached his elbow should have brought him to his knees. 'Don't change the subject, Rosie,' he snapped. 'I'm still waiting for an explanation.'

'Which I don't believe I'm contractually obliged to give you.'

He almost laughed but glared instead. 'I'm waiting,' he said, in his most frosty and regal tone.

She breathed out an unsteady sigh and shrugged her bare shoulders. 'It just never happened for me, that's all. Mum...she needed a lot of support when we first moved back to England, so there was always that. Obviously, I've been asked out on dates before but none of them, well...obviously none of them progressed to the stage where I might have been tempted to take it further.' She pushed a handful of hair away from her flushed cheek. 'You didn't guess?'

Corso didn't trust himself to answer immediately—afraid that to do so might reveal too much, for it was beginning to dawn on him that he behaved differently with her than he did with anyone else. Perhaps because he had known her as well as a prince could know any commoner—at a time in their lives before duty or age had imposed their particular demands on him. Just after his mother had died, when he had undoubtedly been vulnerable, she and her family had helped him sample a simpler life. And yes, he'd caught a glimpse of her un-doubted innocence at his birthday ball—with her gawky and ungainly appearance—but he'd been so busy being angry with her that he'd imagined such a stage was only transitory.

One of the reasons he had considered her the per-fect candidate for this role—apart from her undoubted knowledge of the subject—was because he'd never re-ally thought of her as a *woman*. She had been the sweet daughter of his mentor. The girl who always had her head in a book. He certainly hadn't been prepared for the tan-gible sexiness she exuded when he'd come to find her in England, even though she'd been wearing the most unflattering clothes he'd ever seen. Or for her behaviour when he'd turned up at her suite tonight.

'Nobody would expect a virgin to conveniently produce packs of condoms!' he snapped.

'Really?' Lying back against the pillows, she cushioned her head against her folded arms. 'I thought that was the way things were done. Of course women must take responsibility for contraception and not just leave it up to the man. So why not carry some around—just in case?'

'Is that the reason you had them, Rosie?' he questioned moodily. *Just in case?*'

She shrugged again and he wished she hadn't because it made her magnificent breasts wiggle in a way which made him want to lick his tongue all over them.

'Actually, my sister gave them to me as a part of my birthday present, as a joke. Only it wasn't really a joke.' She hesitated. 'She thought it was time I started doing things that other women of my age were doing.'

'So you chose me as your initiation project?' His mouth thinned. 'Aiming a little high, weren't you?'

'Actually—' indignantly, she sat up in bed to glare at him and the flicker of fire in her eyes was uncomfortably attractive '—ignoring the unbelievable arrogance of your last remark, I could say that you chose me. Or that we chose each other. This thing has been building between us for days now—even innocent little me was aware of that. Though I wouldn't have done anything about it— on principle—and not just because your guards make it impossible for anyone to get near you. You were the one who made the running, remember?'

'I came to warn you off,' he raged.

'Of course you did, Corso. You came to my room

at midnight and told me we weren't going to have sex, before taking off your clothes.' Her lips twitched, as if she was trying not to smile. 'But what's happened has happened and there's no need to worry about it. I know how these things work. I've lived around royals for long enough. I'm not expecting to become your queen.'

'Because that would never happen!'

'Obviously. Even if I wanted it to—which I don't— you helpfully spelled it out for me in words of one syllable just the other day. I know you'll be marrying a royal princess some time soon. Lucky woman!' She pinned a smile to her lips. 'So why can't we look on what just happened as a very enjoyable interlude?'

Corso stilled. 'A *very enjoyable interlude*?' he echoed softly. 'Am I now to be damned with faint praise?'

'I didn't mean it that way.'

'No?'

'No!' Some of her bravado left her and she hesitated, not looking at him now, but staring down at the edge of the sheet, which she was rubbing between her finger and thumb. 'It was…amazing, if you must know. Totally amazing. For me, anyway.'

'For me, too,' he said into the silence which followed, then wondered why on earth he had been so unnecessarily transparent. Because she was inexperienced, that was why. Surely it was only fair to reassure her—so that with future lovers she would be filled with confidence in her own sexuality. And then Corso scowled, unprepared for the territorial twist of jealousy which clenched at his gut at the thought of her being in the arms of another man.

'I'm just surprised…'

'Mmm?' he said distractedly as her words broke into his uncomfortable reverie.

She looked up from her study of the sheet, her teeth digging into the rosy cushion of her bottom lip. 'I'm surprised you chose me, that's all. There must be loads of other women who would have made a much more suitable sexual partner. Why me?'

This was usually the kind of thing a woman asked when she was fishing for a compliment, but Corso suspected that wasn't true in this case. He thought about ignoring her question—of deftly batting it away, confident in the knowledge that nobody ever asked a king something twice. But Rosie was different. She had known him before he'd acceded to the throne. She'd once seen him with tear-bright eyes and when he'd complained about the grit which had flown in them while out riding, she had simply squeezed his arm, before swiftly dropping her hand, as if remembering that she had no right to touch the monarch. She hadn't ever mentioned it again. She hadn't come out with endless platitudes about how sorry she was for the loss of his mother and he had been grateful to her for that, because he had been hurting badly.

But she was no longer that young girl, running on instinct and innocence. She was a woman in her prime—poised on the brink of discovering the rich world of her own sexuality. Didn't he owe her the truth? 'You want to know why I couldn't resist you?' he questioned.

'I'm curious.'

He hesitated. 'You are obviously very attractive.'

'But not your usual type?'

'Well, no.' It had been so long since he'd had a 'type' that Corso found himself wondering whether his preferences might have changed over the years. 'If you really want an explanation, I guess you'd have to put it down to proximity.'

'Proximity?' she echoed, unable to keep the tang of disappointment from her voice. 'And that's all?'

Yes, of course that was all. Close contact plus rampaging hormones equalled explosive physical chemistry. It was no more complex than that. She needed to understand that. And he needed to understand it, too. 'And when proximity is mixed with abstinence—it makes a very potent cocktail. You see, I haven't been intimate with a woman for a very long time, Rosie,' he added huskily. 'Not for over seven years, in fact. Ring any bells?'

It took a few seconds before she answered and he saw the confusion clear from her face as she nodded. 'You're talking about that woman I overheard just before your party?' she breathed. 'What was her name?'

'I don't remember.'

'Tiffany!' she said triumphantly. 'That was it. Tiffany Sackler. I warned you that she was telling a friend she wanted to have your baby. And you were very angry with me.'

'I was more angry with myself,' he admitted.

'And that was enough to put you off sex?'

'It didn't *put me off* sex. It made me re-evaluate my life. It made me consider that maybe I hadn't been thinking through my position properly. I realised I had been placing myself in an invidious position and could easily be compromised by people whose motives were not, shall we say…pure.'

'And was it very hard?' she ventured. 'To go without sex for so long?'

'Hard would not be my adjective of choice,' he commented drily, a reluctant smile tugging at the edges of his mouth. 'You know, you really are going to have to stop blushing like that when you're in bed with me. It's really very distracting.'

'I'm serious,' she said, seeming to hesitate before forging on. 'It's just quite a lot to take on board because you were so well known for being a...'

'A what, Rosie?' he challenged.

She clasped her fingers together. 'A sex symbol, I suppose. A bit of a player. It must have been like a chocoholic deciding they weren't going to eat sugar for the foreseeable.'

He stared out of the window, where the Eiffel Tower was currently lit up with the purple and turquoise colours of the Monterossian flag, as it had been since his arrival in France. 'If you must know, at first I enjoyed the discipline of self-denial. I have always enjoyed testing myself, especially when it's difficult. It's like basic training when you're in the military. No one wants to get out of bed at six a.m. and take an icy shower, before running miles with a heavy pack on your back—but that's what makes your body into a powerful machine. Abstinence helped keep my mind focussed and it coincided with my accession to the throne, and the discovery of exactly what I had inherited.'

This time she didn't prompt him. Not even when he couldn't prevent his voice from distorting with the vein of bitterness he usually kept buried deep inside him. She just tucked a strand of pale hair behind her ear and gazed at him and he thought how much of her father there was in her—for didn't she seem to share his uncanny ability of knowing when to speak and when to remain silent?

And suddenly he found himself telling her. Not all of it, no, but some. Some things he would never tell. 'Countries are like people,' he ground out. 'They evolve and grow. And I didn't like the country which mine had become. The world had moved on and the casinos, which were licensed a long time ago, had begun to attract the worst kinds of people. When I looked closely, I discovered an underbelly which sickened me. Money-laundering. Prostitution. Drugs.' He saw her wince. 'I knew I had to bring about a profound change. I wanted to make Monterosso into a beacon of sustainability and culture. So I shut down some of the more dubious establishments, poured money into social projects and rewilded many of our forests. I knew we had the potential to become a World Heritage site, if we could just clean up our act.'

'That's a pretty incredible thing you've done,' she put in eagerly. 'And that's why you wanted to show the Forrester artefacts to the world.'

Her eyes looked so shining and full of life and in that moment she appeared so utterly idealistic—and, yes, *beautiful*—that Corso couldn't bring himself to disillusion her about his motives. He had told her enough. More than enough. He knew only too well that information was power and was wary of allowing her to get any closer than she already was. Physical proximity was one thing, but anything else had the potential to be problematic. For her, rather than him. He didn't want verbal confidences to be mistaken for real intimacy, because there was only one kind of intimacy he could guarantee. And maybe it was about time he demonstrated that to her, so there could be no mistake.

'Come here,' he said silkily.

He saw the indecision which flickered over her flushed face and he wondered if she recognised the significance of his request. Because this wasn't about him reaching out to her, even though it would have been ridiculously easy to pull her into his arms and kiss her and have her moaning his name before a minute had elapsed. She had to come to *him*. To acquiesce and to relinquish power to him. If she wanted this, then she needed to play by his rules—for he had been born to rule.

He watched as her eyes darkened and then, with her magnificent breasts swaying a little, she slid across the bed towards him, her body warm and soft as it collided with the hard muscle of his.

'What do you want?' she murmured, wrapping her arms around his neck and pressing herself against him.

Corso's body was programmed to respond instantly to a question like that, and it did. He thought how quickly a woman could learn to be a coquette when a man had satisfied her, and he smiled as he trickled his fingers down over her breast and felt her nipple pucker. 'That isn't a very imaginative question,' he chided. 'I would have expected something better from you, Rosie.'

'Don't they say that people who have expectations are doomed to be disappointed?'

'I promise that disappointment is something you'll never experience when you're in bed with me.'

'That is so...' Her eyelids fluttered to a close. 'So...'

'So what?' he teased, his hand now moving down beyond her belly.

'Egotistical,' she managed, at last. 'Corso! What... what are you doing?'

'I think you know very well what I'm doing. I'm going to have sex with you again because last time was your first time and I feel it's my duty to convince you that the pleasure you experienced wasn't a fluke.'

'You're...you're making it sound like some sort of power game,' she whispered.

He didn't answer. Just dipped his head down past her navel and a rush of carnal satisfaction flooded through him as his tongue found her moist bud. He made her come twice more—with his finger and with his mouth—but still he didn't allow himself the luxury of his own release. He could feel the heightening of tension, the terrible aching at his groin, but still he resisted entering her until she was begging him to. As if he wanted to demonstrate to them both that he had clawed back that steely control which had kept him celibate all these years. That he was still in charge and always would be.

Briefly he relinquished his hold on her when at last he could bear it no more, and reached for a condom.

'Corso?' she questioned, and he could see she was looking at him with something like concern in her eyes. But he said nothing. He didn't want any more analysis, or questions, or explanations. That had never been his way. He didn't want to confront his own feelings, or to question hers. He wanted to be deep inside her and lose himself completely in her tight wet heat and only after that would he consider what happened next.

But when it was all over and he lay there, drained and satisfied, he was overcome by a sudden air of melancholy he couldn't seem to shift. He turned on his side to study her and his heart missed a beat. One arm was splayed above her head in unconscious abandon and her head was pillowed on the pale silk of her hair. Oh, Rosie, he thought sadly, as he looked down at her sleeping face and the soft lashes which feathered her pink cheeks. Far better that you'd kicked me out last night and told me never to darken your door again.

CHAPTER TEN

WHEN ROSIE WOKE next morning, she wondered if she'd dreamt the whole thing. She opened her eyes. The un-shuttered windows showed a cloudy spring day, the Ei-ffel Tower looking more sombre without its night-time glitter of flashing lights. Last night it had looked like an extravagant fairground illumination. Today it was just a giant grey construction of metal.

She looked around the bedroom, as if searching for evidence that Corso had been here last night, making delicious love to her. Or, more accurately, introducing her to sex. Because there was a big difference between the two, and only a fool would forget that.

But there was nothing of him to be seen. The military jacket was no longer hanging on the back of a chair—nor the scarlet striped dark trousers lying in a hastily dis-carded heap at the side of the bed. Not a single sign that the King of Monterosso had been there. She licked her lips, because his presence still permeated the room all the same. She could detect his faint scent on her skin. And inside she was warm and aching from where he had been deep inside her.

She must have fallen asleep because she hadn't heard him leave. There had been no farewell kiss. No promises made, or awkward conversation before he took his leave. Should she be grateful for that? She picked up her watch, which was lying on the locker beside the bed, and saw it was just gone seven.

Now what?

More than anything she needed to get ready to go to work, so she lifted the phone to ask for coffee to be delivered to her suite. It arrived accompanied by the most delicious croissant she'd ever tasted—at least she'd got her appetite back—and soon she was feeling a bit more like herself, rather than someone who had temporarily lost sight of her place in the world. But as Rosie showered and dressed in another museum-suitable outfit, she couldn't help mulling over the surprising things Corso had told her last night. About taking a vow of chastity—which was essentially what it amounted to—after she'd confided what she'd overheard all those years ago. And then pouring his redirected energy into polishing the tarnished reputation of his beloved country and putting it back on track.

She didn't want to hang around the embassy, looking as though she were waiting or expecting something—because surely it would be easier if she just made herself scarce. Less embarrassing that way. She didn't want Corso to feel responsible for her, or to worry about how she was going to react. She wasn't going to blush, or sulk, or melt into a heap when he swept through the embassy with his entourage. She was going to take what had happened completely in her stride. She was going to be modern. After all, Paris was one of the most sophisticated places in the world—so why not allow herself to be influenced by it?

Noticed only by a couple of staff, she slipped from

the residence and caught the Metro to the Jardin des Tuileries and went inside the museum to look for Phillipe. She found him in the office, his head bent over one of the Parisian broadsheets, and he looked up and smiled as she entered, that lock of dark hair flopping attractively into one eye. *'Bonjour,'* he murmured as he pointed to the paper. 'Have you seen this?'

She hadn't. Rosie blinked with surprise as she peered over his shoulder. On the front page was a photo of her, next to one of Corso—both taken at last night's dinner, when she'd been only half aware of a photographer capturing the embassy event for posterity. It was hard to recognise herself. The designer clothes and the jewels glittering at her ears and throat made her look like an expensive stranger. And her *hair*. Would she really have worn it that way if she'd realised it was going to tumble to her waist and look so untamed?

'What does it say?' she asked Phillipe.

He scanned the text. 'It talks about the King's plans for closer ties between our two countries. It mentions at some length your family's long-standing relationship with the da Vignola line and remarks on how beautiful you are. *C'est vrai, chérie,'* he affirmed, when she made a muffled sound of protest. 'You are. And then it talks about the exhibition, and that we will be open later this morning.' He smiled. 'I think we are going to be very busy today, Rosie.'

Phillipe wasn't exaggerating and there was a long line in place before the doors had even opened. But Rosie was furious with herself for feeling a distinct air of disappointment as the day wore on. She kept looking up to scan the entrance, or making an excuse to go to the front desk so she could peer outside and see if the King's car was anywhere to be seen. But it wasn't. And neither was he.

They closed at six and Phillipe invited her to join him and the other staff for a celebratory glass of champagne in a bar around the corner, but Rosie refused. She honestly didn't think she could paste a bright smile to her face any longer and she certainly didn't feel like celebrating.

She wished she were back in her little cottage in the woods but, since that wasn't on the cards, at least she could go back to her suite at the embassy and come to terms with the fact that last night had been a one-off. A big mistake—at least, on Corso's part. He was probably regretting having broken his sexual fast with her, rather than someone amazing and well connected, and famous. But the last thing she was going to do was to fixate on the King. She needed to remind herself that this was the first time she'd ever been in Paris and to make the most of it, because a few weeks from now and she'd be back on the railway.

Pulling out her guidebook, she went for a walk in the Tuileries gardens, thinking how peaceful it was to have this beautiful space, right in the middle of one of the busiest cities in the world. Yet somehow, the sight of the tulips and frothy blossom and the stunning pink of the Judas trees gave the place an air of something unbearably poignant. What *was* it about springtime which made people start thinking about love? wondered Rosie. Love was nothing but a word. A stupid word. People bandied it around and used it when it suited them, for all kinds of reasons. A random stranger had said it to her mother and because of that she'd given away all her life savings.

Her dad had loved his work and because of that, he had taken a risk which had ultimately killed him.

Pushing her troubled thoughts away, she strolled around the gardens until the light began to fade, before catching the Metro—and when she arrived back inside the embassy it was to see Rodrigo, the King's aide, heading towards her, a resolute expression on his face.

'The King requests your company, Miss Forrester,' he said, before she'd even had a chance to take her coat off.

'When?'

'Now.'

'I need to change first,' she said calmly, refusing to be intimidated by Rodrigo's faint frown. She wasn't a well-trained dog who would go running whenever the King whistled! More than that, she wanted to be in control. To impose something of her own agenda onto what was happening, rather than fall in with everything Corso wanted. Because suddenly she was scared. Scared of the way he could make her feel—and even more scared of what could happen if she allowed herself to fall for him.

That was never going to happen.

Because she must never allow it to happen.

'I will wait,' Rodrigo said repressively, standing sentry outside her door.

Rosie took as long as she dared to remove the fine wool trousers and silk shirt she'd worn for work, deliberately rejecting all the other gorgeous clothes hanging inside her wardrobe. She didn't want to wear anything the stylist had chosen. Not now, in her downtime—before a face-to-face with a man she should never have had sex with. She needed to look like herself. To *feel* like herself. Which was why she pulled on a pair of faded jeans and teamed them with an ancient sweater she'd knitted during one of those long winter's nights at the hospital, when her father had been lying in his coma.

Rodrigo hadn't moved from his position outside her door, the narrowing of his eyes his only reaction to her dressed-down appearance. As she followed him to the King's suite on the first floor, Rosie felt like a prisoner being escorted to the cells. But the room he showed her into was nothing like a cell—its gilded splendour indicating the importance of its inhabitant, who stood silhouetted against the window as he stared down at the Rue du Faubourg Saint-Honoré. He turned round as he heard them enter and Rosie's heart gave a powerful leap as she met the gleam of his eyes and memories of last night came rushing back in an erotic flood.

'Miss Forrester, Your Royal Highness,' murmured the King's aide.

'Yes, I can see that for myself,' said Corso impatiently. 'Leave us now, Rodrigo, will you? I don't wish to be disturbed until I give the order. Understand?'

'Perfectly, my liege.'

There was silence even after Rodrigo had slipped from the room and the two of them just remained staring at each another, as if it were the first time they'd ever met.

Corso waited for Rosie's reaction, his impatience growing when still she didn't speak. Because didn't part of him—a big part—want her to rebuke him? To ask why he had slipped from her suite without fanfare and demand to know what he was going to do next? Or even to complain about him sending an aide to escort her here instead of going to find her himself. Because wouldn't that have given him the chance to snap back that she had no right to make demands on him, that she should know her place?

But she didn't. She spoke not one word. Just subjected him to a coolly speculative stare, which was doing dangerous things to his blood pressure. She was very controlled, he thought, with reluctant admiration. And she handled herself very well, looking bizarrely at home in these lavish surroundings, despite wearing the most outrageously old jeans and sweater.

'You say nothing,' he observed.

'I am waiting for your lead, Your Royal Highness.' Her answer was demure but he couldn't mistake the tinge of mockery which underpinned it. 'Isn't that the correct procedure?'

'To hell with procedure,' he said, unable to prevent himself from walking across the room and pulling her into his arms. He looked down into the silvery gleam of her eyes and saw her pupils darken and his body responded instantly. 'You've been away much too long.'

'I've been…' Her breathing had quickened. 'I've been working at the museum all day, which is, after all, what I'm being paid to do. We've had a gratifying number of people through the door, just in case you're interested.'

'Yet you chose to walk alone in the Jardin des Tuileries afterwards, rather than join your colleagues for a drink?' he mused. 'Was Phillipe very disappointed by that, do you think?'

She frowned. 'How do you know what I did, and what does Phillipe have to do with anything?'

He shrugged, his fingers straying beneath her sweater to encounter the warmth of flesh beneath, wanting to distract her with his touch rather than admit that he had been bothered by an uncharacteristic twist of jealousy. 'I had a couple of my bodyguards keep an eye on you.'

'Ah!' She tilted her chin to look at him. 'You mean you've been spying on me?'

'Don't be absurd,' he growled. 'You are a member of my party and therefore warrant my protection.'

'Isn't that—?'

But his kiss suppressed the rest of her words, though he wasn't particularly seeking to silence her—he was simply overcome by a need to connect with her again, and as quickly as possible. He wanted her. Very badly. And judging from the hunger of her own kiss, she was feeling exactly the same way. Her fingers were rubbing frantically through his hair. He could feel the stony jut of her nipples which crowned the soft globes of her breasts. The frenetic beat of his heart, as she pressed against him. All that soft, sweet flesh beneath the deliberately casual clothes she had chosen—yet didn't that subliminal message of independence make him want her even more?

And suddenly Corso wanted to behave wildly—to shrug off the weight of all the duties which had consumed him these past years. To forget the control and restraint and frustration he had imposed upon himself. To smash through the veneer of politeness which governed every move he made. He didn't *want* to be civilised, and take her to the giant arena of his bed. He wanted recklessness and excitement. He wanted to do it to her here. Now. On the floor. And if the truth were known, he wasn't sure if he could make it as far as the bed in his current state of arousal.

It feels this imperative because I'm making up for lost time, he told himself as he tumbled them down onto the Persian rug. But his hand was unsteady as he eased down the zip of her jeans and slid them off to reveal a pair of plain black panties, which were strangely sexy. Moving over the satin of her thighs, he traced his finger over the moist gusset and she quivered as he delved beneath the sensible underwear to find her hot bud.

'Corso!' she gasped as he began to strum her aroused flesh.

'Corso, what?' he demanded silkily, but her eyes had closed and he didn't think she'd even heard him. He liked the fact that her thighs had parted and she was looking as helpless as he felt. He bent his head to her lips, his mouth devouring hers with a hunger which felt elemental as he continued to move his hand against her. Within seconds she was orgasming—moaning his name and writhing beneath him. The scent of her sex was heavy in the air as, with his free hand, he slid down his own zip. He reached for the protection which had been discreetly delivered to his suite earlier, but his fingers were shaking like a drunk's as he lay back on the silken carpet.

And suddenly Rosie was on her knees beside him, smoothing the condom over his erect shaft, and he felt as if he might shatter before he was even inside her. He pulled her on top, so that she was straddling him, and he groaned as she began to ride him. Her eyes were open and they met his gaze unflinchingly and for once he didn't want to look away.

He couldn't look away.

It had never felt like this before. As if the very act of having sex was the lifeblood on which he depended. As if his body needed to feel the heat of hers from the inside. He wanted to know every inch of her. Was it possible to want something at the same time as resenting its power over you? he wondered fleetingly as he she tipped her head back and began to moan, and that was when he let go completely.

When he had recovered his strength, he assumed the dominant position, but even that was not enough to satisfy his carnal hunger as he orgasmed for a second time. The third time left him dazed and utterly replete—and it was only when they were sitting at opposite ends of a steaming bathtub that Corso gave voice to his thoughts.

'I wasn't expecting this,' he said.

She tucked a wet strand of hair behind her ear. 'You mean…the sex?'

'Yes, Rosie,' he replied gravely. The bald word seemed hopelessly inadequate for what had just taken place between them, but he refused to give her false hope by correcting her. 'The sex.'

There was a pause before she answered, a shy smile curving her lips. 'Nor me.'

Life could throw all kinds of things at you, he thought as she lapsed into a contented silence, but it was how you dealt with them which ultimately determined your success, or failure. So much hinged on his forthcoming trip to New York. Things he'd been pushing to the back of his mind, but which had come to haunt him during the hours before dawn, when he'd woken with his heart pounding, his brow wet with sweat, his quest to find his half-brother hazy and nebulous. He still hadn't decided whether or not to initiate a meeting, because to do so could set off a ticking time-bomb. Uncovering the dark secret at the heart of his parents' marriage had taken a lot of discreet detective work but Corso had refused to share his discoveries with anyone else—even the aide who had been with him for longer than he could remember. The fact that it was his secret—and his alone—had allowed him to shrug off the nagging fear that the press might get hold of it. How could they? Nobody could talk to them, because nobody knew.

And the press could always be distracted, couldn't they?

The idea flew into his mind with the blinding certainty of a brainwave and he found himself thinking that the timing of this unforeseen affair could ultimately help his cause. Could his brief relationship with Rosie Forrester provide a smokescreen for the task which lay ahead—and throw any potentially curious journalists off the scent?

And what if that hurts her? nagged the voice of his conscience.

How could it? She'd known from the start that this was only ever going to be temporary. He'd told her so himself, even citing the type of woman he would one day marry. Wouldn't she be honoured if he legitimised their relationship by refusing to hide it away? She might not have any long-term future with him, but she would never be able to say that he had been ashamed of her.

He stared across the steam at the vision she made, with her elbows resting on the sides of the bathtub. Her thick hair was piled high on top of her head, damp tendrils spilling down against her damp cheeks. Although her nipples peeped rosily above the water line, he thought how wholesome she managed to look, and how innocent. Even now. Every time he looked at her, he wanted to be inside her. It was a powerful and visceral instinct. It was unfathomable. And surely, the more he indulged it, the sooner it would go away. *He needed it to go away.* His throat thickened.

'When we go to New York—'

'It's okay, Corso,' she put in quickly. 'I know what you're going to say.'

'Really?' He raised his brows. 'Am I so predictable?'

'You don't have to worry.' She cleared her throat. 'I'm not expecting this to continue when we take the collection to America.'

Beneath the water, he began to massage her ankle. 'Why not?'

'Because…oh! Stop deliberately misunderstanding me!' With a return of customary fire, she slapped her hand on the surface of the water so that bubbles flew above them in disintegrating perfumed clouds. 'You know perfectly well why not! You're a king and I'm your employee.'

'How does that impact on how we spend our downtime?'

'Is that a serious question?'

'Of course it is. There's no need to stop what we're doing—as long as we're both enjoying it.' He slanted her a hooded look. 'And can accept the natural boundaries of such a liaison.'

'You mean we would have to be discreet?' She licked her lips. 'Never be seen in public—that kind of thing?'

He shook his head. 'That's not what I meant, no. We're not doing anything wrong, so I think we should just act normally. And since you're going to be sharing my bed, I see no reason why we shouldn't be seen out together from time to time.' There was a pause. 'But you do need to accept that this is never going to end in a wedding.'

Some people might have considered his words brutal, but not Rosie—because didn't his honesty help squash her occasional pangs of longing for what could never be? He was warning her off. He was advising against nurtur-

ing unrealistic dreams about him. But his warning was
unnecessary. She knew the rules. She knew them better than anyone. Just as she knew there were a million
reasons why she ought to call a halt to this right now.
*Before you get in too deep. Before you get your heart
broken into a million pieces.*

But every single reason was blown out of the water by
the man himself, because who in their right mind would
willingly walk away from Corso Andrea da Vignola?
Even now she could hardly believe he was here. Tiny
droplets of water glittered like diamonds in the fiery
depths of his hair and his skin was like oiled silk. She
could feel one hair-roughened thigh pressing insistently
against hers and already she could sense he wanted her
again. She was sitting in a bathtub with the King of Monterosso—yet his exalted position in the world seemed irrelevant. Because it was *him* she wanted. Not his power
or his privilege, but him. The man, not the King. And
wasn't that the most dangerous thing of all?

'Of course I realise that there isn't going to be a wedding. Even if it's very pompous of you to assume that I'd
even want one,' she said coolly.

'So you wouldn't?'

'Oh, I never deal in hypotheticals—it's such a waste
of time,' she answered airily. 'But if we're seen together
in public, it will invite speculation.'

'Speculation about my love life I can deal with,' he
said roughly.

The sudden harshness of his words brought their ban-
ter to an abrupt end and Rosie wondered what had made
the lines around his mouth deepen like that. But that
was irrelevant. This wasn't about trying to burrow her
way into his heart or his mind. This wasn't about the

future, because they didn't have one. She wasn't going to be needy, or demanding. For the first time in her life she was going to have a bit of fun, with a man who just happened to be a king. And if she found herself back in her cottage in a few weeks' time—alone and missing him—well, surely she'd come through enough stuff in her life to be able to deal with the brief inconvenience of a broken heart.

'So are you going to have dinner with me tonight or not, Rosie?'

'I suppose I am,' she said shakily, because he had started tiptoeing his fingertips all the way up her inner thigh and the bubbled water was slopping over the side of the tub as he found his quivering target.

And suddenly she wasn't thinking at all.

CHAPTER ELEVEN

CORSO DA VIGNOLA WAS AN international superstar.

At least, that was what the New York media were say-ing—a media desperate for a good news story after a year when the international headlines had been increas-ingly grim. It seemed that the slick and very cosmopoli-tan American city couldn't get enough of the striking Mediterranean king and his blonde assistant, who knew so much about his tragic ancestor and her exquisite col-lection of jewels.

This time, the TV interview which preceded the open-ing of the collection was shown on one of the country's biggest networks, to a much wider audience than in France. Rosie had to get up at the crack of dawn to ap-pear on a breakfast show featuring an impossibly glamor-ous presenter with the most perfectly arranged hair she'd ever seen, who seemed much more interested in finding out what the King was *really like*, rather than the prov-enance of the ancient burial jewels.

'Oh, you know,' Rosie answered, her expression polite but non-committal. 'Like most kings, I suppose.'

'I wouldn't know, as I've never met one. So if he's plan-ning on throwing a big party while he's here…' The presenter's smile was as bright as her hair as her voice tailed off suggestively.

But all publicity was good publicity. At least, that was what they said. As the red light flashed, indicating they were live on air, Rosie sucked in a huge breath and prepared to speak. And this time there were no nerves. All she had to do was to think about the way she seemed to thrill Corso whenever they were alone together. Who wouldn't have acquired a new-found confidence when a man like that kept breathing into her ear how much he wanted her and then showing her exactly how much?

Like all the other embassies, the Monterossian delegation was in Washington and, since Corso had no desire to stay in a hotel, he'd borrowed a Manhattan penthouse from a friend. It was situated a short distance from Madison Square Park and the quirky museum where the jewels were being showcased. This time the museum's curator was called Donna Green and Rosie found her and her team helpful, welcoming and easy to work with. The downtown location of the apartment meant it was easy for Corso to access the corporate heads he was meeting throughout the day. But first, he insisted that Rosie approve their temporary accommodation, and she couldn't deny being flattered that her opinion mattered to him.

A glass elevator sped them up thirty levels to the very top of an apartment which was like nothing she'd ever seen. Well, of course she hadn't. Even Corso seemed momentarily impressed, and luxury was stamped into his DNA. Spread over five floors and looking as if it were photo-ready for an interiors magazine shoot, the apartment had eleven bedrooms and *fourteen bathrooms* and Rosie found herself worrying aloud that, if she wasn't careful, she might get lost.

'But you do like it?' questioned Corso, turning back from a wall of windows, which showcased the dazzling skyline of the city and the river which gleamed in the afternoon sunshine.

She walked around in a daze, noting the giant glass dining table and carefully placed bowls of pink flowers, which reminded her of the Judas trees she'd seen in Paris. 'Of course I do,' she said. 'Though it's all so perfect it feels a bit like being on a stage set.'

His eyes narrowed thoughtfully. 'Is that how you thought about my palace?'

She thought how few people could say 'my palace' in that proprietorial tone and get away with it. 'Not really. As a child, everything you know is defined by your own experience and it was all I knew. And our house wasn't actually *in* the palace, was it? But, yeah, I guess that since I grew up seeing servants everywhere and watching my parents go off to the occasional formal banquet—I was never particularly daunted by all the splendour.'

'Did you miss it?' he questioned suddenly. 'After you left?'

When he came out with something like that it took Rosie off guard, because it happened so rarely. Corso's preference was always to stay away from the personal and she liked that, because personal questions ran the risk of blurring reality and making her think he cared. Which he didn't. He wasn't laying down the foundations of a long-term relationship by discovering what made her tick. She was his stopgap lover, that was all. *And if he hadn't been deprived of sex for so long, she wouldn't have got a look-in.*

Sometimes she was afraid that his sizzling gaze would burn right through her, revealing more of herself than she wanted him to see. Scared he might sense that her feelings for him were changing—growing—even if she was doing everything in her power to hold them in check. But surely she should answer him honestly—especially when he had been so honest with her.

'I missed the country,' she said suddenly. 'The beaches and the mountains. And the people, of course. Because nobody makes you feel more welcome than a Monterossian.'

'That's quite some praise, Rosie,' he said softly. 'And on behalf of my people, I thank you.'

The approbation in his voice made her uncomfortable and she couldn't work out why. Because it made her long for more—and then more still? Or because praise made people feel secure and her position with him was anything but secure? 'You're welcome,' she said, determined to maintain a bright façade.

'Let me show you where we'll be sleeping.' His golden eyes glinted. 'I'm reliably informed that the master bedroom has a monster-sized bed.'

But Rosie wasn't interested in the size of the bed, or yet another breathtaking view over the Hudson River. The only thing which commanded her attention was the man who had dropped to his knees in front of her and begun to remove one of the skyscraper heels she was wearing—at his request.

First one, then the other shoe was thrust away across the silken rug, before he lifted her foot to his mouth and whispered his lips over each bare toe. She gasped aloud as he licked them, slowly. She'd never dreamed that having your toes sucked could be so…erotic. As if hearing her unspoken plea, he pulled her down onto the floor and the journey of his kiss became more focussed. He took his time as his mouth moved slowly up the length of one leg before finding her thighs and Rosie thought she was about to lose her mind. And then he was sliding down her panties and pushing them away, before placing his mouth where she most needed him and beginning to lick his tongue over her.

He teased her until she moaned. Screamed. Squirmed. Holding her hips as if to anchor her, he pressed his mouth harder against her as she began pulsing helplessly, increasing the intensity of her pleasure until at last she lay there, breathless and shaking, her heart thundering with disbelief at the way he could make her feel like this. Every. Single. Time. And each time he did it, she felt a little bit more exposed. As if he were peeling away all the different layers behind which she hid, leaving her raw and susceptible. Could he tell that her emotions were being compromised? Was it a sign of weakness or dependence that made her heart want to burst with joy whenever she looked at him? And both those things were dangerous. So concentrate on the physical, she told herself fiercely—and stop longing for things which are never going to happen.

She opened her eyes to find him watching her and, lazily, drifted her fingers to the hard ridge at his groin.

'Teach me what you like best,' she said, tugging at the belt of his trousers, but he shook his head as she freed him.

'You don't need any teaching, Rosie. You're a—' she saw him swallow as her fingers curled around his erection '—*natural*. You seem to know what I want better than I do myself.'

When she didn't respond, he frowned. 'That was a compliment,' he observed. 'And since I don't dish them out very often, I find your lack of appreciation a little... disappointing.'

She focussed on his egotism rather than on words

which threatened to destabilise her because they were making her feel special and different. And she wasn't. She *wasn't*. 'Would you like me to gush my thanks?' she whispered. 'Or perhaps to demonstrate my gratitude in… other ways.' She bent her head, glad for the concealment of the thick fall of her hair as she took him into her mouth.

She enjoyed his helpless moan as she sucked him— then licked him like a lollipop, trickling the tip of her tongue up and down his hard shaft. She teased him until he was demanding release and, after he had spilled his seed into her mouth, he dug his fingers into her hair and pulled her up to lie on top of him.

'That was…good,' he said unevenly and then, after a moment of silence while he recovered his breath, his next words took her completely by surprise. 'Since there's so much space to choose from, I thought we could have the top two floors of this place to ourselves while we're here.'

Her eyes widened. 'No servants?'

'No servants,' he agreed. 'My staff can easily accommodate themselves in the rest of the apartment. It might be…*interesting* not to have anyone else around. Liberating, don't you think?'

'Very,' she said shakily as he began to unbutton her little cashmere cardigan.

It was early evening by the time they roused themselves, waking up to find themselves tangled together in a bed whose size really had lived up to the hype. Corso yawned. 'Shall I ring down and ask one of my aides to get us a dinner reservation?'

She hesitated. 'Or we could have a meal delivered here. They do great take-out in New York, apparently.'

'Is that what you'd like?'

She nodded. 'We could even ask the aides to organise

some shopping so we can make our own breakfast in the mornings.' She rolled onto her stomach, propping herself onto her elbows. 'It means I don't have to dress up and get stared at. It's not very relaxing if all the time you know people are wondering why the King of Monterosso is eating out with someone like me.'

'You don't know what people are thinking, Rosie.'

'Corso,' she said patiently. 'Come on. It's always been that way for you. Every move you make and word you speak is analysed.'

He stared out at the lights of the distant skyscrapers and then reached for her. 'True.'

'So let's stay in.'

Corso nodded. 'Let's stay in,' he echoed, the weight of her breast in his hand driving everything else from his mind.

He was aware that she had won that minor battle in the most subtle of ways but unusually he wasn't unduly perturbed at having made a rare concession. Because, in a way, playing house with her distracted him from the fact that somewhere in this city, his brother was walking around. The unwelcome knowledge hovered like a storm cloud on the horizons of his mind. It twisted darkly at his heart. It reminded him that he was here on a mission he had no real appetite for.

Who could blame him for seeking temporary refuge from reality, by losing himself in Rosie's sweet embrace? He'd never thought of sex as a refuge and a comfort before. That it could be layered with things other than satisfaction. And if, from time to time, the sombre toll of his conscience rang too loudly in his ears, it was all too easy to silence it by listening to the more pressing demands of his body.

On the morning of their penultimate day he walked into the kitchen, feasting his eyes on the voluptuous curve of her bottom as she leaned over to poke at something sizzling in a frying pan. Funny. He'd never realised just how sexy an apron could be.

She switched the hob off and turned round, a frown on her face.

'What's wrong?' he questioned as he reached for the coffee pot, even though several weeks ago it wouldn't have occurred to him to enquire after someone's welfare. Or, indeed, to pour them a cup of coffee.

'I'm a bit nervous about going to this cocktail party later,' she said, as he pushed the cup towards her.

Corso tensed. You and me both he thought grimly, though he would never admit to the weakness of nerves. Instead, he threw her a reflective look. 'Why?'

She wiped her hands down the front of her apron. 'I'm not sure if it's a good idea. It's you they want to see, not me. Why, I might even be cramping your style. Didn't you say that representatives from the royal kingdoms of Maraban and Mardivino are going to be attending?' She gave a smile, which looked distinctly forced. 'You never know—your future spouse might be there.'

'I doubt it,' Corso offered drily, lifting the cup to his lips. Didn't she realise he had eyes for no other woman but her? No, of course she didn't. He'd made certain of that. She was inexperienced enough to mistake sexual compatibility for something deeper, and he had been careful not to give her any false hope. Emotional indifference had been a skill he had refined into a veritable art form over the years, and never had he needed it more than he did tonight.

He could feel adrenaline pumping through his body as

it prepared for what lay ahead. His heart was racing, his mouth dry. Because tonight was the night. The seemingly innocuous social event he'd planned with the dedicated focus of a military campaign, which would at last bring him into contact with the mysterious billionaire he had no real desire to meet. Whose very existence made a mockery of all that he had believed and been taught to believe.

Xanthos Antoniou.

The man whose blood he shared.

'Corso?'

Rosie's puzzled voice broke into his thoughts. 'Why are you frowning like that?'

He shook his head as if rousing himself from a dream. Or a nightmare. As he walked across the kitchen towards her and pulled her into his arms, he felt the beat of apprehension. And, yes, of fear. What would tonight's reception reveal, and would he live to regret his curiosity?

'I want you by my side tonight,' he instructed harshly, before crushing her mouth with a kiss which left them both breathless.

It all got out of hand, very quickly. Summarily, he dealt with their clothing—removing only the most essential items before bending her over the kitchen table and thrusting into her, to the accompaniment of her mewled cries of pleasure. He blamed his own particularly explosive orgasm for his wandering attention during the rest of day, though he disguised it well enough during back-to-back meetings with CEOs, environmentalists and movers and shakers. But he was glad to get back to the penthouse, and to stand beneath the punishing jets of an icy shower, telling himself that at least the wait was over.

He was staring out at the New York skyline when Rosie emerged from the bedroom wearing a floaty dress the colour of claret, shot through with threads of silver which echoed the colour of her eyes. But for once he didn't compliment her, or allow his eyes to linger on the bright fall of blonde hair. His head was too full of conflicting thoughts to offer anything other than the kind of nod he might give to one of his drivers.

'Come on,' he said abruptly. 'We need to go.'

Rosie nodded, bewildered by Corso's sudden coolness and change of attitude towards her and wondering what had caused it, especially as he had been so spontaneous and passionate before he'd left that morning. Was he already winding down the affair and giving her a hint of what lay ahead? Because they were travelling to London the day after tomorrow and once that part of the tour was over…

She shivered as they took the elevator to the underground car park. After that, she would probably never see him again. There would be no reason to. Their very temporary relationship would seamlessly come to an end. They would say goodbye and Corso would jet back to Monterosso, preparing for a life very different from her own. And while he was selecting the woman who would become his queen, she and Bianca would be busy buying Mum a lovely new home. Once that was done she would look round for a job in the art world—for how could she fail to find a decent appointment, with Corso da Vignola as her referee? She ought to be counting her blessings instead of focussing on the dull ache in her heart, which seemed to be growing by the minute. Did she really want to ruin their last few days together by longing for something which could never be hers?

But despite all her attempts at conversation, Corso remained silent and remote during the short car-ride to the exclusive venue and once again she got the sense that he was excluding her. They arrived at the exclusive venue and were shown into an elegant room whose silk-lined walls were studded with old masters. A warm burst of applause greeted Corso's entry and the glittering throng began to converge on her consort.

Rosie listened while he spoke to a couple of prominent politicians, as well as a Hollywood star she recognised—though she'd never seen any of his films—and was ridiculously pleased when a woman came up and told her how much she'd enjoyed going round the exhibition earlier that day.

'The Queen's wedding coronet was just…charming!' she enthused.

Rosie beamed. 'Wasn't it just? All those pearls!'

Dutifully, she ate some sushi and tried to enjoy the beautiful artwork in the room. At one point, she commented on a stunning painting, but Corso didn't appear to have heard her. He had grown completely still and was staring at the door with an expression on his face she'd never seen there before. Following his gaze, she noticed a man who'd just walked in—breaking the cardinal rule that nobody should ever arrive after the royal party.

Rosie blinked, trying to make sense of what was happening. It was weird, because the powerful-looking stranger seemed oddly familiar—even though she was certain she'd never seen him before. He reminded her a bit of Corso, though his hair was black rather than lit with flames and his eyes were black too, not golden. But it wasn't just about his looks. It was the way he held himself—as if he owned the space around him. A woman at his side was gazing up at him with open adoration but he barely seemed to notice her—nor the others of her sex who had turned to study him with predatory interest. Instead, his eyes scanned the room, before coming to rest briefly on Corso. But there was nothing unusual about that because everyone always looked at Corso.

Did she imagine the King's quiet intake of breath or the sudden rigidity of his body as the gazes of the two men clashed? For a moment she thought he was about to walk across the room and greet the stranger—though whether to shake his hand or punch him, she couldn't quite decide—such was the tension radiating from his powerful frame. But instead, he shook his head, as if rousing himself from a deep sleep. Suddenly, he touched his hand to her elbow and let it remain there, the tips of his fingers curving lightly around the crook. It was the most innocent of touches but it was remarkable because it was so unprecedented. And significant. Rosie knew that royals were rarely intimate in public and certainly not with a commoner like her—because such a gesture spoke volumes. She heard a faint murmur as people picked up on it and was aware of heads turning in their direction.

And despite her professed dislike of having people look at her, Rosie felt the warm wash of pleasure sliding over her skin as she started to dream. Who could blame her when he was touching her so proprietorially? She started wondering if maybe this *thing* between them couldn't continue for a while longer and that maybe they could be flexible—or creative—about the future. She didn't want a wedding ring. She wasn't that dumb. She didn't imagine for a moment there could be any kind of permanence in their arrangement—but was it so wrong to want to be with him for as long as possible? If Corso suggested carrying on with the relationship once the tour was over, wouldn't she be crazy not to agree? He had planes, didn't he? And boats. And cars. Travelling between Monterosso and England shouldn't throw up too much of a logistical nightmare. *Why should she give him up if she didn't have to?*

But what if your feelings for him keep growing? taunted a tiny voice inside her head. Aren't you already more than halfway in love with him?

'Come on,' he said, his abrupt tone roughly shattering her reverie. 'We're going.'

'But we've—'

'Don't let me spoil your fun, Rosie. Stay if you want. I can easily arrange for a driver to wait,' he added coolly, dropping his hand from her elbow. 'But I'm leaving.'

It was a terse and inexplicable way to end the evening and Rosie didn't understand. In the space of a few seconds he had elevated and then trampled on her dreams—and the easy atmosphere between them had suddenly evaporated.

'Is something wrong?' she ventured during the journey back to the apartment.

Was something wrong?

Corso wondered what she would say if he told her the truth—that suddenly all his certainties about life had been smashed. He clenched one fist to mimic the hard clench of his heart. He had always thought of himself as unique. The sole heir, born to rule. That had been a given—the one constant, which impacted on everything and everyone around him. Even in his most contemplative moments, he had rationalised that seeing his illegitimate half-brother for the first time would have no real effect on him.

But he had been wrong.

Laying eyes on Xanthos in the flesh had felt visceral. Powerful. Unsettling. A sombre connection to the past, and… He swallowed. Because only a fool would ignore the possibility of how it might impact on his future.

'Corso?' prompted Rosie's voice at his elbow and he looked down at her upturned face, to see concern written in her grey eyes. And, oh, the temptation to confide in her was overwhelming—because didn't he trust her gentle common sense and honesty? Wouldn't her uncomplicated softness be like a soothing balm, taking some of the sting out of his discovery?

But he would not do that. It was not fair. Not to him and especially not to her. She was a temporary fixture who would soon be gone—so why on earth would he tell her?

'Nothing's wrong,' he bit out, turning away from the brief hurt which clouded her expression.

He excused himself when they returned to the penthouse, citing urgent work which required his attention. He was still at his desk at midnight, when she hovered in the doorway, her blonde hair lit from the light in the hallway behind her. She was wearing a silky nightgown the colour of ice, edged with a darker lace which emphasised the creamy swell of her breasts. But if she was hoping to seduce him, he was going to disappoint her. He wanted to be alone with his thoughts, not to answer any of the questions he could see were still written in her eyes.

'You go to bed without me,' he said, and he saw the disappointment which made her bite her lip before nodding and turning away.

It was only after she had gone that he realised this was the first time they hadn't gone to bed together.

CHAPTER TWELVE

ROSIE WOKE JUST as dawn was filtering through the windows, opening her eyes to discover Corso hadn't bothered to activate the electric blinds which usually blotted out the New York morning. He lay beside her, his eyes closed. Dark lashes feathered the autocratic cheekbones and the pale sunlight emphasised the fiery highlights of his dark hair. She thought about snuggling up to him as she usually would have done. Wrapping her arms around his warm body and trailing soft kisses up his neck and reaching down to curl her fingers around his inevitable erection. But something was holding her back. A niggle in the back of her mind, which was refusing to be silenced.

And that was when it hit her.

She thought about Corso's behaviour last night. His tension at the party when the stranger had walked in and the unmistakable mirroring between the two men. The way he had withdrawn from her in the car on the way home and his chilly distance when they'd arrived back at the penthouse. Who *was* the black-eyed incomer who had arrived after the royal party last night? She sucked in a breath and Corso's eyes opened so quickly that she wondered if he'd been awake all along.

'That man,' she said.

The hardening of his mouth became an ugly slash. 'Which man?'

Her heart began to pound, because didn't that sound awfully like evasion? 'The man at the party. The man who arrived after you. With the black hair.'

'What about him?'

But he pushed aside the sheet and got out of bed without touching her and that had never happened before. Rosie blinked. His face was forbidding. His expression icy. And this was a Corso she had forgotten existed—or had conveniently allowed herself to forget. The emotionally distant monarch who ruled everyone around him. Who subtly controlled the comments of others by default—even if he had no power over their thoughts. She felt confused—and vulnerable. But she needed to hold it together. She mustn't jump to conclusions, because perhaps Corso needed her help. He certainly looked as if he needed *something*—for the emptiness in his eyes was making him look so bleak and lost and troubled.

'You know him,' she said.

'I've never met him before in my life.'

She wondered whether she should just shut up, which was obviously what he wanted her to do. But she couldn't just walk away and pretend this wasn't happening. She was in too deep to be able to do that. She wanted to reach out and comfort him—even if she didn't know why he seemed to be in need of comfort. Something was driving her on to find out what this was all about…and what did she have to lose? 'But you know who he is, don't you?'

The silence was so long that Rosie wondered whether he hadn't heard her, or was just choosing to ignore her question.

'Yes, I do,' he ground out and she saw the lines on his

face becoming deep crevices, before he turned away to haul on a pair of jeans and tug a T-shirt over his ripped torso. And when he turned back his eyes were no longer bleak, they were blazing with a pure, bright gold—as if he were about to go into battle. 'His name is Xanthos Antoniou,' he grated. 'And he is my father's son.'

She stared at him in confusion, trying to make sense of his words. 'Your father's son?' she repeated and immediately thought about all the possible repercussions. 'Is he—?'

'Older,' he bit out, as if correctly anticipating her question.

'I don't understand,' she said. 'Why is this the first we've ever heard of him?'

Corso registered her bewilderment and suddenly he wanted to lash out. Wanted to deflect some of his pain and confusion onto someone else. Someone who wasn't him. *'We?'* he echoed imperiously. 'Why would you be privy to such knowledge, Rosie?'

'I'm sorry.' She flushed. 'That was presumptuous of me.'

But to Corso's anger, his icy reaction was not enough to deter her, because she sat up in bed a little, her grey eyes huge in her pinched face.

'Tell me,' she urged softly. 'Tell me what this is all about, Corso.'

He stared at her and felt the tightening of his throat. She looked so soft. So giving. As if she wanted to open up her arms to him and hold him tight. He wanted to tell her to keep her questions to herself and stop being so damned supportive—because he didn't need her support. He didn't need anything or anyone—yet he felt as if he might explode if the words stayed locked inside him much longer.

He drew in a ragged breath before baldly presenting the facts—as if that would minimise their impact. 'It took me a long time to go through my father's papers,' he began slowly. 'And it was only when I was nearing the end that I discovered a letter which had been hidden away. It had been written many years ago.' He paused. 'Thirty-four years, to be exact.'

She nodded, pulling up the duvet so it reached her chin.

'It was a letter from a woman, saying she had just given birth to my father's child.' He turned away because he didn't want to see what was written in Rosie's eyes. Not pity, nor pain, nor empathy. 'And attached to the letter was a note in my mother's handwriting, which ended with the words—*are we ever going to talk about this, Joaquin?*'

'Do you think they ever did?' she questioned at last, into the vast silence which followed.

He shrugged, but his shoulders were heavy. 'Who knows? From the date of the note, my mother must have been very sick because she died soon after that.' His words felt painful. Like stones lodged in the dryness of his throat. 'Nobody knows about it—not even Rodrigo,' he added harshly as he turned again to look at her. 'Only the detective who tracked Xanthos down. And now you.'

'And does he—Xanthos—realise who he really is?'

'I have no idea.'

She pleated her brow, like someone trying to work out the final clue of a crossword puzzle. 'So what were you—are you—planning to do with this information?

Surely it wasn't enough to catch a glimpse of him at a party and then just leave?'

'I hadn't thought it through. I still haven't. It was a greater shock than I had anticipated,' he admitted roughly. 'Seeing him in the flesh like that.'

'Yes. I can imagine it was. But…' She hesitated. 'You can't just let this opportunity go, Corso. You just can't. You've dared to dig the secret out and examine it and that's a really brave thing to do.'

She smiled at him and it was the sweetest smile he'd ever seen. So why had his heart started aching, as if something very sad and inevitable were about to happen? As if he had anticipated what her next words were going to be…

'I mean, it's such an incredible coincidence that he happened to be in the same city at all, isn't it?' And when he didn't answer she searched his face and he saw the beginnings of a frown begin to appear. It happened almost in slow motion. He watched as she stared down at the sheet, as if searching for spots of coffee they might have spilled there, and when she looked up again her mouth was twisted, as if she'd just touched her tongue to her teeth and tasted something very bitter. 'But it wasn't like that, was it, Corso?' she said slowly. 'Bringing the collection to New York and managing to see your half-brother at the same time wasn't just a huge coincidence.'

'Does it matter?'

'Actually, I think it does.' She sat up straight, pushing her untidy hair away from cheeks which were suddenly very flushed. 'The whole tour was planned in order to make that happen, wasn't it?'

There was a moment of complete and breathless quiet.

'What if it was?' he demanded harshly. 'What difference does it make?'

Rosie heard the irritation in his voice and the dismissal, too. Yes, there was definitely dismissal—along with that innate sense of entitlement which was never far from the surface. His royal authority superseded everything and woe betide anyone who allowed themselves to forget that. He might have tolerated her feistiness before—but that had been as lovers, when it was all a bit of a game. And this was no longer a game. He would no longer tolerate her insurrection or advice, because this was too important. This had been his main objective all along and everything else had been an irrelevance.

Including her.

'That's why you didn't mind being seen with me, isn't it?' she said slowly, her gaze not leaving his. 'Why you wanted to eat out when we arrived here. Because you know it would encourage the press to take our photos and wonder about the exact nature of our relationship. It would prevent the media from fishing around and finding out the real reason why you might be in New York, wouldn't it? I suppose I must have put a spanner in the works by telling you I'd prefer to eat in and not make a fuss.' She gave a bitter laugh. 'What a disappointment I must have been, Corso—when any other woman would have moved heaven and earth to be seen with you in public. That's why you touched me at the reception last night, wasn't it? Knowing people would notice and it would send their imaginations into overdrive. It would override the fact that you'd been staring across the room at a stranger who looked like you, and stop anyone from asking why. You're not going to deny that, are you, Corso? At least do me the courtesy of telling the truth.'

She saw a muscle working at his temple but that was the only thing about him which moved, because the tension was making his body look as if it had been carved from rock. How he must loathe this kind of analysis, she thought—trying to convince herself she felt no pity for him as he nodded, his expression grim.

'Yes, you're right. I plead guilty to all your accusations. I saw an opportunity and I took it.' His voice harshened. 'But while I might have decided to capitalise on our relationship once we'd become lovers, I didn't actively set out to seduce you. That was never part of my plan. I didn't have sex with you in order to use you. You must believe that, Rosie.'

No, he had seduced her because he had gone without sex for seven long years, and she had been available—falling into his arms like a ripe piece of fruit dripping from the tree. In a way it might have been a lot more flattering if he *had* intended to seduce her.

And he *had* used her, that was the bottom line. He'd used her just as surely as that scammer had used her mother. He'd used her as a smokescreen. A distraction. All the while she'd been thinking how close they'd become and how easy it would be to love him—he had been busy guarding all his secrets.

Rosie stared at the man who stood like a towering colossus against the glorious New York sunrise. In jeans and T-shirt, with the hint of new beard shadowing his jaw, his outward appearance wasn't the least bit regal—yet his extraordinary power radiated from every pore of his body.

She had often wondered how this strange affair of theirs might end. Whether she would be grown-up enough to wish him well for the dynastic marriage he'd spoken of, which featured somewhere in his future. She'd never imagined it would be like this—with a sense of bitter hurt and betrayal seeping through her veins like poison.

Unwilling to rise naked from the bed in front of him, she gave him a tight smile. 'I wonder if you wouldn't mind leaving me alone now, Corso? Because I'd like to pack.'

His eyes narrowed. 'What are you talking about?'

'What do you think I'm talking about? I'm going back to England. So first I'm going to pack and then I'd like Rodrigo to arrange my transport back home.'

His frown deepened. 'But we still have the London leg of the tour to do.'

He meant it. That was the worst part. He didn't stop to consider how *she* might be feeling after his astonishing revelation. 'Did you honestly think we were just going to carry on as before?' she demanded. 'With me meekly helping mount another major exhibition as if nothing has happened and, what—still sharing your bed at night?'

'I don't see why not.' He shrugged with what looked like genuine confusion. 'I don't understand why you're so angry, Rosie.'

He had her on the spot now and she guessed what was making her most angry was the realisation of how little she really meant to him. But her pride would never let her admit to that. 'I wish you'd told me,' she said stubbornly. 'About your brother.'

'Why should I? That would imply an intimacy between us which I have never sought. Not with you. Not with anyone, if you want the truth.' He lifted up the palms of his hands with an air of impatient query. 'Just what did you expect, Rosie?' he breathed. 'It was only ever intended to be a casual affair, we both knew that. I'm returning to Monterosso imminently and they are lining up suitable princesses for me to make my choice of bride.'

'Already?' she burst out, before she could stop herself.

'It's going to be sooner rather than later.' He paused, his next words very deliberate. 'I need an heir.'

She flinched. She couldn't help herself and, although she knew she had said enough, she couldn't seem to hold back the bitter words. 'And will you promise your future bride your fidelity, even if you can't promise her your heart?'

His face became a disdainful mask as he stopped to consider this, as if she had finally overstepped the line. But maybe he decided to answer her question any-way—as if by doing that he would finally kill off any last, lingering hopes. 'Of course I can,' he said coolly. 'Seven years of total celibacy has reassured me that I need never stray.'

She could have hit him, yet in the midst of Rosie's pain came the knowledge that he was capable of so much more. That he didn't *have* to hide behind the emotional barriers he'd erected during a difficult childhood, spent with a dying mother and a distant father. He *could* learn to love—of that she was sure. Hadn't there been mo-ments when she'd seen a chink in his armour, when he had shown her glimpses of the man she knew he could be?

'You've got to open yourself up to love, Corso,' she whispered, aware of the faint prick of tears in the backs of her eyes. 'You've got to learn to love the woman you marry, or else your life will be empty. Just like you've got to get to know your brother, because he's the only brother you're ever going to have.'

Now the disdain was back, and this time it was here to stay. 'I think we've said enough, don't you? I'll speak to Rodrigo about your transportation. Goodbye, Rosie.'

'Just one more thing,' she said as he turned away, and as he faced her again she could see the flicker of apprehension on his features. Did he think she was about to make a total fool of herself? To beg his forgiveness for her presumptuousness and tell him she'd changed her mind and would take him on whatever terms she could get?

'What is it?'

'I just want to be sure that I'm still going to get paid, even if I'm cutting short my involvement in the tour.'

His mouth twisted, as if her words had in some way reassured him. 'Don't worry, Rosie. You'll still get your money.'

And then he was gone. Tears blurred her eyes but Rosie dashed to the shower and brushed them away with an impatient fist before layering her clothes into her suitcase as fast as she could. The exquisite designer outfits she left hanging there—glittering symbols of a different time. She gave a bitter smile. She would have no need of couture when she was back in her old life.

A chauffeur-driven car was waiting to take her to the airport and somewhere over the Atlantic she was able to get a message to her sister, announcing her arrival time in the UK and wondering if they might be able to meet up next weekend, in order to begin the process of getting their mother settled. She was wondering if—and how much—she was going to tell Bianca. Why rake up something which was probably better left forgotten?

The last thing Rosie expected was to see her sister standing waiting for her at the Arrivals exit, her glossy black hair piled up in a sleek updo, oblivious to the men who were giving her second and sometimes third glances.

'What are you doing here?' whispered Rosie as the two women hugged tightly.

'I thought I'd surprise you as that text from the plane didn't sound like you at all. You look... *Rosie!* What on earth is the matter? You look *terrible*!'

Rosie didn't trust herself to reply, but by the time they'd reached Bianca's car she had started crying and the two of them sat in the airport car park, while outside rain lashed down wildly from a gunmetal sky. She'd held herself in check throughout the flight but now she was home and reality had started sinking in, she couldn't seem to hold back the tears any longer and they streamed down her cheeks.

'You've been having a relationship with Corso?' Bianca verified in amazement, when Rosie's choked words had become comprehensible.

'Yes! It's okay. Call me a fool and I would agree with you—because he's a...brute! A cold-hearted and unfeeling brute and I hate him. *Hate* him!' She waited for guaranteed words of support because Bianca had never been Corso's biggest fan, but to Rosie's surprise, no such words came.

'You do realise,' ventured Bianca cautiously, 'that he sent me a massive cheque to buy Mum a house, a couple of weeks ago?'

Rosie blinked, as if her sister had suddenly started speaking in a foreign language. 'But I hadn't done any work for him then,' she said in confusion. And she certainly hadn't been sleeping with him at that point. 'Why didn't you tell me?'

'He asked me not to. He was very insistent you shouldn't know.'

'What…what did he say?'

'That we should get Mum out of London as quickly as possible, so she could be close to her sister. Only we should put the house in our joint names, in case she was tempted to give all her money away again to some chancer she might meet on the Internet. In fact, I've got a few places lined up. I thought we could go and look at them with her, this weekend. Wasn't that kind of him?'

'Wasn't it?' said Rosie weakly.

'It made me think that maybe I'd misjudged him in the past. Now I'm not so sure.'

Rosie nodded and fumbled in her bag for a tissue. But in a way, it made everything even harder to bear. She didn't want to think of Corso as being considerate, and looking out for her mother. She wanted to think of him as the man who had…

What?

Given her the most blissful time of her life but neglected to tell her something which was deeply personal to him? Wasn't she behaving like a child who looked into a toy-shop window and demanded *all* of the toys?

She tried to put on a cheerful front—not just for her own sake, but for others too. She didn't want Bianca to worry about her, and made her promise not to breathe a word to their mother. And even though she felt empty and distracted, she managed to celebrate getting her degree and resolved to start looking round for a job in the art world, once she felt a bit more like herself.

But then the articles started appearing in the sort of

colourful magazines you found at supermarket check-outs and Rosie found herself buying them and slavishly reading them, despite knowing it was only piling on the agony. Articles about Corso and his hunt for a royal wife. All with the same stomach-churning theme along the lines of: *Who Will Wear the Monterossian Glass Slipper?*

There were accompanying photographs, too—and that made it even worse because Rosie started comparing herself unfavourably to the sleek beauties who seemed practically perfect in every way. Her eyes scanned every image with forensic intensity as she searched Corso's ruggedly handsome features for clues about which one he liked best. For a while it seemed as if the cute red-headed equestrian from Boritavia was a serious con-tender, until she was replaced by a dark-headed beauty from Mardivino.

Rosie screwed up the magazine and hurled it into the recycling bin, telling herself that she needed to face up to reality.

Corso was going to marry somebody else and, yes, her heart was breaking. But so what? One day she would get over it.

And then the invitations started arriving. Old-fash-ioned cards written in black ink and delivered in thick, buff-coloured envelopes—inviting her to attend inter-views at some of London's most famous art galleries. They all mentioned her work in Paris and New York and said she came highly recommended. And you wouldn't need to be a genius to know who was behind these sur-prising requests.

Corso.

He was intervening on her behalf, just as he'd pro-vided the money for her mother's new home. Rosie's fingers were shaking as she put down one of the letters and, several days later, she went along to the prestigious Brian Allen Institute, where her interview went much better than she could ever have imagined.

'We'd like to offer you a job,' said the owner of the famous art gallery.

'Honestly?'

His kind and clever face relaxed into a smile. 'Honestly,' he affirmed. 'If you'd like to accept it?'

'Oh, yes, I would,' said Rosie hastily. 'Yes, please.'

Using her concessionary railcard, she took the train back to Reading and worked out what she would say in her resignation letter to her manager, who had always been so kind to her. She would wait until she was properly settled in her new role and then she could send Corso a beautiful postcard, thanking him for everything he had done—diplomatically avoiding the subject of their brief affair, which in retrospect, should have been avoided. She would choose an old master painting on very expensive card and it would bear a carefully constructed message, which was light and witty, without seeming in the least bit bitter, or resentful.

She would have to choose the time of writing very carefully, of course.

It would be a terrible give-away if the words on her carefully chosen postcard were obliterated by tears.

CHAPTER THIRTEEN

THE SOUND OF the storm split the night. Thunder boomed like the clash of cymbals, while silver-white lightning forked the sky. Heavy rain was lashing relentlessly against the windows when Rosie heard a knock at the door and she frowned—because who in their right mind would be out on a night like this?

It must be the wind, she thought. Perhaps a falling branch tumbling onto the house. The forest demonstrating its own elemental power.

But no.

There it was again. Definitely a knock.

She checked the spyhole and thought she must be hallucinating. That perhaps she had conjured up a rainswept image of the man who was always hovering at the edges of her mind. She battled to open the door against the tug of the wind and when she finally managed it, her breath dried in her throat. Because this was no illusion. It was real. Corso da Vignola standing there like some avenging angel, seemingly oblivious to the rain which poured down on him. Wordlessly, she opened the door wider and he stepped inside, his black overcoat and dark hair completely sodden, and Rosie's heart was pounding as she shut the door on the howling night.

A shot of pain ripped through her like a bullet because it was six months since she'd seen him. Six agonisingly slow months during which she'd thrown herself into her new job—while Corso had been busy choosing his new queen. Half a year of living with a constant ache in her heart and wondering why the world around her seemed so grey, even on the brightest of summer days.

Yet now that he was here, it gave her no real pleasure. What pleasure could be gained from reacquainting herself with the devilish gleam of his eyes, or the muscular power of his body and the quiet strength which emanated from it? Didn't acknowledging his golden-dark beauty only drive home just how desperately she missed him?

'You're soaking,' she said woodenly. 'Put your coat by the fire and I'll make some tea.'

'I don't want tea.'

'Well, I do.'

Actually, what she wanted was the opportunity to prepare herself for what she suspected might be the reason why he had turned up like this, without announcement. What was it he wanted to say? To warn her about something she would soon see in the papers—that he was marrying a suitable princess at last?

I thought it only courteous to let you know myself, he would say.

That was very thoughtful of you, she would reply.

She hurried out into the kitchen and returned a few minutes later, thinking how pathetic it was that she'd loaded up the tray with her best china. Unless she really thought the King of Monterosso was going to be impressed by a few cups and saucers she'd picked up in the Debenhams closing down sale, when in his palace they regularly supped from precious, blood-red porcelain.

But Corso didn't appear to have noticed her return—or, if he did, he didn't acknowledge it. His back was to her as he gazed into the fire burning brightly in the grate, and his body was completely motionless. He was still wearing his coat, she registered dully, so clearly he wasn't planning to stay long. She put the tray down with a clatter and as he turned to look at her she felt a moment of despair, tinged with a much healthier edge of anger. *Why* had he come here today—making her endure all the pain of saying goodbye to him all over again?

'What do you want, Corso?' she questioned quietly. 'I assume you weren't just passing?'

Corso studied her across the distance of the small room, which suddenly seemed as vast as one of the ball-rooms in his palace. The only sound he could hear was the crackle of the fire and the fierce pounding of his heart and as he met her quizzical stare he wondered what she would say if he admitted the truth. That he was here because he had to be. Because it felt as if something were drawing him here, without his permission—like the flights of wild geese which flew north in summer, compelled by a biological imperative outside their control.

Yet for weeks now, he had been fighting an inner battle with himself, asking if what he was about to do was in Rosie Forrester's best interests. Or just his own. He had decided to choose his words with care. To lay down the foundations for what was to be his core message—just as if he were presenting a business meeting to foreign investors. But his mouth was stubbornly refusing to obey his thoughts.

'No.' He paused, unfamiliar with the language of love and need. And scared of it, too. He who had never been scared of anything. 'I've come to tell you how much I've missed you.'

She shook her head and her loose blonde hair swayed like an armful of corn. 'Please don't tell me things which are patently untrue. I've seen the photos, Corso—and I've read the articles in gruesome and gushing detail. You've been working your way through every eligible royal princess on the planet, we both know that.'

'Because I felt I had to!' he declared. 'It was something I needed to do.'

'There's no need to make it sound like some sort of punishment,' she accused hotly. 'Not when every single one of those women was accomplished and beautiful!'

'Yes, they were,' he conceded.

'How wonderful for you.'

He heard the crack of emotion in her voice and he couldn't bear the thought that he had hurt her. *Was* hurting her. And wasn't there the inconceivable possibility she might not find it in her heart to forgive him?

'In New York I was reeling from so many things,' he said slowly. 'Not least, my relationship with you and the way it was making me feel. It had never been that way with a woman before—that simple or that easy. That blissful, if you must know.'

'Corso—'

'And then I saw my half-brother across the room,' he said, cutting through her whispered protest. 'And suddenly, I wasn't thinking straight. I found myself filled with a primitive desire to secure my legacy—a legacy which had been drummed into me for as long as I remember.'

'To produce an heir?' she said, in a small voice.

'To produce an heir,' he echoed. 'So I went back to

Monterosso and did what I considered to be my duty. I was shown princess after princess. There were sheikhas and sultanas. Countesses and duchesses. But none of them...' His voice shook, husky and helpless with intent. 'None of them were you, Rosie. And that's why I can't marry any of them.'

'Corso...please... Don't.'

'Don't what?' he demanded. 'Don't admit you're the only person in the world who tells me the truth? Who is always fighting my corner, even when I don't deserve it. Even when I hurt you—you were still looking out for me. Your jealousy didn't impact on your generosity. You told me that I needed to open up my heart to my future wife, or my life would be empty. But you know something?' He stared at her. 'The only thing which will make my life empty is not having you in it.'

He could see the glimmer of tears which were making her stormy eyes look rain-filled and remembered the quick squeeze of the arm she'd given him, after his mother had died. He wanted to kiss her. To hold her and cradle her against the rapid pounding of his heart. But for too long he had thought about what *he* wanted and this needed to be about her.

'Corso,' she said, but he shook his head.

'Let me finish, Rosie. Please. Because you need to hear this. All of it.' He stared down at the blue Monterossian vase on the table, which was filled with bright sprigs of autumn berries. 'You told me I'd be crazy not to connect with my brother and deep down I knew you were right, even though I baulked at the thought. My father had been a cold and distant man but until the discovery of the letter, I'd always thought his marriage to my mother was completely faithful. That was the version I was led to believe.' He paused. 'I didn't want to confront the reality that he'd been conducting a love affair with another woman, and giving his other son all the attention he never gave me.' He gave a bitter smile. 'But I pushed aside the residual traces of childhood jealousy and telephoned Xanthos, suggesting we meet up.'

She nodded, her gaze intent. 'What did he say?'

'He agreed—reluctantly. I flew to Berlin, and so did he.'

'And was the meeting…a success?'

Corso heard the breath of hope in her voice. He shook his head. 'Not really. It seems my construct of the whole situation was completely wrong. Xanthos had never even met my—our—father. His mother had been only eighteen when she'd had him and I gather it was…' suddenly it was difficult to hold back his disdain and his judgement '…a transactional, rather than an emotional relationship. He *paid* to have sex with her,' he explained baldly and saw her look of bafflement turn into shock. 'That's all he would tell me,' he concluded grimly. 'And I don't blame him.'

She nodded, her blonde hair shimmering in the firelight. He could practically see her mind working. But unsurprisingly, she didn't fixate on any of the more salacious aspects of the whole affair. Instead she turned her ocean-grey gaze to him. 'Do you think you'll meet again?'

Corso shrugged. 'Who knows? We'll have to wait and see. He had a tough time.'

'You didn't have it so great yourself,' she pointed out. 'Your dad was never around and when he was, he was remote—we all knew that. And then your mum died.'

'That's why I used to hang around at your place,' he

said, his next admission coming from somewhere he'd never dared access before. 'Because it felt like home.'

'Oh, Corso.'

But he steeled his heart against the tenderness in her voice because he still wasn't done. 'My last royal date took place three months ago, which might make you wonder why I didn't come and explain all this before. But I wanted you to make the most of your new job and your new life. To have the opportunity to work in your chosen field and decide whether or not you wanted to continue in it.' He paused and suddenly his throat was so dry that he was finding it difficult to breathe. 'Or whether you would be prepared to give it all up and marry me.'

There was the clattering sound of a teaspoon being dropped to the floor. 'What are you saying?' she demanded suspiciously, as if he were having a joke at her expense.

'I want to marry you, Rosie Forrester. Because I love you and the thought of not being with you is unendurable. I need to know if you can ever forgive me for my lack of insight. For my arrogance and stupidity. For the way I rode roughshod over your feelings and didn't take them into account. I need you to know that I'm sorry, truly sorry. But most of all, I need to know if you'll be my wife.'

'But we…can't, Corso. You know we can't.'

'Why not?'

'Because Monterosso wants you to marry a royal princess.'

'Monterosso wants their king to be happy and you are the key to my happiness.' He let out a ragged sigh. 'I'd convinced myself I didn't feel the things which other men claim to feel—that I was immune to love and to emotion—but I was wrong. Because you brought something to life in me, Rosie Forrester. You took my cold and unfeeling heart and opened it up. You made me love you and I need...' He sucked in a deep breath. 'I need to know how you feel about me.'

Her gaze was very bright and very clear. 'You know exactly how I feel about you, Corso,' she whispered.

'Tell me,' he whispered back.

'I love you,' she said simply. 'You. The man. And that's all I want. To live with you and lie with you.' Her voice trembled. 'To be your support by day and your lover at night. To feel your child moving within me—many children, if we're lucky enough to have them. To fill that big palace of yours with love and make it a real home. That's what I want.'

His lips curved. 'Not palaces, nor diamonds, or fancy yachts which skim the ocean?'

She shook her head. 'Those things aren't important.'

'To some people they are.' He brushed a strand of hair away from her cheek. 'Me included, if you must know.'

She frowned. 'I didn't think you were into status symbols.'

'Status symbol or not, you're going to need a very big diamond if you're going to become my wife,' he said drily. 'But you do realise what you're taking on, don't you? Because you know better than anyone the demands of royal life. Constantly being on show. Having every look and word you utter analysed for nuance, or meaning. You're going to have to learn never to give too much of yourself away, Rosie, and I'm afraid that your trust in people will inevitably become eroded—'

'And you're going to have to learn to stop being so suspicious and start giving people the benefit of the doubt,' she interrupted passionately. 'To realise it's not the end of the world if sometimes you wear your heart on your sleeve—because your people will respect a king who isn't afraid of being in touch with his own feelings, rather than someone buttoned-up and inflexible.'

'Am I buttoned-up and inflexible?' he questioned gravely.

'Sometimes. But I can show you how to change. We can help each other grow, can't we?'

'Is that a yes to my proposal?' he questioned wryly.

'It is,' she agreed, looking suddenly shy as he reached into his pocket and produced a small box before withdrawing a ring of radiant brilliance—the incandescent diamond flashing like an explosion of white fire within the tiny room.

'Oh, Corso,' she said as he got down onto one knee before her.

'You're going to tell me that you've changed your mind about big diamonds after all?'

She shook her head. 'I'm going to tell you that I love you,' she whispered as he slid the mighty rock onto her finger. 'I love you more than words can ever say.'

EPILOGUE

A LOUD POP woke her, and Rosie blinked open her lashes to focus on the glorious room. The setting sun gilded the sofa on which she lay, naked and replete beneath a soft, cashmere blanket. From here she could see the lake and the mighty mountain which dominated the distant horizon. At the far end of the room stood an enormous fir tree, decked with tiny star-like lights and gleaming silver baubles, for in two days time it would be Christmas.

And there was her husband, his magnificent body bare save for a small white towel slung low on his sexy hips, holding two crystal flutes filled with champagne, which he carried across the room towards her.

'Happy honeymoon,' he said softly.

Rosie smiled a little giddily as he put the glasses down, before dropping the tiny towel to the floor and getting underneath the blanket next to her.

'I can hardly believe we're married,' she admitted, reveling in the warmth of his delicious flesh.

He cupped one breast, stroking his thumb over the nipple. 'Did you enjoy the day?'

'Every moment,' she said, her voice catching a little. Because it had been an emotional experience. A wedding just before Christmas was always going to tug at the heartstrings, even before you factored in the significance of this particular ceremony.

They'd been married in the Monterossian cathedral—a magnificent structure which towered over the city of Esmelagu, and from which you could see the capital's famous lake. Watched by her mother, sister, aunt and some of her co-workers from the railway—Rosie had spoken the solemn vows which had made her Corso's queen.

She had worn a lavishly embroidered white gown—her flowing veil held in place by Queen Aurelia's ancient coronet. There had been tears in her mother's eyes at that point, as she'd whispered how proud Rosie's father would have been.

But despite the rejoicing of the wedding guests, and of the Monterossian people who had taken Rosie into their hearts—the wedding day hadn't passed without a faint sense of uncertainty and of matters unresolved.

Because Xanthos—the King's half-brother, had been there—looking as if it were the last place on earth he wanted to be. His attendance had been grudging and loaded with conditions, some of which had stretched Corso's patience at the time. Unwilling to publicly acknowledge his fraternal link with the Monterossian King, it seemed the half-Greek billionaire had no desire to trade on his royal connections.

He hadn't seemed to hit it off with Bianca either, which was a bit unfortunate, as Rosie had arranged for Xanthos to fly her sister back to England. Bianca had reacted badly to this piece of news—behaving as if she was being expected to slum it, instead of travelling in total luxury on a private jet.

'Why are you frowning?' questioned Corso, as he turned his attention to her other breast.

'I'm just thinking how difficult siblings can be at times.'

'That much is true,' he said softly. 'I guess we just have to let some things go. At least, that's what you always tell me.'

Corso narrowed his eyes as he tried not to be distracted by the pert thrust of her nipple. What was it she'd said to him when he had wondered aloud why Xanthos seemed so determined to dislike him? 'Everything has its time, my darling. We just have to be patient, and wait.'

He believed her. Just like he believed everything she said, because Rosie was the most honest and decent person he had ever met and it was the first time he had ever truly trusted another person. Sometimes he felt like pinching himself because he'd never believed that life could be this good. This easy. And it was all down to her. To this woman who loved him in a way he'd never thought he could be loved. Who had broken down the barriers with which he had surrounded himself and let the light in.

His people loved her and he loved her and one day soon he wanted her to have his baby.

He turned his head to study her blonde head, which was resting comfortably on his shoulder, and she lifted her gaze to his. 'You haven't touched your champagne,' he observed.

'Neither have you.'

'Because I can think of things I'd much rather do than drink,' he growled as he drifted his fingertips to her peaking breast. 'Like making love to my wife.'

'But we've only just—'

He silenced her half-hearted protest with first one kiss and then another and soon she was straddling him on the gilded sofa and tossing back her mane of magnificent hair.

Outside, the setting sun was turning the mountain into the startling colour which had given the country its name.

And, within the sanctuary of their bedroom, the King and Queen of Monterosso made sweet love.

* * * * *\

THE KISS
SHE CLAIMED
FROM THE GREEK

ABBY GREEN

MILLS & BOON

This is for Brian O'Donnell,
one of my favourite people on this planet.

I hope we always live within 2 km of each other. xx

CHAPTER ONE

HE WAS STILL HERE. Sofie MacKenzie's heart thumped hard as her feet took her over the threshold into the small private room before she'd even consciously decided to go in. She knew she shouldn't be here. She wasn't a nurse. Or a doctor. She was a cleaner and tea lady.

And this man was in no position to have tea. He was unconscious, and he'd been unconscious since he'd been brought into the small island community hospital a few days ago. He'd been found on a rocky ledge on Ben Kincraig, Gallinvach's famous mountain, which people came from all over the world to climb.

He wasn't a local, and he had no identifying documents with him or on his person. The climbers who'd found him assumed his bag had disappeared into a crevasse.

Apart from a small bump to his head, he had not sustained any other injuries. He just wasn't waking up.

Sofie was standing at the bottom of the bed now. The man was bare-chested, with a tube extending from his hand to a drip nearby. The steady *beep-beep* of the heart monitor was surprisingly comforting. Which was ridiculous because he was a complete stranger to her.

But he was all alone—he had no one here who loved him or knew him—and that struck at Sofie's heart. She felt an affinity. Even though she'd been born on this island, and had lived here all her life, as the only child of parents who had both died in recent years, and with no other family to call her own, Sofie had always felt a sense of loneliness and isolation.

It was something that not even good friends could penetrate. It went too deep. And so she'd found herself gravitating back to this man with no name, pulled by something too strong to resist.

She'd even, over the past couple of days, when her shift was over, found herself sitting with him in silence, as if to reassure him that someone did care about him.

But her conscience pricked and she had to acknowledge that her interest wasn't entirely altruistic.

He was the most beautiful man she'd ever laid eyes on, and his impressive physicality had impacted her like a punch to the gut, in a way no other man's had ever affected her.

It was as if she'd been encased in ice all her life and suddenly was feeling things—sensations, aches and needs—that she'd never experienced before. Her sexuality was finally stirring. At the age of twenty-three.

She knew people on the island jokingly and affectionately referred to her as 'Sister Sofie', because she'd led such a sheltered existence. Living with parents who had suffered various health issues all their lives had curtailed her movements. They had always favoured staying close to home, due to their ill health, but also because of a mutual fear of air travel that Sofie had never shared.

So she'd never really travelled further afield than places she could go via train or boat. They'd all taken a trip to Northern France one summer, when she'd been a teenager. That was about as exotic as it had got.

When Sofie's friends had been taking their ubiqui-
tous trips to a holiday island in the sun after graduating
from secondary school her father had been dying, so she
hadn't been able to go. She hadn't resented it, though.
She'd been all her parents had had, and she'd felt that responsibility keenly.

Most people her age left the island as soon as it was
possible, or else settled down and started a family. She
hadn't done either. She'd been consumed with caring for
her dying mother until recently, and had only just started
to re-emerge from that cocoon of pain.

Maybe, Sofie told herself, that was why she was so
transfixed by the figure on the bed. She wasn't distracted
or full of grief for the first time in a long time. But she
knew, if she was being honest, that it was more than that.

Even lying down, it was clear that he must stand well
over six feet and that he had the body of an athlete. There
was not an ounce of excess flesh over hard and well-de-
veloped muscles.

He had thick dark hair that looked as if it hadn't been
cut lately. Dark eyebrows over deep-set eyes. Closed. She
wondered what colour they were. Dark, like the rest of
him, she imagined, feeling a tiny thrill at the thought of
them opening right now, seeking her out... *Ridiculous.*

He had a strong, noble nose. Aquiline.

A growth of heavy stubble covered the lower half of
his face, but it couldn't hide the very masculine jawline.
Or his lips.

Sofie's heart thumped again.

His lips were full and sensual. Almost too pretty to belong to a man. But on a man such as this they were pure
provocation. Sinful. *Tempting.*

Sofie's gaze skittered away from his mouth, snagging

on the tattoo high on his left arm. She didn't dare look too closely, but she thought it resembled some kind of howling animal—a wolf?—within a circle shape.

Unable to help herself, she let her gaze continue down over his broad chest, covered with a light smattering of dark hair. And down further, over the ridged muscles of his abdomen.

The sheet was pulled up neatly over his hips, stopping Sofie's far too curious gaze from seeing any more.

She turned away in sudden agitation, aghast at her own uncharacteristic behaviour. She went over to the locker and rearranged some items: a glass of water, a box of tissues. As if to justify her reason for being here.

But the fact was that since this man had appeared in the hospital all sense and reason seemed to have left her, turning her into some kind of a hormonal mess. It wasn't just her. She knew many of the female staff and some of the men were as fascinated by this dark fallen angel as she was.

Except, dangerously, she felt as if she had some sort of ownership over him. As if only she could understand how lonely he must be. Which was crazy because, being unconscious, he was obviously unaware of his state of loneliness. And when he woke up he would immediately call those nearest and dearest to him, making a total mockery of Sofie's fantastical imaginings.

His dark skin looked even darker against the pristine white sheets. Perhaps it was also the fact that he so obviously wasn't from here that connected with her. As if he'd appeared from some parallel dimension to lure her away...

Sofie rolled her eyes at herself. The man was unconscious. He was in no position to lure anyone anywhere. She was in danger of losing the plot altogether.

She knew she should leave, but she hesitated for a moment by the bed. He looked peaceful, but she had an impression of a sleeping panther, full of coiled energy. Just waiting to be unleashed. Her skin prickled with awareness and her gaze fell on his mouth again. The most perfect mouth. She wondered how it would feel to the touch. Warm? Firm?

Never in a million years would a woman like her—the epitome of average—get close to a man like this.

A dangerous sense of recklessness pulsed through her, from the core of her body outwards. She'd never felt anything like it. She was overcome with an urgent desire to know what his mouth felt like under hers. Too strong to ignore.

Before reason and sanity could stop her, she bent down and hovered with her head a couple of inches away from the man's mouth, looking into his face. And then she closed her eyes and pressed her mouth to his.

It was exactly as she'd imagined, but *more.* Firm. But soft. And warm. Lifeblood was in this man, just under the surface. Waiting to be woken.

Sofie stayed for a long moment, eyes shut tight, mouth pressed against his, almost willing him to wake so that she could feel him moving under her. Taking the kiss from her and turning it into something that she'd never experienced before...

But of course he wasn't moving, and she suddenly realised she had overstepped about a million boundaries—professional and personal.

Sofie sprang back, face flaming. As if coming out of a trance she looked around. The room was still empty. She let out a shuddery breath. She needed to leave *now* and put this enigmatic stranger out of her addled mind. Good thing that she had two days off coming up—she needed to clear her head.

She was turning away from the bed when suddenly her wrist was grabbed, stopping her. She let out a squeal and looked back at the man on the bed. She might have fallen to the floor in a dead faint if he hadn't been holding on to her with such a strong grip, keeping her standing there. Captive.

Her first thought was: *His eyes aren't dark brown, they're green.* And then his mouth opened. The mouth that she'd just been willing to open under hers. It was too much to take in. Sofie's head buzzed. Was she dreaming? Hallucinating?

He was frowning. When he spoke it was with a deep rough voice, saying something in a guttural language she'd never heard.

She wasn't hallucinating. She forced herself to suck in air. To focus. 'I'm sorry, what did you say?'

The man frowned more deeply. Awake, he was even more spectacular. His eyes narrowed on her face, focused, and then he said, very clearly in English, 'Where the hell am I?'

Sofie absently touched her wrist where the man had gripped her two days ago. She could still feel those long fingers…her skin had tingled for a long time afterwards. Long after she'd rung the bell and nurses and doctors had come running.

She'd gladly stepped back and let them take over, slipping out of the room before anyone could think to question why she'd been there.

Had she done that? Had her illicit kiss woken him up?

Sofie shook her head. Crazy. This wasn't a fairy tale.

She finished buttoning up her uniform, sighing when she caught the reflection of herself in a mirror in the changing room.

She was too pale, and her dark hair didn't help. Even though it was the height of summer in Scotland, there was little chance of getting a tan. Sofie had never been anywhere in her life that had the kind of heat she'd read about in books or seen in movies. She couldn't imagine it.

The shirt of her uniform strained over her chest. She sighed again, and tried to adjust it so that it sat better. She'd often thought that if she could stretch herself a few more inches above her five foot four her curves might actually make sense and fit her body better. But unfortunately she'd inherited her beloved Granny Morag's diminutive and well-endowed figure. Not to mention her hips. And there was nothing she could do about it.

She closed the door of her locker and tried not to let her mind go to *him*. Even though as soon as she'd walked into the hospital just a short time before the whole place had been buzzing with whispers about the mystery man, who had apparently lost his memory. He had no idea who he was. And neither did anyone else. He hadn't been reported missing, and it didn't appear as if he'd been travelling with anyone else.

But apart from the memory loss and a superficial bump on the head he was in perfect health. Sofie blushed when she thought of how healthy he'd looked. And felt. Under her mouth.

The door to the changing room opened abruptly and Sofie looked around, feeling inordinately guilty. It was a friend of hers—a nurse called Claire. 'They need you in the private room, Sofe. Someone knocked over a vase of flowers and it needs cleaning.'

Sofie gulped. 'The room where that patient is…?'

Claire rolled her eyes. 'That'll be the one. Our one and only private room.'

'He's still here, then?'

Her friend frowned at her. 'Yes, he's still here. What's up with you?'

Sofie clamped down on the panic she felt at the thought of seeing him again. 'Nothing—nothing at all. I'll go right away.'

Sofie gathered a few things and made her way to the room. When she got to the door she heard voices and hesitated, but then the door opened fully and a harried-looking matron saw her and said, 'Oh, good, Sofie. Come in and clean up this mess before someone slips and breaks an ankle.'

Sofie wanted to run in the opposite direction but she couldn't. So she stepped over the threshold. She didn't immediately see the man, as there was a doctor in the room, along with the hospital director, and they stood between her and the bed.

They were talking in low voices, but then someone moved and suddenly the man was revealed. He was sitting up in bed, no longer bare-chested. Wearing a hospital gown. Alert and awake. His impact on Sofie was like a punch to the gut, driving the air out of her lungs.

He was looking right at her with those incredible green eyes. His skin looked darker. His hair longer and more unruly, as if he'd been running a hand through it. The unshaved growth of beard made him look even more masculine. And that mouth…it was in a grim line now. Not soft. She remembered how firm it had felt under the cushiony softness of her lips.

'Sofie?'

Sofie blinked and saw that the hospital director and the doctor were looking at her. The matron said impatiently, 'The broken vase is on the other side of the bed.'

Face flaming, she ducked her head and hurried around to where water, flowers and broken glass lay strewn on the floor.

The dark-haired woman who had just appeared in the room was familiar, and because nothing else was familiar the man's attention was piqued. She pierced through the fog blurring his consciousness like a shaft of light. The stubborn haze in his head suddenly didn't seem so frustratingly pervasive.

He watched as she hurried around to the side of the bed with a mop, brushes and a bucket.

He wanted to look at her more than he wanted to keep listening to the interminable conversation he was being subjected to. He wanted to tell her to come closer so he could inspect her. But she was picking up bits of glass, putting them carefully into a bag. Her uniform shirt gaped when she bent over, and he caught a glimpse of an abundance of pale flesh encased in lace.

When she straightened again he could fully appreciate the fact that she had the figure of a lush pint-sized goddess. Generous breasts and womanly hips. A tiny waist. Silky jet-black hair, tied back, and pale skin. She'd looked at him with wide eyes a few moments ago as if she'd never seen a man before. Huge dark blue eyes—they were the colour of dark violets. Unusual.

But how could he know that when she wasn't close enough for him to see them? *Had* he seen her before? Why was she familiar? His head throbbed with the mental effort he was exerting.

He willed her to look at him—but her gaze stayed resolutely down, fixed on her task. A sense of irritation caught him unawares, as if he wasn't used to any woman avoiding his eye. He had a sense that it was usually the other way around. Her cheeks were pink. And suddenly he felt a surge of awareness in his lower body. A thrum of blood. Excitement. *Sexual.*

The doctor cleared his throat pointedly and he had to reluctantly take his gaze off the intriguing woman and move it back to the trio of people who were making his head hurt with their endless questions.

The doctor said, 'We have no reason to keep you here in the hospital, but obviously you can't just leave when you have nowhere to go and don't even know your own name…'

The man felt a sense of frustration. These people were offering him problems, not solutions.

They started to talk amongst themselves. The director of the hospital said, 'All the hotels and B&Bs are booked this time of year…'

The doctor: 'I would offer to take him in myself, but we've got a full house…'

The matron: 'My mother is coming…'

'What about the Simmonds family? They always have a spare room or two…'

'They've rented out their house for the summer while they visit family down south…'

'Oh, really? I didn't know they'd gone. Julie was working on a new quilt for the community arts and craft shop, but if she's not even here—'

The man put up a hand, stopping their incessant babble. He looked at the girl who was now mopping the floor, the long coil of her silky black ponytail curling over one shoulder, almost long enough to touch her breast. He pointed at her. 'I'll stay with her.'

Everyone stopped at the audacity of his statement. Including the girl. Slowly, she looked up and saw him pointing at her. Those eyes widened again. Dark blue. Definitely dark blue. And suddenly he remembered something.

He spoke without thinking. 'You were in the room when I woke up. It was you.'

Her face went bright pink. Fascinating reaction. Her eyes were even bigger now.

'I… Yes, I was here when you woke. I went and got the doctors and nurses.'

He felt as if there was something else. He remembered the sensation of a tiny wrist in his hand. Cool skin. Soft skin. But the rest eluded him.

Someone cleared their throat. The matron. Sounding very officious, she said, 'I'm afraid that staying with Sofie is not an appropriate suggestion.'

Sofie. It suited her. Soft. Like her curves. But then she looked back at him and he had an impression of something much steelier than *soft*. He gritted his jaw. It was not helping to curb his arousal.

He couldn't look away from her. He ignored what the matron had said and asked, 'Can I stay with you?'

She blinked. He noticed that she had long black lashes. She wore practically no make-up, yet her skin was like porcelain. Showing every fleeting emotion under the delicate surface.

His blood surged again and he put his hand down over his lap. *He didn't usually respond like this in public.* The assertion flitted through his head.

She looked away from him to the others, biting her lip, 'I...um... I don't see why not.'

Her voice was low and clear. Melodic. Pleasing. It hummed over his nerve-endings. No wonder it was familiar to him. They'd met before.

The matron stepped forward. 'Sofie, please don't feel you have to say yes—this is a most unorthodox situation.'

She shrugged. 'I live alone, and since Mother died I have plenty of spare rooms. It seems like an obvious solution.'

The doctor said, 'You really would be prepared to do this? He needs monitoring, because his memory could come back at any time and it might be traumatic. He'll also need to be checked every couple of days, just to ensure he's fully back to good health and there are no lingering effects from his injuries.'

Before the young woman could respond to this the matron said, 'We could arrange to have the community nurse stop by on a regular basis. And if you *are* willing to accommodate him, Sofie, we would give you leave from work to do so.'

'Paid leave?' the man heard himself saying automatically, surprising himself with his need to ensure her welfare was looked after, and also an innate sense that being assertive and being obeyed was as natural as breathing for him.

Someone made a huffing sound. 'Well, of course that goes without saying. Sofie would be doing us all a favour, until we can establish your identity...'

A name popped into his head at that moment. He felt fairly sure it wasn't *his* name, and it brought with it a sense of disquiet, but he said it anyway. 'Darius. You can call me Darius.'

There was silence for a moment in the room, and then Sofie directed a question to the doctor. 'How long do you think it'll take for his memory to come back?'

The doctor said, 'In all honesty it's hard to tell. His memory loss is due to trauma, so it could come back over time in bits and pieces, or it could return all at once, with no warning, at any time from now.'

The man looked at her and saw the conflict on her face. Fascinating that she wasn't trying to hide it. She looked back at him and he saw something that it took him a moment to recognise. Compassion. Pity.

Just as he was bristling at the notion of anyone pitying him, tempted to tell her he'd changed his mind, she said briskly, 'Okay, fine. He—that is, Mr Darius—can stay with me.'

'Are you crazy, Sofe? He could be a serial killer!'

Sofie rolled her eyes at her friend Claire. She'd just changed out of her uniform and back into her jeans and long-sleeved top. She picked up her bag and resisted the urge to check her reflection. She didn't need to. She wouldn't have magically grown five inches and lost a stone.

'I doubt that very much, Claire. Anyway, you live at the bottom of my lane. If I scream loud enough you'll be able to hear me and come running.'

Her friend looked worried. 'I'll check on you every day after work.'

'I'm not the one who fell down a mountain. *He* needs to be checked.'

Claire waved a hand. 'Matron has already put me on that duty. But I don't care about him. I care about you. Are you sure you're not being bullied into this?'

Sofie thought of how his voice had impacted on her when he'd said so assertively, *'I'll stay with her.'* She'd looked up to find him staring at her intently. Her first reaction had been one of a deep electric thrill inside her at the very thought of him entering her house. Sharing her space.

Then he'd remembered seeing her in the room, and she'd gone hot and cold all over. Had he remembered her kissing him? Just not said it? Was that why he'd suggested staying with her? Because he thought that she was offering extra…*benefits*?

But then she'd noticed that he was looking at her quizzically, so she'd calmed herself down. He'd still been unconscious when she'd kissed him. And she really wasn't that memorable.

She looked at her friend. 'He doesn't know who he is. He could have family, friends who are worried about him.'

He could have a wife. Children. A lover.

Sofie's mind skittered away from that—it was all too easy to imagine a man like that in a passionate embrace with some lissom beauty.

Her friend snorted. 'He was climbing a mountain alone. If he has family then they're not beating down the door to find him.'

That made Sofie's chest contract even more.

Her friend's gaze narrowed. 'You're too soft-hearted, Sofe. It'll get you into trouble one of these days.'

Into trouble. Sofie felt an illicit flutter of something very unfamiliar. Rebelliousness. She'd never got into trouble in her life. Yet here she was, inviting a total stranger into her home. A mouthwateringly gorgeous sexy stranger.

'Promise you'll ring me if he starts acting weird.'

Sofie blinked out of her trance. She took a breath. 'Of course I will. I'm sure his memory will come back in a few days and he'll turn out to be some money man from a London City firm who's having a crisis of conscience.'

They got those types up here all the time. Searching for some kind of meaning by climbing a mountain.

Claire made a rude sound. 'If he's a mere "money man" then my Graham is a cast member from *Magic Mike*.'

Sofie thought of Claire's husband and bit back a snort. With his portly belly and thinning hair he was about as far removed from *Magic Mike* as it was possible to get. But he and Claire adored each other.

Sofie sighed inwardly. Some day she hoped to have that too. Maybe that was why she was so eager to host the stranger. Shake her life up a bit. She told herself it had nothing to do with the fact that he affected her on every level it was possible for a man to affect a woman.

At that moment the matron stuck her head around the door. 'Sofie? He's ready to go.'

Her heart palpitated and she suddenly wondered if her friend was right to be concerned about her.

Claire said gently, 'Are you sure about this, Sofe? Don't feel under pressure—we can sort something else out if necessary. I can chuck the kids out of their room and put them on the sofa, and he could stay with us...'

Sofie's trepidation vanished. She felt an almost violently negative reaction to that suggestion. It unnerved her, this sudden feeling of...possessiveness. She shook her head and forced a smile. 'No, it'll be fine.'

Sofie repeated this to herself as she walked out of the changing room and assured herself that his memory would probably return within twenty-four hours.

Then he would be gone so fast that her head would be spinning. Because one thing was certain: that man did not belong in this place.

I shouldn't be here.

The words and the assertion resounded in Darius's head. He frowned. But he had obviously come here. For some reason he couldn't fathom. The fact that he had apparently been climbing a mountain seemed incomprehensible to him. As was the fact that he was now standing in a very pedestrian car park, holding a plastic bag containing his few possessions.

He felt slightly naked in the clothes that had been returned to him, washed and dried. Lightweight trousers, a long-sleeved top with a sleeveless fleece gilet and a rain jacket. Hiking boots. The clothes looked new. Felt new. Evidence that this wasn't something he did on a regular basis?

He didn't notice the group of nurses almost tripping over themselves as they passed him by on their way into work.

He saw movement and his eyes widened on a small blue car as it careened around the corner and came to a stop in front of him with a shriek of brakes. The passenger door opened. He bent down to see Sofie looking up at him. She really did have the most amazing eyes.

'Okay, this is me. In you get.'

He looked at her incredulously. He felt pretty certain he'd never seen a car so small up close. 'I don't think I'll fit.'

'My father wasn't much smaller than you and he fitted just fine.'

Feeling seriously doubtful, Darius contorted himself

into the passenger seat. He did fit. Just. Knees almost up to his chest and his head touching the underside of the roof. He closed the door and tried to find a lever to push the chair back a bit, but it only moved about an inch.

The car didn't move. Sofie was looking at him. He looked at her. He could smell her scent. Clean and un-manufactured. It was alluring just for that reason.

She was still looking at him.

'Why aren't we moving?'

'You need to put on your seatbelt.'

He thought of how she'd careened around the corner and hit the brakes. He felt like pointing out that he was unlikely to move too far if they did crash, wedged in as he was, but instead he just reached for the belt and pulled it across his body. It reached the buckle-holder after a bit of a tug.

Sofie smiled brightly and looked ahead—and then pressed down on the accelerator so hard that they jerked forward and the engine cut out.

Her cheeks went bright pink as she fumbled and started the engine again, muttering something under her breath. A lock of inky black hair had escaped her ponytail and he had to curb the urge to reach out and tuck it behind her ear. He wondered what her hair would be like down. Over her shoulders.

Awareness, hot and thick, coursed through his blood. He gritted his jaw and looked away. Very dimly a voice was telling him that he shouldn't be finding her attrac-tive. But he found himself resisting it. He obviously did find her attractive. Why should he deny it?

They were driving out of the hospital now and through a pretty village. Sofie was talking, pointing things out. He found he wasn't very much interested in what she was saying—he was happy to listen to her soft, lilting voice. He found it curiously soothing. He also found the vast open sky and small clusters of one and two-storey buildings somehow pleasing. As if he wasn't used to seeing the sky like this.

Soon they were on a coast road, with the sea on one side and the mountains on the other. Sofie pointed to a peak in the distance. 'That's Ben Kincraig, where you were found.'

Darius looked at the impressively high peak. He felt nothing. Certainly had no idea why he would have felt the need to try and climb it. 'Did I get far?'

'Apparently you were on your way down from the summit.'

Darius made a satisfied sound. He'd mastered it at least. Sofie glanced at him, and when he caught her eye she blushed again. She really was remarkably pretty. A small pert nose. Surprisingly high cheekbones. Plump lips. Like other parts of her... His gaze drifted down to where the seatbelt cut across her breasts.

Her hands were small and soft. Nails short and practical. Unvarnished. He had a sudden very carnal image of her naked, with her hair tumbled around her shoulders like black silk, breasts full and heavy—

'Here we are. It's really not far from everything, as you can see.'

Darius pulled his gaze from her to see that they were driving down a small driveway towards a two-storey whitewashed house. With its row of windows top and bottom and a slated roof, it looked big enough to house a family, but also modest at the same time. There were some stone outbuildings, and a lake behind the house. A small hill rose from the other side of the water in the distance. Green fields either side. Heather. Small stone walls. It was unbelievably picturesque. Flowers spilled from pots by the front door, bright and colourful. It looked homely and welcoming.

Darius frowned. He instinctively felt a resistance to this scene, even though it also called to something inside him.

Sofie brought the car to a stop by the door, painted a welcoming bright yellow. He opened the door of the car and uncoiled his body slowly, still feeling a slight stiffness in some of his muscles.

And then a dark blur bounded around the corner, almost knocking Sofie off her feet where she was standing on the other side of the car. It was a dog—a big, shaggy, indeterminate breed. It spotted Darius and went very still for a moment, nose twitching. A flash of memory assailed him. A dog not unlike this one. Happy voices. Barking. An excursion. Bright sun. Blue sky. An intense feeling of—

Oof! Darius was nearly knocked backwards when two big paws landed on his chest.

'Pluto, get *down*.'

The dog dropped immediately and looked up at Darius with big soulful brown eyes and a wagging tail.

Sofie came around and took him by the collar. She was flustered. 'Sorry, I forgot about him. You probably don't like dogs…you might even be allergic—'

'I…' Darius stopped. Blank. 'The truth is I don't know.' Frustration bit at the edges of his brain.

Sofie said something to the dog and he trotted away obediently.

Darius looked at her. 'Pluto?'

She made a face. 'My father was an amateur astronomer. He called all our dogs after planets.'

'All your dogs?'

She ticked off fingers. 'First there was Mercury, then Saturn, Jupiter, and now Pluto. He's almost ten years old.'

Darius looked at the woman in front of him and knew in that moment with a certainty he hadn't felt since he'd woken up in the hospital that he had definitely landed in some kind of alternative universe. And that he did not belong here. Even though he found it appealing in ways that he sensed he should not.

Sofie started walking towards the house. 'Come on, let me show you around. You'll be needing to rest.'

Darius felt a flash of assertion—he never rested. He usually pitied people who displayed such mortal frailties. And yet…she was right. He could feel uncustomary fatigue deep in his bones.

For a moment Darius hesitated, frustration biting again at the dense fogginess in his brain. The truth was he didn't really know anything about himself. He resented this awful weakness, this *not knowing*.

Sofie was standing in the doorway, waiting. As much as she intrigued him, he suddenly wanted to flee, as if sensing that by stepping through that door he would be risking never going back to who he was. Never knowing.

He saw the car in his peripheral vision and was filled with an impulse to just get in and drive away. But he didn't even know if he could drive. And where would he go? He was on an island. He had no money. No ID.

He had no choice but to stay. For now.

After a moment's hesitation Darius went towards Sofie, not liking the fact that she was literally the only solid thing he had to latch on to for the moment. Not liking the sense of powerlessness he felt. At all.

Not even she, with her soft curves and violet eyes, could eclipse that right now.

CHAPTER TWO

SOFIE WATCHED DARIUS walk towards the house, struck anew by how tall he was. How big. She didn't feel intimidated, though. She felt jittery. On edge. Especially after that car journey. She cringed inwardly now to think of how ridiculously inappropriate her car was for a man like him. He belonged in a sleek sports car, or an SUV that could accommodate his height and build.

Being in such close proximity to him had been almost overwhelming. The scent of the man still clung to her. Woodsy and masculine. Sensual. And he'd been in a hospital for days! It hadn't dented his appeal.

For a moment just now he'd looked conflicted, as if wondering if he had any other options. Her heart contracted at the thought of how traumatic it must be to remember nothing of who you were. To be at the mercy of total strangers.

As he came closer, Sofie focused on that. Anything to avoid noticing the sheer physicality of the man. But it was hard when he had to duck his head slightly to come in the front door. Into the hall. She wondered what it looked like through his eyes. An old house, it was clean as a pin, but nothing could really disguise the lovingly worn décor, about twenty years out of date. Her parents, bless them, hadn't cared all that much for aesthetics, and they hadn't had much to leave Sofie in the way of funds to do it up as she'd have loved to.

Feeling slightly defensive about her home, even though the man was looking around with no discernible expression other than mild curiosity, Sofie said, 'I'll give you a quick tour.'

She showed him into the spacious living room with its couches and armchairs, its walls lined with bookshelves, a TV in the corner. He went over to the fireplace and looked at a photograph of Sofie as a teenager with her parents. Her face burned to think of how young and innocent she looked. *Still innocent.* Her face burned even more, and she was glad he had his back to her.

'How old are you here?'

'About thirteen.'

'No brothers and sisters?'

He turned around and Sofie willed the heat to die down. She shook her head. 'No. My mother… There were complications during her labour with me and afterwards she couldn't have any more children.'

The stark explanation hid the almost palpable cloud of grief and sorrow that her parents hadn't been able to fulfil their dream of having a big family. They had both been only children, and when they'd married they'd pledged to have a big family to fill the gap that they'd felt growing up.

Sofie knew it was irrational, but she'd always somehow blamed herself, and that had fed into her sense of responsibility towards them—especially when they'd been ill in the years before their deaths. As if she owed them. As if maybe if it hadn't been her who'd been born—if it had been another baby—then things might have been different...

She turned jerkily. 'Let me show you the rest of downstairs.'

He followed her dutifully into the dining room that she explained wasn't really used except for special occasions, and then into the large and homely kitchen with its Aga and massive wooden table. Automatically Sofie felt herself relax slightly. The kitchen was the heart of the house and where she'd always felt safest. It was where she'd done her homework down the years, and where she curled up in a chair near the Aga to read her favourite romance novels.

She said, 'I'll make some lunch soon, but if you're ever hungry just help yourself to anything you'd like from the fridge, or pantry...'

Darius made a sound that might have been assent. Sofie wasn't sure. She moved on, taking him out of the kitchen and back into the main part of the house and up the stairs that brought them to the first floor.

She led him down a corridor with doors off each side. She thought quickly about which room would be best for him and opened one door, going over to the window to open it and let some air in. It was a nice room, in spite of the worn carpet and slightly threadbare curtains. Muted colours. It had always been the main guest room as it had an en suite bathroom with a shower and a bath. The height of luxury in a house like this.

Darius followed her into the room, which suddenly felt claustrophobically small. 'I'll make up the bed.' She gestured towards the bare mattress. 'We—' She stopped, faltered. 'That is, *I* haven't had guests here for a while.'

And certainly never one like this.

Sofie thought of the various distant relatives and paying guests who had come and stayed down the years during peak tourist season. All fairly normal mortals. No one who had possessed proportions close to a Greek god's.

That made her think of something. 'They said in the hospital that the language you can speak…it's Greek. So you're… Greek?'

He looked at her, those dark green eyes far too mesmerising. 'It would appear so.'

Sofie became self-conscious under that intense gaze. It was as if he was searching *her* for answers. Answers she didn't have. She saw him holding the small plastic bag. His only possessions.

She said, 'I have a bag in the boot of the car—clothes that staff in the hospital donated for you.'

At his quizzical look she clarified, 'You only have one set of clothes.'

'I hadn't thought of that.'

'Why don't you come downstairs and I'll fix lunch? You must be hungry. The hospital isn't exactly renowned for its culinary expertise.'

'I'm starving.'

Sofie felt a frisson of something very hot go through her blood and then she cursed herself. He didn't mean starving for *her*. Was she so desperately in thrall to this man that everything he said sounded like an illicit suggestion? She backed out of the room quickly, before he might see something of his effect on her.

She tried to put all inappropriate thoughts out of her mind as they went back into the kitchen and she pulled a container of soup she'd made out of the fridge. She said over her shoulder, 'It's just some soup and bread and salad, if that's okay?'

'I'm sure it'll be a vast improvement on the hospital fare.'

He said that with such a withering tone that Sofie looked at him, amused. 'Maybe that's a sign that you're used to a far higher standard of food?'

'Maybe.'

'Please, sit down...make yourself at home.' Sofie realised then that she couldn't exactly fall back on small talk because Darius didn't know anything about himself.

Then he surprised her, saying, 'I've been dreaming about coffee. Real coffee. *Good* coffee.'

She turned around. 'Ah, now, that I can definitely help with.'

She went over to her state-of-the-art coffee machine. Probably the most expensive thing in the house. Sofie's love of decent coffee was legendary on the island. She made a small cup for Darius and handed it to him where he sat on the other side of the table. At a safe distance.

He took it and looked suspicious. Sniffed it, and then took a sip. What could only be described as a look of pure appreciation came over his face. He closed his eyes. Sofie's pulse tripped. She'd never seen anyone exude such effortless sensuality.

His eyes opened again, and he lifted the cup towards her. 'This is perfect, thank you.'

Pluto ambled into the kitchen and went over to sniff at Darius. Sofie held her breath for a second. When he'd first seen the dog he'd had an arrested look on his face. But now he put out a hand and ruffled the dog's fur. Pluto's tail wagged vigorously. Sofie could sympathise.

She turned away and busied herself with heating the soup and tossing the salad, taking the bread out of the oven at the last minute. She placed soup in a bowl in front of

Darius and put the salad and bread between them. 'Help yourself. There's no ceremony in this house.'

He took some bread, ripping it apart before dunking some in the soup and taking a bite. He made an appreciative sound that once again connected directly with Sofie's pulse.

'This is good, thank you.'

She blushed. 'It's nothing, really—just some leftover vegetables with a chicken stock that I had in the freezer—' She stopped abruptly. She was babbling. She took a mouthful of her own soup before she could say anything else, and winced when she burned the roof of her mouth.

Luckily he didn't seem to have noticed her lack of sophistication, intent on his food.

Sofie had a sneaking suspicion, based on not only his charisma but also his innate confidence, that he was *somebody.* And she suspected that whoever he was, he wasn't just some rich City financier looking to get in touch with his inner child.

He was more than that.

He had something more than confidence. An air of arrogance. It had been evident in the way he'd spoken to the doctors. The way he'd declared that he would stay with her. As if he was used to issuing orders and to those orders being followed without question.

He put down his spoon, the bowl cleared. Sofie had barely touched her own food, too distracted by her guest. She stood up and took his bowl before he could notice how fascinating he was to her. She said, over her shoulder, 'Help yourself to more coffee or anything else. I'll get your room ready.'

She left the things in the sink and went upstairs, taking a deep breath to try and calm her beating heart. Shaking her head at herself, because she was behaving like a giddy teenager, she got fresh sheets out of the cupboard and set to making Darius's bed.

And then she got the bag of clothes out of the car and hoped that there might be at least a couple of items that would fit him—even though she knew for a fact there weren't many men on the island who matched him for height and breadth.

Darius stood at the open back door. The air was mild. Fragrant with freshly cut grass somewhere nearby. The view really was spectacular. With the back lawn sloping down to the lake and then the mountain rising behind it. Gently majestic. Sky so blue it hurt to look at. It almost reminded him of…

He shook his head after a moment, unable to catch the memory. He'd felt heat, though. A far greater heat than was coming from this sun.

Something nudged against his thigh and he looked down to see a pair of soulful brown eyes looking up. The shaggy dog. Instinctively he reached down, patting his head. This time there was no flash of disjointed memory.

The sense of powerlessness he'd felt a short while before was fading. He felt a curious sense of…acceptance. Peace. Sitting with Sofie, eating simple food had been pleasant. More than pleasant. Her soft, lilting voice smoothed the ragged edges of his nerves. While also heating his blood.

It was mildly disturbing that he couldn't look at her without immediately imagining carnal things. Maybe it was something about how fresh-faced she was. How innocent. Because any fool could tell that she was not experienced. Every time their eyes met she blushed and looked away. Darius had a strong sense that he was used to women holding his gaze boldly. That a woman like Sofie was not part of his world.

He heard a sound behind him and looked around. Sofie was standing in the kitchen, long tendrils of black hair framing her pretty face. Once again Darius had to control his body. He gritted his jaw.

'I've left the clothes in your bedroom. Help yourself to whatever fits.'

Suddenly, in spite of the desire this woman triggered in his blood, Darius felt a wave of weariness wash over him. The doctors had warned him that it would take a little more time before he was back to normal.

As if spotting his weakness, Sofie frowned. 'Are you okay?'

Hating to admit to such frailty, Darius had no choice but to say, 'I think I'll lie down for a while.'

'Of course. The bed is all made up. The water is hot, so feel free to have a shower—' Sofie broke off, blushing profusely before continuing, 'I'm not suggesting you need to wash…just do whatever you want. Make yourself at home, Darius.'

Sofie waited until Darius had left the kitchen area and closed the door and then thudded her head softly against the wood. She was so gauche! Literally couldn't even tell the man to help himself to the facilities without turning into a blushing, stuttering wreck because at the mere mention of something so innocuous she'd been unable to help imagining hot water sluicing over taut naked muscles, his ridged abdomen and down lower—

Sofie hit her head harder this time. Hard enough to shock her out of her wayward thoughts.

Enough. She had to get it together and try to curb her newly rampaging hormones. She'd been entrusted with this stranger's care and he was vulnerable. If the poor man knew where her thoughts went every time she looked at him he'd be disgusted.

Darius woke sweating, the sheets tangled around his naked body. His heart was racing. And his body was hard. He grimaced. He'd been dreaming about *her.* Sofie. Dreaming about her curvaceous pale body moving over his, her black hair falling around him as she took him into her slick body and gripped him so tight—

Darius threw back the covers and surged up from the bed.

Frustration at his lack of memory bit at him. Was he usually like this around women he wanted? Was he so highly sexed that every waking and sleeping moment was dominated by carnal thoughts? If so, how did he ever get any work done?

Tendrils of pink light touched the sky outside. It was very early dawn. He felt thoroughly disorientated. Had he slept right through the previous afternoon and evening?

His body still pulsed with desire, and he went into the en suite bathroom and stepped under the shower, having to duck his head a little. He grimaced under the cold water but it had the desired effect, dousing some of the residual heat.

After drying himself roughly Darius went back into the bedroom. He felt restless. He spied some of the clothes donated by the locals and pulled on a pair of sweatpants. They were a little too snug, but they'd have to do.

He went downstairs to get himself some water. A low light was burning in the kitchen. The dog was there, in a huge bed, and he got up and ambled over to Darius, seemingly content with this new guest. Something about the dog's easy acceptance made Darius feel absurdly emotional for a moment as he put a hand on the dog's head. It made him wonder if he had a family. He didn't think he had a family of his own, a wife, or children—when he thought of that he felt a surge of rejection—but he wondered about parents…siblings?

Nothing. Just that dense frustrating fog.

He went over to the sink and poured himself a glass of water, it was ice-cold and unbelievably refreshing. He imagined it coming straight from a pure mountain stream.

He went to the back door and opened it. A cool breeze skated over his skin. The vast sky was turning lighter by the second. There was not a sound except for the dawn chorus of birds. Darius knew instinctively that it was a long time since he'd experienced this kind of peace and quiet.

He heard a sound behind him and turned around to see Sofie standing in the doorway to the kitchen. She was wearing a knee-length silk robe, belted at her unbelievably small waist. A waist she hid under her baggy clothes. He could see bare shapely legs from the knee down. Her hair was loose and tumbling over her shoulders, exactly as it had been in his—

'Sorry,' he said abruptly, desperately trying to regain some control. 'I didn't mean to wake you.'

Sofie was regretting following her guest downstairs. Clearly he was fine. More than fine. He was bare-chested and wearing a pair of sweatpants from the bag of donated clothing. They confirmed her suspicion that none of the local men matched his build. They clung to his slim hips and strong thigh muscles like a second skin. Finished about an inch above his ankles. He should have looked ridiculous. He looked sexier than sin.

'It's okay. I was a little worried because you slept right through the afternoon and evening, but you're feeling okay?'

He seemed to consider this for a moment. 'I'm feeling good. I feel better than I have in days, actually.'

Sofie made a face. 'It's impossible to rest properly in hospital. You obviously needed to sleep.'

'I'm usually up before dawn.'

He looked almost surprised that he'd said this. Sofie took a step into the kitchen. Pluto ambled over and she rubbed his head absently. 'Do you think you're remembering something?'

Darius frowned. 'I think it's not usual for me to sleep like that. Dead to the world. For hours. I feel like I've had my first taste of real sleep in years.'

'That's a good thing… I think?' Sofie said tentatively.

Darius's expression was shuttered, as if he didn't like what he was revealing. 'It can't hurt, I guess.'

'Sometimes you sound quite American,' Sofie observed. 'Maybe you've spent time there.'

He shrugged. 'Possibly. Depending on what I do for a living.'

Sofie felt a rush of sympathy. 'I can't imagine what it must be like to have everything you know…who you are… wiped from your head.'

'I wouldn't recommend it.' His tone was dry.

'Sorry,' she said quickly, mortified that she'd reminded him of his predicament—as if he wasn't already aware of it every second.

'Do you want coffee? I'd be getting up soon to make some anyway.'

'Sure.'

Sofie busied herself with the coffee machine, cursing herself that she hadn't put on more clothes before coming down. But she hadn't been sure if she'd actually heard Darius moving about or not. And she had been mildly worried about him. So when she'd seen his open bedroom door she'd just come downstairs without thinking.

Now her skin prickled all over, and she was conscious that he must be looking at her and finding her wholly average. No matter what he did in his life, there was no doubt that he was the kind of man who would be used to interacting with only the most beautiful women. It would be impossible for a man like him not to.

When the coffee was made she handed him a cup and tried not to stare at his bare chest.

They sipped their coffee in a mutual appreciative silence. Sofie never felt as if she was fully functioning until she'd got that first hit of caffeine. She couldn't help noticing Darius's hands. Square. Masculine. Long fingers. Short nails. But neat.

She asked impulsively, 'Can I see your hands?'

Darius looked at her for a moment, but held out his left hand. Sofie put down her coffee cup and took it in hers, not prepared for the jolt of sensation that arrowed all the way down to the pit of her belly. She did her best to ignore it.

Her hands were very small and pale next to his. She did her best to control her reaction to touching him, even chastely like this. She turned his hand over and back, observing, 'Your nails are neat, not bitten. You're not a nervous person. Your hands are unmarked, but they're not soft. You might work in an office, but it's not your only domain.'

She became aware of her own short, unmanicured nails and skin slightly callused from the work she did. Not the kind of hands he would be used to in a woman, she'd wager.

She dropped his hand and picked up her coffee again, cradling it in two hands, slightly aghast that she'd just done that. She took a step back, as if terrified that she might try and touch some other part of him.

'You're a palm reader in your spare time?'

Darius's tone was faintly mocking. He'd curled his left hand into a fist. Embarrassed heat rose in an inexorable wave and Sofie couldn't stop it. What had she been thinking? She hadn't. That was the problem. Around him she didn't function normally.

'No,' she said. 'Not a palm reader as such…but my granny used to do it. She taught me that it's more about being a good observer than any kind of magic.'

Darius settled back against the kitchen counter. 'She sounds interesting.'

Sofie nodded, her heart aching a little. 'She was. I adored her. She died when I was still quite young, though.'

'What did you parents do?'

'My father was the local postman for years. My mother was a homemaker. We rented out rooms in the house in peak tourist season.'

Sofie thought of the days when she would find her mother standing at the kitchen sink and staring out at the garden. Sighing. Lamenting the lack of siblings for Sofie.

'All my mother wanted was a big family,' she found herself divulging. 'She'd grown up an only child, as had my father.'

'Have you always worked at the hospital?'

She nodded, glad to move away from painful memories. 'I had intended studying to become a nurse, but then my father fell ill and died, and shortly after that my mother became terminally ill. I cared for them both, so I put off doing my degree.'

'There's nothing stopping you now.'

'No,' Sofie agreed.

Her mother's death was still recent enough to be an excuse not to make any big changes, but Sofie knew there was more to why she hadn't jumped at the first opportunity to follow her dream. She'd started to feel restless for something else—something she wasn't even able to articulate. A desire to see the world. She'd only realised this while caring for her mother.

'The truth is that I'm not sure what I want any more.' She hadn't even admitted that to her closest friends.

'So in the meantime you clean?'

There was no judgement in his tone, but Sofie prickled anyway, meeting his dark green gaze. 'It's a perfectly noble profession.'

'For someone with zero ambition and no talent for anything else. That's not you.'

Sofie was momentarily blindsided by his assertion that there was more to her. She felt defensive. 'How do you know?'

He shrugged. 'Maybe, like your grandmother, I can sense things.'

Now she felt exposed. 'You're making fun of me.'

He shook his head. 'Not at all. I think you have more to offer. A lot more.'

Sofie clamped her mouth shut. How could this man who was a complete stranger see right into her, where she harboured that very nebulous desire for more than she'd experienced or seen around her? Whether that was to have the big family that her parents had failed to have, or to pursue a career far outside this small island...

And how had this dawn conversation suddenly become so personal? The sense of exposure prickled over her skin, reminding her she was half-naked. And that he was half-naked.

She stepped back. 'I should get changed. I'll have breakfast ready in about half an hour. Is there anything in particular you'd like?'

Darius frowned. 'Breakfast... I don't think I *do* breakfast.'

Sofie forced a bright smile, as if this impromptu dawn confessional hadn't just happened. 'Whatever you prefer. It'll be here anyway if you're hungry.'

An hour later Darius realised he did do breakfast. When he'd smelled the frying bacon and eggs he'd been suddenly ravenous. He seemed to be consistently hungry—and not just for his curvy and intriguing hostess. As he swallowed the last morsel of the delicious fried breakfast Sofie had made, he felt as if he'd been hungry for years and was only just starting to sate his appetite.

He sat back. 'You could be a chef.'

Sofie made a dissenting sound as she cleared away the plates. 'Hardly. I'm competent, not talented. I don't really enjoy cooking, but it became a necessary skill when we took in guests. I'm very proficient at doing breakfast for eight people.'

'Don't feel under any pressure to cook for me.'

Sofie turned around from the sink. She was dressed now, in jeans and a loose shirt. Darius lamented her hiding those luscious curves again. Her hair was pulled back into a loose bun. No make-up. She didn't need it. Her lips were naturally full and pink. Her eyes were glowing like two sapphires, framed by long black lashes. Dark, arched brows.

'Can you cook?' she asked.

Darius looked around the kitchen and felt nothing but blankness. He shook his head. 'Nothing looks familiar. I don't have a sense that I do.'

Sofie smiled. 'I think it's a safe bet to imagine that you inhabit a world where you don't have to concern yourself with domesticity.'

'You say that like it's a bad thing.'

'Not at all. Believe me, if I could be transported out of this existence, where I'm far too intimately acquainted with the most effective products to use to get toilets sparkling clean, I'd be delighted.'

'I don't doubt you'll do it.'

Sofie looked away, her cheeks going pink.

Darius cursed silently as he shifted in response. It had taken his blood a long time to cool after she'd taken his hand in hers earlier. The sudden shock of physical contact had surprised him as much as it had aroused him. The easy way she'd taken his hand in hers and turned it over and back, inspecting it…

His first reaction, even amidst the arousal, had been to pull away. Instinctively he'd wanted to retreat from such casual contact. But he hadn't. He'd liked her touching him. It had felt…soothing. As well as erotic.

He sensed that he wasn't a tactile person. That in fact he never welcomed contact unless it was initiated by him. And controlled by him.

Sofie wiped her hands on a towel. 'I have to go into town to get some things. Is there anything you'd like?'

Darius was tempted to make a quick retort about her picking up his memory en route, but he curbed his tongue and fought off the frustration at the dense fog in his head. 'I don't think so.'

'You could come with me if you like?'

Darius thought of folding his frame into the small confines of her car. 'No, thanks. I think I'll stay here.'

'Okay.' Sofie got a piece of paper and wrote something down. She handed it to him. 'Look, that's my mobile number. I won't be long, but in case you need anything just use the landline to call me.'

As Darius heard Sofie start the car and drive off he knew with certainty that he really wasn't used to being at the mercy of anyone. Because this was what chafed the most. This sense of being *stuck*. He was used to moving. Doing. But he had to swallow the frustration again.

His memory would come back soon. *It had to.*

When Sofie returned from doing the shopping there was no sign of Darius. Or Pluto. It was amazing how, within such a short space of time, it already felt as if the house was empty without him. As if he'd been there for years.

Sofie snorted at herself. As if a man like Darius would be content in a place like this. In a house like this. The only reason he was here was because his identity had effectively been wiped.

She put away the shopping and explored outside, walking down towards the lake. Darius was there. In jeans—a little too snug—and a shirt that did nothing to conceal his lean body. Pluto was standing faithfully beside him, already totally loyal and besotted. Sofie's heart constricted.

He'd adored her father. Maybe he was just relating to a male presence again.

Seeing him from behind, even in the ill-fitting clothes, and with his tall, lean build, Sofie fancied for a second that he could fit in here, among this wild and dramatic landscape. It might not be his usual milieu, but she sensed a ruggedness about him that might ordinarily be hidden.

Or was she just being completely fanciful? *Yes*, she scolded herself. As soon as this man had his memory returned he would no doubt look around and flee in horror.

And yet, pointed out a small voice, *he came here in the first place, didn't he?*

Darius turned as she approached. Sofie's heart skipped and her breath quickened when she saw that he'd shaved off the growth of beard. He looked no less masculine. The hard plains of his face were revealed now. Nothing to hide that sensual mouth.

She went to stand beside him on the small wooden jetty, very aware of the disparity in their sizes. Before she could stop herself, she said, 'You shaved.'

He touched his jaw. 'Yes.'

Embarrassed that she'd mentioned it, she nodded her head towards the lake. 'I wouldn't recommend contemplating a swim. The lake is deep and freezing, even in the summer.'

'It'd be one way of finding out quickly if I can swim.'

'I'm sure you can swim. Especially if you come from Greece.'

He made a face. 'I can speak the language—that's all we know.'

'You spoke in Greek first…to me. It seems like it's your mother tongue.'

They were silent for a moment, and then Darius said,

'It's so quiet here. A kind of quiet I feel like I haven't experienced for a long time. If ever.'

Sofie made a face. 'Sometimes it's *too* quiet.'

'It's peaceful.'

At that moment, as if to prove Darius wrong, a low, puttering engine noise filled the air. Sofie saw her neighbour's small fishing boat appear. She waved a hand and he waved back.

She said, 'That's Jamie. He fishes here most days.'

When there was no response from Darius she looked at him. His face was ashen, his eyes fixed on the boat.

She turned to him, concerned. 'Are you okay?'

For a long moment he didn't speak, and then colour returned to his face. He said tersely, 'I'm fine.'

'Are you remembering something?'

He shook his head, jaw gritted. 'No. Nothing.'

He turned and walked back up the lawn to the house, Pluto trotting loyally by his side.

Sofie frowned and looked back out to where her neighbour had stopped his boat and was getting his fishing gear organised. She waved again and turned away herself, wondering what had made Darius react like that.

That night, when Darius lay in bed trying to sleep, he still had that awful sick sense of dread in his gut. The sense of dread that had gripped him as soon as he'd seen the boat earlier. The smallest, most innocent-looking boat. And yet that first sight of it had impacted him like a punch to his gut, and it had loomed large in his mind all day and evening. Like a malevolent thing.

He was disgusted with himself. How could he be scared of a boat? Especially if he did come from Greece, where shipping was one of the most important industries and where island-hopping via boat was as common as taking a bus for most commuters.

He didn't understand it and he hated not understanding it. It had ruined his appetite, in spite of the delicious stew Sofie had cooked. Not even the couple of glasses of wine seemed to be blurring the edges of this dread that coiled inside him like a live thing.

Sofie's concerned gaze had caught at him too. Making him feel exposed and claustrophobic. The pity she'd so clearly felt had scraped along his nerve-endings. He despised pity. He had a visceral reaction to any hint of pity. Utter rejection.

He'd wanted to haul her up against his body so that she wouldn't be looking at him with pity or concern any more. But with something far more appealing. Surprise. *Desire.* He knew she felt it too. It throbbed in the air between them like a live current.

So he'd come to bed to avoid temptation. But now he still couldn't relax. He craved oblivion, but the oblivion he craved was with his sweet, kind, compassionate hostess. His innocent hostess. Darius might not remember the first thing about himself, but he knew with bone-deep certainty that he was as experienced as she was innocent, and therefore seducing her was *not* an option.

Maybe, he surmised grimly, being aware that it would be wrong to seduce her was an indication that he had some kind of a conscience. It didn't bring much comfort.

CHAPTER THREE

SOFIE WOKE WITH a start. Her heart was pounding. Had she been having a bad dream? Then she heard it. A low, moaning sound. Tortured. Then a shout.

Darius.

She got out of bed and pulled on her robe, belting it loosely, then went out into the corridor.

It was pitch-black outside. The middle of the night. Darius had been in a brooding mood all the previous evening. She'd put it down to frustration at his memory loss.

She hesitated at his door when she didn't hear another sound. But then it came again and she jumped. A shout—something that sounded like *No!*—and other words in that same guttural language he'd spoken first. Greek.

She still hesitated. Clearly he was having a nightmare. Should she intrude?

But then he made the most heart-wrenching sound and cried out, *'Mama... Papa!'*

Acting on instinct, Sofie pushed open the door. There was one low light burning near the bed. Darius's sheets were twisted around his waist and legs. He was bare-chested and his muscles were sheened with perspiration. His face was stark with pain.

Sofie's heart went out to him.

She went over to the side of the bed and hesitated again, not knowing if it was a good idea to wake someone in the middle of a nightmare. Maybe she could just soothe him with her presence without waking him.

She put out her hand and touched Darius's brow, just as he said brokenly, 'Darius...*óchi*...'

Sofie sat down gingerly on the side of the bed. He seemed to be calming a little. He'd stopped thrashing. His jaw was still gritted, though, and she moved her hand down to his chin, her fingers tracing the tense line, willing him to relax. Stubble prickled against her skin, making her a little breathless.

She thought she'd done it. She thought she'd somehow communicated to him that he was safe, that he was okay. She was just lifting her hand, about to stand up, when Darius suddenly stiffened and his eyes snapped open.

She was caught midway between standing and sitting by the intensity of his gaze. He was looking straight at her. Unfocused at first. And then, as if coming out of a trance, his eyes narrowed on her.

His hands reached up and wrapped around her upper arms. Not gripping, just holding her lightly. He said roughly, *'You.'*

Sofie swallowed. This was the second time she'd disturbed this man out of a sleeping state. 'Sorry, I heard you shouting. You were having a bad dream.'

A 'bad dream' sounded far too benign for what Darius had just experienced. A nightmare about a hellscape would be more accurate. He couldn't even remember the images. All he could remember was the feeling of utter helplessness and terror. Horror. And then a feeling of grief and loss so profound that it lingered in his gut even now, pervading every organ and making his skin clammy.

Yet *she* was here. Once again at his side. Pulling him out of the depths of unconsciousness.

The cool touch of her hand lingered on his jaw. He wanted her hand on him again. He needed it as he needed air to keep breathing. She was the only one who could defuse this awful dread in his gut. The clammy feeling on his skin.

She was already having an effect. All he could see was her. Those huge blue eyes so full of concern. The thin silk robe gaping open to show full breasts barely contained by the lace and cotton of a sleep vest. Thighs bare. Black hair tumbling around her shoulders…

'Darius…' she said softly.

It wasn't an entreaty to stop. It sounded like a question.

'You feel it too, don't you?' he said. 'This attraction between us.'

She did nothing for a long moment. Eyes huge. Then she nodded. Her breathing quickened.

'I want you, Sofie. I *need* you.'

That word *need*—it felt alien on his tongue. In his mouth. Clearly it was not something he said regularly. But he couldn't care less about the implication of that now. Or anything else. All he knew was that Sofie was the one solid thing in his life that he could hold on to and that he wanted way more than that. He wanted to lose himself in her.

She opened her mouth. He saw the pink of her tongue and desire raged through his blood, hardening his flesh.

'I… I haven't done this before. With anyone. I mean, I'm…'

'You're innocent.'

He'd known this. Hadn't suspected how innocent, though. Curiously, it made him feel protective. Possessive. He didn't want any other man touching her for her first time.

'Do you want this?'

Sofie's heart was pounding so hard she felt sure that he had to hear it. Feel it. *'Do you want this?'* She realised that this was exactly what she wanted. Through her own reticence, and then the poor health of her parents, she hadn't had a boyfriend, and she did not live in a place where casual sex went unnoticed. But also, crucially, she'd never met anyone who'd made her *want* like this. Who'd made her so aware of herself as a woman. The fact that this man desired her…it was overwhelming.

Sofie nodded before she lost her nerve. 'I… Yes, I want this. I want you.'

She saw the flash of fire in his eyes and her blood leapt in response. Her breasts felt tight. A pulse between her legs throbbed.

But then a strange expression crossed his face. He grimaced. 'Protection. We need protection.'

For a second Sofie had no idea what he was talking about, and then she understood. Protection against pregnancy. Relief made her feel light-headed. 'It's okay, I'm on the pill. For painful periods.'

She cringed slightly. He didn't need to know about her periods. But he'd probably wonder why she was on the pill if she hadn't had sex before.

He said, 'The hospital gave me a clean bill of health. Of course I can't guarantee that—'

Sofie cut him off. 'I'm sure you're fine.' She was afraid that if he rationalised it for too long he would realise that this was just a desire born of these strange circumstances and that he didn't really want her after all.

She knew she would never meet a man like him again but her conscience pricked. Was she taking advantage of him in his weakened state? When he was vulnerable? She was meant to be providing a safe haven—not jumping his bones because she fancied him.

She said, 'Are you sure that this is what *you* want?'

That flash of fire again. His gaze dropped down to her mouth, and lower to her breasts. Bare thighs. His hands tightened on her arms. He looked back up. Sofie was trembling all over. After just a look.

'I've never wanted anything more than this.'

She made a face. 'Well, you don't actually know that.'

'Yes, I do.'

'But you were having a nightmare. Do you need to talk about it?'

A look of what could only be described as utter rejection passed over his face. '*No*. I do not need to talk about it. I need you.'

Sofie looked at him, torn between wanting to throw caution to the wind and exercising some control, because she felt sure that by the morning he would be looking at her and wondering what the hell he'd been thinking.

He said, 'If you're worried that it'll be painful, it might be at first, but I'll be gentle.'

Her insides melted into liquid heat. A heat she couldn't ignore or deny. She couldn't speak.

She bent forward and pressed an inexpert kiss against Darius's mouth. A sense of déjà vu from when she'd done this the first time around hit her. But then he'd been unconscious. Now he was very much conscious.

When she tried to pull back he held her there. Her

eyes opened and she looked straight into two dark pools of green. His mouth moved under hers softly, coaxing. Lips firm but soft.

He enticed her to open up to him and she did so instinctively, breathing him in. His tongue touched hers and it was like an electric shock going right down to the pulse between her legs. She moaned softly, eyes closing again, as Darius made it very clear that he was the one with the skills.

He took the kiss from coaxing and gentle to something far more explicit and masterful. Sofie's head was spinning, and it was only when she opened her eyes again that she realised she was on her back on the bed and Darius was beside her, a hand on her belly, over her robe.

Her mouth felt swollen. Her pulse was racing. It took a second for her eyes to focus. Darius was above her, hair messy, cheeks slashed with colour. Chest huge. Eyes burning. He looked…magnificent.

He moved his hand under the hem of her vest and then he was touching her. Hand to skin. She breathed in, little fires racing all over her.

He said, 'Okay?'

Something about his consideration made her feel emotional. To block it out she nodded her head vigorously.

His hand moved up to the underside of her breast, and then he was cupping the plump flesh. He looked down. Her vest was ruched up. She could only imagine what he saw. A very average body. Breasts that were too big.

Then his thumb moved back and forth over her nipple and Sofie promptly stopped thinking about anything. The sensation was incredible. Like a wire pulling straight from the centre of her breast to between her legs.

And then he put his mouth on her, and her back arched almost off the bed. She didn't even realise that her hands were gripping Darius's hair. Her entire consciousness was consumed by the blazing sensation of wet heat surrounding her nipple and the tugging of Darius's mouth on her flesh.

He lifted his head and Sofie opened her eyes.

He said, 'You're so responsive.'

'Is that a good thing?'

He nodded. 'Very.'

He undid her robe and pulled it off, throwing it somewhere to the side of the bed. Then he was pulling Sofie's vest all the way up and off. She was too full of growing, aching need to be embarrassed that she was now naked from the waist up.

Darius threw back the sheet and Sofie looked down, her eyes widening as she took in the sleek, taut muscles of Darius's body. And one in particular. Thick and hard. Before she knew what she was doing she'd reached out and touched him. He sucked in a breath.

She snatched her hand back and looked up. 'Sorry, does it hurt?'

He smiled tightly. 'Yes, but not because you touched me.'

A wave of heat pulsed through her body as his meaning sank in. He hurt for her. The thought that she had this much of an effect on him was almost impossible to comprehend.

'Touch me again.'

He lay back. Sofie's gaze drifted down and she reached out again, encircling him with her hand. She was fascinated by the steely strength encased in silken skin. He was hot. She had an urge to bend down and put her mouth to him but she didn't have the nerve.

Darius sat up. 'Lie down.'

Sofie was happy to comply. This was all so over-whelming. Amazing. She couldn't quite believe what was happening, but she didn't want it to stop.

He tugged her shorts down over her hips and off. Now she was naked. She'd never been naked with a man before—with anyone!—and yet she felt completely at ease with him.

He looked at her for a long moment, his eyes devouring her entire body with such blatant appreciation that she didn't have time to feel self-conscious. Then his hands followed his eyes. Cupping her breasts, trapping her nipples between his fingers before surrounding them in the sucking wet heat of his mouth.

A tension was building at Sofie's core, making her feel restless, making her hips twitch. Darius put a hand on her belly and then slid it down slowly. Almost of their own volition, Sofie's legs parted.

He explored her there, his fingers sliding into the soft folds hiding her sex. Sofie's back arched again. Her hands gripped the sheet and she bit her lip as Darius's fingers slid inside her, causing a spike of acute pleasure.

His fingers moved in and out, and Sofie could feel how ready she was. Impossible to hide. His thumb moved against her too, in a circling motion, and then he bent his head and took her mouth in a deep, drugging kiss.

When the building tension peaked and broke over her she cried out into Darius's mouth. And then, while the waves of pleasure were still ebbing through her body, he moved over her, his hips forcing her legs apart even more.

She looked up, dizzy. He took himself in his hand and said, 'This might hurt a little, but I promise it'll get better.'

Sofie was incapable of speech. She just nodded.

Darius breached her body with his, and then in one cataclysmic movement seated himself deep inside her.

Sofie sucked in a breath. It wasn't painful…it was amazing. She felt so full. She wanted to move to alleviate the pressure. But Darius was withdrawing, and instinctively she moved with him, as if loath to let him go.

He huffed out a short laugh and took her hand. He laced his fingers with hers and raised them over her head. That brought her breasts into contact with his chest. Sensitised nipples scraping against his chest. And slowly and inexorably he continued to move in and out.

She could feel her body adapting to his. Inner muscles tight around him. The tension built again, like a storm gathering deep inside her, until it could no longer be contained. Darius thrust deep and Sofie shattered into pieces, crying out, legs wrapped tight around his waist as if that would help contain more pleasure than she'd ever known was possible.

Darius thrust again, one more time, and then went still, his entire body locked in its own paroxysm of pleasure. She felt his release pump inside her and her legs gripped him even tighter. She was filled with a very primal urge to take his seed in as deep as she could.

When Sofie woke it was dawn outside, the sky streaked with pink. She was alone and completely disorientated for a long moment. Then it all came back.

Darius having the nightmare, waking up…telling her he wanted her. Her acquiescence. Making love. It felt like a dream, but she knew it wasn't because she was naked in his bed and her body was feeling totally alien and yet still hers. She was no longer a virgin.

She'd never felt such intense pleasure. She'd never known it could be like that. She'd not even hesitated to acquiesce. But the speed with which Sofie had capitulated to Darius's seduction made her cringe now, in the morning light.

Where was he?

Sofie sat up, only realising then that he must have pulled the sheet over her body as she slept. She couldn't remember anything much after she'd passed out from an overload of pleasure. She cringed again and stole out of the bed. She saw her robe and night things neatly draped on a chair nearby and grabbed them, shoving her arms into the robe and belting it tightly around her waist, terrified that Darius would walk in at any second, before she was ready to see him again.

She ducked into the bathroom and groaned when she caught sight of her reflection. Her hair was a wild black tangle over her shoulders. Her eyes were huge and awed-looking. Her skin was pink. She had a little stubble rash along her jaw. Her mouth looked swollen. She touched it and her skin tingled.

She pulled the robe open and looked down. She remembered Darius cupping her breasts, squeezing the flesh...

Before she could die in a pool of embarrassment, Sofie took off the robe and dived under a hot shower, lamenting the washing away of Darius's touch even as she wanted to try and gather her wits.

When she got out of the shower and went back to

her own room she dressed in jeans and a shirt, her hair still damp.

She went downstairs and found Darius in the kitchen, sipping coffee. Thankfully he was dressed in jeans and a shirt, like her. He saw her and displayed no sense of the emotional turmoil Sofie was feeling—but then he was vastly more experienced than her. Used to this. Even if he didn't remember.

'The coffee is fresh.'

Sofie went in, forcing herself to sound as blasé as possible. 'That sounds good.'

He poured her a cup and handed it to her. She took it and breathed in the aroma. Something familiar when suddenly everything seemed strange and new. Disconcertingly, it didn't even feel like her own house any more. It was as if Darius had been here for ever and had ownership. Because he'd taken ownership of her body?

That rogue thought made her duck her head, averting her gaze in case he saw anything.

'How are you?' he asked.

She looked up again, taken aback. She hadn't expected solicitude. She wasn't sure what she'd expected. To wake up in his arms? She knew she was glad it hadn't happened like that. She'd needed to get her head around it all.

She probably never would.

'I'm okay.'

'Just okay?'

She blushed, because she knew she was more than okay. She was changed. Awed. Still in shock. But she couldn't help a sudden small smile as the enormity of what had happened hit her.

'That was… I didn't know it could be like that. So powerful.'

Something occurred to Sofie and she went cold. 'You could be married. Have a family…'

A snarky voice pointed out that she hadn't been thinking about that when she'd been jumping into bed with him at the speed of light.

He made a face and shook his head almost violently. 'Definitely not married.' He held up his hand. 'No ring and no mark of a ring.'

'Lots of people don't wear rings. That doesn't necessarily mean anything.'

'Trust me. I know I can't know for sure, but I can feel it. I'm not married. I feel a strong sense of rejection at the mere thought of it.'

Sofie recalled the sensation of his release inside her, and how she'd felt that primal urge to trap him there, ensuring that she accepted his essence inside her.

'Maybe you're divorced.'

He made a non-committal sound and then put his cup down on the table. 'Are you sore?' he asked. 'After last night?'

Sofie thought of the hot water of the shower hitting her sensitised skin and blushed and shook her head. 'No, not sore…just a little tender.'

He took a step towards her and cupped her jaw. Instant flames licked across her skin, and deep inside a newly familiar tension coiled like a hungry beast. He bent down and pressed a light kiss to her mouth, she tasted him—and coffee.

He pulled back. 'Too tender for that?'

She shook her head.

He kissed her again, a little harder this time. Pulled back again. 'Too tender?'

She shook her head again. He took the coffee cup out of her hand and put it down. Put his hands on her waist and pulled her close. Close enough that she could feel his body responding to hers.

He squeezed her waist. 'How about that?'

She shook her head, frustration building. He kissed her again and she wrapped her arms around his neck. This time the kiss was deeper, harder. She was losing herself all over again. Now she'd forgiven herself for acquiescing so easily last night, she was about to do it again.

But Darius had pulled back. His hand hovered close to her breast. On the edge of cupping it. She could feel her nipples respond, growing tight. Hard. Aching. *Needing.*

'Too much?'

She saw the heat in his eyes and the glint of devilry. He was playing with her. Frustration boiled over. 'No, nowhere is too tender. I want you, Darius.'

He cupped her breast and she groaned softly. He said, 'Good, because we've only just begun.'

It was much later that day when Darius surfaced from the sensual idyll of indulging in Sofie's luscious body. He'd just taken a shower and now stood by the bed with a towel wrapped around his waist, looking at his lover on the bed. For a novice she was a fast learner. Voracious. It was incredibly sexy and impossible to resist.

He didn't have any memory of his sexual history, but he felt a skin-prickling suspicion that what was happening here with her was not usual for him. It was not that he hadn't had great sex before—*had it always been this amazing?*—but that there was a serious lack of boundaries with this woman.

They'd never really had any boundaries in place, due to the strange circumstances that had brought them together, but he felt sure that boundaries with the women he made love to were of paramount importance to him. Because in much the same way as he was convinced he wasn't married, or remotely interested in being married, he also felt a strong instinct to put some emotional distance between them.

Was he used to women using sex as a means to foster emotional intimacy? That was the only explanation for the way he felt right now. Except he was torn. Torn between wanting to put distance between them and wanting to just slide back between the sheets and rouse her back to urgent life with his hands and his mouth.

At that moment she stirred on the bed and Darius's blood leapt all over again. Hot. She was a naked vision, all soft curves and silky skin. That jet-black hair spread over the pillow. Long black lashes rested on her cheeks. Her mouth made a little moue, tempting him back. So tempting.

But Darius took a step back and obeyed his instincts. Plus, he knew she'd be sore now. He'd tried to remain mindful that this was all new to her, but trying to make sure he was gentle had been a battle he feared he'd lost when she'd sat astride his body and taken him deep inside her, sending him spiralling into an orbit of pleasure so intense that he'd had to hold her hips as he'd thrust up and into her over and over again, shouting out his release when it came, hot and urgent.

It was disconcerting to have nothing to compare this

lovemaking to and yet to feel deep in his bones that this was not like anything he'd experienced before.

Reluctantly he pulled the sheet up over her body, hiding it from his gaze.

'Blood pressure is normal and all vital signs are good. The residual fatigue will pass the more rest and recuperation you have.'

Sofie's face flamed like a furnace when her nurse friend Claire said that to Darius, who was sitting on a chair at right angles to her at the kitchen table.

Claire had popped in after work to do a check-up on Darius, and Sofie went cold and then hot again when she thought of how close she'd come to still being in a very uncharacteristically dishevelled state when she arrived.

What if Darius hadn't woken her and handed her her phone, saying, 'Someone is trying to contact you.'

She'd slept the entire day away, almost in a coma after an overload of sensual pleasure that defied any attempt to try and understand it. Even now she felt dangerously languorous, and was assiduously averting her gaze from her guest.

Eventually, after tea and small talk, Claire got up to leave. Sofie saw her out, feeling as if her friend must surely see right through her.

Claire turned to her in the doorway, eyes narrowing. Sofie's stomach plummeted.

'Is everything okay?' Claire asked.

Sofie balked. 'Fine. Why wouldn't it be?'

'Your guest is…behaving himself? Not giving you any trouble?'

A bubble of hysteria rose up inside Sofie. He wasn't giving her trouble—quite the opposite. She swallowed down the urge to giggle. This was ridiculous—she wasn't a teenager!

'He is being a perfect gentleman,' she said. Not quite true either.

Her friend's eyes narrowed even more. 'I would have to have been unconscious not to have noticed the zing between you in there. You were both trying so hard not to look at each other that your eyes were almost falling out of your heads.' Her tone turned dry. 'I'll admit it's been a while since I felt it myself, but I do remember what it's like.'

Sofie's heart skipped a beat. She blushed. Started to babble.

But her friend put her hand up. 'No judgement here at all. Believe me, if I was in your situation with *that* man, and if he wanted me, wild horses wouldn't stop me from indulging. But we both know that he is not from here. And I mean that literally and metaphorically. Anyone can see that he's a huge fish out of water. Before too long he'll remember that himself and we'll have a fleet of shiny sleek cars coming to take him back to where he comes from.' Claire's voice gentled. 'I just don't want you to be hurt.'

Sofie bit her lip, all hysteria gone now. 'I'm okay, really. I'm under no illusions about what this is.'

But the truth was that she had no idea what this was. All she knew was that she didn't want it to stop.

'Was your friend warning you to be careful?'

Sofie looked at Darius where he stood by a bookcase in the lounge. They'd just had dinner and had come in here to watch a movie. Darius had expressed interest in trying to see if any of the classics might jog his memory. He'd actually managed to find a pair of faded jeans that more or less fitted him, albeit snugly, and a long-sleeved top that did little to disguise the power of his leanly muscular chest.

He was far too distracting.

'Claire?' Sofie asked, stalling for time. She'd deliberately chosen an armchair to sit in, trying to take Claire's advice and not forget herself completely.

Darius's tone was dry. 'Unless anyone else popped in today, yes, that friend.'

Reluctantly, Sofie said, 'She sensed something between us and she was a little concerned, yes.'

'She'd be a bad friend if she wasn't. After all, I'm a complete stranger.'

'I know you won't hurt me.' Sofie was surprised to find she really meant it. She trusted him.

'Not intentionally, no,' he said.

His dark green gaze found hers. Held it. He was sending her a message, she thought. Even though he had no idea who he was, or what his life was about, he somehow knew that he could hurt her emotionally. It had to be a muscle memory. Maybe he was used to telling women not to grow too attached? After all, he'd more or less kept his distance from her today.

Maybe he was already bored with her?

That thought made her feel exposed. She knew how average she was. That this attraction between them was an anomaly. A flash in the pan. She was so far out of his league—

'So, what are we watching?'

Darius came back over to the couch. Sofie shut the circling thoughts out of her head and reached for the remote at the same time as Darius reached for her hand and tugged her over to the couch, to sit beside him.

Instantly her blood leapt and fizzed as he growled, 'You're too far away.'

She couldn't help saying, 'I thought for a moment that maybe you didn't want this any more…'

'"This"? You mean you?'

Sofie winced at how bald and needy that sounded. 'Really, it's okay, I know this is just a temporary madness induced by—'

He stopped her words by kissing her. He pulled back. 'I still want you. I was attempting to put some space between us, so as not to overwhelm you, but it seems impossible for me to resist touching you.'

He started kissing her again, trailing his mouth across her jaw and down her neck, pushing her hair aside.

Sofie attempted to stay in control. 'What about the movie?'

Darius lifted his head. 'I find I'm more interested right now in making love to you than investigating what I remember. But if you insist…?'

Sofie battled for a second, before throwing caution to the wind. She wrapped her arms around his neck and let him lead her back into the fire. Darius's memory and the outside world existed, and would have to be dealt with, but just for now, right here, she could pretend that they didn't.

And she could pretend that Darius was choosing her for *her*, and not just because he had no choice.

Some hours later…

'You are *so* curvaceous.'

This pronouncement was followed by a firm squeeze of Sofie's naked buttock.

She rolled her eyes. 'You mean plump.'

'Succulent.'

This was followed by a gentle bite of the same buttock.

She giggled. 'Now you're making me sound like food.'

Darius felt fairly sure he hadn't ever made a woman giggle in bed. It wasn't altogether unpleasant. It sparked a warm feeling in his chest.

'You are food,' Darius breathed. 'The most succulent, juiciest morsel of flesh I have ever tasted.'

Sofie made a huffing noise.

Darius lifted his head. He was drunk on the scent and the feel of Sofie. 'What?'

She made a face. 'I'm sure you've had juicier than me. You just can't remember, that's all.'

She blushed, and he marvelled that she could still blush after what they'd just been doing. There was not an inch of this woman that he didn't know intimately by now. And he wanted to know again and again. He realised at that moment that he was quite unconcerned about the fact that he had no idea who he was. It was as if he really didn't want to deal with whatever reality awaited him.

He cocked his head to one side. 'Technically, you're correct. I can't know. But does it matter?'

They were sprawled on the bed in a haze of post-coital pleasure, Darius's head near Sofie's lap, hence his proximity to her bottom, and her head near his feet. Black hair tumbled over one creamy shoulder. Her breasts were full and perfectly shaped, nipples rosy. The curve of her waist was an enticement to touch.

Darius was reaching for her when she said, 'Do you wonder why you were on the mountain alone?'

His hand stilled. 'Alone?'

'Most people do that climb in a group or with a buddy. It's safer.'

Darius didn't know why but he suddenly felt a chill go down his back and felt exposed. 'Maybe I don't have any friends.'

Sofie bit her lip. She looked concerned. 'Of course you have friends. Everyone has friends. I'm your friend.'

Darius pushed aside the onset of something very brittle that he'd felt at her mention of friends and the hollow ache it evoked. Was he some kind of lone wolf? Was that why he had a tattoo of a wolf on his arm? A tattoo he had no memory of getting...

His brain started to throb a little. He manoeuvred himself so he was alongside Sofie's delectable body again. 'You say you're my friend...just how friendly are we talking?'

Sofie took his cue and reached for him, smiling shyly. 'Very friendly. Some would say *over*-friendly.'

Darius allowed himself to sink into her embrace, and when she pulled back for a moment he wanted to growl in protest. He opened his eyes. She was looking at him with an expression on her face that was something like...guilt.

'What is it?' he asked.

'It's something I have to tell you. I have a confession to make.'

Darius felt amused at the thought of this woman committing any kind of transgression. 'By all means confess.'

Sofie bit her lip for a moment, almost distracting Darius from hearing what she had to say. But then she said, 'When you were unconscious...just before you woke up... I... I kissed you. You were so beautiful I couldn't resist.'

He had a vague impression of a cool mouth on his... then going away...of himself reaching out to grab onto something. *Her*. Those big eyes. Wide and shocked. Guilty.

Almost to himself he said, 'I remember...you woke me up.'

She blushed. 'It was an unforgivable intrusion of your privacy. I don't know what came over me.'

There was a dull throb in Darius's head, and a niggling sensation that images and words were trying to break through the fog. But he wasn't ready for that. Not yet.

He pulled Sofie close again, willing her to keep the world at bay for a little longer. He said, 'Isn't the Prince supposed to wake the Princess with a kiss?'

Sofie huffed a short laugh. 'We both know I'm no princess.'

Darius wasn't sure how to respond to that. She wasn't a princess, and this wasn't a fairy tale. But the knowledge that her kiss had precipitated his awakening unsettled him.

The throbbing in his head intensified.

Feeling a sense of desperation, and not sure where it was coming from, Darius pulled Sofie close again and said into her soft skin, 'I forgive you for your transgression...now, where were we?'

When Sofie woke she deliberately didn't open her eyes straight away. She took a moment to enjoy the heavy, sated feeling in her body, to revel in the memory of Darius's masterful lovemaking, to go hot and cold and then hot again all over thinking of what had happened here over the past few days. She was no longer an innocent. No matter what happened, Darius had given her that. The gift of knowing she was a sensual, sexual woman. The gift of feeling beautiful, desired. And by such a man...

She stretched luxuriously under the sheet and smiled at the thought that she hadn't slept in her own room since she and Darius had started sleeping together.

'Sofie?'

Darius. Sofie's eyes snapped open. He was standing by the window, fully dressed in those slightly too snug jeans and a shirt that strained ever so slightly across his chest. He looked serious, but she hardly noticed that.

Feeling emboldened by the lingering heat in her veins, which was fast growing, Sofie pulled the sheet back, exposing herself, and patted the bed. 'What's the rush to get dressed? Come back to bed...' she said, in what she hoped was a sultry kind of purr.

But Darius's serious expression didn't change or break. He didn't shed his clothes with flattering speed, as he had been doing. He just looked at her with a kind of stony expression that was a little scary.

Feeling exposed, Sofie pulled the sheet back over her and sat up. 'What is it...? Darius?'

Finally he spoke. 'My name isn't Darius, it's Achilles. I remember who I am. I remember everything. I need to use your phone.'

CHAPTER FOUR

SOFIE GOT WASHED and dressed in record time, while Darius—*Achilles?*—made his phone call. Or a series of them. When she came downstairs he was still on the phone, his voice deep and authoritative. He was speaking French now, and it sounded pretty fluent to Sofie.

She was reeling at the speed with which everything had flipped. Her house no longer felt like a sensual cocoon. There was a new energy in the air. The outside world was creeping into this isolated corner of the country.

She didn't even want to allow her mind to go to who *Achilles* was. He hadn't seemed all that shocked to have his memory returned. Just…grim.

The door to the small study off the living room opened and Sofie sprang back, feeling guilty even though this was her house. She looked up at the man she knew more intimately than herself and he was a stranger. Expressionless face.

She said all she could think of right then. 'Coffee?'

Something in his expression cracked enough to show her a glimpse of the man she had come to know.

He said, 'Yes. Please.'

When they'd both taken a sip of coffee Sofie sat down

at the kitchen table. Afraid that her legs wouldn't keep holding her up.

'So…you are Greek?'

He nodded.

'But you speak French fluently.'

His mouth twisted slightly and that made Sofie think of how only a few hours ago it had been on her body, exploring every inch— She clamped down on that rogue imagery.

He said, 'I also speak Spanish, Italian, and passable Portuguese and Cantonese.'

Sofie's eyes widened. 'Who are you?'

'My name is Achilles Lykaios. I run a business based in Athens.'

Sofie frowned. 'Lykaios…is that something to do with a wolf?'

Achilles nodded. '*Lykos* is wolf in Greek, so it's a derivation of that, yes.'

Sofie said, 'Your tattoo…of the wolf. It's very personal, then.' She'd been fascinated by the tattoo high on his right arm ever since she'd first seen it in the hospital, but hadn't asked about it because she'd known Darius—*Achilles*—would hardly remember why he'd got that if he couldn't remember anything else.

Achilles's head was still throbbing, as if it was hard to contain all the information he'd recovered. As soon as he'd woken up he'd known exactly who he was and where he was. It was as if the knowledge had been there all along and some mischievous force had decided that enough was enough and pulled back a curtain.

There were some things he shied away from, though. He didn't need to go all the way back to the past. Just having had his memory taken and now given back was cruel enough. For the last few days he hadn't been the man who had lost—

'Your tattoo is linked to your name, then?' Sofie said.

She must have thought he hadn't heard her. He looked at her. She'd put her hair up in a knot on her head that his fingers itched to undo. She wore a plain shirt and jeans. Even now, even when he *knew* everything, he was still consumed by her.

It hadn't been an anomaly due to extreme circumstances. They had a powerful chemistry. And she was beautiful. Just not in the way he was used to women being beautiful. She was earthy. Real. Unmanufactured.

The tattoo. Achilles remembered getting it. Stumbling—drunk—into a tattooist's parlour in Paris, yanking off his jacket and shirt and giving them the instructions before he'd all but passed out on the bed. He'd woken up and realised that he'd imprinted his family pain—an eternal howl of pain—on his arm, and pure stubbornness had made him leave it there even though his advisors had begged him to get it removed.

Pictures of him getting the tattoo had, of course, surfaced online, with the main focus being on his shirtless state. Thankfully no one had seemed to notice his inebriated state. And certainly no one knew anything about why he'd chosen to get a tattoo. About his need to inflict some kind of pain on himself…to have a constant reminder of the fact that he was still alive while others weren't.

Achilles's attention came back to Sofie out of the past. He said starkly, 'Yes, it's linked to my name.'

A pain spiked through his head at that moment and he put a hand to his forehead.

Immediately Sofie was standing, 'I think we should go to the hospital and get you checked out.'

But Achilles shook his head. 'No need. My physician in London will check me over.'

'Oh. Okay. You'll be leaving then?'

Thankfully the sharp pain receded, and Achilles said, 'Yes, my assistant is organising my pick-up as we speak. A driver will be here within the hour.'

Sofie's face paled. 'Within the hour? That fast?'

Achilles realised she had no idea who he was. If he was quick he could avert a story appearing in the papers about this entire episode. The last thing he needed now, when he was doing his best to restore people's opinion of him, was to bring about more headlines.

His memory had returned just in time.

He was leaving. In an hour. He'd be gone as if he'd never been here at all. Exactly as her friend Claire had predicted. For one fantastical second Sofie wondered if she was in the middle of some lurid hallucination. Maybe she was the one who'd fallen down the mountain and this was all some sort of coma-induced fantasy?

After all, that was nearly easier to believe than the reality. And what she really didn't like to acknowledge was the awful wrenching feeling in her gut. She hardly knew this man and yet she felt as if she'd never *not* known him.

But he was more of a stranger than ever. Gone was the teasing, sexy man of last night. This man was guarded and stern. Businesslike. Not inclined to loll in bed and tell a woman she was like a succulent food.

Sofie fought down the wave of heat accompanying that memory and forced herself to focus on practicalities. 'Do you want to change into your original clothes? They might be more comfortable…'

'These are fine. I'll be able to change when I get to my house in London.'

Sofie frowned. 'I thought you said you were based in Athens.'

'I am, but I also have a place in London.'

He was more successful than she'd thought. But it wasn't necessarily unusual for a businessman to have some kind of pied-à-terre in London. It was a huge hub for business after all.

Sofie felt the huge chasm of distance between them in that moment. He knew everything about himself now. She knew nothing. At least before they'd both known nothing. And then she felt churlish. It must have been awful not to know anything about himself. He deserved to have his memory back.

She forced herself to ask, '*Are* you married?'

He shook his head. 'No. Definitely not married.'

'You must have a girlfriend…' But when she said that word she cringed inwardly. Even she could see that Achilles didn't seem like a man who had *girlfriends*.

He shook his head again and his gaze narrowed on her. She felt the sense of self-consciousness which she'd all but lost over the last few days. When she'd been lulled into some sensual sense of complacency, basking under the sun of his all-encompassing regard.

'What is it?'

'I want you to come with me.'

What the hell are you thinking? The question resounded in his head as the words hung in the air. The shock on Sofie's face should be making Achilles realise he was being ridiculously impetuous. If he said something quickly now, like, *No, sorry, it's not a good idea*, she would most likely agree with him.

But his mouth stayed stubbornly closed. He knew exactly who he was, and the world he moved in, and it was a world away from here. A world away from her and the type of woman she was. He should leave and just put Sofie MacKenzie out of his mind.

But something in him was resisting fiercely. He'd never met a woman like Sofie before. She was utterly unique. He felt a delicious sense of anticipation at the prospect of taking her with him. Showing her his world. *Having her in his bed.*

With the benefit of the return of his memory he now knew that what he'd shared these past few brief days with her was not usual. He'd never experienced chemistry like this before. Never. Or the sex. He'd always prided himself on being a consummate lover, and he'd certainly gained a reputation for being a masterful one, but with Sofie it was different. It was raw. Mind-blowing. Unprecedented.

Dangerous, whispered a voice. He quashed it. Ridiculous. He was impermeable. It was just sex.

And there was another reason to want her by his side. He remembered now why he'd gone off-grid for a brief time. To avoid the fall-out of a salacious press story—for once not of his making. It was becoming more and more apparent that his lingering playboy reputation was damaging the Lykaios name and legacy and, as much as he hated to admit it, it was time to put an end to it.

What better way than to reappear with a woman on his arm? And not just any woman, but someone who would take everyone by surprise. Someone they wouldn't be able to quantify or contextualise or, even better, recognise.

Sofie opened her mouth. 'You want me to come with you…where?'

She looked totally blindsided. Achilles's conscience pricked. Then an all-too-familiar feeling of ruthlessness reminded him of who he was. How he did things. He told himself that he wasn't being entirely selfish or ruthless—she could gain something out of this too.

'I want you to come to London with me, and then Athens.'

'But… I can't afford to just…leave. I have a job. Pluto… I…' She looked at him, dazed. 'Why?'

Achilles realised in that moment that there was another reason he wanted her to come. She'd been the only solid thing in his life since the moment he'd woken up and looked into her eyes. He wasn't sure he was ready to let her go—and not just because it suited him and he wanted her.

He answered her. 'Because the chemistry we share is very rare and I still want you.'

'Then why can't you stay here?'

'Because I run a business.'

'I have a job too.'

He arched a brow. 'Cleaning in a hospital.'

She flushed. 'I know it's not as fancy as running a business.'

'I have people depending on me for their livelihoods.' That was a slight understatement, but Achilles wasn't going to elaborate now. He was quite enjoying the novelty of a woman who wasn't tripping over herself to jump at his offer.

'I don't even really know you.' Her flush deepened. 'You know…in spite of the last few days.'

He took her hand and led her into the study, which housed a computer. He let her hand go and sat down and typed in a few words. A website popped up: Lykaios Industries. There was a picture of Achilles wearing a three-piece suit, standing with folded arms in front of a massive steel and glass building in Athens. Underneath it said: Achilles Lykaios, CEO of Lykaios Industries.

He stood up and faced Sofie, who was still staring at his image on the screen. He said, 'I am who I say I am. And we know each other intimately.'

Sofie looked at him. 'Yes, but that's just physical.'

He folded his arms. 'You said you wanted to travel.'

She frowned. 'I did?'

'You told me that you envied your friends leaving and travelling when you never could because of your commitment to your parents. But there's nothing stopping you now.'

Achilles could see her chest rising and falling with her breath, more rapidly. 'I can't afford to go to Europe.'

'You wouldn't have to pay for a thing.'

'But I can't just...' She trailed off.

Achilles seized on her obvious indecision. 'Why can't you? I'm sure the hospital can replace you, and someone can take care of the dog. This is a once-in-a-lifetime opportunity. When I leave here I won't be back, Sofie. This is it.' He closed the distance between them and tipped her chin up so she couldn't escape his gaze. He marvelled again at her unadorned beauty. 'It would be an awful shame to let this end here, now. Come with me and I'll show you the world.'

She drew in a shaky breath. 'But for how long?'

Achilles shrugged. 'For as long as it lasts.'

Sofie was up in her bedroom. Somehow she'd managed to break away from Achilles's mesmerising gaze and seductive words and was trying to inject some oxygen and rationale into her brain. She looked around the room—the bedroom she hadn't slept in for a few nights. Because she'd been too busy losing her virginity with a sexy stranger.

Who was no longer a stranger, as he'd rightly pointed out.

Except he still was in so many respects. And he would be for ever if she didn't leave with him, whispered a little voice.

'I want you to come with me.' Had she hallucinated that? He couldn't possibly have said such an audacious thing. But he had. And it was clear he'd expected her to say yes. He hadn't looked remotely nervous or unsure.

But she'd found herself resisting his pull, reacting to an arrogance that had become more pronounced with the return of his memory. She couldn't get the picture of him on that website out of her head. He'd looked so gorgeous in a three-piece suit. Gorgeous and obviously very important. It made sense now—she'd suspected he was *someone.*

She felt slightly insulted that he obviously thought her life was so inconsequential that she could just leave on the spur of the moment because he asked her to.

It is inconsequential, whispered a little voice.

She scowled at herself. And then caught sight of her reflection in the mirror. Shapeless shirt. Faded jeans. Hair up in a messy knot. No make-up. And yet he saw something in her that made him still want her? Even after his memory had returned and he must surely be comparing her to the other women he'd been with?

It was a very flattering thought—that even when the real world was about to reappear and whisk him back to his life he wanted to take her with him. She hadn't ever ventured further than France.

It was too seductive. Dangerously so.

Sofie had always felt a little invisible. Her parents had loved her, but she'd always felt as if her presence just reminded them of the loss of a large family, so she'd got used to tucking herself out of sight or keeping busy so she didn't encroach on their sadness. Not even when she'd been caring for them had she felt 'seen'. And sometimes, when she was among her peers, she felt as if they were so busy with their own lives and families that they wouldn't notice if she just got up and walked out of the room and left the island behind.

But, if she was to believe what had just happened, the most charismatic and exciting man she'd ever met really *saw* her, and still wanted her to come with him. It was huge.

A frisson of excitement prickled over her skin. Could she really do this? What Achilles was offering was everything she'd secretly been dreaming about. Getting away from this place and seeing the world. She'd told him that. She'd revealed so much to him. It shocked her now to realise how comfortable she'd felt with him. How much she'd trusted him.

Of course, she reminded herself, she didn't need a man to take her away from here to fulfil her dreams. She could do it all by herself. But suddenly that thought didn't appeal—setting out on her own.

She thought of watching him walk away and felt panicky. Was he right? Was this a once-in-a-lifetime opportunity?

She heard a noise outside and looked out of the window to see a very sleek black SUV coming down the drive. Tinted windows. No one had a car like that around here. More evidence of the outside world. *His car.*

The panicky sensation became heart-pounding adrenalin. This man would not wait around. He meant what he said. She knew the answer to her question. This *was* a once-in-a-lifetime opportunity. She had no idea how long it would take for him to realise he'd made a massive mistake, asking her to come with him, but she was going to do the craziest and most spontaneous thing she'd ever done in her life and seize this opportunity and make the most of it.

Before Sofie lost her nerve, she went back downstairs. Achilles was in the hall, with Pluto by his side. That image alone solidified her resolve.

The SUV was pulling to a stop outside the door. Achilles turned around and Sofie stopped on the last stair. She was breathless. 'Okay,' she blurted out. 'I'll come with you.'

Achilles's expression didn't change, and for a gut-churning second Sofie thought that maybe he'd changed his mind, but then he smiled and reached for her.

'You've made the right decision.'

'What did you say your business was, exactly?' Sofie asked a short while later. They had stepped out of the back of the SUV onto a cleared area of greenery not far from the hospital. A place where Achilles's team had been told they could land the helicopter.

'I didn't say.'

'Do you want to elaborate now, maybe?'

She sounded a little shaken. Achilles looked down at her and bit back a smile. She had no idea.

Her eyes were huge. She'd pulled her hair back into a loose plait. She was wearing what he figured were her 'smart casual' clothes. A pair of dark trousers and a wrap-around sleeveless silk top. Sling-back shoes with pointy toes. She could have passed for one of his assistants. But he was going to make her his mistress.

She needed to know exactly who he was and what she was heading into.

He said, 'Sofie, look at me.'

She tore her gaze off the sleek modern helicopter on the ground and turned to face Achilles, tipping her face up. He wanted to kiss her. But he restrained himself.

'I should probably tell you that I'm not just a CEO. I'm the heir and owner of Lykaios Industries.'

She frowned a little. He elaborated, 'It's a steel and construction company. We're one of the biggest in the world.' *And would become the biggest again very soon,* Achilles reminded himself. 'It's been in my family for generations.'

Sofie considered this. 'That picture of you on the website, outside that building...'

'I own that building. It's our head office in Athens. We also have offices in London and New York.'

Sofie blanched a little. 'So...you're a big deal?'

Achilles bit back another smile. 'Some would say so. We're very successful.'

'You're...rich?'

'I'm a billionaire.'

Sofie took a step back, going even more pale. Not the reaction Achilles had been expecting.

She shook her head. 'Look, Achilles, I don't know if this is such a good idea after all. You're clearly very important and I'm—'

Achilles reached for Sofie's hand, surprised at the dart of panic he felt. 'You're not backing out now. All this doesn't mean anything. I'm still *me.*'

She looked at him as if trying to ascertain who that *me* was. Eventually she said, 'Maybe, but you come with a little more baggage than I'd imagined. I thought we were going to be taking the car ferry to the mainland so we could drive down to London, or maybe get the train.' She frowned, looking suspicious. 'How exactly are we getting to London?'

She was like a skittish foal. He said, 'We're taking the helicopter to Glasgow, I believe, and then my private jet will take us to London.'

'Private jet… Achilles, I've never been on a plane, never mind a helicopter.'

'Then what are you waiting for?'

'Champagne, Miss MacKenzie?'

Sofie was dizzy. All she could do was nod and accept the ridiculously elegant and delicate glass flute containing honey-coloured sparkling wine. She took a sip and wrinkled her nose at the sensation of the bubbles. The wine was fragrant and sweet and dry all at once. It was heady. Like this whole situation, which had morphed out of her control from the moment she'd laid eyes on the helicopter.

And found out that Achilles was a billionaire.

And that they were flying by private jet.

She looked out of the small window beside her plush seat. They'd left Glasgow behind some time ago and were high above the clouds. This at least felt a bit more solid than the helicopter, which had swayed precariously as it had lifted into the air.

Her friend Claire had come to wave goodbye. Her parting words still rang in Sofie's head: *I think what you're doing is crazy, but brave. Enjoy the adventure and just don't fall for him.'*

Claire was going to watch the house and take care of Pluto. And she'd agreed to smooth things over with Sofie's boss at the hospital—in any case, it wasn't as if she had much of a job to lose, if it came to it.

For a second she let herself feel the giddiness of behaving totally out of character and uprooting her life exactly as she'd dreamt of doing.

'Happy you made the right decision?'

Sofie turned to look at Achilles. He was on the other side of the aisle in his own very plush leather seat. He'd been on the phone since they boarded. He was drinking coffee.

Weakly avoiding answering his question, because the giddy, light feeling inside her was all too disturbing, she said, 'You're not having champagne?'

He made a face. 'Not yet. I need to keep my wits about me.'

Sofie turned towards him in her seat. They were alone except for the discreet cabin staff, who had greeted Achilles by name when they'd boarded.

'How was it that someone like you was able to have an accident and lose your memory and no one came looking for you?'

Sofie's eyes were huge and very blue. And full of concern. Once again Achilles's conscience pricked when he thought of the world he was about to introduce her to. It was quickly followed by a sense of protectiveness. An alien sensation. But not altogether unappealing.

She was looking at him, waiting for a response. Achilles decided she didn't need to know the full extent of his reasons for going off-grid.

He shrugged minutely. 'I needed some space and time to think about things. I have a lot on my plate.'

Sofie's eyes filled with compassion. 'I understand.'

'You do?'

She nodded. 'Lots of people come to the island and

climb that particular mountain because they're searching for something. Because they're…disillusioned. Or tired.'

'You're suggesting I was burnt out?'

She looked earnest. 'It's really not that uncommon for people to go there to challenge themselves by doing something physical. To get out of their own heads.'

Achilles was surprised at how incensed he was by her suggestion that his actions had displayed any kind of weakness. 'I wasn't burnt out. I am *not* burnt out.'

But then, unbidden, a slew of images came into his head: brokering deals that took far too much mental energy and yet left him not much further along on his path to achieving his ultimate ambition; glittering parties where he'd felt more and more removed from everything around him; an endless parade of faceless lovers who had left him momentarily sated but far from satisfied.

It rankled that Sofie had intuited something he hadn't even admitted to himself. And something else struck him then—something he'd avoided looking at too closely before now. There was another reason he'd asked Sofie to come with him. Even though he had his memory back, he still felt as if a part of him was hidden, unknown. As if some vital piece of information was yet to be revealed… some piece of a puzzle. An important revelation that he couldn't pin down. It was disconcerting.

Sofie alleviated that feeling. Once she was near him that creeping sense of something hiding just out of view diminished. She had been his anchor since he'd woken up. And, even though he would die before he admitted to needing anyone, right now he needed her. He assured himself it was purely physical.

He saw something over Sofie's shoulder and undid his

seatbelt and held out a hand. He was done with this discussion. 'Come here.'

Pink came into her cheeks. She darted a look up the cabin towards where the staff were. 'But I'm not allowed to move around, am I?'

'You're allowed to do whatever you want. This is my plane. We're not bound by normal rules here.'

Still looking endearingly uncertain, Sofie undid her belt and let Achilles take her hand. He tugged her out of her seat and over to him, so that she fell with a soft *oof* into his lap, all tantalising curves and silky hair. Smelling of roses and musk. Wholesome. His body reacted to hers instantly in a very unwholesome way.

He turned her towards the window and put his arms around her, feeling the weight of her full breasts close enough to cup in his palms if he chose to. He heard the change in her breathing. More rapid. He lamented the fact that it was a short flight, otherwise he knew exactly where they would be.

He kept his hands off her breasts and said, 'Look down there.'

She did, and he heard her awed intake of breath. 'That's the Thames and the London Eye...and Big Ben and Buckingham Palace!' She turned her head to Achilles. 'Have you ever been to the palace?'

'A couple of times.'

Sofie rolled her eyes. 'Oh, only a *couple of times*?'

Achilles smiled, automatically relishing the thought of Sofie's reaction if he was to take her to a place like that. He shifted slightly so she fell into his lap a little more, where she would be in no doubt as to her effect on him.

Her eyes widened and she said, 'Oh.'

'Oh, indeed. We have just a minute or so.'

'For what?' She was breathless.

'For this.' Achilles funnelled his fingers into her hair and pulled her head down, capturing her soft mouth with his. She opened without hesitation, allowing him access to all that sweetness. A sweetness that made his blood go on fire.

Only when the sound of a discreet cough managed to break through the heat haze in his brain did he disengage and pull back. Sofie's eyes were still closed. Her mouth swollen. Achilles wanted to snarl at the air steward who said officiously, 'Coming in to land, sir. You need to put on your seatbelts.'

Sofie's eyes snapped open and she scrambled out of Achilles's lap, bundling herself back into her seat and doing up her belt, face bright pink, hair mussed. She was adorable. And she was *his*—for as long as he wanted her.

Sofie was still mortified when they reached Achilles's house in the centre of London. She'd got so caught up in his kiss that she hadn't even noticed the steward trying to get their attention. Achilles had been totally unfazed, of course. Smiling sexily at Sofie's embarrassment. She'd just scowled at him, piqued that he'd managed to eclipse the fact that she was on a private jet.

They'd landed in a small airfield and had been met by another sleek SUV with tinted windows. The driver had whisked them straight into the city, to an area of wide leafy streets with huge white houses, one of which belonged to Achilles.

They'd been admitted into an impressive marble foyer by a uniformed woman around Sofie's age just seconds ago. Achilles's cell phone had rung and he'd looked at the screen before making a face and saying, 'I'm sorry but I have to take this call. Céline will show you around.'

Sofie had watched him walk away, filled with a kind

of panic at being left alone, but then she'd realised she was also glad to have a little respite from his far too distracting presence.

And now, as she followed Céline around the house, she was relieved that she was alone—because she really didn't want him to witness her reaction.

It was like something from an interiors magazine. A very exclusive designer interiors magazine. Everything was in muted colours. Sleek lines. A careful juxtaposition of classic décor befitting the age of the house alongside modern art on the walls.

She knocked her hip against a table and what looked like a Ming vase wobbled precariously. Sofie's heart almost leapt out of her chest as she put her hands out to steady the vase.

'Don't worry,' said Céline airily.

Sofie took her hands off the vase only when it was steady again. Her palms were sweating. The young woman was leading her upstairs now, where a plush carpet led down a corridor.

Céline opened a door and stood back. 'This is the master suite. We'll have your bags brought up and clothes put away.'

Sofie was horrified. 'I only have one bag and I can unpack myself...it's no trouble.'

The girl smiled. 'As you wish.'

Sofie stood on the threshold of the room for a second. It was dramatic. Dressed in dark brown and gold. Very masculine. A massive bed dominated one wall. Sofie had never seen a bed so big. Dark sheets with gold trim.

She stepped inside gingerly. Céline breezed past her, saying, 'There's an en suite bathroom and a dressing room through here.'

She was indicating another door. Sofie had a peek and

nearly fainted. The dressing room was the size of the bedroom Achilles had used in her house.

The bathroom wasn't much smaller. The colour scheme echoed that of the bedroom. Dark colours. Two sinks. A massive bath. Walk-in shower.

The views from the bedroom and bathroom looked over an expanse of green lawn. Presumably the house's private back garden. She saw a gazebo in the distance, and a small, manicured maze.

Sofie struggled to find something to say. 'This is…lovely.'

'Can I offer you some refreshments? Champagne? Caviar?'

Sofie looked at the woman and wondered just who she was used to entertaining on Achilles's behalf. She didn't like the images that popped into her head.

She said almost apologetically, 'I'd really like a cup of tea, if it's not too much trouble?'

The girl blinked for a second, as if not computing a request for something as simple as tea, and then she smiled. 'Of course. Come with me and I'll show you to the lounge.'

A few minutes later Sofie was ensconced in a charming room, relatively cosy compared with the other rooms she'd seen. Céline had just delivered tea and biscuits that looked more like art than anything edible.

When she was alone again, Sofie took her phone out of her bag and did what she should have done before she'd allowed herself to be whisked away from her life—looked up Achilles Lykaios to see for herself in detail exactly who he was.

CHAPTER FIVE

THE PHONE CALL had taken Achilles longer than he would have liked. But after his absence he had things to attend to. He'd been distracted for the last ten minutes of the call, wondering where Sofie was. What she was doing. How she was reacting.

He'd been told she was in the lounge having tea, and as he pushed open the door anticipation rose high in his blood and his chest. Something that ordinarily would have disturbed him if he'd stopped to think about it.

She was sitting in a chair, her bag in her lap. Looking at her mobile phone. But when she heard him she turned her head and Achilles saw that she looked stricken. Her face was white. Eyes huge.

'What is it? Did something happen?'

Achilles was by her side in an instant but she recoiled slightly. She shook her head. She held up her phone. 'I looked you up.'

He was surprised at the prickling sense of betrayal he felt. Which he knew was ridiculous. It would have been weird if she hadn't wanted to know more about who he was. Before, it would have been customary for him to have his team look into not only his business colleagues and rivals, but also prospective lovers. It was imperative for him. The experience that had sent him to that remote island in Scotland was a perfect example of his team giving him information to protect his reputation. What was left of it.

And yet since he'd regained his memory it hadn't occurred to him once to have Sofie checked out. A woman who seemed too pure to be true. No one was that pure. He made a mental note to rectify that situation, not liking his sudden sense of exposure.

'So tell me,' he asked easily, belying the tension he felt, 'what did you find out about me?'

She blushed, and it eased the sense of betrayal inside him. She said, 'I read that you're a…a playboy. There were pictures of you with women. Lots of women.'

'I won't lie. I'm not a monk, Sofie. But I'm also not as promiscuous as those headlines would have you believe. Maybe when I was younger…but now? No.'

'You're also an adrenalin junkie. Jumping out of planes. Taking part in celebrity car races across the desert. Extreme skiing.'

He shrugged minutely. 'I can't deny I like a thrill.'

Liar, you do it to constantly risk your own life because you don't feel you deserve to be here.

Achilles recalled the moments of terror he would feel just before he did any of those things, and the words that would go through his mind. *Now my time will be up. Surely now I'll pay the price I should have paid all those years ago…*

But in each instance he would emerge unscathed, with fate laughing mockingly in his ear.

Sofie cocked her head and looked at him. She wasn't cooing at how brave he was, or how strong. 'I guess it makes sense, then, why you would try to conquer the mountain on your own…and yet when you saw a small fishing boat on a placid lake you looked as if you'd seen a ghost.'

Achilles went very still. It was as if she'd just slid a knife between his ribs to the deepest heart of him. The boat on the lake had precipitated that nightmare. Except it hadn't been a nightmare. It was real.

Sofie was frowning. 'What did I say? Are you okay?'

He realised that she obviously hadn't looked online for long enough to delve into his tragic family past. She'd only skimmed the first headlines and pictures that had popped up. The thought of her knowing what had happened…of how she would inevitably look at him with pity and compassion…made Achilles feel even more exposed.

Before he could respond to her question she was saying, 'Look, your life is your business. How you live… play… But it's made me realise that I really don't belong here.' She gestured vaguely around her. She sat forward. 'What happened on the island was amazing, but it came out of extreme circumstances. I think it should just end here. I've had a really nice time. I got to ride in a helicopter and private plane… But there's a train leaving for Glasgow in a couple of hours. I could be home by tonight if I take it. Tomorrow morning at the latest. Honestly, I don't mind. Clearly I'm a bit of a novelty, and I get it. But you're probably already regretting—'

Achilles put a hand over Sofie's mouth, stopping the torrent of words. He could feel her breath against his palm. The softness of her mouth. In spite of that sense of exposure he felt a stronger sense of resistance to her leaving.

He took his hand away. Then he said something he'd

never had to say to a woman before. 'I know. It's a lot to take in.'

She gave him a look as if to say, *You think?*

'You're a lot more than a novelty. I don't want you to go. Not yet.'

She looked doubtful.

He said, 'Look, you're here now. Give me one more night. And then, if you still want to go home tomorrow, I'll arrange it. Now I have to go and see my physician and have some tests done, just to make sure that I'm okay after the memory loss. But there's an event this evening. I'd like you to come with me.'

Now she looked suspicious. 'What kind of event?'

'A black-tie charity ball.'

'I'd love to—really. But I don't have anything remotely suitable to wear and it really isn't my scene. I think there's a tube stop not far from here, isn't there? I'm sure I saw one from the car—'

'Sofie.'

She stopped. For the first time in his life Achilles was actually not certain of an outcome. And he was pretty sure Sofie wasn't playing games. But he'd be a fool not to keep his wits about him.

He heard himself utter a word he'd never had to say to a woman before. 'Please.'

She sucked in a breath and searched his face, her eyes wide and full of concern. There was a long moment when he could see her wrestle with herself.

He said, 'Don't overthink it. Consider it a date.'

Sofie huffed a little laugh. 'The most lavish date in the world?'

He shrugged nonchalantly. 'Why not?'

Eventually her expression cleared. He saw the tension leave her shoulders. She said, 'Okay, then. One night.'

Achilles smiled. 'Good.' He was more relieved than he liked to admit at her acquiescence.

Now she looked worried again. 'I'll have to get a dress.'

He was back on familiar territory. 'Leave that to me.'

'I don't want you paying for me.'

'Trust me,' he said. 'I know what will be expected. It's one night. Let me do this. You put me up in your home, took care of me.'

Sofie blushed. 'I feel like I took advantage of you.'

Achilles marvelled at the way her brain worked. So different from everyone he knew. He shook his head. 'If anyone was taking advantage it was me.'

'Okay, I'll let you get a dress, because you know better than me how these things work, but only if you hire it.'

Achilles held out a hand. 'Deal.'

Sofie put her hand into his, and before she could say anything he tugged her forward and cupped the back of her head, capturing her mouth with his. Letting her soft sweetness morph into something much more carnal and sexual.

She was falling into him, and he was ready to scoop her up and take her to the nearest soft flat surface, but then she pulled back. 'You have to go to the doctor.'

There was a discreet knock on the door.

Achilles called out with a bite of frustration, 'I'm coming.' He looked at Sofie. 'Do not move. I'll be back in a few hours. I'll have the dress delivered.'

'Okay.'

Sofie watched Achilles stand up and walk out. She'd been so ready to leave and go home just a short while before, beyond intimidated by what she'd seen when she'd searched for Achilles Lykaios online. So many pictures and headlines. Each one landing in her solar plexus like a punch to the gut.

World's richest industrialist makes a new acquisition!

Can anything stop Lykaios Industries from taking over the world?

Achilles Lykaios takes part in another death-defying stunt—how many lives does this man have?

Achilles Lykaios refuses to answer questions about his love life...

Achilles Lykaios plays as hard as he works...

This last headline was accompanied by pictures of Achilles attending a different glittering event every night of one week, each time with a different woman on his arm.

And yet more headlines:

Achilles Lykaios at world exclusive premiere with latest lover, top model Cassandra Nunez...

And then, mere days later...

Cassandra Nunez is seen out and about after split with Lykaios... 'The man is incapable of feeling anything. He's a robot.'

Sofie had felt sick as her head had filled with the image of the stunning dark-haired Spanish beauty. All flashing eyes, alluring curves and pouting mouth. She hadn't looked happy.

This definitely wasn't Sofie's world. But maybe it could be for just one more night. Achilles made it sound so simple. And, as intimidated as she was, she didn't want to walk away from him yet.

She knew that as soon as Achilles saw her in his milieu he would understand that she had to go home. But she vowed in that moment that she would see this experience as a portal into doing something about her ambitions to travel and see the world. To find meaningful work and maybe, one day, settle down and create the family she'd never experienced. And even if that didn't happen it would be okay. Because just being around Achilles made her feel a sense of worth and visibility that she'd never felt before, and she would always cherish that.

So, really, what harm was one more night living the fantasy?

A few hours later, after being given the all-clear from his doctor, but with no explanation as to how and why his memory had chosen to come back at that particular moment, Achilles strode back into his Mayfair townhouse, welcoming the distraction of wondering about Sofie. The thought of her having left by now sent a wave of rejection through his body. He wasn't ready to let her go. He'd asked her for one more night. She would stay for more. He was renowned for his powers of persuasion. In the bedroom and the boardroom.

He stopped at the door to the master suite. It was ajar.

Sofie was inside, because he'd instructed that she be put in his room. She was facing away from him and was wearing a black dress that was cut away to the middle of her bare back. Straight shoulders. That fall of inky black hair against her pale skin.

As if sensing him, she turned around and his breath caught in his throat. The dress was held up by a jewelled collar, but his eyes skimmed over that detail and down to where a keyhole cut-out exposed the voluptuous curves of her bare breasts.

Gathered at the waist, the dress fell to the floor in soft drapes. It was daring, yet simple and elegant. She wore minimal make-up and her hair was loose and artfully tousled.

When she spoke she sounded nervous. 'The stylist helped me with hair and make-up. I wouldn't have a clue about that sort of thing.' She picked at the sides of the hole at the front of the dress, as if to pull it closed over her breasts.

'Stop,' Achilles growled, suddenly feeling a little feral. 'It's meant to be like that.'

'I feel naked.'

Achilles walked towards her. 'Believe me, you're not naked enough.'

She blushed.

He stopped just in front of her, a little surprised at the powerful rush of need in his blood. Enough to make him *not* act on impulse. Not to rip open that collar so that the dress fell open and he could feast on her luscious breasts. *Later.*

'You look perfect. Plenty of women will be dressed in far more revealing dresses.'

'Achilles, are you really sure you want to do this? I mean it's not too late—there's another sleeper train—'

Unable to stop himself, Achilles stepped up to Sofie and stopped her words with his mouth, his hands on her small waist. The dress was silky and slippery under his hands, making his blood surge as he imagined what she would feel like under his fingers, between her legs where heat throbbed, how she would cry out when he tasted her.

Dizzy at the speed with which a mere kiss was about to morph into something far more carnal, Achilles pulled back. When he could speak he said, 'You are not leaving. Not yet.'

He took his hands off her waist. Her eyes looked a little blurry. Mouth pink.

'Okay. Not leaving.'

'I have to change. Why don't you wait for me downstairs? I won't be long.' First, he needed to take a very cold shower.

Sofie floated downstairs, her blood still rushing giddily through her veins after that kiss. She was unsteady in heels at the best of times, and these strappy sandals were vertiginous, so she was happy to sit and wait in the lounge, as suggested by another of Achilles's house staff.

Céline must have gone home… Sofie missed a familiar face in such intimidating surroundings.

When the stylist had suggested she try on this dress earlier, she'd protested. It had looked like a mere sliver of black silk on the hanger. It couldn't possibly be a full garment. But then she'd put it on and looked at herself in the mirror and had genuinely not recognised herself.

She'd never imagined she could look like this. Kind of…sleek and sultry. She looked down and saw the curves of her bare breasts and fought back the urge to pull the dress closed over them again.

As Achilles had pointed out, there would be women dressed in less. She wasn't a total hick—she read the gossip magazines like everyone else—so she knew what people wore to exclusive parties.

At that moment she heard low voices outside the room and stood up just as Achilles entered. Her legs immediately felt weak. He was wearing a classic black tuxedo and he'd shaved. He was all sharp angles and hard bones. And that beautiful mouth. But his hair was still a little overlong. He looked exactly like what he was. A modern-day titan of industry.

'Ready to go?'

'No,' Sofie responded honestly.

Achilles smiled and held out a hand. 'Trust me, it'll be fine.'

Sofie walked forward and put her hand in his. She very much doubted that, but she couldn't deny she was curious to get a little taste of a life she would never experience again after tonight.

'Close your mouth.'

This instruction was delivered with a dry tone. Sofie immediately clamped her mouth shut, feeling heat rise into her face. She couldn't help her awe and wonder, though. They were in one of the country's most famous museums, which had been transformed into a glittering, golden wonderland populated by a species of human that Sofie had never seen before. Tall, sleek, beautiful.

The air smelled rich. Rarefied. Waiters moved so smoothly through the crowd it was as if they were on invisible wheels. Did they get training to move like that?

Sofie wondered, just as Achilles took two glasses of champagne from one of the proffered trays and handed her a glass.

Sofie took a sip of the sparkling wine. Her second glass in one day. She'd only ever had sparkling wine before when she'd turned twenty-one, and it hadn't been champagne. •

At that moment a tall, beautiful woman glided out of the crowd to come and stand in front of Achilles. She was very blonde and very tall. And thin.

'Achilles,' she purred, 'where have you been hiding? You weren't at the opening of Nick's new club in Paris…'

She pouted, and looked so ridiculous that Sofie almost laughed. But then she realised the woman was being serious.

The woman flicked her a dismissive up-and-down glance and then fake-smiled. 'I'm sorry, I'm intruding. I didn't realise you'd brought your assistant this evening. No rest for the wicked, eh?'

Achilles snaked an arm around Sofie's waist and pulled her close. He said smoothly, 'She's not my assistant. Sofie MacKenzie, I'd like you to meet Naomi Winters.'

Sofie held out her right hand and smiled. 'Nice to meet you.'

The woman's eyes grew huge, and then she spluttered something unintelligible and melted back into the crowd.

Sofie hated to admit to the lance of insecurity and, worse, jealousy. 'One of your ex-lovers?' she asked.

Achilles made a sound. 'Please credit me with some discernment. That woman has edges sharper than a knife.'

That only made Sofie think of the ex-lover she had

seen online—the sultry Spanish beauty. *'The man is incapable of feeling anything.'*

She shivered slightly and Achilles's arm tightened. 'Cold?'

She looked up at him and felt dizzy at his beauty. No wonder the other woman had been so dismissive of Sofie. She must be standing out like a sore thumb. Sofie shook her head. 'I'm fine.'

She let Achilles take her hand and lead her deeper into the crowd towards where music was playing and tried to keep her mouth shut.

Sofie was in Achilles's arms on the dance floor. He was barely aware of the slow, jazzy music coming from the world-famous band. He was very aware of how Sofie felt in his arms. Soft and unbelievably sexy. He'd seen many people here this evening—contemporaries. Adversaries. Normally he would have engaged, but he'd found himself swerving away to steal more time with this woman.

Her reaction to their surroundings had been enthralling to him. She'd looked like a child in the middle of the world's most expensive toyshop. He was so used to this type of venue himself that he barely took them in any more. And everyone he knew affected the same blasé attitude. They wouldn't dare look impressed, even if they were.

Sofie was totally unaware of the social mores of a milieu like this. And in a way that should be a sign that perhaps she was right, and she should go home after one fantastical night, but still Achilles resisted.

He wanted more than one night.

He looked down at her. She was gaping at someone gliding past on the dance floor. He recognised her just as Sofie whispered, 'Do you know who that is? She won an Oscar last year!'

'Eyes up.'

Sofie dragged her gaze away and up to Achilles. He felt the effect of those huge dark blue eyes right in his gut. And lower.

She ducked her head. 'Sorry, I'm embarrassing you.'

He tipped up her chin with his finger and shook his head. 'No, you couldn't embarrass me. I'm enjoying it.'

A glint came into Sofie's eye, reminding him of that steely strength he'd noticed about her when they'd first met. She said, 'The novelty factor?'

'Not novel. Charming.'

'Oh, you're a smooth one.'

He found himself smiling, and it felt strange. He realised he was used to having to curb most of his emotions around women, not wanting them to get the wrong idea.

She looked a bit nervous. He found being able to read her equally enthralling. 'Spit it out.'

She bit her lip, and then she said, 'Earlier, I didn't see any mention of your family...parents...siblings...'

That knife was slicing back through his ribs. Achilles fought not to tense. 'My family are dead.'

The concern he'd imagined earlier came into Sofie's eyes and the knife between his ribs twisted. 'Oh, Achilles, I'm so sorry. I had no idea.'

He ungritted his jaw. 'It was a long time ago.'

Before she could keep looking at him like that or say anything else, he took her hand and led her off the dance floor.

She picked up her skirts and followed him. 'Where are we going?'

He looked back at her. 'Home. We've got one night and I don't intend to waste it.'

She was right. She didn't belong here. With him. But it was just for one more night. He would let her go tomorrow and get on with his life. Put her, the island and his brief memory lapse out of his head for good.

Achilles didn't say a word on the way back to the house. Sofie's brain buzzed as she tried to think of what he'd meant by his family being dead. The obvious, clearly— but had they all died at the same time? Parents? Siblings? Clearly it was traumatic, and he did not want to talk about it. And she was not in a position to question him. Not when she was here for just one more night.

She felt a pang near her heart at that thought.

She sneaked a glance at his granite-hard profile. It was unreadable. This man was hidden behind layers. A world away from the more approachable version of himself when he'd lost his memory. Then she felt guilty for comparing him to how he'd been before. This was who he was. Not that other man.

He might look remote, but she could feel the sizzle in the air and in her blood. Her hand was in his. Captured. She had no desire for him to free it.

One more night of this fantasy.

The car drew to a stop outside the house, and before the driver could open her door Achilles had got out and was there, holding out his hand again. She let him help her out. She was feeling breathless at the intensity he was exuding and she tried desperately to put out of her head all her questions about his family.

It didn't matter. Achilles and his life were too big

for her. They would have these few hours and then she would leave. Still in one piece.

Are you sure about that?

Her heart squeezed, as if to tell her that she'd become a lot more invested than she'd realised.

The front door to the house opened just as they reached it. Nothing as mundane as having to let himself in with a key for Achilles.

Sofie felt like giggling at the absurdity of it all. It was better than allowing herself to feel intimidated. But once they were in the dimly lit front hall and the staff member who had opened the door had melted away discreetly, Achilles turned to Sofie and she didn't feel like giggling any more. She felt a sense of urgency.

They moved towards each other at the same time, Sofie's arms reaching up and Achilles's hands funnelling into her hair. Mouths meeting, tongues tangling.

Sofie felt herself being lifted against Achilles's chest and then he was carrying her up the stairs to the bedroom, kicking open the door. Only putting her down by the bed. She was breathless, as if she'd been the one carrying him.

A couple of lamps were on, sending out golden haloes of light. Sofie barely noticed. Her hands itched to undress Achilles but she felt suddenly shy.

He shrugged off his jacket and it fell to the ground. He pulled apart his bow-tie and said, 'Undress me, Sofie.' As if he'd read her mind.

She lifted her hands to the buttons of his shirt, fingers clumsy as she moved down his chest, revealing the wide muscled expanse bit by torturous bit. She pushed apart the shirt and left her palms on his chest. It was warm and hard. Hair prickling her skin.

'Keep going.' His voice was rough.

Sofie's pulse jumped and her blood went on fire. She dropped her hands and put them to his trousers. Undoing the button and then the zip. She could feel the heat of him through the material. She grazed the ridge of his erection with her fingers and he sucked in a breath. She looked up. He looked at if he was in pain.

She opened her mouth to ask if he was okay, but he put his hands over hers. 'You're going to kill me before we've even started.'

Sofie blushed. She couldn't believe she had such an effect on a man like this. Especially after seeing him in his own habitat.

He finished opening his trousers and pushed them down off his hips, taking his underwear with them. He stood before her, naked and proud. Aroused. For her. It was enough to make her legs almost buckle.

Achilles put his hands on her shoulders and turned her around. He pushed her hair over one shoulder and she felt him undo the clasp at the back of the collar. The dress loosened around her chest and Achilles peeled it away, so now she was bared from the waist up.

He came and stood behind her, brought his hands around to her chest, cupping her breasts and moulding them to fit in his big palms. Thumbs scraping her hard nipples. She moaned. She'd thought the other morning— had it only been *this* morning?—that on recovering his memory he would leave and she would never experience his hands on her again.

She wanted to imprint this onto her memory like a brand, so she would never forget how he made her feel. So desired, so beautiful. So extraordinary when she was nothing special. Just a girl from a small island in Scotland.

Feeling that sense of urgency again, afraid she might see signs of the dawn heralding the next day already, Sofie turned around, dislodging Achilles's hands. She pressed close and reached up. 'Achilles, make love to me.'

He found the side clasp of her dress and undid it, and it fell in a pool of silk to the floor. Now she only wore skimpy underwear and her shoes. Achilles gently pushed her back onto the bed and tugged her underwear down, slipped off her shoes.

Draped over the edge of the bed, Sofie felt very naked and very decadent as Achilles's gaze moved over her. He took himself in his hand and started to stroke up and down. Sofie's eyes widened on him. He was so unashamedly sexy. She wished she had the confidence to sit up and replace her hand with his—but before she could even think about doing it he was moving towards the bed and she couldn't breathe.

She was about to move back a little on the bed when he said, 'Stay there.'

He disappeared from her view for a moment and she felt him pushing her legs apart, his big body resting between her thighs. Hands shaping her waist, coming under her buttocks. And then his breath was *there*, feathering over her heated flesh. Sofie moaned softly. He pressed kisses up along one inner thigh and then he put his mouth to her, hot breath and devilish tongue. Exploring and teasing her aching flesh. A hand reached up and squeezed her breast, fingers trapping a nipple.

That was all it took to send Sofie flying over the edge, her whole body pulsating on the crescendo of an orgasm so intense that when Achilles moved and replaced his mouth with his erection, seating himself deep, Sofie climaxed again.

She looked up at Achilles, dazed. Drowning in pleasure. The expression on his face was intent as he moved in and out slowly, letting her get used to his body. He was big. Stretching her wide. But she wanted more already. Again.

He lifted her leg and his movements became more urgent, harder. Sofie embraced it and wrapped her other leg around his waist. 'Achilles…' she breathed, just needing to say his name. As if that could keep her anchored when every part of her was spinning wildly out of control.

Achilles's big body tensed and jerked against Sofie's. She could feel him deep inside, her legs stretched wide around his hips. And as his body released its own climax she responded with another spontaneous wave of pleasure, muscles contracting powerfully around his. An age-old dance that Sofie had no choice but to submit to.

For a long moment Achilles's weight crushed her to the bed. She felt as if she never wanted to move again. But eventually he did. She winced a little when her muscles didn't seem to want to release him. Everything in her wanted to cling to this moment.

He manoeuvred them onto the bed properly and drew a sheet over Sofie's deeply sated body. She could barely move, and was asleep before she could notice that Achilles looked at her for a long time, before he got up, threw on some clothes and left the bedroom.

CHAPTER SIX

WHEN SOFIE WOKE she was disorientated for a moment. There was a heavy feeling in her body and a hum of noise outside. She kept her eyes closed and frowned, trying to place it. And then her eyes snapped open.

Traffic. London. Last night.

She was alone in the bedroom with a sheet pulled over her naked body. She remembered Achilles pulling it over her and after that…nothing.

Along with waking came another realisation. *It was over.* They'd had their one night. She would get up, walk out, enter the world of mortal people again and go back to her wee island and try to forget about—

There was a knock on the door and Sofie sprang up to sit clutching the sheet around her. 'Yes? Hello?'

The door opened and it was Céline, with a breakfast tray. Sofie was so glad to see a familiar face that she smiled. The young woman came in and put down the tray on the other side of the rumpled bed.

Sofie realised she must look a sight—she could feel that her hair was all over the place. Her smile faded. 'I could have come downstairs…there's no need for this effort.'

'Don't be silly—it's no problem.' The girl gave her

a look before going to the curtains and drawing them open fully.

Sofie squinted a little in the bright sunlight. She interpreted Céline's look and said, 'Ah, I guess this is the routine?'

The girl came back and stood at the end of the bed. Now she looked a little embarrassed. 'It's a courtesy usually offered...' She trailed off.

Sofie made a face and picked up a grape. 'Don't worry—you don't have to say it. I'm under no illusions that I'm the first woman to appear in Achilles's bed.'

Céline's expression was half confirmation and half pity. Sofie wasn't the first by a long stretch, and she wouldn't be the last. That galvanised her to get moving. After all, Achilles hadn't even stuck around to say goodbye. He might not even be in the country any more!

But before she could do anything Céline gestured to the tray. 'There's a note for you from Mr Lykaios.'

The girl left the room.

Sofie looked at the tray and saw a folded piece of paper nestling against a small vase with a posy of flowers. She opened it out, fully expecting to see a message saying something like *Bye, now. Enjoy your life, Sofie. Don't call me, I'll call you. Never.*

But it said:

Good morning. I have to attend a meeting at my offices, but I would like to talk to you. Please wait for me at the house? I won't be long. A

Sofie's heart thumped. He wanted to see her before she left. Suddenly there were butterflies in her belly when a moment ago she'd been planning a quick and as elegant an exit as possible, considering she would be doing a kind of walk of shame to the nearest tube station and getting the train back up north.

She realised she was still sitting naked but for a sheet in Achilles's bed. And she had no idea if his *I won't be long* meant he was about to walk back through the door any second. Sofie took a quick, fortifying gulp of coffee and then sprang from the bed and into the bathroom, washing herself in record time.

Thankfully the bedroom was still empty when she re-emerged and quickly dressed in a pair of jeans and a sleeveless top. She dug her feet into wedge sandals and pulled her hair back roughly.

When she went downstairs it was quiet. She wondered what happened in this house if Achilles wasn't in residence? It seemed very wasteful—but then what did Sofie know about the requirements of international billionaires?

With no one in sight, Sofie gave in to a slightly rogue urge to explore and went towards a door that was partially open. When she peeked inside she could see that it was a study. Shelves lined the walls from floor to ceiling and a big window looked out over a lawn.

There was a faint musty smell in the air, as if the room wasn't used much, and an even fainter smell of tobacco. Sofie noticed framed pictures on a wall behind the desk and went over. They were mostly of a handsome couple. Both dark-haired, the man was tall and dashing and the woman was…stunning. Not just because she was physically beautiful but also because she was smiling, grinning. They looked so happy it was almost palpable.

Sofie put her hand to her chest, where her heart ached a little.

There was another picture of the man, this time on the deck of a small boat with a young boy of about ten who was holding a big fish aloft with a massive grin on his face. Again their happiness leapt out of the frame and touched Sofie.

Was this Achilles? And his father?

She admonished herself. It was none of her business— as Achilles had made quite clear.

A sound from behind her made her whirl around guiltily. It was Céline. Sofie said, 'I'm sorry. The door was open and I was curious.'

Céline said, 'Don't worry about it…the door is usually locked. I just came to tell you that Mr Lykaios is on his way home, if you want to wait in the lounge?'

Sofie followed Céline to the lounge, even more curious now about the room and why it wasn't in use. Why it was normally locked? She told herself again it was none of her business. She switched her mind to Achilles and what he might want. If he was coming to say goodbye in person it would make it harder to walk away. But, as civil and gentlemanly as he was, he didn't strike her as the type of person to go out of his way to bid adieu to a temporary lover.

On that slightly uncharitable thought, Sofie heard a noise outside and footsteps. She couldn't help the little jump of her heart and the buzzing in her solar plexus. Honestly, it was ridiculous. As if she needed more evidence of how out of her depth she was in this place, she had the reactions of a teenager in the full throes of a crush.

The door opened and Achilles filled the frame in a pristine three-piece suit complete with tie. Every bit of Sofie's skin prickled with awareness and excitement.

'Morning.' Her voice sounded rusty.

'Good morning.' He closed the door behind him. 'Thank you for waiting to see me.'

'That's okay. It's not as if I'm in a huge rush...' *To get back to my lonely house on the island.*

For the first time in Sofie's life she was aware of how lonely her life was. Not the best epiphany to be having in front of a man who was going out of his way to be polite and say goodbye in person.

Sofie felt she should make it easier on him. She said, 'You really didn't have to interrupt your day to come back here. We don't have to do this in person.'

Achilles arched a brow. 'You would be happy to leave without saying goodbye?'

Guilt and heat filled Sofie. 'Well, no, obviously I didn't mean it like that... It's just that if you were too busy, that would have been okay with me.'

'You don't put much value on yourself.'

That put a hitch in Sofie's chest. She felt simultaneously surprised at his perspicacity and defensive. 'I have plenty of value for myself... I just don't like to put people out.'

He's right, though, isn't he? a little voice said.

Sofie thought about how she never asked for anything. Or let people know her dreams. Preferring to fade into the background, as if apologising for her presence. Not wanting to take up space, to remind her parents of their lack of family.

'There's something I should explain,' he said.

Sofie shook her head, dislodging her unwelcome thoughts. 'Why do you need to explain anything?'

'I didn't go to Scotland just to clear my head. It was

to escape—get off the grid for a while to dim the heat of a news story about me.'

Sofie recalled the salacious headlines she'd seen and remarked dryly, 'It must have been pretty dramatic to force you to make that decision.' She remembered how she'd suggested he was burnt out. The thought was laughable.

Achilles made a face. 'It wasn't anything that would have fazed me before, but things have changed recently.'

Sofie sat on the arm of a chair. 'Like what?'

He hesitated, and she had the sense that he resented having to spell this out, because he wasn't used to having to explain his motives or actions to anyone. The thought gave her some sense of satisfaction. Of some kind of control being restored.

He said, 'Like the fact that my actions have a direct effect on my business and my employees. Apparently my bad reputation has exceeded its sell-by date and people are less willing to indulge me. I couldn't care less what people think, but when opinion starts affecting my bottom line it's time to reassess.'

Sofie squinted at him. 'So no more jumping out of planes?'

Achilles was dry. 'Apparently it doesn't inspire confidence in my commitment to Lykaios Industries.'

Or yourself, Sofie was tempted to add, still smarting a little after his own insight into her self-esteem, or lack of it.

He said, 'I know a very high-profile couple—not well, but well enough. She wants a divorce. He doesn't. The woman used my name in her reasons for wanting to divorce, exploiting my notoriety as a way to bring her very conservative husband as much adverse public exposure as possible.'

Sofie's mouth opened. 'But you—?'

He was already shaking his head and Sofie had to admit to a flash of relief.

'No, of course not. I don't get involved with married women. Apparently it was actually their pool boy, but he's an unknown. I decided to absent myself from the scene to take the heat out of the story and in the end, after a warning from my legal team, she dropped the claim.'

'Okay...' Sofie was wondering why Achilles was telling her all this now. 'What does this have to do with me?'

Achilles looked at Sofie. Last night he'd been fully prepared to say goodbye to her. One last night. She didn't belong here, and he shouldn't have led her on by asking her to come to London with him. He should cut it off now. Let her go. Get on with his life.

But...he couldn't. Last night had only proved that he wanted her with a passion he hadn't felt in a long time. If ever. So, as a man who had never denied himself anything pleasurable, why would he start now?

She was a grown woman. As long as he was very clear about what to expect, if she decided to stay then there should be no concerns.

'There's an event in a few days on one of the Greek islands. It's an art exhibition showcasing some of the world's biggest artists. The woman who was naming me in her bid for a divorce will be there and, while she's no longer using my name, the rumours made some waves and it would deflect the lingering gossip if I had someone with me.'

'Me...?'

'Yes.' Achilles cursed silently. Usually he was a lot more suave about getting his message across. Women usually met him halfway. More than halfway. Eager to pick up any crumb he threw them.

'I want you to stay, Sofie, and come with me.'

She blinked. Her cheeks coloured. 'I… You want me to stay just because you need a date to create a diversion from gossip and this woman?'

Her lilting Scottish accent caught at Achilles's gut. He cursed inwardly again. 'It's not just that. I don't want you to go. I'm not ready to let you go.'

Again, not words that Achilles had ever uttered to a woman. But this was different. Sofie was different. She would understand what he meant. She wouldn't get the wrong idea.

'I'm not ready to let you go.'

But I will be as soon as I don't want you any more.

Sofie picked up the message hidden between his words loud and clear. A pang of vulnerability reminded her of the loneliness she'd always felt. The loneliness waiting in the wings. She would be mad to pretend it didn't exist.

She felt very clearly in that moment that if she left now she might, just *might*, be able to get on with her life and put him behind her. But if she stayed and succumbed to the all too seductive temptation to revel in his attention for longer, it would be a different story.

She shook her head. 'I don't know if that's a good idea.'

Achilles took off his jacket and pulled at his tie, undoing it. He came towards Sofie and she stood up, every part of her body quivering with anticipation. A little voice mocked her. *It's already too late.*

But he stopped a couple of feet away. 'When was the last time you took a holiday?'

Sofie's mind was blank for a moment. Then she said, 'I went to Edinburgh for a weekend with my mother before she died.'

He shook his head. 'No, I mean the kind of holiday where there is nothing asked of you except that you are indulged. Where the sun warms your whole body from the inside out and when it gets too much you jump into the refreshing waves of the sea or the pool. Where by the evening your skin is golden and sandblasted. Where you eat the finest, freshest foods and get drunk on the best wines. Where the sunsets colour the entire sky in red and gold.'

Sofie desperately resisted the picture he was painting. It was far too compelling. She folded her arms across her chest. 'Gallinvach has some amazing sunsets too, you know.'

His mouth quirked, as if he knew he was getting to her. He came closer, but still kept a little distance between them. He cupped her elbows with his hands and tugged her gently towards him. She could smell him… that unique and very masculine scent. It was probably bespoke, made especially for him.

He said, 'I don't think you've ever been indulged, Sofie. Let me indulge you. Let me spoil you. Let's enjoy this chemistry, because it is rare and it won't last for long. I need someone by my side and we still want each other. Let's have some fun.'

Fun. There it was. The explicit warning. It untangled something inside Sofie. At least he wasn't making her any promises. Leading her on to think that something was going on here more than pure physical compatibility. Lust. And when was the last time she'd had *fun?* She felt a pang. She didn't know if she'd ever really had fun in her life.

If Achilles hadn't appeared in a hospital bed on her tiny island, in a coma, then right about now Sofie would probably be changing a bed or cleaning out toilets. And—not that she'd resented that work for a second—something inside her chafed at the life she'd been living. Doing menial work that didn't ask her to step out of the shadows or question what she wanted. Using her grief as a shield to hide behind.

She knew she should resist prolonging this fantasy. She knew she didn't belong here. But his words were weaving a spell around her and inside her. Luring her further along the path. *'Let me spoil you.'* Words that she'd never heard in her life. *'Let me indulge you.'* It was shockingly decadent. The thought of being indulged. Spoiled.

Achilles was looking at her. Really looking. He saw her in a way no one else ever had, not even her parents. It was dangerous. But it was also exhilarating. Too exhilarating. Fatally, she knew she couldn't resist. She wanted to have fun.

'Okay.'

Achilles's hands tightened on her elbows. 'Yes?'

Sofie nodded. He tugged her towards him and pulled her right into his body. Everything melted and went on fire at the same time. Sofie undid her arms and put her hands on Achilles's chest.

Achilles looked at her mouth and then kissed her,

stealing her breath and her sanity. When he pulled back it took a second for her eyes to open. She felt dizzy.

'What happens now?'

Achilles said, 'Now we go to Athens.'

'What are you smiling at?'

Sofie looked at Achilles on the other side of her in the back of the car. 'I was thinking that I've been completely spoilt…flying by private jet before I've even been on a commercial flight.'

Achilles shrugged. 'It's the most practical way to travel for me.'

Sofie rolled her eyes. 'No, you just travel like that because you can.'

'If you're thinking of giving me a lecture about climate change, don't. My plane is being used in an experiment to pioneer more eco-friendly fuels.'

'Very commendable.' Sofie tried to stop herself smiling at Achilles's defensive tone.

He reached for her, tugging her across the back seat towards him. 'Have I met the one woman in the world who literally cannot be impressed by me, or anything I do?'

Sofie felt light and buoyant—a totally alien sensation. 'On the contrary, parts of you are very…impressive.'

Sofie's hand was resting on Achilles's thigh and she moved it a little higher. He caught her hand in his, trapping it. His jaw tightened but there was a glint in his eye. 'You'll pay for that.'

He caught the back of her head with his other hand and pulled her towards him, covering her mouth with his. He took her trapped hand and brought it to where his anatomy was responding very impressively.

Sofie melted into him, her fingers exploring the hard flesh under her hand, under his clothes.

It was only when there was a discreet but persistent cough that Achilles pulled back and broke the kiss.

Sofie opened her eyes and blinked. They were outside what looked like an exclusive hotel. She sprang back when she realised people were moving about just outside the car.

Achilles said roughly, 'Don't worry, the windows are tinted.'

Still… She felt exposed. And, worse, when she saw the elegance and refinement of the women entering the hotel she felt thoroughly and utterly out of place. The driver was outside the car, clearly waiting for a movement from Achilles before opening the door. Her face flamed. Maybe he was used to this kind of thing because it happened on such a regular basis? She cursed herself. *Not* the time to be getting paranoid and jealous.

Achilles adjusted his clothing and was about to open the door when Sofie grabbed his arm. He looked at her. 'They won't let me into that place looking like this!' she said. 'I look like a bag lady compared to those women.'

Two women were walking past in clothes that screamed *designer*.

Achilles just took her hand, opened his door, and pulled her out behind him. Immediately there was a suited official-looking man approaching them. 'Mr Lykaios, we are so happy to have you back with us again. Everything is ready for you in your apartment.'

Sofie kept silent but absorbed that fact. He had an apartment in a *hotel?* How decadent.

Achilles said something to the man, who looked at Sofie and then away again, then said, 'Of course, right away.'

Achilles was leading Sofie into the most palatial space she'd ever seen. Vast. Built out of what looked like golden-hued marble. There were tables with flower displays as big as small trees. Elaborate chandeliers sparkled and glittered high in the ceiling. And all around them milled the kind of people Sofie had seen at the event in London. Except this time they weren't in evening dress. Most of the men were in suits, and even if they weren't in suits they were in elegantly casual clothes.

A woman walked past her in a white trouser suit, dripping in diamonds and leaving a cloud of strong perfume in her wake. A bellboy followed her with a trolley full of monogrammed luggage.

Sofie couldn't help sneezing when the scent stuck in the back of her nose. A few people looked around. She went puce. Achilles led her into a lift. The doors closed.

Sofie said, 'These people don't even sneeze, do they?'

Achilles leaned back against the mirrored wall of the lift. He was blocking her view of herself and she was glad. People probably thought she was his assistant, like that woman had in London.

His mouth quirked. 'They're as mortal as you and me, even if they don't like to think they are.'

'I don't think you've thought this through, Achilles.' She had to say it, as much as it pained and humiliated her. 'Even if you dress me up in a nice dress, I'm going to stick out like a sore thumb among these people.'

'Which is why I've arranged for you to be pampered tomorrow.'

The lift doors opened before she could fully absorb what that might mean, and he caught her hand again and pulled her straight into a vast reception room. Sofie gasped. It was exquisitely furnished. Expensive antiques perched on shelves and small tables. They were probably priceless. There were murals on the ceiling. Cherubs and birds and clouds.

Achilles led her over to a set of French doors and let her hand go to open them. The heat slapped her in the face, much as it had when she'd stepped off the plane. She felt overdressed. The sun thankfully wasn't too high in the sky as it was early evening. Sofie walked out onto a wide terrace bordered by a stone wall. Straight ahead of her, on a hill, was the Acropolis.

She'd caught glimpses of it on her way through the ancient city in Achilles's car, but to see it like this was... breathtaking. Tourists as small as ants clambered all over the site.

'It's so majestic,' Sofie said quietly. Awed.

Achilles came and stood beside her. She looked at him. He'd taken off his suit jacket and his tie and had opened a button, rolled up his sleeves. His profile was regal. He looked like what he was: a Greek god of a man, back where he belonged.

Below them, the Athens streets thronged with people and traffic. A giddiness at finding herself here rose up inside Sofie. She turned to Achilles. 'Thank you.'

He looked at her. 'For what?'

She waved a hand around her. 'For this. For bringing me here.'

His expression became quizzical, as if he'd never seen her before. 'But we haven't even left the apartment yet.'

Sofie looked back out at the view. 'It's enough—believe me. I've never seen anything like this.'

He took her hand and raised it to his mouth. 'Then you'd better get used to it.'

His mouth on her hand made her pulse trip. Achilles pulled her closer and looked down. 'First, we need to get you out of those clothes. I plan on burning them, if you're not too attached?'

Sofie felt like giggling. 'But then I'll be naked.'

When it was like this with just the two of them, in spite of the fantastical surroundings, she could almost believe he was the man he'd been before his memory had returned. Less stern. Carefree.

Achilles responded, 'You say that like it's a bad thing.'

'Um… I don't know if the elegant specimens who inhabit your world are quite ready for the reality of an average body.'

He pulled back for a moment and looked her up and down. When he looked into her eyes her knees felt weak. His gaze was smouldering. 'Your body is far from average—and, believe me, I know.'

That struck like a sharp dart. A compliment inside a reminder of who she was with. An international billionaire playboy with more sexual experience than she would probably accrue in two lifetimes. She pushed her misgivings aside. She knew who he was now. She knew this was just a temporary indulgence.

'Come here,' Achilles commanded.

Sofie let him pull her into his arms and kiss her, moulding her body with his hands as if she was some precious thing. *This* was what was so dangerous and what she couldn't resist. So she didn't.

Later that evening, after the sun had set, with a lingering hum of pleasure in his blood Achilles sat in a chair on the terrace and let the sounds of Athens wash over him.

He'd showered and thrown on a pair of faded jeans and a loose shirt. It felt good to have his own things again.

People were laughing far below. Shouting. Cars honking. Alarms. And above it all, lit up, the Acropolis presided eternally over this teeming city.

Achilles had mixed feelings about being back in Athens. He always had mixed feelings in his home country. Because he loved and resented it all at the same time.

Diverting his mind away from the shadows, he thought of the awe and delight on Sofie's face earlier, when she'd said *Thank you*. Just for bringing her here. Nothing else. Not for jewellery, or clothes. For an experience that most took for granted.

That he'd taken for granted for years. More than taken for granted. He'd treated his privilege with a cavalier attitude that pricked at his conscience now.

Irritated with his line of thought and the fact that he seemed to have developed a conscience along with the return of his memory, Achilles got up and went inside, pouring himself a shot of whisky. It burned down his throat. He hadn't come back here to examine his conscience. He'd come to repair his reputation, to continue building Lykaios Industries into the most successful company in the world, and to prove to everyone that he wasn't a messed-up product of his past.

So far, so on track. And with a lover warming his bed who would only enhance his plans. A totally unexpected lover. Someone inexperienced and yet someone who made him feel like a novice.

Achilles's body was already responding to the recent memory of how she'd straddled him, taking him so deep he'd seen stars. The way she'd moved, getting used to the sensation of riding him. Killing him in the process.

It had taken all his restraint and skill not to explode like a virgin with his first woman.

He'd shaped her beautiful full breasts, his hands moving down to that small waist and then to her hips, holding her still, finally, because he had reached the limit of his control.

He cursed and poured another shot of whisky, and then walked out to the terrace again, to try and get some oxygen to his brain. In spite of the heat from the drink filling his throat and belly, he felt a cold finger trail its way down his spine as something occurred to him.

Was he being taken for a ride—literally—by someone who had seen him in a moment of weakness and decided to use it to her advantage? She might come from an island on the edge of Europe, but she couldn't be *that* pure and sweet...

The memory of her awe and gratitude earlier mocked him now. Was he the biggest fool to have brought her here? To have believed everything she'd uttered? To have believed in the picture of innocence she'd presented, thanks to her humble job and her home on that small rural island? After all, she had shown little hesitation in agreeing to let him stay with her. Maybe even then she'd been hedging her bets and taking a gamble on Achilles being indebted to her? Maybe she'd counted on him as a means of escape from the drudgery of her life?

He'd instructed his team to look into her earlier, but instead of making him feel more in control it had made him feel guilty. Ridiculous. Achilles never second-guessed himself. If anything, it was proof he was doing the right thing and was right to be on his guard around her.

He thought of something she'd said when he'd offered

to get her a dress in London: *'I feel like I took advantage of you.'* Perhaps she'd meant it literally, and had been all but telling him that he was being a fool, guided by his hormones rather than his well-honed instincts.

He felt a slight surge of revolt in his belly to be casting Sofie in this light, but he pushed it down ruthlessly. No. He did not regret bringing her here—after all, he wanted her more than he'd ever wanted another woman and he would not deny himself that pleasure—but from now on he wouldn't let himself forget who he was and who he'd become out of necessity. Because he knew the world wasn't fair, and he knew that if he let his guard drop for a minute he could be annihilated.

At that moment, as if on cue, he heard a noise.

Sofie.

CHAPTER SEVEN

ACHILLES LOOKED AROUND from where he was standing with the glass in his hand on the terrace. He tried to curb his response but it was useless.

Sofie was a few feet away, swaddled in a robe, black hair tumbled around her shoulders. She looked sleepy and sexy and delicious. *And potentially treacherous*, reminded a voice.

She smiled shyly. 'Hi, I didn't hear you leave the bed. What time is it?'

'It's late...after midnight.'

She looked embarrassed. 'We never even had dinner.'

Achilles steeled himself against this portrait of innocence. He had to. 'I can order food up now, if you're hungry?'

She shook her head. 'No, don't put anyone to that kind of trouble. I can wait for breakfast.' She came out to the terrace and gave him a look. 'Are you okay? You seem...tense.'

'I'm fine.'

Sofie asked, 'What are you drinking?'

Achilles cursed silently. He would be wise not to take Sofie's innocent persona at face value, but he didn't need to lose sight of his manners in the process.

'It's whisky—would you like some?'

'Maybe just a little, with some water—thanks.'

Achilles went and poured her a small glass and brought it back, handed it to her. Noted her small hands and neat unvarnished nails.

She went over to the wall and held the glass in both hands looking out over the view. 'It's so warm even at night. It's lovely.'

He went and stood beside her.

She said, 'My father used to give me a dram of whisky on special occasions. I had my own wee glass for it.'

Achilles said, 'I drank a bottle of whisky when I was fifteen and I was sick for a week.'

Sofie looked at him, eyes wide. 'Why on earth did you do that?'

Achilles shrugged and fought not to remember the awful sense of rage and recklessness he'd felt in those years. 'A dare at school.'

'I'm surprised you still drink it after that experience. It'd be enough to put anyone off.'

He lifted his glass. 'I learnt to respect it.'

Sofie turned her back to the view and leaned against the wall. 'So this is where you live? Or do you have another home here? A family home?'

Achilles's skin prickled. 'This is where I live when I'm in Greece.'

'You own this apartment, then, in a hotel?'

He nodded. 'Why so curious?'

She looked a little embarrassed. 'Sorry... I just thought that, coming from Greece, you'd have a family home here.'

He thought of the island that housed his family home. He'd been back to the island, but he hadn't visited the property since that fateful day. He'd sold every other property but that one and the property in London, something always stopping him at the last minute.

'Actually, the house in London was more of a family home. I went to school in England and spent a lot of time there.'

The London townhouse had been in his family for a couple of generations. His mother had loved it. He'd loved it as a child. Playing in the garden with the dog. Going to the zoo with his father—just the two of them, because his brother and sister had been too small.

'Ah...that makes sense.'

'What's that supposed to mean?' Achilles welcomed this diversion from his memories.

Sofie wrinkled her nose. 'Not that I'm acquainted with many men of your...er...status, but I'd kind of assumed you might own a flash penthouse apartment.'

'Isn't that a bit of a cliché?' Achilles was amused, but also wary. Her perspicacity only seemed to be confirming that he was right to be more suspicious than he had been.

She shrugged. A small rueful smile played around her mouth. 'Clearly I've read too many books featuring clichéd characters.'

They were silent for a couple of minutes, letting the sounds of the city wash up and over them. In spite of himself Achilles could feel himself start to relax. It was so easy to forget everything when he was with her.

He could sense her building up to saying something. She looked at him.

'There was a room in the house in London...the door was open and I went in. It was a study.'

Achilles's insides turned to ice. He said nothing.

His father's study.

She continued, 'I know I shouldn't have been in there...but I saw a picture on the wall—a couple of pictures. Your parents? And you and your father on a boat with a fish?'

Images flooded Achilles's head. The boat. His parents on board with his younger brother and sister. He on another smaller launch, headed back to Athens. They'd all been waving at him, and then his brother and sister had unfurled a banner that read *We'll see you soon, Achilles! We love you very much!*

And then...

Before Sofie could say another word, Achilles responded curtly, 'My family are not up for discussion. Like I said, they're dead.'

She looked contrite. 'Of course. I'm sorry. I'm too nosy for my own good.'

Full of volatile emotions, mixed with the passion he couldn't control around her, Achilles said, 'Yes, you are...but I know just the punishment.'

He caught the lapels of her robe and pulled her to him, needing desperately to remind them both of why she was here and to get rid of unwelcome memories.

He felt a moment of nostalgia for the peace he'd felt while his memory had been gone. No toxic history. No grief. No loss. No pain. The only way he could achieve that state again was right now and here.

He undid Sofie's robe and it fell open.

She gasped, 'Someone will see us.'

He took the glass out of her hand and put it down. Then he pushed the robe off her shoulders completely and it fell to the ground, baring her. She was exquisite. And already the heat of desire was burning away the past.

She covered her breasts with her arms and Achilles gently pulled her arms away. 'No one can see. Trust me.'

Sofie glanced around, but he already knew there were no high-rise buildings around them. She looked at him, and for a moment the way she looked at him so trustingly almost undid all his recent rationale. *Almost.* But he was stronger than that.

He traced his hands down her arms and saw how her nipples pebbled into hard points. He led her over to a chair and sat her down. He went down onto his knees in front of her and pushed her thighs apart, baring her to his gaze.

His erection strained at his jeans but he ignored it, set to showing Sofie all he was interested in. Pleasure. Nothing but pleasure.

'Okay, Sofie, you can turn around now.'

Sofie turned and looked at the reflection in the mirror and stopped breathing. She looked…she looked so different. And yet the same.

She was wearing a long black dress with a black mesh panel between her breasts. There was a diamanté detail down the edging of the front of the dress and under her chest, framing her waist. It fell in loose flowing folds to the floor, chiffon overlaying silk. She could see a tantalising glimpse of her cleavage through the mesh at the front of the dress.

It was sexy, and modern, and had a rock and roll edge that she never in a million years would have considered might suit her. Black patent heels with distinctive red soles were on her feet, adding a couple of much-needed inches to her height.

Her hair had been trimmed by a few inches. A lot of the heaviness had been taken out, so now it feathered over her shoulders in a wavy, choppy style. But it was the make-up that really made her look a little closer. Her eyes looked huge, framed by dramatic kohl, dark eyeshadow and lots of mascara. And her mouth was very red. Had her lips always been so…full? And her waist so small?

Sofie had always been aware of men's interest in her, and she'd put it down to the curves that were out of proportion with her frame. She knew she was no great beauty. But now, for the first time, she had a sense that Achilles saw something in her that she'd never had the confidence to acknowledge herself.

Ridiculously, she felt emotion rising and swallowed it down, conscious of the stylist and the hair and make-up people who had appeared in the apartment just a couple of hours ago, after she'd spent a morning in the hotel spa, being massaged and generally primped and plucked in places that had never been primped and plucked before.

She hadn't seen Achilles all day. He'd been gone that morning, leaving a note detailing the spa appointments, and telling her that he would see her this evening and that they had a 'small function' to attend.

If this dress was evidence, his idea of a 'small function' was something that required full evening dress.

A woman appeared in the door. She'd been in the kitchen that morning and had introduced herself as Elena, Achilles's housekeeper. Elena caught Sofie's eye now and said, 'Mr Lykaios is running late. The driver will take you to the venue and he will meet you there.'

Immediately Sofie felt panicked, but the woman disappeared before she could ask what she should do if she couldn't find him, or if she would even be admitted if she was on her own. In a foreign city. Where she didn't speak the language.

The stylist touched her arm. 'You look stunning. Mr Lykaios will be there to meet you, I'm sure.'

Sofie smiled gratefully. 'Is it that obvious I'm not used to this?'

The woman smiled, but it was a little awkward, and Sofie felt a dull flush rising when she realised that probably this woman had come here before, to dress Achilles's other lovers.

Good, she told herself stoutly. She needed reminders like this so she didn't get completely lost in the fantasy.

The stylist became businesslike. 'I've left the rest of your clothes in the dressing room. We were instructed that you needed to have a range of casual daywear and evening clothes. If you need anything else, please don't hesitate to call. Here is the jewellery for this evening, and your bag.'

She pointed to a pair of diamond earrings, a chunky diamond bracelet and a black clutch bag.

Sofie touched them reverently, and then something occurred to her and she pulled her hand back as if burned. 'They're real, aren't they?'

'Of course.' The stylist almost sounded insulted.

'I can't wear these—what if I lose an earring?'

'Don't be silly. You must accessorise, and if you don't wear precious stones, everyone will notice. And,' the stylist added with a flourish, 'you'll need to wear this.'

Sofie took the mask handed to her. It was black, with tiny diamond detail around the edges, and an elastic band to hold it to her head. 'What's this for?'

'It's a masquerade ball.'

Sofie's levels of anxiety shot up another few notches at the words *masquerade* and *ball*.

The stylist and her team left and Sofie, after a moment's hesitation, put on the jewellery. The earrings felt heavy and the bracelet even heavier.

At that moment Elena appeared again. 'The driver is waiting outside when you're ready, Miss MacKenzie.'

'Please, call me Sofie,' she said, before the woman disappeared again. Being constantly called *Miss MacKenzie* wasn't helping her feel any more grounded.

Sofie took a deep breath and picked up the mask and the clutch bag. She wasn't near ready, but she didn't think she would ever feel ready for this world. She just had to enjoy the moment and try not to feel too intimidated.

Achilles saw her as soon as she entered through the central arch of one of Athens's most glamorous locations. An ancient temple that had been turned into an exclusive space for cultural and charity events.

He could actually have made it back to the apartment in time to pick her up, but at the last minute he'd decided it would be no harm to set in place some boundaries, some distance. So he'd resisted the urge to change his plans.

She looked very pale from a distance. Luminous, almost, next to the darker skin tones around her. The naturally sun-kissed skin of Athenians.

He could see that her hair looked lighter, slightly shorter. It sat in glossy waves over her shoulders. A mask covered the top half of her face, much like everyone else, but left the bottom half exposed. The plump outline of her mouth. The delicate jaw.

His insides tightened as he acknowledged just how

beautiful she was. Naturally. Her body was like a siren call. Curvy and shapely in a way that seemed almost provocative next to women who were as thin as stick insects.

And with an instinct born of years of tracking beautiful women he could see men noticing Sofie. Starting to circle her. As if this was not a civilised gathering but something far more elemental.

Before any of them could make a move, Achilles closed the distance between them and snaked an arm around her waist.

She tensed and looked up, and then relaxed again. 'It's you.'

'Sorry I had to let you arrive on your own.'

He realised he really meant it. He couldn't understand why he had thought it would be a good idea to put some space between them. He was fully in control of this situation, even if Sofie did turn out to have an agenda.

'I won't lie and say I'm not intimidated—this is so impressive. How do you ever get used to places like this?'

Achilles looked around at the spectacular surroundings and the monied glittering crowd. Like the party in London, it was a scene he'd experienced a million times before and would experience a million times more. No matter how many times he threw himself out of planes or down the steepest ski runs in Europe it seemed there was no escaping his destiny.

He felt jaded all of a sudden. An emptiness. And with that realisation came again that sense of something just out of reach. A thread of memory he hadn't recovered yet. Some revelation. Having Sofie by his side usually eclipsed that niggling sense of something still hidden, but not tonight.

A waiter came with a tray and Achilles let Sofie go momentarily to take two glasses of sparkling wine, hand-ing her one and shutting the rogue thoughts out of his head. He clinked his glass to Sofie's and regretted that half her face was obscured by the mask. He wanted to see those fascinating expressions.

His eyes drifted down over the dress and his blood heated even more. It showcased her sexy body to perfection. He said, 'You look…stunning.'

She blushed. Would she ever *not* blush?

Then she said, 'Thank you for arranging the spa treatments and the hair and everything. I hope it's made me more presentable.'

Achilles might have assumed she was fishing for compliments, but he knew she wasn't. 'Everyone is wondering who you are.'

'Because it's obvious I don't belong here.' She looked down.

Achilles put a finger under her chin and tipped it up. He acted on instinct, pressing a swift kiss to her mouth that had nothing to do with claiming her publicly and more to do with something far more disturbing. A need to reassure her.

He said, 'You're with me. You belong here just as much as these people around us.'

She looked up at him. Eyes wide and dark blue under her mask. For a second he thought he saw the sheen of moisture, but she blinked and it was gone. Her voice was husky, though, when she said, 'Thank you for that.'

He took Sofie's hand and led her into the crowd, determined to make the most of being seen with a new lover. And a wholly unexpected one at that.

The function in London hadn't remotely prepared Sofie for this. This was next level. The sheer opulence made her think of the Greek and Roman empires.

The air was thick with the scent of exotic flowers and a mixture of priceless manufactured perfumes and colognes.

At one point Achilles caught her wrinkling her nose and said, 'Okay?'

In spite of the majestic surroundings, Sofie was beginning to feel increasingly hot and suffocated. She said apologetically, 'I think I need to get some air, but you stay here. I'll find my way outside.'

'No, I'll—'

'Lykaios—there you are. We need to talk about the deal in New York. Where have you been for the last few weeks? No, don't tell me... I can only imagine...'

The man interrupting them barely glanced at Sofie. She sent a look to Achilles, telling him to stay, and stepped away before he could stop her. He let her go.

Sofie spied open doors in the distance and made her way through the crowd, who all seemed to be infinitely taller than her. When she got outside to a terrace she pulled off her mask and sucked in the evening air. It wasn't cool, but at least there was a bit of a breeze and she felt she could breathe again.

Manicured gardens stretched out before her. People were moving around the garden: women in long dresses, men in suits. If she closed her eyes and opened them again she could almost imagine she had slipped back a century. Flaming lanterns lit pathways. Fairy lights were strung along bushes and in trees. It was magical.

Classical music floated on the breeze from inside. She turned around and leaned back against the terrace wall. From here she could see Achilles as he easily stood head and shoulders above almost everyone else.

She thought of what he'd said to her: *'You belong*

here.' Not true, obviously, and yet emotion had risen before she could hide it. Hopefully she had, though. Achilles wouldn't understand how or why those words had impacted her so deeply.

To have a man like him really look at her, say such a thing and make her feel so *visible*, so wanted...it was more seductive than any designer dress, spa treatment or glittering event. And that was why she had to be so careful. A man like him was used to issuing platitudes to women. To saying what was required in the moment. He was an expert. It didn't mean anything.

And yet...the warm glow still burned in her belly.

She noticed now that he looked tense. Tense in a way he hadn't been on the island. But then that was to be expected when he had so much responsibility. An entire industry in his name.

He was talking to another man now and his jaw was tight. He must be so used to these kinds of situations that they barely impinged on his consciousness any more. That made Sofie feel sad. For him. That nothing impressed him any more. If it ever had.

She saw women circling Achilles, waiting for an opportunity. One came when the man he'd been talking to walked away. But just as one of the women approached Achilles looked around and caught Sofie's eye where she stood outside.

Without even acknowledging the woman, Achilles moved towards her. Sofie couldn't deny the very feminine thrill she felt that *she* was the object of his attention—however briefly. And in a place like this, surrounded by the most beautiful people in the world.

It was surreal and it was heady.

And it was about to get headier.

Achilles came close and pulled off his mask, revealing his face. He put hands either side of her on the wall, trapping her. 'I've had enough…ready to go?'

Sofie's heart thumped. 'But we only arrived a short while ago. Don't you need to talk to people? Network? Dance?'

'I don't need to do anything.'

Sofie rolled her eyes. 'You said yourself you need to improve your reputation. If we leave now it's hardly going to improve things.'

Achilles lifted her hand and raised it to his mouth, kissing her palm. It felt unbelievably erotic. As if he'd kissed a far more intimate part of her body.

'Perhaps,' he conceded. 'But when we appear in public again and again people will see that I'm reforming.'

Sofie was about to ask, *How many 'agains' will that be?* But she held her tongue. That way lay brutal truths she wasn't ready to face up to yet.

Weakly, she allowed Achilles to take her hand and lead her back through the throng.

People whispered as they passed by. Sofie tried not to be too self-conscious. She lifted her chin and thought to herself how exhausting it must be to be under this kind of scrutiny all the time.

The following day Achilles was working from the office in the apartment. Because he'd woken late. On account of indulging in a hedonistic night of sensual pleasure. It was something he was renowned for, but this time it was different.

Before, he would have walked away from the lover in question without a backward glance. Momentarily sated. He'd woken this morning to find the bed empty and had felt a gnawing sense of hunger. For Sofie. Again. Already.

He was insatiable. It had never been like this.

He'd found her eating breakfast and chatting to Elena, his housekeeper. As he'd come into the room Sofie had said, 'Did you know that Elena's son has just graduated with a law degree?'

Achilles had looked at the woman he'd only ever greeted in passing before, or issued instructions to. He had felt ashamed to admit in that moment that he'd had no idea if the woman was married, had family, or any other personal information.

Achilles had made an appropriate response, but it had been a reminder that Sofie came from another world, where a conversation between two people wasn't a transaction but a pleasantry. It wasn't an altogether unwelcome reminder.

She'd informed him that she intended to go sightseeing that day. 'I don't want to waste any time. There's so much to see.'

Achilles had found himself curbing an urge to tell her he'd go with her. He had too much to do. He couldn't afford to forget that he had a business that needed serious tending if it was to become even more successful.

He certainly couldn't afford to let a woman make him forget that.

He saw movement on the street far below. As if conjured up out of his imaginings, Sofie appeared outside the hotel.

Her jet-black hair was pulled up into a knot on the top of her head. She was wearing a simple dark blue sundress with a ruched bodice. Thin straps. It fell to just below her knee. Perfectly regular attire for this part of the world. But all he could see was acres of pale bare flesh. The slender slope of her shoulders. The back of her neck. Top of her back. Her shapely legs. Feet bare, in a pair of wedge sandals.

She had a bag across her body and was looking at a map. The doorman of the hotel went over to her and said something, and Achilles saw her grin and turn the map the right way around. He saw the effect of her smile on the doorman—normally a taciturn man, he was grinning now too. And pointing to somewhere in the distance.

As she waved and started to walk away Achilles felt a spurt of panic. He shouldn't let her go alone. Was she even wearing sunscreen?

A knock came on his door. He bit out a curt, 'Yes?'

'Your client is here for the meeting.'

Achilles had to battle for a long moment to restrain himself from throwing his schedule out and following Sofie into the streets of Athens. She would be fine. He'd already instructed his very discreet security guards to keep an eye on her in case she got lost.

She disappeared around a corner. Achilles turned away from the window. 'Send him in.'

'So where did you visit today?'

Sofie looked at Achilles, who was sitting to her right at a long dinner table on the open rooftop of a restaurant in the centre of Athens. Apparently the dinner tonight was in aid of a local charity. Thankfully it wasn't that formal an event.

Achilles was just wearing a simple suit with no tie, yet he still managed to look as if he'd stepped out of the pages of a men's magazine. She was wearing a black jumpsuit that was cut so low that she'd been in the process of taking it off again when Achilles had appeared in the bedroom and said, 'No, leave it on.'

What he'd meant was that *he* would take it off her and then make love to her and then she could put it back on. Her skin still tingled from the lingering after-effects.

He'd cupped her face in his hands after their frantic coupling and said incredulously, almost angrily, 'What do you do to me? You are like an unquenchable fire in my blood.'

She would have said the same thing to him if she'd been able to put two words together. It made her feel prickly now.

'You know where I visited because you had me followed.'

'By my security team.'

'I didn't even know you had security. They weren't with you in Scotland. If they had been then you might have not fallen down the mountain.'

And she might not ever have met him.

'That's because I instructed them to stay behind.' His gaze narrowed on her. 'What's wrong?'

Sofie sighed. Nothing. And everything. She was a million miles out of her comfort zone and yet she'd never been so exhilarated. Walking around Athens today and soaking in all the sights and sounds had been truly amazing. But she was ashamed to admit she'd felt a bit lonely. Missing Achilles. Wishing he was the one showing her around.

'Nothing, I'm just a bit…out of my depth, I think.'

'I heard you tried to get into the Acropolis.'

'It was too busy. I can try again—it's no big deal.'

'We leave for the island tomorrow, where the art exhibition is being held.'

Sofie tried to hide her disappointment that she wouldn't see one of the wonders of the world. 'Oh…which island?'

'It's privately owned. It's near Santorini.'

'How long will we be there?' Her life felt very strange now. Days were melting into days and almost a week had gone by since she'd left her own very humdrum life behind. She could get used to this timelessness.

Achilles shrugged. 'A couple of days…then I have to go to New York for a meeting.'

Sofie almost made a sound. New York had always been her number one wish list destination. But Achilles had said *I*. Maybe he was already planning on letting her go after the island.

Hating the feeling of powerlessness, she needed to prove to herself that she wasn't just a piece of flotsam on the current of Achilles's life. Stoutly, she said, 'New York will be exciting and I'm sure you'll be busy. It's about time I arranged a flight home anyway, I'll look into it tomorrow.'

Achilles looked at her. 'What are you talking about? You're coming with me.'

Her heart palpitated. 'What?'

'You're coming with me, of course.' Achilles popped an olive into his mouth, as unconcerned as if he suggested taking someone to New York with him every day of the week. Which, Sofie had to concede, perhaps he did.

His arrogant assumption that she would agree warred with the sense of pure excitement that a) he didn't want her to leave yet, and b) she could see New York after all.

But she couldn't afford to forget that sense of powerlessness—because *that* was the reality. She was here only while she still held interest for Achilles, and if she had any control it would be in deciding her own fate.

It almost killed her to say, 'That sounds amazing. Thank you. But I think it would be best for me to return home after Greece.'

Achilles smiled at her and it was dazzling. 'You don't have to decide now.'

Sofie wanted to hit him. He oozed an arrogance that told her they both knew he would all too easily bend her to his will. And if he wanted her to go to New York then it would be nigh on impossible for her to resist.

His smile widened, as if he knew exactly what she was thinking. And that smile did her in, because he rarely smiled like that. Not even on Gallinvach before his memory had returned. Too often he wore a brooding air—which, when she thought about it now, didn't really fit with his persona as a debauched devil-may-care playboy.

But to think that she could make him smile like that, even once… Her heart thumped ominously. She was in trouble.

A couple of hours later they were nowhere near the hotel and the car had pulled up on a quiet side street that looked vaguely familiar. Achilles had been on his phone and now he was off it.

Sofie asked, 'Where are we?'

Achilles said mysteriously, 'Rectifying a situation.'

He came around to her door and pulled her out. And then he handed her a pair of flat slip-on trainers.

Sofie looked at them. 'Was it that obvious I couldn't walk in those heels?'

Achilles pushed them towards her. 'Just swap your shoes.'

.

Sofie had had a couple of glasses of champagne and felt a little giddy. As she slipped off her shoes with relish and stepped into the flat ones she said, 'You know, you're very bossy. You were bossy like this before your memory returned. It's obviously an inherent trait.'

He said nothing, but when she straightened up to hand him her shoes she could see a smile playing around his mouth. *Oh, boy.*

He put the shoes in the boot and caught Sofie's hand, leading her to a huge set of gates where a man was waiting. It was only when they were through the gates and walking up some wide steps that Sofie realised where they were.

She stopped, and made Achilles stop too. She looked at him. 'No way.'

He looked at her. 'Yes, way. This is the Acropolis.'

'But it's closed.'

'Not for us.'

Struck dumb with awe, Sofie let herself be led up to the majestic ancient site. Floodlit. Soaring over them with its tall columns and spectacular statues. Athens lay around them, glittering like a bauble. They couldn't even hear the traffic from here.

The man who had met them led them around, giving them a tour in perfect English. All Sofie could think about was how hot it had been earlier and how many people had been clamouring to get on the site. This, in comparison, was magical. And cool. With stars overhead in a clear sky.

When the tour was over, Sofie floated back down to the car by Achilles's side. Impulsively she threw her arms around his neck to say thank you, and for the first time she noticed that he tensed a little bit. As if caught off guard by her spontaneity.

She drew back, her buoyant mood pierced. 'Sorry, I just… That was the most beautiful thing I've ever experienced.' She tried to lighten the suddenly brooding mood by saying, 'It's a good move. Very smooth. I bet it goes down well with everyone.'

He frowned. 'Everyone?'

Now Sofie felt uncomfortable. 'Other women?'

Achilles shook his head. 'I've never done this before.'

'Oh.' Now Sofie felt crass. But right now she didn't know where she stood with this man. He'd smiled at her earlier and it had sparked a scary feeling of joy inside her. And then he'd just done possibly the most romantic thing she would ever experience in her life. But now he was looking at her with an undecipherable expression.

'Sorry, I just thought maybe…' She trailed off weakly. 'It was a lovely gesture. Thank you.' She couldn't help feeling that she'd ruined it now.

Achilles helped her back into the car and they went back to the hotel and his apartment. When they got inside, Sofie holding her high-heeled shoes in one hand, Achilles shrugged off his jacket and said, 'I have to make some calls. You should go to bed, Sofie. We'll leave for the island first thing in the morning.'

CHAPTER EIGHT

ACHILLES PACED RESTLESSLY in his office, all thoughts of making calls gone from his mind. All he could see was Sofie. The awestruck wonder on her face as she'd turned in a circle, taking in the Acropolis around her.

The idea to take her there had occurred to him after he'd noticed how obviously disappointed she was not to have seen it. It had taken a mere phone call for him to arrange it. As it did most things. A fact he was starting to realise for the first time in his life.

He'd surprised himself with the gesture. Usually he was loath to do anything that might send the wrong signal.

Sofie hadn't taken it like that. She'd assumed that it must be some kind of signature move on his part. A flamboyant coda to an evening date.

The thing that had surprised him most about her assumption was that it had *hurt*. Her low opinion. When it shouldn't. Because he'd been living down to people's low opinions of him for a long time. Revelling in them, almost. Until he'd decided to reform his reputation.

Achilles's relationship with Sofie had already smashed through about a hundred of the boundaries he usually insisted on. They'd been pushed aside when she'd taken him in and treated him with such kindness when he was at his most vulnerable.

And even though she'd been innocent—physically—and was unworldly, she had a pragmatism about her that he'd never encountered before. A groundedness that had reassured him that she knew not to spin castles in the air about what was happening between them.

Which was good, given his insistence that she come to New York with him. The words had tripped out of his mouth before he'd even had time to really register what he was saying.

But then he thought of how she'd managed to make him *feel* something earlier—hurt. By her opinion. Perhaps she'd been right to resist his invitation to New York—which, admittedly, had been less of an invitation and more of a decree, he realised now with a little wince.

Maybe it was a bad idea to prolong this...this madness. Maybe he should let her go after the island. After all, he could take his pick of women to continue in his campaign of reformation. As it was, Sofie's appearance on his arm more than once was making people talk—in a good way.

A soft knock came on his door, dislodging his thoughts. 'Come in.'

Sofie appeared in the doorway, black hair tumbling around her shoulders, wearing some sort of silk sleep suit. Shorts and a short-sleeved button-down top. And everything Achilles had just been thinking about was blanked from his mind.

She sounded hesitant as she said, 'Sorry, I didn't want to disturb you.'

'Yet here you are,' Achilles pointed out dryly. Shadows hid her face, but he could imagine her blushing.

'I just wanted to say I'm sorry about earlier—I never

wanted to give you the impression that what you did wasn't amazing. It was. I had no right to assume that it was something you did all the time.'

Once again Achilles felt a piercing sensation in his chest. Damn her. He said, 'Come here.'

She walked towards him and he saw her breasts swaying gently under her top. And just like that his body was inflamed. He put his hands on her waist and tugged her into him, relishing her soft curves against his hardening body.

Her hands were on his arms. Small. Capable. He wanted them on him. Encircling him. Moving up and down. Followed by her mouth. And tongue. He knew just how to punish her for making him feel…

'You had every reason to make that assumption. I have a reputation.'

'A reputation you're working hard to reform.'

Achilles slid his hand around Sofie's neck, the fall of her hair a silken caress on his skin. 'I think we could work much harder.'

'We?' She arched a brow.

Achilles's brain went red-hot. In these moments when Sofie played with him he could imagine that she was every inch the experienced coquette. He seized on it to remind himself to keep his guard up and to counteract anything deeper.

'Yes, *we*,' he growled. 'I want you on your knees. Now.'

Sofie's eyes widened and flamed at his command, but she wasn't shocked or intimidated. He could see that she was excited. Colour poured into her cheeks. Her breath got faster. Achilles undid the buttons on her top and it swung open, revealing the ripe globes of her breasts. He almost forgot the need for restraint. *No.* This was how she would pay.

He put his hands on her shoulders and gently pushed her down. He undid his belt and trousers and pulled them down with his underwear, releasing his erection.

Sofie's gaze fixed on it. Eyes wide. Before he lost the ability to speak, Achilles said roughly, 'Touch me. Taste me.'

And she did.

And even though he'd been with countless women before, Achilles knew that what he was about to experience, as inexpert as it was, would blow everything he'd experienced out of the water.

Damn her.

It was late in the afternoon and that was about the only concrete thing Sofie knew. All other concerns had melted away in the heat of the sun beating onto and under her skin, warming her bones in a way they'd never been warmed before.

This late in the day was the only time Sofie felt it was comfortable enough and safe enough for her to lie in the sun. Slathered in factor fifty sun cream. Under strict instructions from Achilles.

The only sounds were the chirruping of birds and insects in the undergrowth near the infinity pool. Boats in the far distance. The lapping of the waves on the beach far below where she was.

They'd arrived on the island a couple of days ago and were staying in a modern villa perched on the edge of a bluff overlooking the Aegean Sea. Dark blue and endless, and broken only by the sight of other islands in the distance.

While Achilles worked in the villa's home office, Sofie behaved like a sybarite. Lounging by the pool, eating delicious snacks provided by the discreet staff. Drinking homemade lemonade and then, in the evening, delicious Greek wines. And even more delicious food.

She was being thoroughly indulged, exactly as Achilles had promised.

It made her feel a little ashamed, how quickly she was getting used to being served. When that had been her job up until a very short time ago; serving tea and toast to patients in the hospital.

It felt like another life now. But she needed to remember that *that* was real life. Not this.

She sat up on the lounger and hugged her knees into her chest. She looked out over the view and sighed deeply, trying to imprint it onto her mind for ever. But she knew that in spite of her best efforts it would fade. Would *he* fade too? Impossible to believe.

She heard a sound and looked around to see Achilles appear on the terrace. He was naked but for a pair of short swim-shorts and Sofie couldn't take her eyes off him. She was glad she was wearing sunglasses.

He went to the deep end of the pool and dropped the towel he was carrying, dived in with innately graceful athleticism. Sofie sighed with appreciation. Her efforts in the pool were more akin to a dog doing its best to keep its head above water.

After an impressive set of lengths, with his strong arms scissoring in and out of the water, Achilles stopped and came to the edge of the pool nearest where Sofie was still sitting, ogling him. Too late to act cool.

'Come and join me,' Achilles said.

Sofie shivered inwardly. She would never forget the

way he'd commanded her the other evening. *'I want you on your knees. Now.'* What had followed had shown her that up until that moment Achilles had merely been toying with her. Keeping her in the shallow end of the pool. But that night…taking him in her hand and then tasting his very essence, feeling him grow even harder against her tongue…had changed her. Matured her. Given her a sense of her own power and femininity like nothing else had until that moment.

He'd made himself vulnerable to her, and yet he'd never seemed more powerful and commanding. By the time he'd finally touched her she'd exploded into a million pieces. She still felt the shock of it now. The pleasure she hadn't been able to contain.

And this…for him…was normal.

He gestured with his hand for her to come to him. Knowing that if she didn't obey he would just come and get her, Sofie stood up and tried not to feel self-conscious when his dark green gaze dipped over her body, bared in all its disproportionately curvy glory in a bikini.

She sat on the edge of the pool a little away from him, and then squealed when he reached for her and pulled her into the water. She splashed inelegantly and spat out water, but she no longer cared how she might be compared with his other, much more svelte lovers because her legs were around his waist, breasts crushed to his chest, and his mouth was on hers, eclipsing every annoying thought.

'Wow.'

Sofie couldn't be more articulate than that. The scene before her was like something out of a dream.

The vast villa on a hill had all its windows and doors open. Music playing. The sun had set and the vast clear sky was painted in shades from orange to lavender. People milled around with glasses of sparkling wine in their hands. The scent of herbs and flowers infused the air.

Tables were set with elaborate floral centrepieces down the middle, groaning under the weight of the food being offered. Vast canvases of art were hung on huge walls inside and Sofie could see people appraising the paintings, looking very serious and appreciative.

'What's this event in aid of again?' she whispered to Achilles.

'It's an annual private art event, with proceeds going to fund the arts in different communities. This year the money is going to fund scholarships for underprivileged students in London, Athens and Paris.'

'Oh, that's nice.'

A stunningly beautiful and impossibly tall black woman glided past Sofie at that moment, dressed in a silver trouser suit. It was only afterwards that Sofie recognised her as a legendary supermodel.

Sofie had felt her red cocktail dress with its deep vee was too revealing, but now she felt positively overdressed compared to what some of the women were wearing. Or not wearing. The dress was sleeveless, and gathered to her waist, from where it fell in soft folds to her knees. She wore matching red high-heeled sandals.

Achilles had surprised her by asking a hair and make-up stylist to come to the villa to help get her ready. She wasn't under any illusions that, much as it was a nice gesture, it wasn't necessary. Her own best efforts wouldn't be up to par with a sophisticated crowd like this. As it was, she was half expecting a tap on her shoulder and to be escorted off the very exclusive premises.

When she stopped rubbernecking for a moment she

realised that a couple were standing in front of Achilles. A tall and very distinguished-looking older gentleman and a woman who had to be his wife. Younger by a few decades. Closer to Achilles's age. Blonde. Skin stretched across her face in a way that made it look totally expressionless. Cold blue eyes. Improbably pert-looking breasts under a sheath of what looked like liquid gold.

Sofie knew instantly who she was. Even before she felt Achilles tensing and pulling her closer.

'Athena… Georgiou,' Achilles said smoothly. No one shook hands.

The man offered a tight smile. The women spoke in Greek, and Achilles said with unmistakable steel in his voice, 'I'm afraid Sofie doesn't speak Greek.'

The women cast a dismissive glance at Sofie. 'Forgive me. I shouldn't assume everyone is multi-lingual.'

Ouch.

They exchanged pleasantries, laced with venom from Athena, and then the other couple were gone.

Sofie looked up at Achilles. 'I think I've guessed who that was. The reason for our presence here this evening?'

Achilles grimaced. 'Yes. Sorry for subjecting you to Athena's very particular brand of toxicity. She's determined to move on to a new husband and she'll do anything—even paint herself as an adulterer. Because of course she ensured in the prenuptial agreement that she would still receive a hefty pay-out. But her husband isn't going to let her go without a fight.'

'What a lovely situation.'

'Not an uncommon one. For every genuine marriage there are about a hundred as toxic as the Demetrious's.'

Sofie balked at that. It made most of the marital strife she'd heard of look positively Disneyesque in comparison. Suddenly she was aware of the cynicism in the air like a scent. Aware of the women looking around them, eyeing up the men. The men with wives appraising other women. The general air of discontent.

She shivered a little and Achilles said, 'You can't be cold?'

She shook her head, 'No, I'm fine. I think I'll just go and look at the paintings for a minute.'

A man was approaching Achilles, looking very determined. Achilles said, 'I'll follow you in. If you see something you like, let me know. I'll buy it.'

About a minute later, when Sofie was standing in front of one of the paintings and saw the price tag, she almost choked on her drink.

A friendly voice beside her said, 'I had much the same reaction the first time I came to this event.'

Sofie looked around warily, and then had to look up at the tall woman beside her. Very pretty, with dark hair and blue eyes. Pale skin. She looked friendly. Eyes twinkling.

Sofie said, 'You sound English?'

The woman nodded and held out her hand. 'Guilty as charged! Lucy Levakis. And you sound Scottish?'

Sofie shook her hand. She smiled. 'Yes, from Gallinvach—a small island to the very north of Scotland.'

Lucy frowned. 'Isn't that famous for one of Scotland's highest mountains?'

'Yes, Ben Kincraig—that's it.'

Lucy let her hand go. 'I've never been, but I believe it's beautiful.'

Sofie felt shy all of a sudden, as she realised how polished and glamorous this woman was. 'It is pretty.'

'I see that you're here with Achilles Lykaios?'

Sofie nodded. 'I… Yes… We're…together.' She felt so awkward.

The other woman said conspiratorially, 'You're not his usual type.'

Sofie made a face. 'You don't need to remind me.'

Lucy Levakis laughed. 'No, I mean that in a good way. I've always thought there was more to that man than the hedonistic playboy he presented to the world.'

'Do you know him?'

'He's done some business with my husband, Ari Levakis, over the years. We've met socially. But I guess it's understandable that he would go off the rails after such an awful tragedy.' She winked at Sofie. 'You're a breath of fresh air—and a good sign that he's not totally unredeemable.'

Sofie smiled weakly. She was dying to ask if the 'tragedy' referred to Achilles's family and how they'd died.

'Darling, there you are. I need you to help me deal with the Demetrious couple—that woman is insufferable.'

A very handsome man, about the same height as Achilles, appeared by Lucy's side. The zing of love and passion between them was almost palpable.

Lucy tore her gaze off her husband and looked back at Sofie. She introduced her husband and then said, 'It was really nice to meet you, Sofie. Good luck. I hope to see you again.'

She winked at her and then they were gone, hand in hand. Clearly one of the very rare couples that Achilles had referred to as being genuine.

It made Sofie feel a little off-centre to have met someone so normal. As if the real world had collided with this fantasy existence for a moment, giving her a tantalising sense that perhaps it worked for some people…

At that moment Achilles appeared, and Sofie had to

force that rogue notion out of her head. Her existence in Achilles's world would only ever be transitory.

He stopped beside her and slipped his arm around her waist. He looked at the painting she was still standing before. 'You like this one?'

She pointed to the notice beside it. 'It's a million euros.'

'If you like it I'll buy it for you.'

Sofie thought for a moment. 'No, let someone else buy it. You can just donate the money to the charity.'

'Done.'

She rolled her eyes. 'It's like Monopoly money to you, isn't it?'

Achilles shrugged. 'I can't apologise for what I was born into. It's a legacy.'

'One I think you don't exactly relish...'

Achilles's face hardened. 'I have no problem with the legacy. I have an issue with how it came to me.'

'Your family...?'

More people came into the space around them and Achilles caught her hand, pulling her outside to a quiet terrace, where flaming lanterns flickered over the space throwing out golden light.

He let her hand go. 'Did you look it up?'

Sofie shook her head. 'No... I wouldn't do that after the last time. Achilles, look...you don't have to tell me anything, but clearly it's out there. Maybe it's better I hear it coming from you than someone else?'

Achilles's mouth tightened. He turned away and looked out over the view. Soft jazz music drifted on the breeze. People were laughing.

He said, after a long moment, 'My family had a yacht. Me and my parents and my younger brother and sister, Darius and Olympia—'

'Darius…' breathed Sofie. 'That's where the name came from.'

'Yes. It popped into my head. But I didn't remember the significance. Obviously. We were all on the yacht—it was about this time of year, the end of summer. I was leaving the yacht early, because I was due to go to Athens and from there back to London to school. My family were going to follow me in a couple of weeks. I was thirteen, my brother was nine and my sister six.'

It was as if Achilles was speaking from a script. Sofie wanted to touch him but he seemed too remote. Caught in memory.

'I had just got onto the launch and was heading away from the yacht. They were all waving. Darius and Olympia had made a banner, saying how much they loved me and would miss me. Even though I'd see them again in two weeks. They held it up so I could read it just before…'

He stopped. Gritted his jaw.

'Just before the explosion.'

Sofie was very still.

'Everyone on the yacht was killed instantly. It was an accident. A fault in the engine. Leaking fuel that caught fire. We were hit by debris. I woke up in a hospital in Athens about a day later. I thought it had been a bad dream, but it wasn't. They were all gone. In an instant. For ever.'

'That's why you had that nightmare after seeing the boat on the lake. You hate boats…' Sofie realised then that she hadn't seen any pictures of Achilles on boats or near them. Apart from the one in his father's study in London.

It was as if Achilles didn't hear her. He gestured with his head to the dark sea around the island. 'It happened out there. I own this island. This event was devised by my mother because she loved the arts so much. She took great pleasure in separating the cynical masses from as much of their money as possible, encouraging them to outdo each other.'

Sofie was trying to absorb the fact that this was his family's island. 'She sounds like she was a lot of fun.'

'She was. She didn't take any of this too seriously. She really didn't care about wealth, or status. Our family villa is on the other side of the island...'

Sofie said nothing. She was reading between the lines. Achilles hadn't been back there in years. If ever.

Achilles continued, 'My parents were one of those few couples who really adored each other. And us. We were a very happy family. I loved my brother and sister. I would have done anything for them. I would have died for them.'

'But you survived.'

'Yes. I survived. So that I could live with the reminder every day that I have inherited a legacy that was theirs as much as mine.'

Before Sofie could even try to articulate a response to that he looked at her.

'I live with the reminder that what I lost can never be recreated,' he said. 'I had a family and I lost it. I will never suffer such loss again.'

Sofie's heart ached. 'But, Achilles, no matter what you do there's no guarantee that—'

'Of course there is. It's very simple. I will never marry. Never have a family.'

'What about the Lykaios legacy? Don't you owe it to your family to keep it alive?'

Achilles's mouth twisted. Sofie had never seen him so bleak.

'I owe it to them to make the company successful. I owe it to the employees who trust in me to guard their livelihoods. When I leave this company it will be more successful than it's ever been, and it will be run by a board who will protect its interests—not a family who can be destroyed in a second.'

'But you weren't destroyed.'

'Wasn't I?' He shook his head. 'Don't look at me like that, Sofie. I'm not looking for sympathy.'

Sofie tried her hardest to push the emotion down. But it was hard. She knew in that moment, fatefully, that she'd gone way past a point of fooling herself that she could walk away from Achilles unscathed.

Feeling almost angry with him for getting under her skin so comprehensively, she said, 'I can't pretend not to be affected, Achilles. I'm a normal person with normal reactions. I care about you. I wouldn't be with you if I didn't.'

'You're too nice.'

'No, I'm just normal. You're too used to being surrounded by people who are twisted and cynical. They've forgotten what it is to feel anything.'

'I'm one of them.'

'I don't think you are.'

He looked at her and said, very carefully, 'Yes, I am, Sofie. I can't promise anything beyond *this*. I don't want to. It's not what I want. Something broke inside me a long time ago and it can't be fixed. That's okay.'

It wasn't, though. Sofie knew that as Achilles took her by the hand and led her back into the throng of the party. Soon they were inundated with more of Achilles's ardent followers.

She felt queasy inside and couldn't shake it.

She had a better understanding of why he behaved the way he did. Why he'd gone off the rails—clearly chafing at receiving an inheritance that shouldn't be solely his.

But he'd then stepped up to the plate because of the responsibility he had to his family legacy.

Was that the reason he was drawn to extreme sports
and hedonistic living? Some kind of survivor guilt? She
went cold inside to think of how he taunted death. But
Sofie got it. She understood.

Maybe some day a woman would be able to break him
free of his past—someone who understood this world as
well as he did. Who could rouse the need in him to overcome his demons.

But it evidently wouldn't be her. She realised after that
exchange and those revelations that she needed to protect
herself, because Achilles had really meant every word
he'd said back there. He'd been warning her. Spelling it
out in massive letters.

I am damaged and I have no desire to be healed by you.

She'd told Achilles that she cared for him—massive
understatement—and he'd barely blinked. It hadn't made
even a dent of impact.

She'd indulged in fantasy for too long. Basked in the
sun of Achilles's regard. Fooled herself into believing that
he really saw her. And he did. But not in the way she
needed. He saw her—but only as a temporary diversion.

She didn't want someone to see her only temporarily. She wanted someone to see her for ever. To want to
get to know her deeply and with love. *That* was what she
wanted—more than finding herself through travel, or escaping the confines of her small island.

That would all mean nothing unless she could share it
with someone she loved, who loved her back.

When they arrived back at the villa after the party Achilles felt tired. As if he'd been running for miles and finally

stopped. As if a weight had been simultaneously lifted and replaced on his shoulders. The strangest sensation.

He shrugged off his jacket and went straight to the drinks cabinet to pour himself a nightcap.

He looked over his shoulder to where Sofie was slipping off her shoes. She'd been quiet the whole way back. Not like her. Usually she was chattering about the people she'd met, the ridiculous things they'd said or done.

He frowned. 'Do you want a drink?'

She held her sandals in her hands and shook her head. 'No, thanks. Actually, I think I'll just go to bed. I'm quite tired.'

Already imagining sliding between cool sheets and curving his body around hers, moulding her breasts with his hands, Achilles felt anticipation fire up his blood and said, 'I'll join you shortly.'

He turned away, but from behind him Sofie said hesitantly, 'I think I'd like to sleep alone tonight.'

Achilles went still, the drink halfway to his mouth. He put the glass down and turned around. 'What's going on?'

He noticed now that she looked nervous. Pale in spite of the lightly golden glow her skin had acquired in the sun.

'I think it's best if I make my way home from Athens when we return. And you go on to New York.'

Achilles wasn't stupid. He had registered Sofie saying, *'I care about you'*, but he'd pushed it down deep, where it wouldn't impact. He suddenly felt unbalanced, as if the earth had shifted slightly.

'Is this because of what I said? It wasn't anything you didn't already know.'

'I didn't know the details of how you lost your family.'

'They don't have anything to do with this.'

Sofie looked at him with those huge dark blue eyes.

He realised now that they reminded him of the sky just before the dusk disappeared completely.

'No, I guess they don't. This is to do with me. Not you.'

Achilles smiled, but it was mirthless. 'Isn't that line a bit outdated?'

'It's not a line.'

Colour flared in her cheeks, which only made Achilles's blood hotter.

'I care about you, Achilles. More than I should. And I know you didn't promise me anything at all. Your parameters were very clear. Fun and adventure. And I've had an amazing time. But I can't pretend to not be affected by my emotions, and if we continue this...this affair, when it ends—as it inevitably will—I don't think I'll cope very well. Whereas you... I think you'll cope just fine. And you'll get on with your life.'

Achilles absorbed Sofie's words. She wasn't saying anything remotely unreasonable. She was just being honest. It struck him that in any other situation with a lover telling him she had feelings for him he would not still be standing here.

But her words weren't evoking panic or claustrophobia. They just evoked a kind of numbness. He couldn't quite believe she was saying she wanted to leave. She couldn't leave. Not yet.

CHAPTER NINE

'I'D STILL LIKE you to come to New York with me.'

Sofie sucked in a breath. She'd more or less told him she loved him without actually saying it and he'd barely blinked. Further evidence, if she needed it, that his emotions were encased in ice. Exactly what he'd been accused of by one of his previous lovers. As if she needed that reminder now.

'But…why?' Her heart thumped. Maybe she had got through to him, but on a level he wasn't ready to accept. Maybe—

'Because our relationship has been good for business. I have an event to attend and I'd appreciate you by my side, to really affirm for people that things are changing.'

'Oh.'

'You said that New York was one of the places you wanted to visit most.'

She had. But she hadn't really envisaged visiting with her ex-lover while he was using her to maximise a PR opportunity. Did she really mean so little to him after all these weeks?

He ran a hand through his hair. 'Look, the last thing I want to do is hurt you, Sofie. We won't sleep together again. But I have enjoyed…being with you. Let me treat you to one last trip and then we can go our separate ways. No harm, no foul.'

No, Sofie thought. *Not for him. Just a broken heart for her.*

She knew it was madness even to think about agreeing. That his offer only demonstrated just how walled-off his emotions were, if he couldn't even appreciate how hard it would be for her…

He said, 'Pictures are already on the internet of us meeting Athena and Georgiou at the party, with renewed speculation as to whether or not I actually had an affair with her. Your presence has obviously mitigated that. But if you go home now, and if I appear in New York alone, it'll fuel the speculation even more.'

Sofie felt a lead weight in her belly. Along with that queasiness again. 'Wow. I mean, I know you're ruthless, because you'd have to be to thrive in a world like this, but I hadn't expected to experience it first-hand.'

You saw those headlines, didn't you? mocked a small voice.

The picture of that Spanish beauty's petulant face came back into her mind's eye.

At least he wasn't dumping her.

But, perversely, what Achilles was saying, even if he was driving a knife into the heart of her with every word, actually made things easier. Surely she could be as ruthless as him, couldn't she? Seize the opportunity for a free trip to one of the cities she'd most wanted to visit ever since she was a little girl?

Could she put her emotions on ice too? Just for a few days?

The thought of insisting on leaving and of Achilles having an idea of just how much he meant to her, of returning home to her house alone, was suddenly anathema to her. Even though she refused to admit it to herself.

Then he said, 'I would really appreciate it.' And she knew that she didn't have the strength to say goodbye forever, just yet.

She lifted her chin and said, with as much dignity as she could muster, 'Fine, I'll come to New York with you and I'll go home from there.'

'Thank you.'

'Okay. Goodnight, Achilles.'

Sofie turned and left the room, escaping into one of the spare bedrooms before she did something stupid like throwing herself into his arms and begging him to make love to her one last time.

She was doing the right thing, she assured herself. Seizing an opportunity to broaden her horizons and putting down some clear boundaries with Achilles. She should be proud of how she was handling this, even when she knew that she was fooling herself by believing for a second that she had things under control.

'Are you okay?'

Sofie looked at Achilles where he sat across the aisle from her on the private jet. They'd taken off from Athens airport a short while ago, after picking up some things from Achilles's apartment at the hotel.

She nodded her head vigorously. 'Fine. Just a little queasy. Something I ate from the buffet last night, maybe.'

A light flutter of concern resided in her belly as she acknowledged that the queasiness she'd felt the previous evening was lingering. She'd felt properly nauseous that morning, but hadn't actually been sick. She wasn't even allowing her head to go in the direction of scary speculation, because it was impossible. She was on the pill and she took it religiously every day. She never missed.

She told herself it was due to the emotional turmoil of deciding to be a masochist by agreeing to stay a few days longer with a man who was quite unperturbed that their relationship was over.

They'd returned to Athens that morning and Achilles had been perfectly civil. As if Sofie was now in the role of employee. Which in a way she was.

Part of her was seriously impressed with Achilles's ability to switch from red-hot lover to distantly polite companion, and another part of her wanted to bang her fists against his chest, demanding that he show some tiny vestige of emotion. To show that he'd cared. That he was so overcome with desire that he simply couldn't *not* touch her.

Feeling prickly more than queasy now, she looked out the window at the brown earth far below. A stewardess approached with a glass of champagne and another surge of nausea took Sofie by surprise.

She shook her head. 'No, thank you.' She undid her seatbelt and went to the bathroom before Achilles might see her reaction.

Inside the luxurious cubicle she took deep breaths to stave off the nausea and splashed cold water on her face. She looked at herself in the mirror and barely noticed the spray of freckles across her sun-kissed nose.

A very ominous suspicion was taking root in her belly.

Queasiness.

Reacting violently to the thought of alcohol.

This was more than food poisoning or emotional turmoil.

But she wasn't going to go there. It was too potentially huge even to contemplate. If there was one thing
she knew for certain after last night it was that Achilles
Lykaios was possibly the most family-averse person on
the planet. And for very understandable reasons. He'd
seen his entire family disappear right in front of him.
The scars of that trauma were not scars he was willing
to heal. And certainly not with a baby.

Sofie felt sick again and sat down on the closed toilet
seat. She put her head between her legs until the nausea
passed. And then she vowed not to think of it again. Because the universe could not be that cruel.

She'd already suffered the trauma of not having siblings and living with the weight of her parents' sadness.
Achilles had suffered an even more unspeakable trauma.
Bringing a lone, illegitimate child into that equation was
not an option, so maybe if she just ignored the ominous
signs it would go away.

Achilles watched Sofie come back down the aisle of
the plane. She was avoiding his eye. Something twisted
in his chest. Did she want to be gone that badly? Even
though she had said she cared for him?

But then in his world words were cheap. He'd been
told dozens of times by lovers that they adored him and
couldn't live without him, only for them to turn and
show their real feelings were far less than adoring when
he called it quits.

Sofie hadn't even said she adored him. She'd said she
cared for him and, considering how considerate she was
with everyone around her, from his housekeeper to the
concierge of the hotel whom she'd hugged goodbye before promising to send him some Scottish shortbread,

Achilles figured he might sit somewhere in her affections just above those two. She was just a caring person.

She sat down in her seat and Achilles couldn't stop his gaze straying to her silky-smooth bare legs. She was wearing a button-down silk shirt dress with a belt around her waist. Gladiator style sandals.

His fingers itched to slip off the belt and undo those buttons, baring her soft curves to his gaze. He could pull across the privacy curtain and have her straddle his lap, draw her mouth down to his and kiss her while he released his aching—

Enough. He looked away and cursed his lack of control. He needed her for one thing now—to consolidate his improved image. That was all. He had more control than this.

'This is…spectacular,' Sofie said faintly as she took in the view from Achilles's penthouse apartment at the top of one of Manhattan's skyscrapers just a couple of blocks south of Central Park. She was gazing at a skyline she'd only ever seen in movies or read about in books. And it didn't disappoint.

'I suppose this is more what you expected?'

She dragged her gaze away to look at Achilles. But not too closely. She found it was easier to avoid looking at him at all if possible. Especially when stubble lined his jaw and reminded her of the beard he'd had when they'd first met.

'It's stunning. But you might have to give it up now that you're a reformed man.'

'Pity. I like the view.'

'It's some view…' Once again Sofie was trying to imprint it on her mind. A futile exercise.

Achilles went back inside. Staff had greeted them and taken their bags to the bedrooms. There were so many rooms that Sofie had grown dizzy. There was even a gym with a lap pool.

She followed him. 'What's the event this week and why is it so important?'

Achilles was pouring himself a drink at an art deco cabinet. He said over his shoulder, 'It's the biggest charity event of the season and it heralds everyone coming back from their summer holiday homes and getting back to work. It's a major networking event as much as a fundraiser for charity.' He turned around to face her. 'Drink?'

Sofie shook her head quickly. 'No, thank you.'

Achilles went over to the window and looked out. 'It's held in one of Manhattan's most iconic museums. The publicity is always intense. That's why it's important for me right now.'

As lightly as she could, Sofie said, 'And afterwards you'll go back to Europe?'

Achilles shrugged. 'I might stay here for a while. I have some business to attend to here and in South America.'

She couldn't stop pictures forming in her mind of some sinuous Brazilian beauty twining herself around Achilles's hard body. Sofie would be back in her homely *lonely* house with Pluto by then, and—

Stop, she admonished herself. Self-pity had never been her thing.

'I might go out and explore a little before it gets too dark, if that's all right?'

Achilles faced her. 'Do whatever you want, Sofie. You're my guest here this week. My driver is at your disposal. He'll take you anywhere you like. I can order tickets for any Broadway show you'd like to see too—just name it.'

'Would *you* like to see a show?' The words were out before she could stop them, and there was an embarrassingly wistful tone in her voice.

Achilles shook his head. 'Not really my thing.'

'Sure…of course.'

Sofie left before she could put her foot in it even more. Of course Broadway shows weren't Achilles's thing. He wouldn't be seen dead at something so popular.

The driver indulged her whim and drove around Manhattan from Central Park to Times Square. She opened the window wide and soaked it all in. Only allowing herself to feel marginally sad that she was doing it on her own and not with Achilles. He'd been to Manhattan a million times.

But no. She had one more week of being indulged with this five-star treatment and she had done the mature thing and nipped her affair with Achilles in the bud to reduce her emotional pain as much as possible. All in all, she was being thoroughly adult.

That was when she spotted a drugstore, and suddenly didn't feel so adult any more.

As the week progressed Achilles found that the control he'd thought he was wielding was beginning to seriously fray at the edges. And that was because Sofie wasn't behaving the way he had expected.

She was being thoroughly independent. Sightseeing every day from morning till afternoon. Not slightly fazed by the fact that she and Achilles had broken up.

You were the one who asked her to come to New York with you, a voice pointed out.

Achilles scowled at himself. He was in his office downtown, near One World Trade Center. The views encompassed the East and Hudson rivers. The Statue of Liberty.

The world was at his feet.

But he couldn't have cared less about that right now.

Admittedly this was not a situation he'd faced before. Usually he'd rather swim in a pool full of sharks than spend time with an ex-lover. And on some level he realised now that he'd believed Sofie wouldn't be able to hold out against the chemistry that still crackled like electricity whenever they were near each other. That she would be the one to give in and admit defeat, admit that she still wanted him.

But then he'd hardly seen her. Maybe that was her strategy. Avoid him at all costs.

Perversely it made him feel slightly better to think that she was struggling too. That perhaps her nights—in a bedroom on the other side of the apartment from his— were also populated by X-rated dreams from which she woke sweating, her heart pounding as if she'd run a marathon and her body aching for fulfilment. And then meet him over breakfast in the morning as if everything was totally fine. While her hormones raged under the surface.

He'd arrived back at the apartment late last night to find Sofie curled up in a chair dressed in soft sweats, with a shawl wrapped around her shoulders, hair loose and face scrubbed clean. Her fresh-faced beauty had nearly bowled him over—and then he'd realised she was on the phone. She hadn't even noticed him.

She was talking to her friend Claire in Scotland and raving about the show she'd seen that night, speaking so enthusiastically that Achilles had felt jealous that he hadn't been with her to experience it. She'd sounded like a joyful child, describing everything down to the bathrooms in the theatre.

Broadway reminded him of London's West End, and the shows his parents had taken him and his brother and sister to—the reason why he hadn't been to a show since. But for once the memory wasn't as acutely painful as it had been in the past. It felt more nostalgic.

And then he'd felt like a voyeur, eavesdropping on her conversation, so he'd left and made some calls. By the time he'd gone looking for her again she had gone to bed.

And now he couldn't concentrate on work because he was too fixated on what she was doing.

He picked up his phone and made a call.

Sofie felt a prickling sensation on the back of her neck and looked up to see Achilles standing in the doorway. Her heart palpitated. He was clean-shaven and wearing a three-piece suit.

She noticed the frisson of awareness rippling around the room full of women as they too clocked him.

The flower-arranging teacher clapped her hands together softly. 'Okay, your ten minutes are up. I'll inspect your displays now.'

Sofie stopped faffing with her flowers and stood back. Achilles leaned against the doorframe and arched a brow at her. She scowled at him. For the whole week she'd been doing her best to avoid him and pretend she wasn't being driven mad by sexual frustration. As if she was completely okay with this arrangement. With denying herself the pleasure of his lovemaking just to protect her heart.

And now he looked as if he knew exactly how hard it

was for her and was enjoying every moment of her self-inflicted torture.

He'd come home last night after she'd returned from a show and she'd been talking to Claire on the phone. She'd seen him in the reflection of the window in the lounge and deliberately emphasised what an amazing show it had been, to make it sound as if she couldn't possibly have had a better time if he'd been with her.

But then he'd disappeared, and she'd felt deflated, and she'd had to deflect questions from her friend about their relationship for ten minutes.

'Beautiful, Sofie. I like the way you've framed your arrangement with the eucalyptus.'

The class ended shortly after and the others filed out. Sofie took her time, simultaneously annoyed and excited that Achilles had tracked her down. He was still at the door, waiting.

She smiled brightly. 'Work must be very boring if you're looking to join a flower-arranging class.'

'I had no idea it was even a thing,' Achilles remarked.

The class had taken place only a few blocks from Achilles's apartment building. He walked out with her. The sun was setting, imbuing everything with a golden glow. The city was still baking. Sofie was glad of her linen shorts and sleeveless shirt. She'd pulled her hair back into a ponytail.

'There's a great pizza restaurant near here if you're hungry?'

Sofie looked at Achilles suspiciously. 'Don't you have meetings or calls or stuff to do?'

He shook his head. 'Nope.'

'Aren't you a little overdressed for a pizzeria?' Great—now she sounded churlish. She said, 'Sorry, I just wasn't expecting you to appear and want to have dinner...'

Achilles shrugged. 'I'm hungry. I called my driver to see where you were.'

'Okay, that sounds nice.' She was reading too much into it.

As they walked down the street together Sofie felt ridiculously shy. She realised that for all the time she'd spent with Achilles they'd never really just had a date. Or spent any time together that hadn't been charged with sex or an appearance in public at an event.

It had been a rollercoaster. Since the moment he'd looked at her that day in the hospital and said, *'I'll stay with her.'*

'Here it is.'

Sofie found they'd stopped in front of a very humble-looking pizzeria. Tables outside. Couples and families having dinner. Casual. Relaxed.

They got a table inside, near an open window. Sofie lifted her face to the breeze.

'So, flower-arranging...?'

Sofie looked at Achilles. 'What? I saw a sign in a local coffee shop window. I fancied learning a new skill. Plus,' she confided, 'I've seen most of the major sights.' She looked around the restaurant. Unpretentious, but very homely. 'This is nice.'

'I guessed you'd like it.'

She sent him a look. 'I'll take that as a compliment and not a reference to the fact that I don't have a sophisticated palate.' She picked up a bread stick and nibbled at it. 'How do you know about it? It seems a little out of your league...'

'My father used to bring me here. After a baseball game.'

Sofie tensed inwardly at his mention of his father. 'You had a good relationship?' she asked.

Achilles nodded. 'The best. He wasn't corrupted by the legacy he'd inherited. He cared about the business, but the money was superfluous to him. He cared more about the staff and creating a happy family.'

'That's pretty amazing, considering he could have been a total brat.'

'Like I was a brat?'

Sofie's heart clenched. 'I don't think you were half as bad as you think you were. And I can understand how you probably wanted nothing to do with it after—'

'Drinks?'

Sofie looked up. She hadn't even noticed the waiter.

Achilles ordered wine and Sofie's stomach roiled. She said quickly, 'Just sparkling water for me.'

Achilles looked at her. 'Okay?'

She nodded and avoided his eye. 'The heat and wine don't really agree with me.'

She thought of the unopened boxes she'd bought in the drugstore the other night. She hadn't had the nerve even to look at them yet.

Achilles took off his jacket and waistcoat and Sofie had to fight not to let her gaze linger on the way his muscles moved under the thin material of his shirt. Especially when he rolled up his sleeves.

When the waiter had delivered their drinks and taken their order, Sofie diverted the conversation away from Achilles's family into more neutral territory.

She was surprised to find a couple of hours passing so easily that it reminded her of how it had been on the island, when Achilles had still been Darius.

'So what are you going to do now?' he asked.

Sofie took a sip of coffee and put her cup down. 'I don't think I'll go back to the hospital. I think I might open up the house as a B&B for a while…think about what I want to do.'

'You could do a degree in flower-arranging.'

Sofie scowled and threw a morsel of bread at Achilles. He grinned. Her heart broke and swelled at the same time. He liked her. She knew that. But she was still a novelty to him, and after being in his world for a while she could understand why.

He wanted her. She could feel it now, humming between them like a charge of electricity. But without a deeper emotion it would destroy her.

She looked at her watch. 'It's late. Maybe we should head back.'

'Early start tomorrow?'

'It's my last day. I want to pack as much in as I can.'

'Last day?'

Achilles was about to put some money on the table but Sofie stopped him and said, 'Please, let me get this. It's not even a dent in what you've spent on me, but I'd like to.'

He looked at her for a long moment and then put his money back in his pocket. 'Sure.'

Sofie couldn't imagine that many of his women offered to pay for their dinner. She put the money down and they walked out of the nearly empty restaurant.

She said, after a minute of walking companionably with him down the street, 'I've booked a flight home to Glasgow for Saturday morning. A taxi is picking me up early.'

Achilles walked beside her, his waistcoat back on but open, his jacket slung over his shoulder. She noticed everyone he passed doing a double take—men, women, children, older people... No one was immune to his magnetism.

'I told you I would organise it for you.'

Achilles's voice was a little abrupt. But Sofie told herself she was imagining things. Even if he still wanted her, he had to be looking forward to moving on and seeking out fresh thrills. This was the man who threw himself down the blackest ski runs, after all.

'It's fine. I have savings. It's not that expensive.'

They were back at his building now. Entering. Heading up in the lift. The doors opened and they stepped into the corridor outside the apartment. Achilles opened the door. Sofie went in. She felt the tension mounting.

Achilles closed the door behind her and she turned around and looked at him warily. The easy camaraderie of dinner had dissipated. There was a sense of danger and excitement in the air.

He leaned back against the door. Totally relaxed and yet coiled. 'I still want you, Sofie.'

Sofie's blood leapt. Sizzled. Every cell in her body was aligning to his like magnets. She was so tempted. But the emotion rising in her chest and throat reminded her of what was at stake. This wouldn't be just sex for her.

'I want you too. But I don't think it's a good idea.'

A muscle pulsed in Achilles's jaw. He straightened up. 'You're probably right. I have early meetings tomorrow, all the way through to the afternoon. I'll meet you back here at six to go to the function. I've arranged for a hair and make-up team to come and help get you ready.'

Sofie felt sick. A different kind of nausea this time. Regret and heartache. 'Okay, thank you.'

This was it. They'd go to the function tomorrow night and then she'd never see him again.

Sofie went into the bedroom and the first thing she saw was the bag from the drugstore. She instantly felt nauseous again.

If she did see Achilles after tomorrow night, it wouldn't be because he still wanted her.

Achilles felt a dangerous sense of volatility. No other woman who admitted to wanting him would deny herself. *Or him.* And it wasn't just about the sex, Achilles knew. It was about the fact that Sofie was exerting a level of self-control that he could only admire.

This evening had been unexpected. He hadn't known what he'd planned on doing when he'd tracked Sofie down to the flower-arranging class. He hadn't quite believed what his driver had said she was doing. It was so far beyond the realms of what any of his other lovers had done.

And then he'd realised the pizzeria was nearby. A place he wouldn't dream of taking a lover. Because none of his other lovers would have stepped over the threshold. They would have been horrified by the lack of luxury. But he loved it. Because it had been his and his father's place. And he'd known Sofie would love it too.

Achilles stood on the private terrace outside his bedroom. Hands on the wall. He bunched them into fists. If anything, his instinct to take Sofie to such a sacred place was a wake-up call.

She'd told him she wouldn't sleep with him because her emotions were involved. His were still on ice. But he was coming perilously close to breaking all his own rules. The rules that protected him from risking losing his loved ones all over again.

He didn't have loved ones and he wasn't about to lose his mind completely and change that. Not for anyone. No matter how good the sex.

Sofie was waiting for Achilles to appear in the main drawing room the following evening just before six. She was wearing a deep royal blue strapless dress. Ruched over her chest, it had a high waist and fell to the floor in silken folds with a chiffon overlay. It was dreamy and romantic and not helping her state of mind.

The hair and make-up team had applied make-up that made her glow. Her eyes looked huge and her mouth looked plump, as if she'd just been kissed. Her hair had been pulled back into a chignon. She wore a diamond necklace and matching bracelet. Matching blue clutch and high-heeled sandals.

She'd never felt so elegant. So far removed from herself. It only compounded the numbness she felt. At the thought that this was *it*. And also the earth-shattering discovery she'd made just a while ago.

Numbness was good. Protective.

There was a sound and Achilles appeared in the doorway. He was doing up a cufflink, so he didn't see her at first. It gave Sofie a moment to gather herself, to observe him.

In a black tuxedo, he was breathtakingly handsome. Broad-shoulders. Narrow waist. Long legs. She drank him in greedily. Knowing it wouldn't be long before everything changed. But, weakly, she diverted her mind from that now.

He looked up. Stopped moving. Eyes narrowed.

Looked her up and down. Sofie's skin tingled. Her blood grew hot.

'You look beautiful,' he said.

She felt beautiful. For the first time in her life. 'Thank you.'

He led her downstairs to the car and they made the relatively short journey to the museum. It was thronged outside, with glamorous guests arriving and paparazzi with flashing cameras.

There was a red carpet. This was definitely the highest profile event they'd attended. As soon as Sofie joined Achilles at the bottom of the red-carpeted steps there was a hush, and then an explosion of lights. Sofie flinched.

Achilles took her hand and said, 'Stick close to me.'

She had no intention of going anywhere else.

Somehow they made it to the top of the steps and the furore died down a little.

Inside the museum it was a magical wonderland. Everything was gold and glittered. The vast ceilings were elaborately frescoed. Discreet waiters moved through the crowd offering sparkling wine and hors d'oeuvres.

Sofie was too scared to eat.

After moving through the crowd and stopping to talk to people, they were gently guided into another vast room, with round tables that had elaborate central floral displays. Achilles led her to a table near the front, where there was a small stage. A tuxedoed trio were playing classical music. As the guests took their seats they stopped playing and a well-known movie star got up and spoke.

Sofie realised it was an auction, with lots ranging from yachts to even a small island. This really was the domain of the richest people in the world.

Achilles's arm was across the back of her chair and his fingers brushed her bare shoulder from time to time. She knew it was for the benefit of the crowd and any stray photographers, but she wanted to beg him to stop it. He was causing havoc in her body. She'd survived the week pretty well up to now, precisely because there had been little to no physical contact.

And then a lot came up and she felt Achilles tense beside her. It was to be part of a world-renowned team in a catamaran race. There was some footage of the incredibly delicate-looking craft shown, and to Sofie it looked terrifying. It seemed only the skill of the sailors stopped it from flipping and breaking into a thousand pieces in the sea.

When the bidding started she nearly fell off her chair when Achilles put in a bid for a stupid amount of money. Monopoly money. She heard people gasp around them. She wasn't the only one to realise the significance, apparently.

Achilles kept bidding. Sofie looked at him. His face was stony. The movie star tried to raise another bid but none was coming. The gavel went down on Achilles's last bid.

Sofie sensed eyes on her and Achilles even as the auction moved on and other lots were announced.

When she felt as if they were under slightly less scrutiny, she said, 'What were you thinking? You hate boats. And not only that—it looks terrifyingly dangerous.'

He turned to her and picked up her hand and brought it to his mouth, pressing a kiss to the palm of her hand. Sofie shivered inwardly. There was something bleak in Achilles's gaze.

He said, 'Haven't you heard of facing your fears?'

'Yes,' said Sofie weakly, hating herself for being so distracted. 'But I think you could have started by taking a ferry trip across the Hudson or down the Thames.'

She couldn't hide her concern. Not anymore. Not when there was more at stake. So much more. She said, 'Achilles, look, there's something I need to tell you...'

But the auction was drawing to a close and he was tugging her out of her seat and saying, 'Let's dance.'

Sofie let herself be led, sensing a strange volatility in Achilles. They followed the sounds of music to another room with dimmed lighting and couples dancing. He pulled her into his body on the dance floor and, weakly, Sofie couldn't help herself melting against his much harder contours.

For a moment she almost forgot. Or tried to fool herself into thinking she could forget. She looked up at Achilles's jaw. It was hard...unyielding. She hated the idea of him doing something as dangerous as taking part in a catamaran race purely to test himself. Even though her opinion probably didn't mean all that much.

'You don't have to do it, you know,' she said.

He looked down at her. 'Yes, I do.'

'You once told me I don't put much value on myself. I could accuse you of the same.'

'How's that?' A muscle pulsed in his jaw.

'It's not your fault you survived, Achilles. It was sheer luck and fortune. You could have just as easily died that day.'

The thought made her go cold inside.

'I know that.'

She felt the tension in his body. 'Do you?'

Being welded to his body like this was torture. Exquisite torture. Surrounded by people, yet cocooned in their own embrace. Sofie knew that she had to tell him now. Before she lost her nerve.

'Achilles…'

He looked down again, face stark. 'More pearls of wisdom?'

Sofie took a breath and quelled the tremor in her legs as best she could. 'There's something I need to tell you. It's not directly related to the catamaran race, but it might make you think differently about it. Actually, it might make you think differently about…a lot more than that.'

He stopped moving. 'What is it?'

Sofie swallowed. Opened her mouth. 'I'm pregnant.'

CHAPTER TEN

THE JOURNEY BACK to the apartment was conducted in icy silence. Sofie would never forget the look on Achilles's face as her words had sunk in. Disbelief, horror. Utter rejection.

When they got into the apartment he went straight to the drinks cabinet and poured himself a drink. Downed it in one. Then another. Sofie slipped off her shoes, feeling unstable enough as it was.

He turned around and uttered one word. 'How?'

She regretted taking off the shoes then, feeling far too small next to the sheer stark rejection all over his face. He looked drawn. Older.

'The pill… I take it every day. I haven't forgotten once. I think maybe the travelling…the time zones… might have affected it.' A weak excuse even to her ears, but she had no better idea of why it might have failed.

'How do I even know you took the pill? You just gave me your word and, like a fool, I believed you.'

Sofie left the room, went to the bedroom and got her washbag. She brought it back into the lounge and took out the foil packet and handed it to Achilles. He could see for himself all the days marked off where she'd taken the contraceptive tablet.

He handed it back. 'That means nothing.'

He was morphing in front of her eyes, turning into someone cold and remote and cynical.

She said, 'I know this isn't what you wanted.'

'Want. It's not what I *want*. Ever.'

Sofie put her hand over her belly. 'I'm not getting rid of the baby.' Already, only hours after finding out herself, she felt a sense of protection that stunned her. It was primal.

Achilles's mouth twisted. 'Of course you're not. Why would you? You're set for life now. It's survival and I know all about that.'

There was something so utterly cold and bleak in Achilles's voice that Sofie shrivelled up inside. 'Believe me, I wouldn't have planned it like this either. The last thing I want is to bring a lone child into the world without a family.'

'Next you'll be suggesting we get married.'

Sofie shook her head. She was seeing the very brutal depths of Achilles's pain and cynicism now and she had to try and stay strong. 'No, of course I wouldn't suggest that. I know you want that as little as you want a family.'

'And yet we're bound together for ever now. No matter what.'

There it was. The true lack of his regard for her. Sofie sat down on the edge of a chair behind her before her legs could give way. 'Yes.'

Even if he didn't want involvement, she'd have to have some contact with him. She had an image of herself, a single mother with her child, on their own in the house in Gallinvach, and it sliced right into her. Another lonely child. Except she vowed then and there to do everything in her power to make sure her child didn't feel invisible or responsible for the lack of a family.

* * *

Achilles was barely aware of Sofie's distress. All he could see was her betrayal and his own rage at himself for being so stupid.

Here was this woman he had trusted implicitly since he'd become aware of her in the hospital. A young innocent from the wilds of Scotland—she'd never been anywhere in her life—and yet now here she was with the oldest trick in the book, making a complete mockery of everything they'd shared.

Half to himself he said, 'You learned fast.'

'What?'

He looked at her and forced ice into his veins. Even now she affected him. Damn her. 'You heard me.'

'What are you suggesting?'

Achilles shrugged, a kind of icy calm descending over him as the first shock waned a little. 'It's understandable. Like I said, it's survival. To be honest, it would have been more remarkable if you *had* been everything you seemed. A total innocent with no agenda.'

Sofie stood up from the chair. Her voice shook. 'I do not—did not—have an agenda. You were the one who invited me to leave Gallinvach with you.'

'And you hesitated the requisite amount of time not to appear too eager.'

'Stop it, Achilles. This isn't you. This is your past talking. Your fear. Trauma.'

There was something dark and twisted writhing in Achilles's gut. Threatening to devour him completely. The thought of a baby was beyond terrifying. When he pictured a baby he remembered his mother coming home from hospital and holding a bundle in her arms, bending down so he could see the scrunched-up face of his baby brother, and then his baby sister.

He'd been the perfect older brother. No jealousy. Just utter adoration. And protection. He would have died for them if he could. But he hadn't been able to save them.

Sofie was just a few feet away, looking stricken. Achilles could only see an act. Treachery. He felt utterly conflicted. He wanted to pull her to him, sink into her softness and let her help him lose himself, and at the same time he despised her for articulating his worst fears. For bringing them to life. Literally.

He went to the door and didn't look back at her. 'I'm going out. You'll be gone by the time I get back.'

He opened the door, but before he could walk through it she said from behind him, 'Achilles, wait.'

Against every instinct urging him to run, he did.

She said brokenly, 'I love you, Achilles.'

The darkness inside him threatened to drown him. He bit out, 'Don't, Sofie. Just don't.'

And he left.

The following morning Sofie couldn't have been more certain that she was back in the land of reality. She was in the middle of three seats on a packed plane to Glasgow. There was a squalling baby in front of her and a child kicking the seat behind her. If she hadn't been so miserable she might almost have smiled at the juxtaposition.

When she'd woken this morning, after a restless night, a note had been on her bedside table. So at some point Achilles had come back and into her room. The thought of him watching her sleep made her feel alternately hot and then frustrated. Maybe if he'd woken her...if they could have just talked...

But the note had told her there was no hope. It had read:

Once you have confirmation from a doctor that you are pregnant let my solicitor know. He will make arrangements for maintenance. You will want for nothing. A

Sofie had been surprised at the anger that had surged up. She'd never really felt anger in her life.

She'd gone looking for Achilles, but he hadn't been in the apartment and the housekeeper had informed her that he was on his way to Rio de Janeiro on business.

So she'd ripped up his note and left one of her own:

Achilles, I do not need confirmation of what I already know. I am pregnant. We need nothing from you. S

The child kicked her seat again. She put her head back against the headrest. It was going to be a long flight.

Achilles saw Sofie's note when he got back from Rio de Janeiro a couple of days later. He scowled. He'd believe her *we need nothing from you* until the moment she sued for maintenance.

It had occurred to him that perhaps she wasn't even pregnant. It could be a bluff. But, to his surprise, that thought hadn't made him feel a sense of relief. It had made him feel even more conflicted.

There was a knock on the door. His housekeeper put his head around it. 'Sir, the car is ready downstairs.'

'Thank you.' The man had almost disappeared again when Achilles said, 'Wait… Tommy…?'

'Sir?'

'Did Sofie—that is, Miss MacKenzie—take anything with her when she left?'

The man blinked. Achilles realised he'd never really noticed him before. But Sofie had probably got his life story out of him.

'She just had a small suitcase with her, sir. It looked… er…not that new.'

In other words she'd taken her own case and nothing else. And the stylist hadn't left any messages about missing jewellery, as had happened with other women in the past.

Other women. Achilles's face felt as if it was in a permanent scowl as he went downstairs and got into the car. People coming towards him diverted in another direction. The thought of other women made bile rise. He couldn't even countenance the thought of going through the motions. To what end? It all seemed so futile to him now, and that revelation made the back of his neck prickle and his head throb, as if something was trying to break through in his head. But it wouldn't come.

Achilles shook his head as the car arrived at his office. He got out and went in, stony-faced.

When he got up to his office his PR team were waiting, their faces wreathed in smiles. 'It's all good news, sir. Sofie MacKenzie is great for business. Your stock value has never been higher.'

Achilles looked at the paper that had been thrown on his desk. There were a couple of pictures. Him with Sofie at the charity auction, and also a more grainy picture of them going into the pizzeria. He hated it that they'd been seen in that moment.

The headline read: *A changed man! Is Achilles Lykaios finally settling down?*

This was exactly what he'd wanted. So why did he feel so hollow, and as if he'd lost instead of won?

The jubilant PR team left and there was another knock on the door. His assistant. Achilles did his best to be civil. 'Yes?'

'That report you asked for. A couple of weeks ago. On that woman.'

A heavy weight lodged in his gut. If anything, it was more relevant now than ever. 'I don't want to see it—just tell me what it says. Briefly.'

His assistant came into the office and pushed the door closed so no one could hear. 'It's a short report, sir. She's completely clean. Two parents, both deceased. No siblings. School and then straight into work at the hospital. She cared for her parents before they died. No evidence of boyfriends. A pretty quiet life.'

Achilles absorbed that and heard a dull roaring in his head. 'Why did it take so long if there's nothing in it?'

'Because we were afraid we'd missed something. We couldn't really believe someone could be this clean. It's not what we're used to.'

No. Because Sofie came from the real world, where people were normal and nice and lived lives of contentment far beyond the reaches of him or anyone he knew. He was the anomaly. Him and his peers. They were the outliers. People with vacuous lives that others pitied.

But his parents hadn't been like that. They'd carved out a relationship built on love and a family. He'd always vowed he would have that too. Until it had blown up in his face. Literally.

And just like that a sense of déjà vu almost made

him sway on his feet. The niggling sensation of something hiding on the fringes of his memory became clear. He remembered now. He remembered it all. The reason why he'd lost his footing on the mountain. The reason why he'd fallen.

His assistant stepped forward, looking concerned, 'Mr Lykaios, are you all right?'

Achilles shook his head. 'No, I'm not all right.'

Sofie was taking advantage of the last of the late summer sun to wash and dry every bedsheet in the house. She needed to get her B&B up and running if she was going to make any money out of the next few weeks, before the high season ended.

When she'd returned a few days ago, her friend Claire had picked her up from the ferry at the harbour, taken one look at Sofie's face and pulled her in for a hug.

Sofie had said to her, 'Don't say a word, Claire. Please.'

And her friend hadn't. Sofie hadn't told her about the pregnancy yet. She was too raw. Too angry. Part of her wanted to get right back onto another plane and march into Achilles's office and demand that he…*what*? Admit that he loved her too? When he didn't? Admit he actually wanted children? When he didn't?

Sofie pinned the last sheet on the line with more force than necessary. She heard Pluto barking at the front of the house. The sound of crunching gravel. She frowned. That couldn't be Claire, and it couldn't possibly be someone looking for a room because she hadn't put up a sign or advertised online yet.

She walked through the kitchen and out into the hall. The front door was open. She stopped in her tracks when she saw a blacked-out SUV. And a familiar tall figure climbing out of the driver's seat.

Pluto was jumping up and down, tail wagging vigorously. Almost giving Achilles a more rapturous welcome than he had Sofie. Achilles bent down to greet the dog. It was such an incongruous sight that Sofie couldn't move.

He was wearing jeans and a dark T-shirt and he looked mouthwateringly sexy. Sofie scowled and folded her arms across her chest even as her heart threatened to jump out of her chest. 'What are you doing here?'

'I heard you were renting rooms.'

'Not ready yet. Come back never.'

She turned around and went to go back into the house, but Achilles said, 'Sofie...'

She stopped. She realised she was shaking. Trembling. She turned around again, and emotion made her volatile. 'What is it you want, Achilles? I think your note was very clear. We don't need to communicate at all.'

'We need to talk.'

'About what? There's nothing to discuss.'

'I think a baby is something to discuss.'

'It's early days...too early to be safe. Something could happen.'

Achilles went pale. 'Don't say that.'

That floored Sofie. Achilles came towards her and she couldn't move.

'Can we go inside?'

Sofie made her legs move. Backwards. Into the house. Into the faded and threadbare lounge. Where the picture of teenage her was still on the mantelpiece.

Achilles dominated the space too easily—a painful reminder of how it had felt as if he belonged here before.

'What is it you've come to talk about?'

'You. This. Us.'

Sofie shook her head. 'There is no "us". There never was.'

Achilles looked at her. She realised now belatedly that he looked a little unkempt. Wild. Tired.

'That's funny,' he said. 'Because, as the papers and gossips are pointing out, you are my longest relationship.'

Her insides dipped. 'That was just to prove to people that you were reforming.'

'And yet was it a hardship, our spending time together?'

Sofie wanted to stamp her foot. 'No, of course not. But we both knew it wasn't a relationship because it wasn't going anywhere.'

'And yet I'm here and you're pregnant.'

Sofie said, 'Look, if you've just come to terms with this news, and feel like it's your duty to take some responsibility, then—'

'You said you loved me.'

Sofie's mouth shut.

'Did you mean it?'

Sofie's emotions went from volatile to vulnerable. 'What do you think?'

Achilles ran a hand through his hair. He seemed agitated. 'I don't know what to think. I know what I hope, though.'

'What do you hope?'

He looked at her. 'That you meant it.'

'Does it give you some sense of satisfaction to know that I love you—are you that cruel?'

'Sofie. Stop.'

He came closer and put his hands on her arms. She could smell his unique scent and wanted to drop her head against his chest, have his arms wrap around her so tight she wouldn't be able to breathe.

She pulled back, dislodging his hands.

Achilles said, 'No, I'm not so cruel that I'd seek to get some vicarious pleasure out of knowing that you feel more for me than I do for you. It's because I'm a coward.'

Sofie shook her head. 'How are you a coward? You survived one of the worst tragedies anyone could suffer.'

'I'm a coward because I hid behind that tragedy my whole life to avoid more pain.'

Sofie shook her head. 'Anyone would have done the same. Others would have fallen apart completely. You never did.'

Achilles made a sound. 'Didn't I? I almost let it all go.'

'But you didn't.'

'No,' he conceded. 'Sofie… I've never said anything like this to anyone, except my family. But all I know is that since I woke up and saw you in that hospital you've been the centre of my world. My life. I don't want anyone else. I want you. I dream about you. I ache for you.' He shook his head. 'The other evening…when you told me about the baby…it was my worst fears manifesting. And you were articulating them. Someone I had trusted implicitly. I went on the attack and you didn't deserve that.'

Sofie shook her head. 'What are you saying?'

'What I'm trying to say is that I love you and I want to have this baby with you. I don't want us to be apart ever again.'

Sofie's heart swelled so much it almost hurt. But it was too much. 'I don't… I can't believe this. You. I know what you went through, Achilles. You're just here…saying this now…because you've realised that this is good for your bottom line or something… I saw all those headlines about how well your business is doing. I'm not stupid.'

'No, you're far from stupid. The truth is I wanted this before I even met you.'

Sofie frowned. 'You're not making sense.'

'That's why I fell down the mountain.'

Sofie sat down on the couch behind her. Achilles came and sat down too. 'Can you explain that?'

He shook his head. 'It's hard to explain. I came here to escape media attention, as I explained. We figured that if I was off the radar when that story broke it would fizzle out and Athena Demetriou would be scrambling to explain. But all I know is that suddenly I *wanted* to go away. Get off the grid for a while—and that had nothing to do with escaping media attention. It was about escaping a feeling of emptiness that had been plaguing me for some time. So I came here. Didn't even book anywhere. Climbed straight up the mountain. That's the only bit I still couldn't remember—the actual mountain climb and how I came to fall.'

'But now I do remember,' he went on. 'I got to the top and it was beautiful. But for the first time in my life I realised how alone I was. I had no one to share it with. Another man who had climbed the mountain was ahead of me. He had a friend with him. He was video calling his family and showing them the view. He was almost crying, telling them he couldn't wait to see them. That he was coming home.'

Achilles shook his head.

'Normally that would have been a trigger for me. Any mention of happy families usually is. But it wasn't. It made me realise that I'd spent my whole life rejecting happiness and joy for fear of losing it all again. I was lonely. Empty inside. All the carousing and the money meant nothing. It's such a cliché, but in that moment I realised that my life was worth nothing unless I was brave enough to overcome my fears and open up. Drop the cynicism. I was so tired of it all. Jaded. And that's when I missed my footing and fell. And when I woke up you were there.'

Sofie felt shaky. 'Just because I was the first woman you saw it doesn't mean anything.'

Achilles shook his head. 'It means *everything*. You kissed me. You woke me up. It just took me a while to remember.'

Sofie stood up. She felt jittery. As if she was going into shock. 'I don't know if I can trust this...you. This is just you protecting your interests.'

Achilles stood up. He shook his head. 'I couldn't care less about all of that. Truly. I care about the legacy for the sake of my father, who put so much work into it. I care about the employees and I care about creating more jobs. I care about the business growing and succeeding for all our sakes. But that's the extent of it. I've installed a very capable cousin as CEO to manage things for a while, so I can take a break.'

'Take a break?'

'I think we're going to be pretty busy for a while.'

'We...?'

Achilles came closer. Put his hand on Sofie's still-flat belly. 'Us.'

Sofie looked up at him. She was stripped bare emotionally. 'I'm scared that you don't see me. That I'm just a project now, because of the baby. I can't be invisible again, Achilles. It'll kill me.'

He came closer and cupped her face in his hands.

'From the moment I woke in that hospital all I've seen is *you*. You are beautiful and kind and full of so much potential. Not just as a wife and mother. You have an amazing career ahead of you as a flower-arranger.'

Sofie let out a sudden unexpected laugh. A giddy feeling was bubbling up inside her. Achilles did see her. He had always seen her. More than anyone else ever had. She had to trust that.

As if reading her mind, he said more seriously, 'I see you, Sofie. I want you. I love you. I can't promise it'll be easy for me to start a family, but I want this. And I'll do whatever it takes to prove it to you and to overcome any demons in my way.'

Sofie looked at Achilles. 'What about the catamaran race?'

He shook his head. 'The only reason I bid on it was because I'd been feeling so numb ever since that night on the island when you said you cared for me and wanted to leave. And because I knew you were leaving the next day. I felt a sense of desperation to feel something, even fear. I've pulled out of the race.'

'Thank God…' Sofie breathed. 'It looked terrifying.'

'I can't guarantee I won't want to do it at some stage in the future—but maybe after I've had a few trips around your lake in your neighbour's fishing boat first.'

Sofie smiled and tears blurred her vision. She threw her arms around Achilles's neck and pressed her mouth to his. He caught her head, fingers tangling in her hair, holding her there so he could deepen the kiss.

After long minutes of getting reacquainted, Sofie pulled back. Dizzy. 'I love you, Achilles Lykaios. I'll do my best to make you happy.'

'You already do. More than you even know.' Now he

sounded emotional. But then he said, 'But do you know what would make me even happier right now?'

Sofie moved against him, revelling in the evidence of his desire. 'I think I can guess.'

He picked her up and carried her up the stairs. Sofie giggled like a teenager. The fact that there were no sheets on any of the beds wasn't even noticed as they sank into one another and made their vows to each other for a lifetime of commitment and love.

EPILOGUE

Ten years later, Gallinvach, summer

'MUM, LOOK WHAT I caught! Take a picture, quick!'

Darius's voice rang out across the small lake at the back of Sofie's family home. He was on the back of a small fishing boat, wearing a T-shirt, shorts and a life jacket, and was proudly holding up a decent-sized fish.

Nine years old and named after Achilles's beloved brother, he was already up to Sofie's shoulder, clearly taking after his father, who was standing by his side and grinning proudly.

Emotion welled in Sofie's chest when she saw their daughter Ellie, two years younger than Darius, jumping up and down with excitement on the other side of her father.

Sofie did as she was bid, and snapped a shot with her phone, very aware of the significance of this photo and the healing that it depicted in so many ways.

Sofie called out, 'That's amazing! Now put him back before he dies!'

Darius carefully unhooked the fish and threw it back into the water. Sofie sat back down in the wooden chair under the shade of an umbrella in the garden where it sloped down to the lake.

She checked to see that their three-year-old, Cyrus, was still sleeping, spreadeagled on the rug beside her, exhausted after a game of chase earlier. Long dark lashes fanned across his chubby cheeks. Sofie gently stroked a finger across his face, not taking this moment for granted for a second.

She turned back to the lake to watch as Achilles steered the boat back in. The shadows were lengthening, the glorious summer's day coming to a close. Her family home, for so long a place of loneliness and palpable grief, was now full of the kind of sound and energy that her parents had craved so desperately to counteract their own lonely childhoods.

Sofie wished they could be here to witness her family. She no longer blamed herself for their sadness. She should have been enough for them, and the fact that she hadn't been wasn't her fault.

Sofie knew that even if she and Achilles hadn't had children they would have been happy with each other. Not lacking for anything. But they had been blessed, and she gave thanks every day that Achilles had overcome the trauma of his past and his fear of loving again to embrace a future that had terrified him for so long.

They spent every summer here in Gallinvach, with Achilles ensuring that he could work remotely if required. And for the rest of the year they based themselves between Athens and London. It was a lifestyle that Sofie had adapted to with far more ease than she ever would have imagined, navigating the social whirl of Achilles's life by seeking out and making some genuine friends among their peers.

They'd renovated the house on the island and extended it, adding a more modern touch. Sofie had overseen the redecoration of the interior, bringing in an understated elegance, hauling it firmly into the twenty-first century.

Achilles tied the boat off at the jetty and lifted Ellie onto the wooden platform. Darius jumped from the boat as agile as a little goat and came and gave Sofie a quick hug and kiss before saying, 'Can I take your phone to show Jamie the picture?'

Sofie handed him her phone and Darius was gone, speeding up the garden to his neighbouring friend. Cyrus was stirring on the rug and Ellie sat down beside him, giving him a hug.

Then Achilles was stepping out of the boat and striding up the small jetty. As handsome as he'd been the first day Sofie had laid eyes on him. Even with a few grey hairs in his temples that she loved to tease him about.

He stopped where Sofie was sitting and put out a hand. She leaned forward and took it and let him pull her up, letting out a small *oof* as she did so, and looking down ruefully at her massive bump.

Achilles pulled her close and kissed her. Even after all these years, and in her current state, she felt the urge to deepen the kiss. Both of them were helpless against the familiar pull of desire.

'Mama, Cyrus has a dirty nappy.'

Sofie pulled back from Achilles's embrace reluctantly and chuckled at Ellie's scrunched-up face. Nothing like a dirty nappy to kill a mood.

But before she could reach for her now very much awake and cheekily grinning three-year-old, Achilles beat her to it and scooped him up into his arms, making Cyrus squeal with joy.

Sofie watched her husband carry their son into the house to despatch the nappy and gave a sigh of contentment. She and Ellie followed behind them. Ellie took her hand and Sofie looked down. Her daughter had inherited Sofie's blue eyes, and with her dark hair and olive-toned skin, she was going to be a beauty. She'd never feel that she had to hide in the shadows or that she wasn't seen. Sofie felt absurdly emotional at that thought and blamed pregnancy hormones.

'Mama?'

'Yes, love...' Sofie swallowed the emotion.

'Boys are smelly, aren't they?'

Sofie laughed. 'They can be...a little. But so can girls.' She stopped and bent down in front of her daughter. 'But do you know what? Some day you might find that they can smell quite nice.'

Ellie scrunched up her nose again and pulled away. 'Ew, no way!'

She ran back up to the house and Sofie followed behind, smiling to herself. Ellie would feel differently soon. Well, actually, maybe not so soon. With the most over-protective father in the world, it might be some time before Ellie and her little sister, who would be born any day now in the local hospital, would come to appreciate how nice boys could smell.

Sofie felt a sudden contraction around her abdomen

and stopped in her tracks to suck in a breath. Achilles appeared at the back door with Cyrus in his arms and saw her. He was on the alert immediately and came over.

'Was that what I think it was?'

Sofie straightened up. The contraction had passed. She said, 'It might be, but it might be nothing.' Just then she felt a gushing warmth between her legs and looked down stupidly. She'd had three children, but her breaking waters confounded her for a second.

Achilles sprang into action. He helped Sofie into the house and sat her in a chair. He made a phone call that had her old friend Claire arriving with her husband in tow, ready to spring into childminding action.

Sofie felt totally calm. 'Guys, I really appreciate this, but it could be ages before—' Her words were stopped by another sudden powerful contraction.

Claire snorted. 'I don't think so. After three bairns, this one is coming in a hurry. She'll be out before you know it. Your case is by the door—call when you have news.'

Sofie was all but carried out to their car, in spite of her protestations. Achilles got them to the hospital in record time and then it was all a blur as, true to Claire's pronouncement, this one came quickly.

Phoebe Lykaios, named after Achilles's mother, was born just after midnight. Exhausted but ecstatic, Sofie looked at Achilles—very crumpled now in his shorts and T-shirt—as he walked back and forth, holding his swaddled daughter in his arms.

And then suddenly, in spite of her fog of exhaustion, Sofie noticed something and gasped.

Achilles looked at her. 'What is it? Are you okay?'

Sofie started laughing, but had to stop when it hurt her tender insides. She nodded, and managed to choke out, 'Don't you recognise this room?'

The following day, when the other children were allowed in to see their new baby sister, Sofie said to them, 'Do you want to hear a story?'

The two eldest huddled around the end of the bed and Cyrus climbed into her arms, putting his thumb in his mouth. Sofie shared a complicit look with Achilles and said, 'You know the fairy tale *Sleeping Beauty*?'

Ellie sighed. 'I love that story.'

Darius made a face. 'That's a soppy story.'

Cyrus sucked his thumb, just happy to be back with his mother.

The baby made a small mewling sound but then stopped.

'Well,' said Sofie, undaunted, 'that's how I met your daddy—in this very room. He was asleep for a long time, and I kissed him awake.'

Ellie frowned. 'But isn't the Prince meant to kiss the Princess awake?'

Achilles took Phoebe out of the cot and came and sat beside Sofie on the bed, cradling their newborn. He said, 'In this instance the Princess woke the Prince and saved him.'

Darius said grudgingly, 'That's actually kind of cool.'

Achilles leaned over and kissed Sofie. They shared a look full of love and so much more.

Sofie said with a smile, 'And then the Prince rescued her right back.'

Ellie clapped her hands. 'And they all lived happily ever after!'

Sofie laughed again, her heart so full it almost hurt.

'Yes,' she said, looking at her beloved family and then at Achilles. 'Yes, they did.'

* * * * *

COMING SOON!

We really hope you enjoyed reading this book.
If you're looking for more romance, be sure to
head to the shops when new books are
available on

Thursday 7th July

MILLS & BOON®

Coming next month

HIS DESERT BRIDE BY DEMAND
Lela May Wright

"Can you explain what happened?" Akeem asked. "The intensity?"

Could she? Nine years had passed between them—a lifetime and still… No, she couldn't.

"My father had a lifetime of being reckless for his own amusement—"

"And you wanted a taste of it?"

"No," he denied, his voice a harsh rasp.

"Then what did you want?" Charlotte pushed.

"A night—"

"You risked your reputation for a night?" She cut him off, her insides twisting. "And so far, it's been a disaster, and we haven't even got to bed." She blew out a puff of agitated air.

"Make no mistake," he warned, "things have changed."

"Changed?"

"My bed is off limits."

She laughed, a throaty gurgle. "How dare you pull me from my life—fly me who knows how many miles into a kingdom I've never heard of and turn my words back on me?" She fixed him with an exasperated glare. "How dare you try to turn the tables on me?"

"If the tables have turned on anyone," he corrected, "it is me because you will be my wife."

Continue reading
HIS DESERT BRIDE BY DEMAND
Lela May Wright

Available next month
www.millsandboon.co.uk